The Darcy COUSINS

MONICA FAIRVIEW

D0035652

sourcebooks
landmark

Published by Sourcebooks Landmark, an imprint of Sourcebooks, Inc.
P.O. Box 4410, Naperville, Illinois 60567-4410
(630) 961-3900
FAX: (630) 961-2168
www.sourcebooks.com

Library of Congress Cataloging-in-Publication Data

Fairview, Monica.
  The Darcy cousins / Monica Fairview.
      p. cm.
 1. Americans—England--Fiction. 2. Cousins—Fiction. 3. Young women—Fiction.
I. Title.
  PR6106.A38D37 2010
  823'.92—dc22
                              2010001463

Printed and bound in the United States of America.
      VP 10 9 8 7 6 5 4 3 2 1

To Joseph, "sun of my life, gilder of every pleasure,
soother of every sorrow," lover and editor,
and Meena, my tumbling turbulent
mountain stream of joy

Chapter 1

THE CHURCH DOOR FLEW OPEN AND FOOTSTEPS RESOUNDED through the church, forcing its lethargic inmates into sudden animation. Mr Collins, whose sermon on fire and brimstone had taken on a decidedly monotonous rhythm, was awakened into new fervour. His eyes rounded and his voice rose, ringing with conviction now that he had found a target for his wrath. Even his conviction, however, did not regain him his audience, for the congregation turned *en masse* to survey the newcomers. Heads turned, necks stretched, and hats fluttered. Twittering echoed around the stone pillars.

Mr Collins tried his best to ignore these disturbing signs of inattention. He proved himself worthy of his position indeed, for he did not falter for an instant and, when the restlessness of his flock became too apparent, he turned his eyes on the one person who was worthy of the benefit of his words—indeed, had had a hand in suggesting those very words—his noble patroness Lady Catherine de Bourgh. She sat rigidly upright in her pew and kept her gaze calmly fixed upon him. Her daughter Anne, though generally too sickly to be curious, shifted in her seat so that she could sneak a glance at the new arrivals, until a sharp pinch forced her to recall the gravity of their elevated stature.

But, at last, even Lady Catherine de Bourgh herself could not ignore the disturbance, for the newcomers, instead of squeezing silently into whatever empty bench they could find, came straight in her direction and signalled for her to shift down towards the other side of the family pew. Lady Catherine, torn between the diminished dignity of moving from her accustomed seat or the prospect of causing a scene in the Lord's presence, moved closer to her daughter. At this insult to his dear patroness, Mr Collins stuttered, not once, but twice, an event of such unprecedented magnitude that he succeeded in drawing all attention back to himself again.

"I am sorry we were tardy, Lady Catherine. I know we wrote that we would arrive before church today," said a cheerful young voice in a loud whisper. Those closest to Lady Catherine's pew strained to listen above Mr Collins's voice, and a few turned to convey her words to the ears of their less fortunate neighbours.

An elderly lady's voice could be heard complaining forcefully that no one ever told her anything. "What is the young lady saying?"

She received several disgruntled looks.

"One of our horses was lamed," continued the young lady, "and we had to wait until a fresh one could be brought. It took forever."

Mr Collins fixed a quelling look at the young lady in question. She was apparently chastised, for she said nothing more. But no sooner had Mr Collins resumed the familiar flow of his sermon than the young gentleman leaned across his sister and added in a whisper, "I hope we have not missed too much of the service," he remarked. "My watch must have been stolen by pickpockets when we stopped in Bromley, for I could not find it, and I have no idea of the time."

Lady Catherine did not deign to reply. Mr Collins paused in the middle of a sentence and cleared his throat.

Georgiana Darcy, who was sitting to the right of Anne, wished

Mr Collins would simply ignore the newcomers, instead of drawing even more attention to them. Her party seemed to have become the focus of all eyes. If only their pew faced forward, instead of standing sideways where everyone in the congregation could see them! She squirmed in her seat, trying her best to look unruffled. If only she were sitting with her brother, Darcy, whose tall form was partly hidden by a pillar.

Such thoughts did not avail her, however, for there she was, with all eyes turned towards her group. She needed to project an air of calm dignity. She grasped her hands together in her lap and concentrated on practising serenity.

One pair of eyes—dark and insistent—stood out from the sea of eyes turned towards her. Her tremulous serenity collapsed. A glance across the empty space to the pew opposite theirs—one of the pillars of the community, clearly—revealed the source. A dark-haired, impeccably dressed young gentleman was watching her—not the others, but her in particular. His knowing gaze rested on her deliberately, and she had the uncomfortable sensation of being evaluated.

She looked away quickly at the sea of eyes to her left. She preferred them to that one single evaluation. But looking away did not help, for she could still feel the touch of that steady gaze upon her. Unable to resist, she turned to him again. He nodded at her politely, with a hint of a smile that suggested sympathy with her predicament. She flushed this time, flustered more by his pity than by anything else that had transpired.

Fortunately, by now the new arrivals appeared sufficiently cowed by Mr Collins or Lady Catherine or both, for neither of them uttered a sound until it was time to sing the next hymn, upon which they sang with voices like angels.

At least, that was what old Miss Alton said to her sister, Miss

Emily, when they had left the church behind them and started on the path towards their cottage. Miss Emily, who was partially deaf, could neither agree nor disagree, but acknowledged generally that they appeared to be very agreeable young people.

This seemed to be the general consensus in the village of Hunsford. Much was made of the fact that they had requested Lady Catherine to move. But the explanation given for such an obvious social *faux pas* was that it was only to be expected, since they were Americans. This explanation seemed enough to satisfy most people. A few less easily persuaded souls, however, pointed out that though Mr Robert Darcy was American, he was as fine a gentleman as could be, and married to an English lady, moreover, and he would never have thought of forcing Lady Catherine to move. Nothing remained to be said except that, since the two young people in question were actually Mr Robert's brother and sister, one would have to blame their extreme youth for the mistake. They were by no means to be condemned in any case, for how could they know that Lady Catherine de Bourgh had occupied that exact same seat for at least the last thirty years, since the Sunday after Sir Lewis de Bourgh had brought her home as a new bride?

The mistake was even more quickly forgiven when it became known that they possessed respectable fortunes. The young lady, Miss Clarissa Darcy, was worth at least £25,000 a year, while the young man, Mr Frederick Darcy, was worth far more.

It was Mrs Channing who put her finger on the pulse of the matter as she addressed her son, who had not attended the service, and so had to be apprised of all the excitement he had missed.

"Their behaviour would be enormously presumptuous were it not for the fact that they are known to be cousins of Mr Darcy. Any cousins of Mr Darcy must be respectable enough to be received in any household in the county. The fact that they are American pales in significance to that very important connection."

"But, Mama," said Mr Channing, an easy, cheerful young man whom his mother fondly described as the handsomest young man in Kent, "you have told me nothing at all of Miss Clarissa Darcy's appearance. For all you have said will weigh nothing with me, unless you can tell me she is pretty."

"Weigh nothing?" replied his mother. "What can be more important than family connections, especially when they come with a considerable fortune? A young lady can look like a toad and still receive offers of marriage when blessed with such advantages."

"Still, Mama, I am not so desperate as to try my luck with a young lady who looks like a toad."

This threw his mama into an agony of confusion. "But I did not say she looked like a toad, Percy. If I did, I did not mean it."

Mr Channing smiled at her obligingly. "You did not say it. But you have not told me either if you think her handsome enough to tempt me."

His mother sniffed. "She is not unpleasant looking. Not as fine-looking as you, but acceptable."

"You sound unsure, Mama."

"That is because I am not sure she would suit you," said Mrs Channing. She picked up her work and pierced the cloth with quick, tight stitches. "You would do better to cast your line at Miss Georgiana Darcy. *She* combines all the advantages we have spoken of, and she is a biddable type of girl, the type who will not cause you any trouble. I suspect Miss Clarissa Darcy has a mind of her own."

"You pique my interest, Mama. I must meet such a paragon, for I quite admire a young lady of spirit."

Mrs Channing jabbed her finger with a needle. Peevishly, she tossed her needlework to the side. "You will do as you wish, I know. You have never set much store by anything I say. But I think such a young lady would not do well for a wife." She was quite out of breath by the end of her little speech.

Her son's astonishment was readily apparent. "I have not heard you express such a strong opinion for a long time, Mama. You need not worry! I do not intend to marry any time in the near future. But that does not mean I will abstain from meeting young ladies of fortune."

Mrs Channing, satisfied that he was in no immediate danger of riding over to Rosings to propose to Miss Clarissa Darcy, took up the discarded needlework and fell back into old habits. She was generally inclined to agree with others who were more forceful than she and rarely took her own position on anything. Only the most dire fears moved her to express her opinion openly. "No, of course not. It is advisable to foster good connections whenever one can," she observed placidly.

"Then we are in agreement," said Mr Channing. "I am to meet the young lady in question. But since Lady Catherine has issued no invitation for me to visit her at Rosings Park, I fear that my chances of becoming acquainted with the Darcy ladies are rather reduced." He paused a moment to let her mull over his words, knowing full well that Lady Catherine's failure to invite the Channings for more than two weeks while her relations were visiting was a sore point to his mother.

"I cannot force Lady Catherine to invite us if she does not wish to," replied Mrs Channing, once again stabbing at her needlework.

"Of course not. But I have a perfect solution. If I cannot go to Miss Darcy, Miss Darcy shall come to us. We shall have an informal dance, and Lady Catherine's guests shall be invited."

However little the idea of organizing a large event for such important guests may have appealed to Mrs Channing, she could not refuse. Her first thought was that such an event, with the presence of such prominent personages, would be food for conversation among the ladies of the neighbourhood for months and would add greatly to her consequence. Her second was that perhaps such an amusement might keep her son longer with them in the country. For she had noticed that her son visited her less and less frequently, and that his friends and London amusements occupied most of his time.

Besides, he was her only child and she was not in the habit of denying him anything.

"But your father…" she protested weakly.

"My father may not approve of lavish entertainment," said Channing, "but he is far away in India and, as long as you refrain from writing to tell him about it, will not know anything about the matter."

Mrs Channing, quickly relieved of her one cause of apprehension, allowed herself to be persuaded.

"There shall be a dance, then, if you insist, and you shall meet everybody." A sudden doubt struck her, and she added, "That is, if Lady Catherine and her guests agree to attend."

Mr Channing grinned. "I can assure you they will, Mama," he said. "For after spending so much time in Lady Catherine's presence, they will be more than ready to seek other company. We must invite the Darcys directly as well as Lady Catherine, for that way, even if Lady Catherine refuses, *they* will not."

❦

Outside the church, Mr Robert Darcy performed the necessary introductions.

Lady Catherine acknowledged Miss Clarissa and Mr Frederick Darcy with gracious condescension. If her nod held a hint of disapproval and her smile did not quite replace the scowl on her face, one could blame it on the weather. For despite the clear sky, a chill wind was blowing. Now was clearly not the time to exchange pleasantries. Her ladyship was eager to reach her waiting carriage.

Behind her, Miss Anne de Bourgh started to extend a hand out of her fur muff but withdrew it quickly as her mother's voice reached her from inside the carriage.

"Stop dawdling, Anne, or you will take a cold."

The dreaded word seemed to have the desired effect, for Miss de Bourgh hurried in quick small steps to the carriage, followed closely by Mrs Jenkinson, who occupied herself running behind Miss de Bourgh and rearranging her multiple shawls.

Mrs Robert Darcy, formerly Miss Caroline Bingley, smiled at Clarissa and Frederick.

"I hope you do not think us unwelcoming," she said, "You must not mind Lady Catherine. She is like that with everyone."

"Oh, no," said Clarissa, "I do not mind her at all, for I have an aunt just like her in Boston. But I am very pleased to meet my brother's wife at last. We have heard so little about you because of the blockade, but I am eager to get to know the lady who took my brother's fancy. He is not easily pleased, you know."

Caroline smiled. "I hope you will not be disappointed. I wish we could have had the opportunity to meet earlier." She turned to the tall young man who stood next to Clarissa. "I have heard a great deal about your business abilities, Mr Frederick."

Frederick grinned. "I have been fortunate enough to be in the right place at the right time," he said, bowing. "As I have now had the fortune to make your acquaintance, Mrs Darcy."

Robert then introduced his cousin Fitzwilliam Darcy, Mrs Elizabeth Darcy, and Miss Georgiana Darcy.

Georgiana, who had prepared some words of welcome and rehearsed them to herself, was startled to find herself pulled forward by both hands and embraced by Clarissa.

"Oh, I am so glad to meet you!" said Clarissa, her eyes shining. "It is wonderful to have a cousin my age, and a girl too. All my cousins from my mother's family are either too old or too young or *boys*, and you know what *they* are like. But look at you! I never imagined you would be so pretty! How tall and straight you are, and what lovely long eyelashes you have! I have plans for us. We will take advantage of Frederick's presence to do all sorts of things, for we cannot rely on Robert anymore now that he is married. I am sure he has become as dull as ditchwater."

"You may depend on me, Miss Darcy. I will endeavour to do what I can to keep you and my sister entertained," said Frederick, bowing over Georgiana's hand.

All the words she had meant to say flew out of her head, but she did not find herself tongue-tied at all. "I have no doubt we shall find plenty to do," she said, laughing. "Though I should warn you that Lady Catherine will have her own ideas about how we should be occupied."

"Then we shall steal out of the window when she is napping," replied Clarissa. Her eyes sparkled, and Georgiana found herself gripped by the same sense of expectation as her cousin. Her eyes went to her cousin Frederick, who was twenty-six and seemed in every way as full of restless energy as his sister.

"You had better wait to plan your mischief until you arrive in Rosings," said Elizabeth, a twinkle in her eye. "Lady Catherine will be greatly displeased if we are late for dinner."

As they left the churchyard and strolled towards the Darcy carriage, a curricle drew up to them and halted. Georgiana immediately recognized the same young gentleman who had stared at her in church.

"Darcy!" said the flawlessly dressed young gentleman. "A very good morning to you."

Darcy greeted him like an old friend. He quickly performed the introductions. The gentleman was Mr Henry Gatley, a property owner from a few miles away.

"And here are my two cousins, newly arrived from Boston."

An amused look passed over the young man's face. "Yes, I am well aware of the fact."

What he did not say, but meant, was that every single member of the congregation was well aware of it.

"You have strong powers of observation, Mr Gatley," remarked Georgiana, stung by his implication. What right had he to judge her cousins when he knew nothing about them?

She regretted the words immediately. Mr Gatley, who had barely acknowledged her beyond a quick bow at their introduction, turned his piercing gaze towards her.

"Indeed?" he said.

She flushed for the second time that morning. As if it was not bad enough that her cousins had drawn so much attention to their party. Now he thought her ill mannered as well. Not that she cared particularly for his opinion.

She raised her chin and met his gaze.

"Your mother is not with you?" said Darcy. "I thought she was most particular about attending church."

"She is unwell," said Mr Gatley.

"I am sorry to hear it. Please give her my regards," said Darcy. "And you must call on us soon, Gatley. We can make up a gentleman's card party." His easy manner bespoke the ease of long acquaintance.

"I would be delighted," said Mr Gatley.

He bowed to everyone and continued on his way.

There is nothing more irritating to one who has just been rude than a person whose manners are spotlessly polished. Georgiana watched his curricle disappear down the road, irked at herself for allowing his superior manner to ruffle her. On impulse, she drew up to her brother, who was walking with Elizabeth at his side.

"Do you know Mr Gatley well?" she asked.

"We were at school together, though not in the same class. He is three years younger than I am. I have always found him very congenial company," said Mr Darcy.

"He appears to me rather opinionated," said Georgiana.

"He is a very orderly type, and can be severe at times, but there is no harm in him."

Her brother's words confirmed her opinion. Mr Gatley was the type of gentleman who took himself too seriously by far.

"I see that you have taken an interest in your brother's friend," said Elizabeth teasingly.

This was so far from the truth that Georgiana laughed.

"Quite the contrary. I have taken a dislike to him."

Darcy regarded her gravely. "It is hardly fair to form an opinion of a person with whom you have hardly exchanged a word."

Georgiana, who did not like her brother to reprimand her, however mildly, replied that one could not help it if one did not take to a person on sight.

At that instant Clarissa hailed her, and she dropped back to join her cousins. The excitement of getting to know them soon took over and she promptly forgot Mr Gatley.

Mr Gatley took off his boots as soon as he stepped into the house, and tiptoed up the stairs. His mother was indeed unwell, as he had told Darcy. She was suffering from one of her rare migraines— the last one had been several months ago—and he was acutely conscious that the slightest sound could be distressing to her. When he reached her bedchamber, however, he sighed with relief. The door was open and the curtains drawn back to allow in the daylight, a sign, surely, that the worst was over. Still, he made every effort to move as quietly as possible, just in case.

She was sitting up in bed, reading.

"I am glad to see you better," he said, smiling. "You have recovered quickly. It usually takes much longer."

"I do believe these attacks are growing less frequent and are no longer so severe. Perhaps some day they may even disappear altogether." She gestured for him to come in. "Anything new at church today? How was Mr Collins's sermon?"

"The same as usual. I suppose Lady Catherine was not particularly inspired today."

It was their joke, a joke they made every Sunday, when he was in the country.

"I do have news though, important news. You will be sorry you missed church with such a poor excuse."

Consternation appeared on her face. "It was not an excuse," she replied firmly, "as you know very well."

"I know," he said affectionately. "But you will regret being ill on this particular Sunday, for you missed the biggest event in Hunsford since Sir Lewis married Lady Catherine."

Mrs Gatley sat up straighter in bed. "When I think of how many sermons I have had to endure and nothing to tell at the end of it! And now, on the only day for years that I have missed church, something big has to happen. What a misfortune!"

Mr Gatley laughed. "It is a misfortune for me, for now I will have to recount every detail, since if I do not, you will be at a disadvantage when the ladies of the neighbourhood come to visit, and you will blame me for it."

"Spare me the commentary and come to the point, please, Henry. Come and sit on the bed where I can see you without twisting my neck, and tell me what happened."

Her son obliged her by recounting the events of the morning in as much detail as he could remember.

He did not mention, however, that he had met Miss Georgiana Darcy. He knew how quickly his mother's mind would leap from one thing to another, and he had no intention of raising any expectations in that direction.

Chapter 2

WHEN A GROUP OF YOUNG PEOPLE COME TOGETHER, THEY are unlikely to be inconvenienced by trivialities such as the weather. Despite the chill in the air which Lady Catherine objected to, the younger Darcys elected to walk from church to Rosings, and refused Darcy's offer of a ride.

Georgiana was more than glad to have the opportunity to come to know her cousins. It was not her first encounter with such enthusiastic youngsters. Elizabeth's sisters Lydia and Kitty Bennet had been animated and headstrong young girls. But since their activities were often restricted to looking for officers and buying new hats, she normally felt awkward around them, and she knew that they were not particularly interested in her. Things were different with these cousins of hers.

It was too early to tell, of course, but she had reason to hope that something would come from the acquaintance. She very much hoped it would. For no matter how much she hesitated to acknowledge this, even to herself, the fact was she found herself at a loss. For it is a truth universally acknowledged that when there is a new baby in the house, one is certain to be ignored.

Or so it seemed to Georgiana, who had always counted on her brother Fitzwilliam's attention when they were together. She now had to accept that an active baby, crawling around everywhere, seemed to occupy a large part of her brother's affections, along with the wife he adored. It was blatantly unfair, since Georgiana had done everything she could to welcome Elizabeth to Pemberley when her brother had fallen unexpectedly in love.

She ought not think that way—she felt guilty the very moment the idea came into her mind. She loved her nephew, of course. He was a delightful little rascal, quite a miniature of his father. And she could not have hoped for a better sister. Elizabeth was a charming companion. She was merry and made her laugh and, with the assistance of her chaotic family, Pemberley had been transformed from a solemn edifice full of ghosts to a warm and affectionate home.

But there could be no doubt that Georgiana was most definitely *de trop*. The fate of unmarried sisters had befallen her. For while she did not for one instant feel unwelcome, her place had shifted in the household, and she now occupied the role of an outsider looking into a happy family circle.

The arrival of Clarissa and Frederick was therefore really very fortunate. An express had arrived a week ago from Liverpool via Derbyshire, informing Robert of his brother and sister's safe arrival in England. It had come as a complete surprise, since Robert had heard nothing at all from Boston for the last six months at least.

The letter had occasioned a great deal of excitement with everyone. Except for Lady Catherine, who had remarked that they had timed their crossing badly, since if they had arrived but one week earlier they would have been in time for Easter.

As if any of the ships crossing the ocean could predict the day of their arrival! In fact, it was only because hostilities had ceased between the two countries that they were coming at all. According to Frederick, who had written the letter, they had sailed on the very first passenger boat to leave Boston since the war.

Robert had immediately proposed opening his London town-house to receive his family, but Lady Catherine would not hear of it. The Darcys had always stayed at Rosings Park for a few weeks over Easter. Any attempt to deviate from this custom would brand him an American Darcy and, therefore, already suspect as a renegade.

Robert would not have cared in the least about such branding. But the peace between Fitzwilliam Darcy and his aunt had been shattered by his marriage to Elizabeth, and it was only with great condescension—after the birth of an heir to Pemberley—that the Darcys were once again welcome at Rosings. Robert's departure would risk putting a fragile reconciliation to the test.

An express message was sent accordingly to the Darcy brother and sister in Liverpool with an invitation from Lady Catherine for them to join everyone in the traditional Easter family visit to Rosings.

And, most importantly, it mentioned that Clarissa was to have her coming-out this Season. Georgiana, whose official coming-out had been postponed because Elizabeth was increasing, could not have been more delighted. She had not particularly been looking forward to the Season, but it would make all the difference to have someone else by her side.

She imagined her American cousin would find their English ways confusing at first. She would be more than happy to assist her and to provide whatever guidance she could. Clarissa was one year younger too. It would be nice to have someone to take care of for a change.

"Do you intend to stay in England for some time?" she asked Frederick.

"Having just endured the long journey from Boston," he said, "I am quite reluctant to undertake another sea voyage any time soon." He sighed. "However, you will not see much of me. I have business interests in the North that I must pursue, and what little time I have left afterwards I will spend in London becoming acquainted with members of the business community with whom I have dealings and, if possible, taking in some of the sights."

He laughed at her bemused expression. "I have not answered your question, have I, Cousin? Let us say that I will remain in England for at least two months. Beyond that, I cannot say, except that I cannot delay my business in Boston too long."

At this, Clarissa slipped her arm through Georgiana's. "As for me, I shall be very glad not to see too much of Frederick. I saw far more of him than I could ever wish during our journey. We were confined to each other's company for *weeks*."

"You wait until I leave, Clarissa," said Frederick, "then you will realise how much you will miss me, and it will be too late, for I will be gone."

"You are very much mistaken, Frederick," said Clarissa, "for I now have a new cousin who is far more interesting to me than you could ever be."

"I am very flattered," said Georgiana, smiling, "but perhaps when you come to know me you will not be of the same opinion at all."

"I cannot imagine such a thing happening," said Clarissa. "I always know immediately whether I am going to like a person or not, and I have not been mistaken yet."

"Setting aside my sister's ability to foresee the future, I must agree that it is very unlikely in any case," said Frederick gallantly.

"I have the feeling you will be a steadying influence on my wayward sister."

Georgiana basked in the glow of her new acquaintances. For the briefest moment, the assessing gaze of Mr Gatley came to her mind, but she was able to dismiss it, thinking instead how very wonderful it was to have such pleasant relations.

❧❧❧

Upon entering the drawing room at Rosings, they beheld Lady Catherine holding sway over the family from a lofty chair painted with oriental designs, with an exceedingly tall back. She wore a great yellow turban with a prominent single feather on her head and a superior expression on her face.

"Does she not resemble an oriental despot?" said Clarissa, in an undertone. "Do you think she will tell the servants to take us away and chop off our heads?"

Georgiana stifled a giggle. "I think she resembles Henry VIII," she replied. "I saw a painting of him once; I am certain she looks like him."

"What are you saying?" demanded Lady Catherine. "Tell me at once."

Clarissa curtseyed prettily, though there was nothing at all meek in her demeanour. She did not reply.

"So these then are your brother and sister," said Lady Catherine, addressing Robert Darcy. Her ladyship's gaze swept over Frederick, then moved on to examine Clarissa from top to bottom. She crooked two fingers.

"Come closer where I can see you properly," she commanded. "You need not hover in the doorway. I am aware that you have not yet changed your travel clothes. Do not worry. I will not blame you for looking dishevelled."

Clarissa approached and stood before Lady Catherine, a half smile lurking on her lips.

"Oh, I would not think of joining the company without refreshing myself first. You have no idea, Lady Catherine. I am *quite* splattered with mud."

To illustrate her point, she raised her foot and placed it on Lady Catherine's footstool. She then pulled up her skirt and petticoats almost to her knees, revealing mud-stained stockings and a very well turned calf.

"I believe my stockings are quite ruined," she said, surveying them dejectedly.

"Dear Lord, child!" exclaimed Lady Catherine, waving her hands about. "Cover yourself immediately!"

The feather on her turban trembled with indignation.

Clarissa, her eyes widely innocent, lowered the petticoats obligingly.

"There are gentlemen present! Surely you know—one does not do such things in England," she announced imperiously. "And, especially, one does not do such things in Rosings!"

Lady Catherine's scandalized gaze shot around the room but found no one to echo her outrage. Caroline was talking to Elizabeth and they had not witnessed the outrageous act. Clarissa's brothers shook their heads at Clarissa and raised their brows but did not show any undue alarm. The only other gentleman present in the room was Mr Darcy. He did not look scandalized. His eyes held a distinct gleam of amusement instead.

Her gaze returned to Clarissa, who seemed oblivious to any wrongdoing.

"I will ring for a maid to show you to your room. Go and change quickly, then. Do *not* keep us waiting."

Clarissa, with a little curtsey, turned and left the room.

"Georgiana, I wish you to help Miss Clarissa settle in. She is not accustomed to our English ways and will benefit from some instruction."

There was no mistaking her ladyship's meaning. It fell upon Georgiana to enlighten Clarissa and advise her that whatever one may do in American society, one ought not to deliberately allow an English gentlemen a view of one's calves—at least, not if one was a well-bred young lady.

Lady Catherine dismissed Georgiana with a flicker of her hand. As she left the room, Georgiana heard her saying to the others, "I would have sent Anne, since Anne's knowledge in matters related to good breeding is far superior, but she is too fatigued today."

As Georgiana stepped into the hallway, she almost ran into Clarissa, who was standing against the wall. Clarissa grinned. "I hoped she would send you after me," she said. "That got us out of her presence quickly! So, are you to instruct me on the mysterious ways of English society?"

"I fear I must," said Georgiana, uncertain what to make of this new cousin. "We have a great many social restrictions here, you know. You may not be aware of them."

Georgiana did not believe that Clarissa would do such a thing if she was really aware of the improper nature of her behaviour.

"You need not bother to explain all that," replied Clarissa, following the maid up the stairs. "I am sure I shall muddle my way through."

Georgiana was not at all satisfied by that statement. "Muddle your way through?" she said, her voice ending in a little squeak.

Ghastly visions rose up in her mind of horrified matrons glowering at them, of fellow debutants whispering and giggling, of gentlemen snubbing them in ballrooms. Did she really want to enter society with Clarissa by her side?

"Oh, do not be such a goose! I have had a proper upbringing, you know. An English governess no less, *and* a finishing school."

Georgiana let out the breath she knew she was holding. "I am glad to hear it. Why then—how then?" She could not think of a way to say it that would not offend.

Clarissa threw her a backwards glance. "I know my behaviour was improper, but I could not help it. Her manner was quite insufferable. How can you endure it?"

"I suppose I have simply become accustomed to it. We always used to visit at Easter—except that I have not visited for some time, though my brother has—and have come to know her ways."

"Well, I am in no hurry to return to the drawing room." She spotted a window seat and went to it. "I shall take my time dressing. After all, my clothes are still in my trunks and they have become very crumpled. I am afraid my dress will have to be pressed before I can wear it." She turned to the maid who had brought them up.

"Could you see to it, please?" she said with a smile.

"Oh, but you cannot!" said Georgiana, as the maid left the room. "Lady Catherine will be expecting us downstairs very soon."

"I love window seats, do you not? I have never seen one in a bedchamber before." Clarissa settled herself on the window seat, drawing her legs up into a tailor position. "This one is particularly charming. What a perfect place to sit and admire the view, or to settle down with a book of poetry!"

Georgiana had never seen a lady sit crossed legged before. With her dark curls and dark, almond eyes, Clarissa exuded a mysterious, exotic air.

"I hope you do not plan to sit like that in public."

Clarissa looked down at the long stretch of leg visible under the hem of her dress.

"Why, is it not acceptable here?"

"Most decidedly not."

"Then I *shall* sit like this in Lady Catherine's presence. She will be obliged to send me from the room again." She laughed at Georgiana's dismayed expression. "I am just teasing. Now that you are responsible for me, I will endeavour to behave very well indeed."

Georgiana was only partly relieved by Clarissa's remark. Meanwhile, she was aware of Lady Catherine downstairs, waiting for them to return. "Perhaps you ought to change. Lady Catherine does not like tardiness."

Clarissa's eyes twinkled with mischief. "Then I am sorry to say that she will have to wait for some time, for I am in no hurry to return to her illustrious presence. Besides, my gown is not yet ready."

Lady Catherine had forestalled them. She did not leave them to their own devices for very long. A few minutes later, her maid Dawson appeared.

"I am Dawson, Miss Clarissa. I have been sent by Lady Catherine to help you dress," she said with a haughty sniff. "You are wanted in the drawing room as quickly as possible."

"My dress has been taken down to be pressed," replied Clarissa, rather smugly, Georgiana thought.

"There is no time for that. There must be something you can wear," replied Dawson.

"I particularly wished to wear that dress. It is my favourite."

But by now, Dawson was rummaging in Clarissa's open trunk. She pulled out a pale yellow dress and, spreading it across the bed, pronounced it reasonably wrinkle-free.

"This one should do for dinner," said Dawson, ignoring Clarissa's protests completely. "If you'd care to turn round, Miss Clarissa, I will help you out of your old dress. Then we can send it downstairs to have it washed. The sooner we get the mud stains off the better."

Clarissa looked for a moment as though she would refuse. But good sense must have prevailed, for what good would it do to quarrel with Dawson, after all? She turned her back to Dawson and with a hugely exaggerated—and very unladylike—grimace directed at Georgiana, she submitted to the maid's ministrations.

"Well then, Dawson. You may do your worst," she said cheerfully.

Meanwhile Georgiana considered her cousin and tried to determine which was stronger—her misgivings that Clarissa may have a harmful effect on her first Season or the sense of anticipation she felt at meeting someone so completely different than that to which she was accustomed.

Chapter 3

LADY CATHERINE WAS HOLDING COURT WHEN THEY RETURNED to the drawing room, advising Mrs Caroline Darcy that she ought not to wear that particular shade of green.

"It is much too dark for someone of your colouring."

Mrs Caroline Darcy, who was known to have exquisite taste in her clothing, looked ready to say something, but restrained herself when the young girls entered. Robert Darcy signalled for them to sit by him, for he was eager for a chance to talk to his sister, but Lady Catherine forestalled him.

"You must not sit too far from me, child," she said, "otherwise you will have to shout across the room to be heard, which is not at all becoming in a young lady."

She indicated a chair close to hers.

Georgiana, who had not been a recipient of her ladyship's favour, took the seat next to Robert.

"Fortunately for you, I have not had the tea tray removed, though if you had delayed any further, you would have had to stay without. I will brew you some tea."

She made a show of inserting her key into the lock of the tea caddy and taking out the tea leaves once again.

"I thank you, Lady Catherine, but I do not like tea. I do not drink it at all. I prefer coffee."

Lady Catherine peered at her as if to determine if she was in earnest.

"Not like tea?" said Lady Catherine. "I have never heard of such a thing in my life!"

"I was not raised to like tea, Lady Catherine," said Clarissa. "Since the Boston Tea Party, I am afraid the inhabitants of Boston have been much more inclined to drink coffee."

Robert, who had been observing the scene with amusement, guffawed loudly at her words.

"What tea party? What *are* you talking about?" She puzzled over this, until understanding dawned suddenly. "I do recall something about the people of Boston tipping all their tea into the harbour. Why could they not have sent the tea back, instead of destroying it? A shocking waste of good tea when it is so very expensive. I always thought it odd, but then, there is no accounting for taste. I like my coffee well enough. But I am afraid you will find that you cannot avoid tea here in England, Miss Clarissa, unless you wish to appear uncommonly rude. I suggest you acquire a taste for it." She paused for a long moment. "Or at the very least, learn to sit on a chair that has a plant next to it."

Georgiana, who would not have thought her aunt capable of such a joke, let out a giggle. Darcy chuckled and both Elizabeth and Caroline smiled. Clarissa, genuinely puzzled, looked around her to determine the reason for the general amusement.

"I am sorry, Lady Catherine, but I do not comprehend you. Why a plant?"

"Why, to pour your tea in. You need not fear that you will kill the plants, for they are generally fond of tea," she said, the slight smile that stretched her lips revealing that she was very pleased with herself for her joke.

It was not in her ladyship's nature to be amused for very long however. She drained her teacup and then returned to her customary mode of interrogation.

"How did you enjoy your journey here, Miss Clarissa?" she demanded.

"I cannot say I enjoyed the journey," replied Clarissa. "Fortunately I did not suffer from sea sickness, which afflicted some of the others, but we experienced some terrifying moments."

"I daresay you must have encountered a gale," remarked Lady Catherine. "*That* would account for you being terrified."

"Quite so," replied Clarissa pertly. "And I can assure you, there is nothing as terrifying as being on a tiny ship in an enormous ocean and being buffeted by the waves."

"Surely you did not come on a tiny ship," said Lady Catherine. "You did not, did you, Mr Frederick?"

"I believe Clarissa was referring to how she felt upon the ship, rather than to its actual size," he replied, with a small smile.

"Then she should have said so," her ladyship asserted. Satisfied with his answer, however, she turned her eyes upon Clarissa again. "Well, child? Do you intend to continue your account or not?"

"Certainly, Lady Catherine. The waves rose higher than a steeple, and they crashed down around us with the force of boulders."

"Boulders?" interrupted Lady Catherine. "How ridiculous!"

"I see you have acquired some literary talent since I last saw you, Sister," said Robert Darcy, with a grin. Lady Catherine sent him a quelling glance.

"Fortunately, the gale did not tear the ship apart as I expected," continued Clarissa, ignoring both interruptions. "In fact, the captain told me afterwards—I do wish he had thought to mention it earlier—that packet boats are made to work well under stormy conditions, as they can sail closer to the wind than other ships and can pick up good speed when the wind is strong. Or something to that effect, for he explained it at great length and I understood only half the nautical terms." She paused and looked round. Georgiana could tell that she enjoyed having an audience.

"However, the gale was not at all the most terrifying aspect of the trip. *That* occurred much earlier."

She paused, whether for effect or to catch her breath was not clear.

"We were assured before we left, you see, that the treaty had been ratified, or Mother would never have put us—particularly me—on a ship bound for England. We never expected to have a military encounter. So you can imagine our terror when we were fired upon by an English naval vessel, just a few days out from Boston!"

"Impossible!" muttered her ladyship, outraged. "No British naval vessel would break the treaty. Are you accusing a British naval officer of acting dishonourably?"

Clarissa flashed her a grin. "I am only recounting what occurred, Lady Catherine, and my brother will support my account." Everyone looked towards Frederick, who nodded in confirmation. "It turned out that they were firing a warning. We were obliged to draw up to them and allow them to come aboard to inspect our ship. I hid in a corner, convinced they would hack us to pieces, for they looked uncommonly grim and harsh in their uniforms. But then they asked us if we had ratified the treaty and the captain said yes and there were smiles and cheers all round."

"I should think so indeed," said Lady Catherine, sitting back in her chair with a relieved expression. But then she sat up straight again.

"What can your mother have been about," she remarked suddenly, "sending you all the way to England without even a maid to accompany you?"

"My sister did have a companion—her governess, no less—a Mrs Morris," said Frederick, "but since Mrs Morris and I are to return to Boston in a short while, I have granted her permission to visit her relations in Lancashire, knowing that a maid will be appointed for Clarissa in London. I trust we will not need to appoint one here?"

Lady Catherine stared at Frederick for a long moment. "You seem very decisive for one so youthful. Exactly how old are you?"

"I am twenty-six, madam."

"I expect you are like all Americans—presumptuous, outspoken, and opinionated. A bad business this, declaring your independence from England. And how do you think you will manage without us, pray? You may depend on it, you will come to realise your folly soon enough."

A sharp gleam entered Frederick's eye. "It has been thirty-nine years since our Declaration of Independence," he remarked. "And I believe no one has had cause to regret it so far, particularly since we have so recently been at war. We have built our own institutions…"

But Lady Catherine's attention was diverted by a message that had been brought in by a footman.

"What can be the meaning of this?"

She scanned the contents and tossed the note aside.

"I had expected to be joined by a gentleman today for dinner," said Lady Catherine. "Colonel Fitzwilliam, Darcy's cousin. He is a very eligible young man," she explained, addressing her words to Clarissa, "and I intend to see him married to Anne or to Georgiana."

Georgiana noted the warning to Clarissa implied in her aunt's words. Since she herself was discovering Lady Catherine's plans for the first time, she was completely taken aback. She made an unsuccessful attempt to hide her reaction.

"You may look surprised, Georgiana, but do not think I will let you go the way of your brother. What objection could you possibly have to Colonel Fitzwilliam? And who else should he marry but one of his own cousins? He may not command a fortune himself, but he is the son of an earl, and *that* signifies a great deal. Well, what do you have to say to that?"

Georgiana had a great deal to say to that, but she did not think any of it would be wise.

"Georgiana is to be presented in London," said Elizabeth firmly. "I am sure there will be plenty of eligible young men there for her to meet."

"She should be presented in London, of course, and should be presented at court, though I am sure *you* will not be able to do so. You must leave it to Darcy to find someone suitable. Georgiana has an old and worthy heritage, and she should be proud of it. But that can have no bearing on the matter at hand. I have quite settled it in my mind: either Georgiana or Anne will marry Colonel Fitzwilliam," she pronounced. "I have not yet determined whether I wish him for Anne. I do not approve of young ladies marrying strangers, nor of all this newfangled business of marrying for love."

She directed a significant dark glance at Elizabeth, then at Darcy, who had not heard a word, since he was deep in discussion with Robert and Frederick. "I have always said it is far better for those who have money to keep the money within the family," she said more loudly, "for why should we benefit other families, when we can benefit our own?"

Darcy still paid her no attention. She was obliged to call out to him. "Darcy! You do not attend to my words."

"Lady Catherine?" he said, respectfully enough, but his lips had tightened.

They were all making a special effort to be polite to Lady Catherine. After Fitzwilliam's marriage to Elizabeth, she had cut them off and only the birth of a Darcy heir had enabled a reconciliation to occur. This was the first time in two years they had visited Lady Catherine and there was a marked tension in the air.

"I hope you do not plan to let Georgiana have any choice in the matter of her marriage."

"On the contrary, she will have a great deal of choice in the matter of her marriage, Aunt," he responded. "But we had better postpone this discussion to another time." He looked meaningfully towards the doorway through which Mr Collins's voice could now be heard.

Lady Catherine, who would never stoop to discussing family matters in front of the lower orders, immediately dropped the subject.

Clarissa, making the most of the Collinses' arrival, came over quickly and took a place next to Georgiana.

"I am very grateful that Lady Catherine has not included me in her plans," she whispered. "Though if I had known that we were expecting an eligible gentleman, I would have waited to show my ankle until later."

Georgiana, trying not to laugh, looked down, for she did not wish to draw the attention of Lady Catherine once more. But, as luck would have it, Lady Catherine noticed her and, misled by her downcast eyes, remarked loudly that Georgiana at least was an obedient, modest girl and thought just as she ought. *She* was not unbecomingly forward.

"In any case, the colonel will not be joining us today. He has written to say he cannot, for with Napoleon running about France gathering an army, one cannot be sure of anything at this time, and none of the officers are permitted to take leave."

"I can see that you have taken my news badly, Anne," she said, looking towards her daughter and frowning. "I am sure, however, that Colonel Fitzwilliam would not have missed this family gathering if he could help it, for he is very attached to me and to Rosings and does not like to stay away."

Georgiana, try as she would, could see nothing in Anne's behaviour to reflect any disappointment. Anne looked tired and pale—precisely as she always did.

"It is, of course, all Napoleon's fault, for he is becoming quite bothersome. He has certainly inconvenienced us, for now there will be too few gentlemen and we will be obliged to change the seating arrangement at the table."

The Collinses were ushered in at that moment. They were followed by a nursemaid carrying a two-month infant—Felicity—who was promptly removed after Lady Catherine had examined her face and remarked that her looks were improving now that her face was no longer so crumpled and she did not look so cross-eyed.

Mr Collins was very gratified by the praise. He bowed low before Lady Catherine and thanked her most earnestly for noticing what must be to her ladyship a very insignificant matter. He then went on to apologise to everyone present, expressing his fear that he had kept them waiting.

"I must lay the blame at Mrs Collins's door, for at the last moment we had to wait while the nurse changed Felicity, since Charlotte was not satisfied that she was presentable. She was convinced that her clothes were wet, though I assured her they were quite dry, with the unfortunate consequence that we have now encroached upon your ladyship's infinite patience by keeping your ladyship waiting."

"Mrs Collins was quite right," replied Lady Catherine decisively. "You could not have brought an infant into my presence in wet clothes. Of course, if you had been truly late, it would have been altogether better to leave the child behind."

Mr Collins expressed his regrets once again and promised that, should such a deplorable event occur another time, he would keep her ladyship's advice in mind.

Lady Catherine now rose, a signal that they would be going into dinner, and, as they gathered to form a line, her imposing voice could be heard correcting everyone in matters of precedence.

"We do not have enough gentlemen," she said. "If I had known the colonel was not coming, I would have invited Mr Gatley to dine with us. He would have evened out the numbers and is the only gentleman in the neighbourhood worthy of being invited to dinner at Rosings. We would still have been short, but that would hardly matter to the younger ladies, since they are not yet fully out. They will have to be content with sitting next to each other."

Georgiana was delighted at the opportunity.

As they were taking their seats, Lady Catherine turned to Georgiana and addressed her from the top of the table.

"Perhaps now you will realise what your fate will be as an old maid—perhaps *now* at least you will regret Colonel Fitzwilliam's absence. You are forced to sit at the bottom of the table and must enter without an escort."

Georgiana made a valiant attempt to keep a straight face, but Clarissa next to her fumbled for a napkin.

Fortunately, the first course was brought in and Lady Catherine did not see her as she collapsed into a fit of giggles.

But when the fit passed, Georgiana was struck by a certain realisation. She might not take Lady Catherine seriously, but she served as a reminder of the change in her status now. For the first time, she considered the implications of Lady Catherine's speech.

She was now old enough to be married. Lady Catherine's words were just the beginning of the pressure that society would bring to bear upon her to choose a husband, and choose quickly. The carefree time of being left to her own devices had gone forever. Whether the gentleman in question was Colonel Fitzwilliam, Mr Gatley, or anyone else she had not yet met, she would before long have to start making decisions. Within a few short months, her future would be determined.

It was a terrifying prospect.

Chapter 4

"WE MUST ENDEAVOUR TO KIDNAP MISS DE BOURGH," announced Clarissa several days later as the three younger Darcy cousins were walking together in the tree-lined grove in Rosings Park. "We have to take her away from here. We cannot allow her to languish like this. I am certain Lady Catherine locks her in a tower when no one is around and forces her to drink some strange herbs that stop her from running away or talking to anyone. Nothing else would account for her condition."

"Something villainous is most certainly afoot," replied Frederick with mock gravity. "Lady Catherine must be in desperate need of her daughter's fortune, having gambled all her husband's money away. I am convinced she is poisoning Miss de Bourgh, slowly but steadily. Would you not agree, Miss Darcy?"

Georgiana laughed. "I cannot imagine my aunt gambling a fortune away, however fond she may be of card games, but I am willing to entertain any idea you put forward as possible."

"You need not make fun, you know," said Clarissa, addressing her brother. "If you are so very clever, *you* may explain to us why Miss de Bourgh says hardly a word and has been reduced to such a pitiful condition. Have you seen how Mrs Jenkinson hovers around her constantly? I am convinced that Mrs Jenkinson is not her companion at all. She is her keeper." She paused to allow her statement to sink in.

"You look sceptical, Georgiana, but can you deny that she is watched every moment? Why is it that Miss de Bourgh cannot wriggle a finger without someone noticing—either Mrs Jenkinson, Lady Catherine, or her maid Dawson? I have never seen the young lady alone. Why, I would not be surprised if someone watches her even when she is on the privy."

Georgiana was suitably shocked at this remark. Clarissa threw her a wicked glance. "Yes, I know I ought not to mention such things. But that is neither here nor there. What explanation do you have, Frederick? Or do you think her quite ordinary and unremarkable?"

"She could be remarkable or odd without being a victim of a devious plot," replied Frederick.

Clarissa made an impatient sound.

"I will grant you that she is not at all ordinary," said Frederick. "Over the last week I have used every skill in conversation I ever learned. I have tried a variety of approaches. I have talked of the snow that fell on the fifteenth—which everyone has discussed most eagerly—but it did not motivate her. I have spoken banalities, uttered trivialities, spewed forth philosophical wisdom, and made the most outrageous remarks hoping that something might prompt her to speak. Nothing worked."

"Oh, Fred, you did not!"

"I most certainly did," replied Frederick. "But it made not a jot of difference. I still could not bring her to say more than two words at a time. Surely, even if she is very sickly, she would welcome some diversion? Unless, of course, she disapproves of our presence in her home, and her silence is prompted by disdain or arrogance. Miss Darcy, you know her better than we do. Is it possible that she despises us?"

Georgiana was at a loss to provide them with more information. She could not imagine that Anne was so very proud. But she was by no means certain. She could only remark, rather guiltily, that she had no idea.

To herself, she admitted uncomfortably that she had not made any genuine effort to speak to her cousin for years. She always enjoyed her visits to Rosings—in spite of her aunt—particularly when she came from school, because she knew her dear brother would be at Rosings at the same time and she saw so little of him generally. So her main objective in visiting Rosings was usually Fitzwilliam, and she rarely communicated with her cousin. To her, Anne was—Anne. Georgiana hardly spared her a moment.

"I do not believe that a sense of consequence motivates her," said Clarissa with certainty. "It is fear and fear alone. Lady Catherine has threatened her. She is afraid to speak lest she reveal the terrible trials she has endured."

Georgiana shook her head at Clarissa's fanciful interpretation. Frederick chuckled.

"Clarissa is always like this," he said to Georgiana. "She has read so many horrid novels she sees the whole of life itself as a never-ending conflict between villains and innocents."

Clarissa frowned at her brother. "I would be grateful if you kept your opinions of me to yourself. You may wish to prejudice Georgiana against me, but I will not permit it."

She turned her back to him and walked on ahead. Georgiana, caught amidst this wrangle between sister and brother, could not determine whether they were in earnest. She remained in an agony of indecision whether to intervene or not.

They continued a few steps in silence, with Clarissa walking in front of them. Very soon, however, she dropped back to join them, the quarrel forgotten, and addressed herself to Georgiana.

"You *must* tell us what occurred to make Anne what she is. Was she always so meek and biddable? She is such a scrawny thing. Yet I think if she were to build up her strength she could be quite taking, for though she is small and thin, her features are quite pleasant. If only she was not always so wet and miserable. With all those furs wrapped around her, she looks like a rain-soaked kitten."

Georgiana laughed. "Oh, Clarissa! I thought you in earnest."

"I *am* in earnest."

Georgiana, recognizing that Clarissa really did want an answer, considered her question. "It seems that she was always like this. Though now that you have brought it up, I seem to recall a time when she was not."

An image sprang to her mind of a girl climbing a tree. It was a distant memory, for Georgiana must have been very young at the time. In her mind's eye she saw Anne laughing. She saw a bright face, with red cheeks and eyes that glowed. Anne had laughed and pelted apples at Georgiana and her brother, until finally Fitzwilliam could bear it no longer. He climbed the tree after her and dragged her down. Yet even then she had laughed. The memory seemed so at variance with the present that Georgiana was ready to dismiss it as nothing more than her imagination.

"I remember she was struck down by a putrid fever," she replied, trying to recall what was vague at best. "It was the same illness that killed Sir Lewis. Anne never recovered her strength afterwards. I think that, for some time, Lady Catherine lived in fear of losing Anne as well. But no one has mentioned it since, so I cannot be sure."

"How long ago was that?" asked Clarissa.

"Sir Lewis died about twelve years ago."

Clarissa shuddered. "*Twelve years* of being smothered and cosseted! That is enough to make anyone sickly and cross."

"You must not say such things!" said Georgiana, coming belatedly to her cousin's defence. "It is not her fault if her health is delicate."

"I did not mean that it was, only that *I* would never have accepted it. I would have fought harder to overcome my weakness."

Georgiana smiled at her cousin's statement. "That is easy to say when one is strong," she said, "but who knows what one would do under the circumstances? Being constitutionally weak is bound to erode one's will."

Frederick stopped at this point and announced his intention to return to the house.

"We know too little about the situation to make a judgement. Clarissa tends to exaggerate, but I would certainly like to discover more, especially as she is almost a cousin of ours. Our best course of action now will be to question Darcy about her, for he will remember a great deal more than Georgiana, since he is much older."

Clarissa grinned at him. "By all means. Anything you can find out will surely help us resolve this puzzle."

With a quick bow to Georgiana, he strode away.

"Your brother is very obliging," remarked Georgiana.

"Oh, I do not believe him for a moment. He has only returned to the house because he is tired of my wild fancies. A game of billiards with Darcy is of far more interest to him than spending time with *us*."

This was hardly flattering for Georgiana, who was enjoying Frederick's company. She must have revealed her disappointment because Clarissa corrected herself at once.

"Oh! I did not mean that he is bored with you! But what young man would choose to stroll around with relations far younger than himself if he can spend time with gentlemen-about-town like Robert and your brother?"

"True enough," said Georgiana, though not particularly convinced.

"In any case, we must make our own plans. We need not depend on my brother for anything. The first thing we must do is find a way to talk with Miss de Bourgh alone. We must draw her away from Mrs Jenkinson, who is no doubt set to spy on her. Then, when she is alone with us, we can convince her to confide her situation to us. Perhaps there is some way we can help her."

Georgiana mulled this over. It was true that Anne was never left alone. And however fanciful it may be to cast Lady Catherine as the villain of a Gothic novel, Georgiana was aware that Lady Catherine was a formidable parent who allowed her daughter very little independence.

She was mortified to think that she had never thought of reaching out to her cousin and helping her before.

❦

Clarissa was certainly right about Frederick, for when Georgiana approached him later to ask if he had found out anything more about Anne, he looked confused at first and then smiled wryly.

"I have not had the chance of a private moment with Darcy yet," he said. "But we are going out together later this afternoon, and I will try to ask him then."

His response confirmed to Georgiana Clarissa's superior knowledge of gentlemen's behaviour.

"You were right about your brother," she said to Clarissa when she saw her a short time later. "You understand people far better than me, even though you are more than a year younger." Her statement held a minute note of envy.

Clarissa immediately dismissed her praise.

"Fiddle-de-dee! Knowing my brother hardly demonstrates superior understanding," she replied. "He is altogether too predictable. Besides, you must remember that I grew up with three brothers." She peered round the edge of the door into the drawing room, and, finding it empty, ran to sit in Lady Catherine's chinoiserie chair.

"I do declare," said Clarissa, "I feel like a monarch."

"You must not, Clarissa!" Georgiana protested, casting an anxious glance towards the door and half laughing. "Suppose she were to come upon us?"

"I cannot imagine what she would do if she does come upon us," said Clarissa. "Is there a rule that no one but Lady Catherine is allowed to sit in that chair?"

"No. At least, there is no spoken rule. But the fact is, nobody does, and it would vex her exceedingly."

"I care little if she is vexed. I also like to sit in this chair." But she sprung up and waved her hand towards the piano forte.

"Do you like music? Or, I should ask, are you a proficient player?"

Playing the piano forte was one of Georgiana's most treasured accomplishments. She could happily spend several hours a day playing and considered herself a good musician. She did not want to appear boastful, however.

"I have been told I am," she replied modestly.

"Good. Then we have something in common, for I am generally deemed to be a talented player," said Clarissa. "We shall have to play for each other. Wait here. I will go up to fetch some music, and we can judge each other's playing for ourselves."

Clarissa returned presently with several sheets of music.

"I have *Les Adieux* by Beethoven. It was the latest piece of his to be had in Boston. I do not know if he has published anything since. Do you not like Mr Beethoven? Is he not sublime?"

"I cannot say I like him. I find him too ponderous."

"You must not have heard him played as I have or you would not say such a thing. Listen!"

She opened the piano, and spreading her fingers across the keys, she began to play.

Georgiana listened as her cousin had bid her and marvelled. She had never heard Beethoven played as her cousin played him, with so many contrasts and in such an evocative manner.

"Well, Cousin? Do you see now how Beethoven's music is not as heavy as you pronounced him? You know, he wrote this piece when Napoleon was marching into Vienna. Fortunately, it has a happy ending."

"I admit myself mistaken," replied Georgiana readily. "But how did you learn to play so well? If only I could aspire to half your skill and expression, I would be happy."

"Tut! When I have heard so much from your brother about your skill. I was worried you would think me beneath your notice. Come," she said, pulling her towards the piano and pressing her to sit on the bench. "I have played for you. Now it is your turn."

Georgiana chose a piece by Cramer she knew very well. She executed it perfectly, with only one minor error, and by the end felt very pleased with herself.

"I see your reputation is not exaggerated," said Clarissa. "Though with your permission, I have a comment to make."

Georgiana was accustomed to receiving general applause whenever she played. So she smiled at her cousin's remark and said that she would be happy to hear anything her cousin had to say. She supposed that it would be an extravagant compliment.

"Your execution is faultless," said Clarissa, "and your playing—perfection itself. Nevertheless, there is something lacking."

Georgiana was quite at a loss as to how to react to this unexpected criticism.

"You would be a far superior player if you could infuse your performance with more feeling."

Georgiana swallowed. "Surely you jest, Clarissa."

"No, I am serious. I believe you are the more skilful player of us two. But when music lacks heart, there is something hollow in the performance. I will show you the difference."

Clarissa turned to the first page of the piece Georgiana had been playing, "You can play this piece in so many ways. You may play it gaily," she said, and her fingers pranced across the piano. The music came out sounding almost comical.

"Or you may be solemn." She played the next few bars in a grave, studied way, and the piece turned ponderous.

Georgiana shook her head. "But you cannot *change* the music from what it is meant to be. You cannot bend it to your will. I do not believe one should force one's own temperament onto the music."

Clarissa put down the piano cover and rose. "I was, of course, exaggerating, to prove my point. I will not try to convince you to play against your will. Indeed, you play remarkably well. Our divergence stems merely from a difference in style. Come, let us leave, for I hear Lady Catherine's voice, and I do not wish to be compelled to play for her. I can put up with opinionated remarks about almost anything, but I like music too much to allow her to instruct me when she knows nothing about it."

That evening two young men arrived at the invitation of Mr Darcy to make up a card party. Georgiana saw them from the stairs as they strode towards the library. One was Mr Gatley, though all she caught of him was a glimpse of broad shoulders and dark hair coiling above a night-blue coat. She had never seen the other gentleman. She had the impression of a lithe form with an easy stride, merry blue eyes under a fashionable sweep of ash hair, and refined features. He nodded to her as he passed by, acknowledging her presence.

The party was intended for the gentlemen alone. Lady Catherine, however, had no intention of allowing the men to disappear from under her jurisdiction for a whole evening.

"Where are you taking that table?" she said to the hapless footman who was carrying a card table that way. "Is that the table from my parlour? Why are you not setting it up in the living room?"

"Mr Darcy requested it, your ladyship. He specifically mentioned the library."

"Nonsense. They cannot intend to neglect the ladies when it is only nine o'clock. They may have their own card game later. Gentlemen keep late hours, in any case. It can be no great sacrifice to postpone their own party until after they have played with us."

Under other circumstances, Georgiana would have been delighted with the opportunity to mix with gentlemen that were unknown to her. But she was wary of Mr Gatley. Something about him put her on the alert—or on the defensive, she was not quite certain which—and made her wish to avoid him. She was quite at a loss to account for it, for she could not put her finger on any particular cause. She had the feeling that he was a person who was quick to judge others and who was only too ready to find fault with them.

It was with some hesitation, therefore, that she agreed to join them in a rubber of whist. Her instincts told her she would do well to excuse herself and retire to her room.

The attraction of mixing with two handsome young gentlemen is a temptation few young ladies can turn resist, however. Georgiana told herself she ought to at least discover what it was about Mr Gatley that disturbed her. And she unquestionably wanted to meet the other gentleman.

So, despite the qualms that whispered at the back of her mind, she allowed herself to be persuaded.

Chapter 5

IF HE HAD KNOWN THEY WERE TO SPEND THE EVENING WITH Lady Catherine, Gatley would never have accepted the invitation. He had dealt with Lady Catherine more than he would ever have wished. Since he had returned from the war to take over his inheritance two years ago, he had come to realise that nothing could be accomplished in the village of Hunsford without Lady Catherine's express approval. As self-appointed magistrate of the parish, nothing was beneath her notice and nothing beyond her interference.

It was the way of things, of course. Sir Lewis de Bourgh's family had held sway in Hunsford for generations. And now Lady Catherine in her own right claimed ascendency. She was the only titled person in the area, and her rank had its privileges. Still, it did not mean he enjoyed his enforced association with her.

His worst encounters with her—and he admitted that his patience threshold was not very high—were at the parish meetings, where the landowners of the area met to discuss common problems. He had quickly realised that the only way to avoid confrontation was to avoid speaking to her ladyship. It was not the best solution, by any means. But he had no other recourse. She was so very determined to have her way that it was impossible to convince her to change her mind about anything.

Naturally, he could not avoid meeting her socially, and on such occasions, he came prepared to be polite.

But he had not come expecting to see Lady Catherine tonight. He regretfully abandoned his vision of brandy, cigars, cards, and good company, and resigned himself to an evening wrought with tension.

He was tempted to tell Darcy he had remembered a previous engagement. But he did not think there was any way to do it without causing offence. He could hardly be impolite to Darcy about his aunt. But the fact was, he could not think of a less pleasurable way to spend the evening.

He was not in the best of moods, therefore, when he entered the drawing room.

Darcy's sister immediately caught his eye. Her light wispy hair floated around her face, and her large hazel eyes stared out at the world like a curious kitten. She was really quite beautiful, in a quiet, ethereal kind of way. In the church, with the light of the stained glass windows on her, she had looked almost otherworldly.

Unfortunately, she had the self-effacing mannerisms that afflicted young chits new out of the schoolroom. She did not meet one's gaze head-on, or if she did, she looked away quickly, as she was doing now. Of course, she was still young—not yet out in Society, he would wager. Very likely she would improve, once she had been through her Season and lost her hesitancy. He hoped so, for he was not one of those men who delighted in blushing young innocents.

Her cousin—Cassandra or Clarissa, he could not remember which—also made a pretty picture. But where Miss Darcy gave the impression of tranquillity, her cousin gave the impression of sharpness. She smiled and laughed but there was an edge to it all—the edge of a blade, well-honed. He sensed that she was unpredictable, and he himself preferred balance too much to find that engaging.

Since they were condemned to an evening with the ladies—and he still resented it, feeling he had agreed to come under false pretences—it was remarkably easy to choose whom he would prefer to spend it with. He strolled over to Miss Darcy and took a seat next to her.

Georgiana was delighted to meet the new gentleman, Mr Channing. His manners were carefree and pleasant, and he gave every sign of being more than happy to spend an evening with the ladies. It surprised her to discover that he was Mr Gatley's cousin, since he did not resemble that daunting gentleman in the least.

As for Mr Gatley, he entered the drawing room with a scowl on his face. She resolved to be civil despite his coldness, reminding herself that she had already been guilty of ill manners in the church-yard. Her determination, however, proved unnecessary. He came over to her as soon as he entered, and she found nothing to fault either in his greeting or in his conduct afterwards. If he lacked the sparkle of his cousin, he could hardly help it. Not everyone could be animated and compelling.

Georgiana secretly decided that he was a little dull.

Meanwhile, Mr Channing expressed an eager desire to learn all about America from Clarissa and Frederick.

"You have to tell me all about it," he said. "It must be quite a change to come to Kent from Boston."

Frederick snorted. "Very different indeed!" But he was little inclined to continue the conversation, and wandered off to talk to enquire of Elizabeth what book she was reading.

"From Boston, yes," replied Clarissa, "for I have never lived in the country. I grew up in town, so it is quite new for me to be in a country environment."

"In that case, you must find it doubly tedious to be here."

"Not at all, Mr Channing. I have discovered a whole new family over here, and I am very glad to become acquainted with them, at least for now." She smiled impishly. "You will have to ask me a year from now, if I continue to live in the country, and then my answer would perhaps be quite different."

"A woman after my own heart!" exclaimed Mr Channing. "For I will admit that I find town living far superior to country living. But then Gatley here will disagree, I am sure."

"For each its season," said Mr Gatley. "I enjoy London for a time when everyone flocks to London. But then when I tire of it, I am more than happy to retire to the country and forget about London entirely."

"How can one forget London?" said Mr Channing. "It is far too amusing. I must tell you, Miss Clarissa, that you will quickly tire of being here."

"What about you, Miss Darcy?" said Mr Gatley. "Which do you prefer?"

Georgiana thought of many lonely hours spent alone in Pemberley, walking through the hallways, staring at the pictures of her ancestors, and feeling like a wraith.

"To me town is infinitely preferable."

"Huzzah, Miss Darcy! So you see, Gatley, you are the odd man out here."

Mr Gatley smiled. "If you hope to make me change my mind because of that, I should tell you from now—you will not. I am certain that when you have reached my age, you will all be in agreement with me."

"So he speaks from the grand old age of twenty-six! With what gravity you must see the world from that lofty vantage-point!"

The young ladies laughed. Mr Gatley merely smiled and insisted that he would remind them of this in the future.

"A wager!" said Mr Channing. "I smell a wager."

"You do not smell anything," replied Mr Gatley, "for I will not wager on a certainty."

❦

It was easy to like Mr Percy Channing. Fortune had bestowed on him everything that could please a young lady, but for Georgiana, he had an ability she longed to have herself and always appreciated in others: the ability to put people at ease. Before she knew it, Georgiana was talking to him as though she had known him all her life.

"I cannot comprehend why we did not meet before, Miss Darcy. I know your brother well, but I never became acquainted with you."

He almost certainly knew the most recent reason for her absence from the neighbourhood. Fitzwilliam and Elizabeth had incurred Lady Catherine's wrath when they married against her will. It was only the birth of little William Lewis—the new Darcy heir—that had softened her towards them. She was grateful to him for not referring to it.

"I was at school until recently and only used to visit at Easter. Afterwards, I settled in Derbyshire. I have not visited my aunt for some time."

"In that case, you must grant me the opportunity to show you and your cousins around the area. You may know it a little, perhaps, but I am sure your cousins will be eager to discover it."

"I am sure they would be delighted," she said sedately, not wishing to sound too eager for his company.

"And you? Would you be delighted?"

She was pleased that he asked.

"Thank you, I would."

"Then we will arrange for something very soon. I wish the weather would settle soon. It is so difficult to arrange outings at this time of the year."

Georgiana agreed. The recent snow had cast a damper on everyone's hopes for a warm spring.

"And we will endeavour to find some amusements for you in the neighbourhood."

His use of the plural made her curious.

"May I ask why you keep saying 'we'? Do you have sisters or brothers?"

"No, I am an only child. I was referring to Gatley as well as myself."

"Are you and your cousin close friends then?"

"In some ways. We deal together very well. We spent the early part of our childhood together, so he is much more like an elder brother to me than a cousin." He lowered his voice to confide in her. "Though sometimes, I will admit, he is difficult to be with. He demands perfection in those around him, and woe to you if you do not measure up to his ideal."

This was so close to Georgiana's own impression that she gave a little laugh.

"Is he always like this then?"

"Not always," said his cousin, "for how would I then tolerate his company? No, he can be very agreeable when he sets his mind to it, but one never knows when the mood will strike him."

Georgiana turned her head to survey the young man occupying the chair next to her. He was talking to Clarissa, a half smile on his lips. Apparently, he was prepared to make himself agreeable, for a while at least.

"I hope I have not given you the wrong impression," said Channing anxiously. "I should not have spoken as I did, for I am very attached to my cousin."

Georgiana assured him that he had not said anything she had not already observed in Mr Gatley, and Channing gave her a look of relief.

"In any case, *you* need not worry about that, for even a stickler such as my cousin would find nothing to fault in *your* behaviour."

Lady Catherine's voice broke unceremoniously into their conversation.

"The card tables have been set. We can now commence our play. Darcy, you may join our table. And Mr Channing. Mr Frederick, you may join Mr Gatley at the other table. I suppose, Mrs Darcy, as usual you prefer reading to card playing?"

"Most definitely," said Elizabeth, her eyes twinkling.

"Or perhaps you would prefer a game of backgammon?" said Robert. "I have a mind to play one myself if anyone would join me."

"I will join you," said Elizabeth. "But I warn you I have every intention of winning this time."

"That remains to be seen," he replied, taking up the challenge.

Meanwhile, Channing rose with exaggerated reluctance from his seat and threw Georgiana a regretful glance, managing at the same time to express his comic distaste for having to sit with Lady Catherine. Georgiana pressed her lips together to prevent a laugh from escaping.

But a moment later her laughter disappeared when she realised that, while she was paying attention to Channing, she had been assigned a partner—Mr Gatley.

Though by no means outstanding, she was generally a competent player. Tonight, however, she played badly, making the wrong call several times, and growing more and more flustered as the evening wore on.

"I take it you do not like cards, Miss Darcy?" said Mr Gatley.

Georgiana—who was on the verge of saying something similar in order to excuse herself and retire—now was provoked into asserting the opposite.

"I am very fond of card playing, Mr Gatley. What gives you the impression that I do not like to play?"

He could not, of course, answer by saying she played badly. She waited to see what he would come up with.

His eyes glinted. "Merely that you appear distracted, and seem more inclined to watch the people around us than the cards."

Touché. He had answered her question, and at the same time reproached her for not paying attention. He was intelligent, she would grant him that much.

"I admit that I find people more interesting than cards," she replied. "Which is fortunate or I would be likely to turn into a hardened player and become the bane of my family's existence."

"I am in a position to assure your family that they need never have a moment's anxiety in that respect."

At the other table, Channing nudged Clarissa, who was not his partner, and she responded mischievously by flashing her cards at him, taunting him with a quick view. Georgiana cursed the luck that had seated Clarissa at his side and not her. She stole glances at him from the corner of her eye. Blue eyes shimmered as he tilted his head backwards and laughed. Fawn hair flew back then fell forward again onto his brow. Supple fingers picked out a card and snapped it onto the table.

It was her turn to set down a card. She put one down at random.

Mr Gatley groaned, while Frederick, who was partnered with Caroline, let out a whoop of joy.

"I do not know why you are being so hen-witted tonight, Georgiana, for when we played a rubber two days ago you were far superior. Of course, I have no objection at all, since it means we have won the game."

"You are her cousin, Mr Frederick Darcy, but is it not rather harsh to call a lady hen-witted?"

For the second time since she knew him, Georgiana did not know whether it was worse to be censored by Mr Gatley or to be at the receiving end of his sympathy.

"My cousin is perfectly entitled to call me hen-witted if he wishes," said Georgiana, "particularly when I know it is only in jest. And to prove I have no ill feelings towards him, I suggest we switch partners."

Determined this time to show Mr Gatley that she was *not* hen-witted, she gave her hand her full concentration. To her delight, she and Frederick took the first game.

"It seems Frederick has all the luck," remarked Mr Gatley.

"I hope he will not call *me* hen-witted as well," said Caroline.

"I would never be so bold as to call my new sister any such thing," said Frederick gallantly. "Besides, *you* did not toss away important cards at crucial moments."

"I believe it was a conspiracy between the cousins to make me lose my money," said Mr Gatley.

"You have a suspicious mind, Mr Gatley," retorted Georgiana.

"Hardly. I can see no other explanation for your carelessness during your round with *me*, and your sudden recovery during your round with Mr Frederick."

Both Georgiana and Frederick protested.

The game at the other table ended. A small intermission followed, during which Mr Channing approached their table.

"Is my cousin giving you a hard time, Miss Georgiana? I should warn you that he demands perfection in everyone and that you will find him very difficult to please."

Georgiana smiled. "Does he really? Then I shall not try, for I know my character is far from perfect, and I will be sure to fail."

Lady Catherine now called for the players to return, and Mr Channing drifted off.

"I fail to see what is wrong in expecting the best of others," said Mr Gatley.

"There is nothing wrong in expecting the best of others," said Georgiana, warming to the subject, "provided you will allow for people's weaknesses. To demand perfection is a sure way to be disappointed in everybody, for you will be bound to think ill of others."

"It is you, Miss Darcy, who thinks ills of others, since you are so sure that I will be disappointed."

"You are twisting my words," she said, vexed.

"I am sorry if I have made you angry," he said evenly.

"I am perfectly calm," she replied crossly.

A hint of a smile touched his lips.

"Then perhaps you may allow that I have become too involved in the argument and would rather postpone it?"

"You may do so, of course."

"You are displeased. What if I admit quite humbly that you are the victor in this case, and that I need time to recoup my energies in order to defend myself better?"

A quick laugh escaped from Georgiana.

"Mr Gatley," she said, "you use politeness far too skilfully for me to stand a chance. Let us end the discussion, then, with no one a victor. But I warn you, I mean to raise the issue again some other time."

"I will be prepared," he replied, with a smile that warmed his eyes.

Frederick once again reprimanded her for not paying attention to the game. "I will not call you hen-witted again, for I dare not," he said, with mock terror. "But I wish you would pay more heed."

Amidst raillery and light conversation, the time passed better than Georgiana had expected. The ice had been broken. Still, she felt on edge around Mr Gatley, and whenever his gaze landed on her, she turned aside.

They played until late. Miss de Bourgh and Mrs Jenkinson, who had not participated, had long since excused themselves, but to Georgiana's surprise, Lady Catherine persevered.

When Lady Catherine finally stood up, she did not retire. Instead, she declared that they were in need of refreshments and that they would resume their playing after a light supper. Meanwhile, she commanded the young ladies to take their place at the piano forte.

"We have two young ladies in the household who are rumoured to be accomplished at the piano forte. Yet, thus far we have not heard a single note from either of them. Pray, what is the good of learning to play if you do not perform in front of others? I hope you play reasonably well, Miss Clarissa?"

"I believe so, Lady Catherine," said Clarissa, tilting one of her brows.

"I do not know if you have any good music masters in Boston, but I suppose you could not. You must benefit from your stay in London to study music with the best masters. Mr Robert, I hope you will ensure that your sister receives the proper instruction."

Robert Darcy, who was about to make a strategic move in his game with Elizabeth, paused and looked up. "I will certainly engage a master for her if I think that she needs it. But you can be sure that my mother, who is very diligent in these matters, has engaged the best master that can be had for her tuition."

"In Boston?" retorted Lady Catherine. "I cannot believe any American music teacher equal to one engaged in London."

"Perhaps my mother engaged an English teaching master," said Robert Darcy with laughter in his voice.

"I think an Italian music master can be hired as well in Boston as in London, Aunt," said Darcy, "for I believe it is the Italians that excel in this art."

Lady Catherine waved a hand dismissively. "I do not hold with hiring foreigners to teach young ladies. Nothing good could come of it. Italians in particular are too inclined to incite sensitive young minds to excitement. Was it not last year that young Miss Preston ran off with her Italian teacher? If *I* were to teach Anne to play, no one but an English music teacher would do for her."

There was no reply. Satisfied that she was the victor on this point, she turned to the young ladies.

"Which of you will play first? I hope neither of you will hold back, for it is very unbecoming for a young lady who is sure of her accomplishments to pretend to be shy."

Her remark seemed calculated to make Clarissa hold back obstinately. Georgiana, fearing that her cousin would say something inopportune if pressed by Lady Catherine, quickly offered to play herself.

She sat down and settled her skirts. When she raised her hand to arrange the music, she grew aware of a presence beside her.

"Allow me to turn the pages for you, Miss Darcy."

She would have preferred Mr Channing, of course, but she could hardly refuse Mr Gatley's offer.

"Very kind of you, Mr Gatley."

Her fingers felt stiff as they hovered over the keys. She did not think she would be able to play a single note, not with him standing so near and looking over her shoulder. She was a confident player, but tonight she was unusually self-conscious. She pretended to select another piece of music and shuffled the sheets again, hoping to restore her equilibrium. Again, she gathered her skirts around her. Then she looked towards her audience. Mr Channing gave her an easy smile. The smile steadied her. There was really nothing to worry about. What did it matter if she was aware of Mr Gatley's presence? She took a deep breath and began to play Kelly's very popular "March in Bluebeard."

As the familiar notes rose up and filled the room, she allowed the music to lead her. Even though Mr Gatley leaned even closer to turn the first sheet and a trace of his cologne reached her, still the music took her along, and she followed.

When the last note had dissipated, she rose and awoke to the crack of applause from her small audience.

"Now *that* is what I would call playing with feeling," said Clarissa, grinning as she took her place at the piano.

Only then did she try—unsuccessfully—to account for the strange sensations that had assailed her.

Chapter 6

THE NEXT MORNING, CLARISSA BURST INTO GEORGIANA'S bedchamber just as she had finished dressing. Her cousin's face glowed with excitement.

"You will never guess what has happened!" she said.

A number of unfeasible possibilities ran through Georgiana's mind, the first being that Mr Channing had proposed to Clarissa.

"Oh, I hate guessing games. I cannot guess, Clarissa. I give up."

Clarissa, who had hoped to keep Georgiana dangling for a while, was now deflated.

"What will you give me if I tell you?"

"Nothing," replied Georgiana. "If you will not tell me the news now, I will refuse to hear it."

"Very well, I will tell you. It is about Miss de Bourgh. I contrived yesterday to give a note to her undetected, and she has answered me! We are to meet her this very morning in the orangery *without Mrs Jenkinson*!"

More than relieved that it had nothing to do with Mr Channing, Georgiana shared immediately in Clarissa's excitement. She was by now completely convinced that Anne needed rescuing, and was delighted that Clarissa had managed to set up a meeting so quickly.

"This is excellent news," she said. "But how is Anne to shake off her keeper?"

Clarissa grimaced. "I do not know. But she is to meet us at eleven, and we only have a few minutes. 'Tis lucky you are dressed, or I would have had to go without you."

They slipped furtively through the house, not wishing to alert anyone about the direction they were taking. They slipped through the door to the orangery, and immediately the warm thick scent of orange blossoms assailed them.

They peered through the vegetation but found no one.

"She is not here," said Clarissa, her voice heavy with disappointment.

"I am here," came a feeble voice in reply.

Anne had chosen a seat in the shade of some citrus trees, where the sun that poured through the glass did not touch her. She sat among the shadows, swathed in various shawls, her hands enclosed in a grey muff.

"We had a hard time finding you, Miss de Bourgh. You certainly know how to choose your spot," said Clarissa.

"Of course," said Anne, a smile flickering on her lips.

"We never seem to have a chance to talk to you," continued Clarissa, "We wanted to take the opportunity to get to know you while we are here."

Anne threw her an odd look, as though she could not possibly believe such a thing.

"Are you cold, Cousin?" said Georgiana, imagining that the muff must be very warm inside a hothouse.

"I tend to feel the chill more than others," replied Anne.

"Oh, let us not talk about the cold," said Clarissa impatiently. "Let us talk about you."

Anne raised an eyebrow. "About me?"

"Well, I know nothing about you. Georgiana told me you fell sick at the same time as your father and have not recovered your strength since."

Anne turned her gaze on Georgiana. "Yes, I suppose that is true. You were small then. Just a little girl."

Georgiana nodded. "Still, I remember that before you fell ill, you used to laugh a lot."

Anne gazed listlessly into the distance. "I suppose I did. It seems so long ago, I barely remember it."

It occurred to Georgiana that the fever may have affected Anne's mind. She spoke in such a monotonous manner that there did not seem to be much point in continuing to question her.

Clarissa, unwavering in her intentions, was not in the least deterred by Anne's vagueness.

"But you must remember *something* of your childhood. Georgiana says you used to climb trees."

A wider smile appeared on Anne's face. "Yes, I do recall that. I used to throw apples at Fitzwilliam. He was always so proper and fussed so much about his clothes, I could not resist it."

"My brother?" said Georgiana. "No, it cannot be." She never recalled her brother fussing.

"He was indeed very particular, though you would not think it now. That was when we were fifteen, of course, and at fifteen one sees the world in a skewed way." Her face became almost animated. "I rather liked him, at the time, but he was too busy being important and growing up. And he knew his aunt intended us for each other, so I was the last person he wanted to be friendly with."

"That must have been difficult for you," said Clarissa.

"Not really," said Anne. "I pelted apples at him, and it made me feel better. What else do you wish to know?"

"I want to know why you talk to no one and why you keep so much to yourself," said Clarissa.

In the long pause that followed, Georgiana was tempted to tell Anne that she did not need to answer Clarissa's questions if she did not wish to. She would not have been surprised if Anne had chastised them for prying.

Clarissa shifted in her seat.

"I find lengthy conversation too tiresome," said Anne.

It was not much of an answer. They were clearly intruding. Really, it was time they left. Georgiana tried to catch Clarissa's eye.

"I enjoy reading, however," continued Anne. "I read anything I can lay my hands on. My father's library, fortunately, is well stocked."

"But I have never seen you read," said Clarissa.

"No. My mother does not approve of reading for females. She believes it corrupts the female brain. I read whenever I have a chance, which is often, when we do not have company, for I can always retreat to my chamber to rest."

"What do you read?"

"Anything, from poetry to botany."

Clarissa digested this. "But are you not always accompanied by Mrs Jenkinson? Does *she* know that you like to read?"

"Of course. How could I conceal such a thing from her? But she has not informed my mother." She rose and rearranged her cumbersome shawls around her. "I must go now, otherwise Mrs Jenkinson will come looking for me."

"But will you meet with us again? Alone?" insisted Clarissa. "We would like to have your company."

Again, a smile flickered. "Of course, if you wish it," said Anne. She made her way slowly back.

"That was a good beginning," said Clarissa. "She answered our questions, and she is willing to meet with us again."

Georgiana hesitated. "I suppose it *is* an improvement. As you said, she is prepared to meet with us again. But you must not press her for answers—promise me that."

"I will not," said Clarissa.

Anne seemed to have appreciated their attempt to reach out to her, for she made it a regular habit to meet with them for a short time every day. This was done stealthily, however, confirming to the young ladies that Anne did not want her mother to know. They would receive a note from a maid or a footman, informing them of a time and place for a meeting. She always seemed to know their plans, for she never set up anything if they were otherwise engaged.

Clarissa did break her promise not to pressure Anne into answering any private questions, but only once.

"How can you bear it?" she asked suddenly, when Anne mentioned something to do with Mrs Jenkinson. "Do you not crave freedom? Do you not long to leave the house whenever you wish and walk wherever you wish, without being followed and reported on all the time? Oh, I could not bear it!"

Anne, to her credit, remained unruffled during this outburst.

"It is a matter of degrees," she said calmly. "*You* cannot leave the house whenever you wish, nor go out without an escort of some kind. You have the freedom of the grounds, perhaps, but you cannot venture too far on your own."

She paused when one of her shawls slipped, and she rearranged it carefully, making sure not to disturb the others.

"Even if you *were* allowed complete freedom to go where you wish, whenever you wish, then you would still be restricted, for you would be open to attack any time by unscrupulous persons. We live in a world where the strong prey upon the vulnerable. If that were to change, then perhaps we would be completely free. But for now, we must live with what we have. We women have always had restrictions placed upon us, and we have dealt with them as best we could."

Clarissa did not ask Anne any private questions again. Instead, they found themselves discussing books they had read and exchanging opinions on poetry and art. Georgiana discovered an Anne she had never imagined existed, who not only had a breadth of knowledge, but also strong opinions on the things she read.

It was difficult to reconcile this opinionated young lady with the pale, quiet daughter who sat in the drawing room under her mother's eye. Georgiana rapidly concluded that, while Lady Catherine may not have locked her daughter in a dark tower, she had certainly driven Anne to hide her true self from the world.

***

Two days later, two ladies called on them, since Lady Catherine had graciously informed the gentlemen that they were welcome to do so. One was Mrs Gatley and the other Mrs Channing.

Mrs Channing was a tall, wiry lady whose clothes did not fit her. They rode up and appeared loose in all the wrong places. Her hunched shoulders amplified this impression. She took a few cautious steps into the drawing room and set about to express her elation at Lady Catherine's generosity in inviting them to call. While she spoke, she looked about her a great deal, as though she wanted to remember any changes to the room so that she could report them to her friends.

"One is very conscious of the privilege, Lady Catherine, especially when you already have a household of guests to entertain."

Lady Catherine inclined her head graciously and waited for Mrs Gatley to approach.

Mrs Gatley, like her sister, was a tall lady. Unlike her sister, however, she seemed to have employed a skillful modiste. She wore a striking purple walking dress with a white ruffled collar and gold braiding. She paused in the doorway, surveyed everyone present, then swept into the room with confident grace.

"Good morning, Lady Catherine," she said, her musical voice carrying across the room. "I have not seen you for some time. We shall have to arrange a vingt-et-un party one of these days at Ansdell."

"Certainly," said Lady Catherine haughtily. "But we would do better to have it here, since the drawing room at Ansdell tends to be draughty."

"Then I take it you do not wish to receive an invitation, when I send them out?" enquired Mrs Gatley politely.

Lady Catherine fixed a stony gaze on her. "Of course I wish to receive one. I can always decline if I do not wish to attend."

Mrs Gatley inclined her head politely and went to sit next to Elizabeth.

"The baby is doing well, I hope?" she asked.

Elizabeth's face brightened.

"He is doing more than well, thank you," said Elizabeth. "Only I feel I do not get enough time with him, for he is always with Nurse."

"I felt the same," said Mrs Gatley. "I used to creep up to the nursery at odd times to see my children, especially my eldest daughter. Nurse had quite an easy time of it, for I used to give her time off, just so I would have the excuse of spending time with them."

"That is the worse thing you can do to a child, especially to a boy," said Lady Catherine. "You will spoil him, and then when it comes to sending him off to school, he will have a most difficult time, and be picked on by the other boys. They must learn to be independent from infancy."

"I am not even sure it is necessary to send them off to school at all," said Elizabeth.

This radical opinion earned a disdainful look from Lady Catherine.

"That is what comes from having been raised without even as much as a governess between five girls. You will learn soon enough what it means for a boy to be an heir to a fortune, and how necessary it is for him to mingle with other males in his social class in order to take his proper place in society." She gave a scornful laugh. "Or did you think to teach him this yourself?"

A militant look entered Elizabeth's eye. Georgiana groaned inwardly. There was going to be trouble.

"I am inclined to agree with Mrs Darcy," said Mrs Gatley serenely. "I think it is cruel to send boys away when they are so young and to have them grow up without a mother's influence."

"A mother's weakness must never be allowed to affect the child's future," said Lady Catherine repressively. "A mother must be strong, in order for the child to be strong. There are mothers, however, who put their own feelings above their child's interest, and that can only lead to ruin."

Mrs Channing, who had become decidedly uncomfortable when her sister had spoken, now nodded in agreement.

"Yes, a mother cannot be selfish. I would have liked to have kept my dear Percy at home, for he was my only child, you know, and with his father away—it quite broke my heart. But I overcame my feelings and sent him away, and look how well he has turned out! Even if he spends most of his time in London and I see very little of him."

Caroline seized the opportunity to turn the conversation.

"Does Mr Channing take lodgings year round in Town, or do you have your own townhouse there?"

"We have a townhouse, but with my husband in India—he is with the Company, you know—and no daughters to bring out, I am little inclined to go there," said Mrs Channing. She had one of those voices that gave the impression of some great grievance, even when she was talking of an ordinary matter. "We open it up whenever Mr Channing comes to England, of course. Percy prefers his own lodgings."

With the conversation safely settled on more mundane matters, Caroline made an observation about the unsettled weather they were having.

"Yes—the weather has turned quite cool again," complained Mrs Channing. "I had hoped it would be warmer."

Georgiana, who had wanted to speak for some time, but could not contribute to a conversation about children, was glad of the change of subject, and pointed out that at least it had been generally dry and that they had had several warm days as well.

"But that is precisely what I object to," replied Mrs Channing. "If the weather had stayed cold, then we would have resigned ourselves to it, but when it is so inconsistent, promising sunshine and blossoms one day, and flurries of snow the other, then how are we to react? Why only the other day I went out wrapped in a cloak with fur trimming, and with an ermine muff besides, and what do you think happened? The sun came out, and the weather turned warm, and I grew so hot in my cloak I was forced to throw it off."

At this moment, Lady Catherine called Georgiana and asked her to hand out tea cups to the ladies. She had fallen into the habit of ignoring Clarissa when it came to this task, as though not liking tea could hinder a person's ability to pass round the teacups.

Georgiana did not like carrying the cups across the room. She worried that she would trip, or that the tea would spill, or that she would splatter the tea onto someone's lap.

"You are too slow, Georgiana," said Lady Catherine impatiently. "You must learn to give the cups out faster. There is nothing worse than lukewarm tea."

Georgiana reddened at this public rebuke, particularly since it was undeserved. There were only a few ladies to be served, and even if she was slow, the tea could hardly have turned cold so quickly.

Mrs Channing took a sip from her cup. "You are quite right, Lady Catherine," she said, "my tea is lukewarm."

Clarissa, noting her cousin's embarrassment, jumped up. "I will hand the cups around, Lady Catherine, for I have a very steady hand, and I am very fast."

Lady Catherine snorted but gave her the next cup. "Perhaps between the two of you, we will manage to have some hot tea."

"Come, sit next to me," said Mrs Gatley, in a friendly manner to Georgiana, "and tell me what you have been doing. You know, your Mama and I go back a long way, for we were debutantes together."

Georgiana had no memory of her mother, but she was curious to learn about her, and before long, Mrs Gatley was entertaining her with little anecdotes about their experiences of the ballroom together.

The visit did not last long after that, and Georgiana, who was enjoying listening to Mrs Gatley, was disappointed when the ladies rose to leave. But her disappointment quickly melted away when

Lady Channing announced that there was to be an informal dance on Thursday—in one week's time—at Millcroft Hall, and that they were all invited.

The two ladies had hardly left when Lady Catherine objected. She proclaimed that, though the older members of the group were naturally free to go, the younger ones—and here she stared severely at Clarissa and Georgiana—were not yet out and should not be attending a ball. Certainly, she said, Clarissa should not attend social events until she learned to conduct herself properly in English society.

The gentlemen, who had just finished a game of billiards, walked into the room at that moment, and, overhearing her last comment, asked the ladies what had happened to provoke it.

Lady Catherine informed them of the invitation and declared that the young ladies should not be permitted to attend.

Robert Darcy responded coolly that he had no objection to his sister attending a small country dance and that he had every faith she would conduct herself as well as any English young lady.

Darcy stated that, as head of the Darcy family, it was surely *his* privilege to determine what the young ladies should do. *He* thought it perfectly acceptable for the two young ladies to attend the dance, and, therefore, he could see no reason why his aunt should object.

Lady Catherine expressed her extreme displeasure by rising quickly. Calling imperiously to Dawson, she sallied forth and exited the room without a word.

Chapter 7

"I CAN ALREADY TELL I WILL ENJOY THIS," SAID CLARISSA, CASTING a practised eye around the room. They had passed through the receiving line and greeted both Mr Channing and Mr Gatley. Now they left them behind, though Georgiana did sneak a backward glance or two.

"I have spotted a number of eligible young gentlemen already. Look at that one standing over there. Is he not a dream?"

He was most certainly a dream. With his patrician nose, the perfect soft curls lining his brow, and his large dark eyes, he resembled a Grecian statue. He was by far the most striking gentleman in the room, even more handsome, Georgiana had to admit, than Mr Channing.

But instead of warming to the situation and becoming more eager, as her cousin did, Georgiana found herself turning cold. The room was not large—not a formal ballroom by any means. But as soon as she stepped in, the clamour of many voices, with the mingled fragrances of candles and colognes, evoked unwanted memories and destroyed all her excitement.

She had not been to many dances. But each and every time, her memory immediately flew back to the day she had first seen George Wickham.

It had happened at an informal dance not very different from this one, held in Ramsgate, the coastal town where she had gone for the summer with her companion, Mrs Younge. Though she was only fifteen at the time, Mrs Younge had persuaded her that there could be no harm in attending such an informal occasion, not if it was a private event held by people Mrs Younge trusted. Wickham had approached her there and expressed his delight in how beautiful she had grown up to be. He reminded her that he had lived on their estate before her father died. She remembered, of course, for he had been kind to her. She still had a doll that he had given her once.

Excited by her first dance and feeling grown up in her very first evening gown, it had been easy for such a charming young man to draw her into his net.

But then he had betrayed her.

She would never forget her brother Fitzwilliam's warnings afterwards. He had spoken to her gently, telling her that she was well out of a situation that was doomed from the start. He had advised a distraught fifteen-year-old to view all men who approached her as fortune seekers, not interested in her at all, but in her thirty thousand pounds—as George Wickham had been—and to guard herself against them.

Wickham was now cold in his grave. But the memory invariably cast a shadow over her whenever she attended a dance. The discordant sounds of instruments being tuned, the mingled odours and scents—overheated candle wax, the press of bodies, the amalgam of clashing colognes and essences—and the incessant din of voices, all these blended themselves into a single distilled image; that of Wickham. For no matter how ignoble his behaviour had been towards her—and towards others, it seemed—she had not been able to make herself dislike him.

It was because of this that she suspected her own judgement. If she could only hate him, she would trust herself better. But in some hidden part of herself—in spite of everything—she still harboured some tenderness towards him. Which made her a fool. And a fool could not be trusted to determine which young gentleman was sincere and which a fraud.

At least she was aware now, as she had not been at fifteen, that thirty thousand pounds was a temptation.

From somewhere behind her, her brother's deep voice rang out, then Elizabeth's lighter one. Their voices reassured her. *They* were there. They would surely step in if they found her acting foolishly. Perhaps she might allow herself to enjoy an innocent dance or two without fearing some hopeless entanglement.

She pressed her fingers together behind her back and took a deep breath.

"I hope you do not intend to stand here all evening looking severe, Georgiana. You will frighten the gentlemen away. It is really too bad Frederick refused to come with us, preferring to go to London. It would have made matters much easier, for he is very good at mingling. Come! You must introduce me."

Clarissa tugged at her arm.

"It is not so very simple," replied Georgiana. "Remember that I do not actually live here, so I am not acquainted with many people in the room. We shall have to wait for one of our hosts to introduce us. In any case, *we* cannot go around the room meeting young men, for it is up to the gentlemen to come and meet us. It is hardly acceptable to cross the room expressly to talk to someone who has caught our fancy."

Clarissa made an impatient gesture. "I am aware of that. You need not read me the rules of ballroom etiquette. I will not stride over to the first gentleman I see and introduce myself. You must grant me more discretion than that, no matter how poor your opinion may be of us Americans," said Clarissa. "I merely intend to stroll about the ballroom. How else do you think we can attract the gentlemen's notice otherwise? How will they find us in this crowd? We must make the effort first."

"If you really wish it so much," said Georgiana, smiling, "then by all means, show me how to do so, as long as you promise you will do it discreetly."

"I will be discretion itself," said her cousin. "Come then."

Arm in arm, the young ladies surveyed the room, their trajectory bringing them very close to the Grecian idol. A crowd of young ladies stood around him, and he gave every appearance of enjoying the attention.

As they walked by, the Sculpture turned his eyes upon them, and Clarissa, casting him a coy sideways glance, ambled past.

"I do believe he's noticed us," said Clarissa, sounding satisfied. "We may head in another direction now, and wait, as you say, for him to come and find us."

The receiving line broke up at that moment. Darcy and Elizabeth, who had been conversing with Gatley, now came to stand with the young ladies.

"So, Georgiana," said Darcy. "You must think of this dance as your last opportunity to test the waters before your launch into society next month. Many of the people here are strangers, so you must practise all the social skills you have learned. You too, Clarissa, though to judge by your manner you have had enough practise at home in Boston."

Clarissa made a face. "'Tis quite a different matter in Boston. There, most members of our circle are known to one another, at least by name, and anyone new who is anybody is quickly introduced to everyone else."

"I think you will discover that things are not so very different in London," remarked Darcy. "Once you have listened to the gossip for some time, you will soon feel you know everyone, even if you have never met them."

"And conversely, *they* will feel that they know *you*," remarked Channing, joining them.

Georgiana's pulse made a little jump. She turned to him with pleasure. "This is a fine affair. You must have worked hard to transform a mere living room into this," she said, indicating the potted palm trees and splashing fountains that had converted the room into an exotic garden.

"I believe you have Mrs Channing to thank for that," said Gatley, who now joined them as well. "You do not think my cousin had a hand in it, do you? He is far too indolent to do anything more than attend the dance, even if it is in his own house."

Channing raised his hands in surrender and laughed. "I admit it readily enough. I would not have known what to do in any case. It is ladies who accomplish clever things such as this. We men lack the imagination to create anything that requires refined taste."

"I cannot agree," said Georgiana, a smile on her lips, "for if you look at most of the great works of art, they are done by men."

"That is only because women have no time to paint or sculpt," said Clarissa. "We are too busy running households and doing *these* kinds of things." She indicated the room. "The results of our labours, alas, are all too fleeting."

Mrs Channing now approached and claimed her son's attention, taking both him and his cousin with her.

"My advice to you, Georgiana," said Darcy, picking up where he had left off earlier, "is to beware of attributing your own goodness to everyone you meet. Not everyone's motivations are as innocent and pure as yours. You cannot afford to be naïve. It is far better to err on the side of caution."

Georgiana cringed at the reminder. Was he, too, remembering Wickham? Or was it something else entirely? Had she been too forward in speaking with Mr Channing?

"Stop, Fitzwilliam, in heaven's name!" said Elizabeth jokingly. "I do believe you are more nervous than Georgiana is. It is not the first time she has been to a dance. You need not be so anxious. You will frighten her so much she will not have any pleasure in it."

Darcy took Elizabeth's arm and settled it on his. "You are quite right, you know. I am sorry, Georgiana. I am fretting when I should be telling you to go and enjoy yourself." He gave her an affectionate smile. "But is it not natural that I should worry about my little sister?"

Mr Gatley once more came up to them, this time bringing with him the Grecian Sculpture and an accompanying young lady.

"What did I tell you?" murmured Clarissa. "I knew I could induce him to meet me."

Introductions were made, and it emerged that the two young people were brother and sister.

"Odysseus Moffet?" said Clarissa when she heard his name. "Is your name really Odysseus, or did I misunderstand?"

The Grecian Statue bowed and assured her that his name was indeed Odysseus.

He was either immune to reactions such as hers—having experienced them too often—or generally apathetic, for he exerted no effort to explain his name. His sister, whose given name was Athena, seemed similarly unconcerned. Gatley, having performed the introductions, took Miss Moffet away to join another group.

The young man asked to be set down for a dance, first with Clarissa, then with Georgiana.

"I would not like to appear partial towards either of you," he explained with a small laugh. "Especially since I have just met you and have had no chance to make any judgement."

Both ladies accordingly put his name down on their dance cards.

"Will you be spending a long time in this area, Miss Darcy?"

Both cousins began to answer at the same time. Clarissa waved her hand in Georgiana's direction playfully.

"I am sorry, Cousin. I am so accustomed to being Miss Darcy at home. I still forget sometimes that I am Miss Clarissa here."

Mr Moffet looked blankly at her.

"My cousin has only recently arrived from Boston."

"Boston?"

"Not the English Boston," said Clarissa. "The American one."

"Ah," said Mr Moffet. "Yes, I heard something of the sort, but I did not credit it. Surely you did not come all the way across the ocean on a ship?"

"There is no other way," replied Clarissa with a smile.

"Just so," said Mr Moffet.

A general pause in the conversation followed

"Well, you have come to the right place," said Mr Moffet heartily. "Kent is known as the Garden of England, and for good reason."

The young ladies waited for him to expound on this, but no clarification followed.

"Did you grow up in Kent, Mr Moffet?" said Clarissa.

"Yes. Born and bred right here, in Dawcott Hall. You must come to visit Dawcott, for our grounds have much to recommend them. My mother has a disposition for the Gothic, and she has had a grotto built, and a sunken garden. Even better, she discovered some old ruins that were overgrown and had them cleared. I can assure you, the result is entirely Romantic."

"I am glad, since I love old ruins," said Clarissa. "We are particularly deprived of them in the United States, for there are none."

"Really?" said Mr Moffet. "Why ever not?"

Clarissa did not have an answer.

"It is too new," said Georgiana, feeling that someone ought to explain.

Mr Moffet seemed perfectly satisfied with the explanation.

"Can you tell me the history of the ruins? The ones on your grounds," said Clarissa.

Mr Moffet drew his brows together and gave her question some consideration. "They are very ruinous, so one cannot make head or tail of them," replied Mr Moffet, and he laughed. The young ladies smiled politely. "But I am sure that they must have a long history. Since you are clearly fascinated, we will most certainly arrange for a picnic. If that will appeal to you, Miss Darcy?"

"Certainly," said Georgiana.

A long pause followed, in which each of them sought for something to say.

Fortunately, Mr Channing reappeared at that very instant, and Georgiana let out a silent sigh of relief.

"Mr Moffet is planning a picnic," she said, then bit her tongue. What made her think Mr Channing would be included in the invitation?

"Is it not too early in the year for a picnic?" said Channing.

"One can never tell with the weather, Channing," said Mr Moffet with a frown. "In any case, we can always arrange for a visit to the ruins, with or without a picnic. Miss Clarissa is most eager to see them."

"I should have guessed that you would like ruins," said Mr Channing, smiling broadly at Clarissa. "You seem just the type of person to do so."

Clarissa's eyes lit up with amusement. "Don't tell me, Mr Channing. Have you already come to know my character?"

"Not as well as I would wish," replied Channing meaningfully.

"I daresay you would, Mr Channing," replied Clarissa, meeting his eye.

Mr Moffet looked from one to another uncertainly. Seemingly reaching his own conclusions, he shifted his attentions exclusively to Georgiana.

"Miss Darcy, if *you* do not care for ruins, you still find much that is agreeable at Dawcott Hall, for Mama has spared no expense on developing the grounds."

"I would be happy to see both the grounds and the ruins," said Georgiana.

Mr Moffet beamed in delight at the prospect. "Then I will speak to Mama immediately," he said, and took off.

"Dear old Moffey," said Channing, watching him go. "He always reminds me of a ferret."

"A ferret?" said Clarissa, "How can you say that, when he is so very handsome?"

"But did you not notice his teeth?" said Mr Channing.

Clarissa denied noticing anything odd about his teeth.

Georgiana *had* noticed that his teeth jutted out very slightly, and she was inclined to agree that there was something ferret-like about Mr Moffet. She had just begun to formulate a witty response when she realised that the conversation had already turned. They were discussing something else entirely.

"I hope you are enjoying the evening, Miss Darcy," said Mr Gatley, appearing suddenly at her side.

Georgiana, who wanted to follow the other conversation, answered dismissively.

"I believe I will enjoy it, once the dancing has started."

"You like dancing, then?"

Georgiana gave up on the possibility of talking with the other two and turned to Mr Gatley. She did not know why he unsettled her so. She grew immediately defensive.

"Yes, I do. Do you consider that unusual?"

"Not at all. I myself am quite neutral about dancing. I neither deliberately seek out dancing, nor do I actively avoid it."

By this time, the banter between Clarissa and Channing had ended.

"One could argue that by not actively seeking something," said Channing, "you are consequently avoiding it."

"That is mere sophistry," replied Gatley.

"Not when it is true of life generally," said Channing. "What would you call someone who neither seeks people's company nor avoids it?"

"I would call such a person a curmudgeon," said Clarissa.

"There you have it. Miss Clarissa, you have struck the nail on the head, for you have found the exact word for my cousin."

"But I did not mean it to refer to your cousin," protested Clarissa. "We were talking in general."

"I will submit to the judgement of Miss Darcy," said Gatley. "Do *you* consider me a curmudgeon?"

Put on the spot in this manner, with three sets of eyes awaiting her expectantly, Georgiana floundered.

"Well, I hardly think I am qualified—I cannot—"

Mr Gatley's very presence reproached her.

"It is hardly fair to put such a question to Miss Darcy, Gatley," said Channing. "You have placed her in an impossible situation."

Georgiana smiled thankfully at him for championing her.

"Can you not see that she agrees with us but is too embarrassed to admit it?"

Georgiana gave a little cry of protest.

"I do not—"

"You should not deny it, Miss Darcy. You need not spare my cousin his feelings. I assure you, he is not a flower that wilts at the slightest harsh word."

Georgiana, not knowing how to extricate herself, wished she could be somewhere else.

She waved to Robert and Caroline, who were strolling round the ballroom, and willed them to come over.

"Besieged by admirers already, I see," said Robert, reaching her in a few easy strides.

Georgiana, whose cheeks already simmered with heat, felt them blaze.

"Two gentlemen hardly qualify as a siege, Robert," remarked Clarissa. "Though I will admit," she said, casting a mischievous sideways look, "some gentlemen are better qualified to fit the description than others."

A grin from Mr Channing rewarded her statement.

"I am too modest to assume you are referring to me," he quizzed. "I am sure you mean Gatley."

"Fie," said Clarissa. "You cannot suppose I would be so ill bred as to single out any one particular gentleman!"

Georgiana, seeing her cousin smile openly at him, envied Clarissa her easy repartee. If only *she* had thought of something clever to say instead of falling into such absurd confusion.

Robert and Caroline, beckoned by someone else, moved away. Clarissa and Mr Channing continued to exchange quips.

She turned to Gatley, wanting to explain somehow that Mr Channing had misinterpreted her silence but unable to find the right words.

"How are you and your cousin coming along, Miss Darcy?" said Gatley, relieving her of the need for apology.

"Very well," she replied. "Clarissa arrived from Boston barely three weeks ago, yet I feel as if I have known her all my life. Of course, I know her brother, Mr Robert Darcy, which no doubt accounts for my sense of familiarity. It is certainly a pleasure to have her around."

"She is very lively, is she not?" he said, contemplating her cousin.

"I own myself quite captivated by her," said Georgiana enthusiastically. "I did not expect to like her so much, but I am very glad she has joined our family."

"Your feelings do you credit, I am sure," said Mr Gatley politely.

Perhaps she ought not to have been so gushing in her praise of Clarissa.

"I have spent a great deal of time in Derbyshire of late," she continued, feeling some explanation was called for. "My sister-in-law was confined, and there was no one to chaperone me about, so I have not been in company very much. I am relishing the chance to spend time with someone closer to me in age."

Mr Gatley nodded, his expression softening. "I am sure it

was also tedious to be with a newly wedded couple all the time. I remember when my sister Isabella married and she and her husband had to live with us while repairs were made to his manor. It seemed they only had eyes for each other, and everything one said or did was an intrusion."

"Yes, that is it exactly!" said Georgiana, relieved to know that she was not alone in experiencing such a thing and that he would not think her peevish to resent her brother's happiness.

The music struck up, and Mr Channing extended his arm to Clarissa.

"May I have this dance, Miss Darcy?" said Mr Gatley, giving her a precise bow.

"Will you overcome your indifference to dancing, then?" said Georgiana with a quick smile. Then she wished the words unsaid. Would he think her too pert?

She was rewarded with an answering smile. "I have to salvage my reputation," he replied. "I must ensure that no one at all thinks me a curmudgeon, not even you."

Georgiana, still embarrassed by the earlier incident, grimaced ruefully.

"I did not handle that very skilfully, did I?"

"You are not expected to handle it skilfully at all," said Gatley. "You are only now making your entrée into society. I should not have asked you that question in the first place. It was I who was at fault. You cannot be expected to be skilful—yet." He smiled kindly as they took their place in the line.

Georgiana looked over to where Clarissa and Channing stood in the line. Clarissa flitted and chattered, perfectly at ease, as though she had attended dances since the day she was born. *She* was skilful. And Channing clearly found her amusing.

He did not look towards Georgiana, not a single, fleeting glance.

She fervently wished she did not like Channing. But even as she determined not to pay him any more attention, she caught herself repeatedly craning her neck to seek him through the gaps between the other dancers. It had been a long time since anyone had captured her interest. She ought to nip this interest in the bud, before it developed into something more difficult to control.

But she had a sinking feeling it was already too late.

Chapter 8

MR CHANNING DID NOT INVITE GEORGIANA TO DANCE. NOT that she lacked partners, for after Mr Moffet came to claim her, a number of other young gentlemen were introduced, and her card was soon almost full. But the perversity of the human spirit is such that when a young lady longs for one specific partner, every other partner counts for nothing. The other young gentlemen with whom she danced might as well have spared themselves the trouble.

Her brother also approached her and asked her if she had room on her dance card for him.

Now here was somebody she did care about.

"Of course there is, Fitz!" she said affectionately.

As the dance started up, they moved into position. Georgiana admired the smooth agility of her brother's movements. He was such a proficient dancer. She had never understood his disinclination to dance. She remembered him saying once that dancing was the most primitive of human instincts—that even savages could dance. Yet no one seeing him on the dance floor could possibly mistake him for a savage. She smiled to herself at the image of everyone in the room in a state of half undress, pounding about on the dance floor.

"I see you are enjoying yourself, Georgie. You seem to be doing very well. You certainly do not need my help in finding partners."

"I suspect that Clarissa has something to do with that," she replied honestly. "She draws gentlemen to her easily."

Darcy frowned. "I would not credit her with that much. You are easily the best looking young lady in the room. Better still, you are a Darcy. And, on top of all that, you have a fortune to your name. What more could any young man wish? I would not be surprised if every gentleman in the room aspired to dance with you."

Georgiana was flattered that he thought her very good looking. Was she, indeed? As for the rest, it was more a liability than an advantage.

"Thank you for encouraging me," she said. "You are the best brother I could ever have hoped for."

"I am not encouraging you. Surely you do not need that? You must be more than satisfied with yourself. I am merely stating the facts of the matter."

As he spoke, his eyes drifted to Elizabeth, as if he wanted to be sure that his wife was safe. She was standing with Lady Catherine.

"You need not worry, Brother," she said with amusement, following the direction of his thoughts. "I am sure Elizabeth is perfectly able to look after herself."

"Of course she is. I do not know what you mean. What nonsense is this, Georgie?"

It was a constant source of wonderment to Georgiana that her brother watched over Elizabeth so anxiously. She herself saw Elizabeth as a poised, outspoken young woman, more than capable of defending herself from attack from any quarter. Darcy, however, seemed convinced that he needed to shield her from any number of snubs and insults, and was in a constant state of vigilance.

The dance parted them for a while. Georgiana could see that her brother had not liked her remark. He was…prickly when it came to Elizabeth. Still, she did not wish to offend him.

The moment the dance allowed it again, Georgiana spoke up, hoping to give his thoughts a different direction.

"Lady Catherine dotes on William Lewis, does she not?"

Fitzwilliam's tension relaxed. "She is delighted to have a Darcy heir, I am sure," was all he said, but he spoke with the pride of a father who has no doubt that his child is adored by everybody.

❦

Gatley had done his duty. He believed strongly that as a host—of sorts, at any rate—his role was to make sure everyone was happy. He had danced with every young lady in the room once and ensured that any lady in danger of becoming a wall flower was introduced to several young gentlemen who could dance with her. Beyond that, he could not do anything more.

His aunt and his mother had also done what they could to make sure everyone intermingled and that nobody was left out.

As for his cousin—now *that* was a different matter. Channing had changed of late. The long absence of his father—almost two years now—was having its effect, along with the indulgence of a mother who could deny her son nothing. Far be it for Gatley to think his uncle's presence desirable. The older Mr Channing was a despicable bully who brought terror to the household, reducing his wife to an imbecile and driving his son quickly away. But the absence of any steadfast figure—male or female—who could bring some direction to the household was beginning to take its toll.

For two years his cousin had been indulging no one but himself.

Which was all very well—men had to sow their wild oats and so on, and Channing was only twenty-three. But here and now, there was a ball, and Channing was the host. Yet instead of helping out, he sought his own amusement, and in the process, carelessly slighted more than one young lady. Channing was careless, Gatley maintained, and not essentially unkind. Despite a selfish streak that reared its ugly head once in a while, his cousin was a decent enough person, when reminded of his duty.

The problem was, there was no one to do it. In so many ways, Gatley had assumed the role of the older brother. So the unpleasant task was his.

To this purpose he took Channing aside and advised him to pay more attention to young ladies who did not have partners.

"I fail to see why," drawled Channing.

"It is what a good host does," said Gatley.

"Young ladies who have no partners have no appeal for me," replied Channing. "Why should I indulge them when no one else wishes to? It will only give them a false sense of vanity."

"Because it is *your* dance, in *your* house. It is expected from a good host," said Gatley patiently.

"It is, as you say, *my* dance. If one cannot enjoy oneself at one's own dance, I can see no reason to have a dance at all. If *you* choose to take pity on every unappealing young lady in the neighbour-hood, I will not prevent you. But do not expect me to follow suit. I prefer to make merry."

"One thing does not necessarily exclude the other," replied Gatley. "Take Miss Darcy, for example. She is a very taking thing—very pretty, as a matter of fact, in a quiet sort of way—yet you have not danced with her once tonight."

"I have danced with her cousin, Miss Clarissa."

Channing could sometimes set his teeth on edge. He could even bring out stronger instincts, truth be told. But Gatley reminded himself that Channing would see reason eventually. It just required patience.

He set out on the unpleasant task of explaining why, exactly, Channing needed to be considerate to young ladies like Miss Darcy.

❧

The time for supper came and went, and still Mr Channing had not stood up with her. Georgiana, with two empty spaces on her card for the first time that night, sought to occupy herself by moving towards the refreshment tables to obtain something to drink. Lemonade in hand, she weaved her way towards Robert and Caroline, who were engaged in conversation next to some potted palms.

"You are too refined in your sense of duty, Cousin," said a voice from behind the palms. She recognized it instantly as Mr Channing's. "I do not need to pretend politeness to anyone. Just because Miss Clarissa is related to her, it does not mean I need to give her my attention."

Mr Gatley, for it was he, said something she could not distinguish.

"Devil take it, Gatley!" responded Channing, "How you *do* love to preach! Miss Darcy has nothing to distinguish her. It is difficult to credit it, when she is a sister to Mr Darcy, who is perfectly agreeable—I have hunted with him and find him good company—but his sister! I have never met such an insipid bore. She's as dull as ditchwater. If even a fortune of thirty thousand is not enough to tempt me, you cannot think your prosing and moralising is likely to have any effect."

With that he walked off. As his footsteps receded, Georgiana, not wishing to be caught eavesdropping, moved away hastily. But by some ill fortune, Mr Gatley emerged from behind the palms at that very moment, moving in the opposite direction, and they collided. The lemonade splattered onto his coat.

"Oh, I am so sorry!" said Georgiana, staring at the stain in distress, struggling to control the impact of Mr Channing's words. It would be ridiculous if she burst into tears for no apparent reason but for spilling some lemonade.

Mr Gatley took out a handkerchief and dabbed calmly at his coat.

"It is nothing at all," he said. "A little lemonade never harmed anyone." At that moment his gaze fell on her face and the handkerchief stopped moving.

He knew she had heard everything.

She waited for him to speak, but he did not. He resumed his dabbing. When he was finished, he quietly put the handkerchief in his pocket. He took her by the elbow and led her to a seat by the window.

"I always find it easier to sip lemonade when sitting down," he said.

She expected him to say something else—to apologise perhaps for his cousin or try to pretend the conversation she overheard had not been about her, but he did not.

"I think lemonade is just the thing," she said, "when one is in a crowded room and has been dancing."

No wonder Mr Channing thought her insipid and boring. She could not have made a remark more calculated to prove him right.

"Lemons," remarked Mr Gatley gravely, "have been known for their restorative traits for centuries. I have heard that they are treasured in the hot climates of the Mediterranean for precisely that reason."

"Are they indeed?" she murmured, wishing more than anything that she could excuse herself, for what could be more banal than this conversation about lemons?

"I have visited the south of Spain in the spring," he continued, "and I can assure you there is nothing more wonderful than the aroma of orange and lemon trees in blossom."

"Yes, there are orange trees in Lady Catherine's orangery. The aroma is wonderful, as you say."

She thought of Anne, hiding under the trees.

In another corner of the room, Clarissa was talking enthusiastically, probably spinning a tale about Boston, to judge by the fascinated interest of the young people around her.

Her eyes sought out Channing. He was not with Clarissa. The throng occupying the centre of the room made it impossible to see him from where she was sitting. She should not seek him in any case—not now. Then she spotted him, bowing to Athena Moffet as a country dance came to an end. His smile was devastating.

A new set was forming, and Mr Gatley asked her to dance. Since no one else had claimed the dance, she had no choice but to stand up with him, though she could hardly put two words together. They met and parted in what Georgiana supposed must have been the correct moves, but beyond that she saw nothing.

At the end, he guided her to where Fitzwilliam and Elizabeth stood, and she felt safe again.

But not for very long. They could do nothing to protect her from Channing's words, after all.

Chapter 9

GEORGIANA RESOLVED TO SPEND THE DAY AFTER THE DANCE in bed. She knew very well that everyone would ask her all kinds of questions. They would expect her to be exuberant, and tease her about her partners and try to discover if she had a favourite admirer. What could she answer? Better to avoid questions altogether—at least until she had recovered her spirits enough to be cheerful. Perhaps then she could honestly say she had found it entertaining. Which she had, in a way, for Mr Gatley had been an agreeable partner, and Mr Moffet had paid her flattering attention, and she had danced a great deal.

But why, oh why had she gone to the refreshments table? If only she had gone to stand with Clarissa instead of Caroline and Robert, she would not have overheard Mr Channing's dreadful words.

Groaning inwardly, she drew the sheet over her head only to have it yanked from her.

"I do not know why you are pretending to be asleep, but whatever your reasons," said Clarissa, "I do not intend to let you get away with it."

Georgiana feigned sleep as hard as she could, hoping Clarissa would go away.

But Clarissa leaned over and tickled her on her sides.

"What!" She sprang up in bed and stared at her.

"Aha!" said Clarissa. "I knew *that* would do the trick."

"How dare you…" Georgiana began to sputter, for no one had done such a thing since she had been ten and new to boarding school.

Clarissa bounced onto the side of the bed and settled there. "Dear Georgie. Have you never been tickled? With three older brothers and one younger sister, I have been tickled more times than I care to recall, though of course now my brothers have become too old to do it." She regarded her as though it was quite pitiful to have missed such an experience. "I suppose your brother Fitzwilliam has always been too old to do it."

"Of course I have been tickled," replied Georgiana indignantly. "Plenty of times."

"It would do you good to be tickled, now and again."

But Georgiana was in no mood for such things. "I do not wish to offend you, Clarissa, but I want to rest."

"I do not understand you. We did not even stay out late last night," said Clarissa. "Did something happen at the dance? You were very quiet in the carriage on the way home. Anything you would like to tell me?"

"There is nothing to tell, Clarissa. Now would you be so kind as to leave me alone?" Georgiana pulled the cover again over her face.

"No," she said. "I will not. I will not force you to tell me, though I can, you know. You will tell me eventually, in your own good time. Everyone does."

With a quick sweep she pulled the cover off the bed entirely and skipped away with it.

"If you want the cover," she said, "you will have to come and get it. I will not allow you to languish in bed all day like a heroine out of a melodrama."

"Very well," said Georgiana half exasperated and half amused. "I will not languish in bed all day. I will complete my toilette and then join you. Does that satisfy you?"

"As long as you do not linger, for I will be back if you do not join me quickly enough. Perhaps I might even send Dawson."

❦

Georgiana came downstairs to find two large baskets of flowers occupying two tables in the hallway. A maid who was passing by smiled and pointed out that one of them was for her, the other for Miss Clarissa. She picked up the note that came with her flowers, hoping—quite illogically, she knew—that it might be from Channing.

> *Dear Miss Darcy,*
> *Thank you for an enjoyable evening. I hope to have the pleasure of another such occasion very soon.*
> *Sincerely,*
> *Gatley*

Georgiana swallowed down her disappointment. The note afforded her little satisfaction. Certainly it went no farther than politeness required, and it was a painful reminder of events she would rather forget.

Curiosity compelled her to look at the other basket. The flowers were similar, no doubt obtained from the same nursery. Looking carefully around to make sure no one would catch her, she furtively pulled out the note attached to the flowers.

Dear Miss Clarissa,
You dance like an angel and float like a cloud. You are the vision that inhabits my dreams.
I await our next encounter with pitiful impatience.
Sincerely,
Channing

If she needed a knife to her pride, that was it.

❧❦❧

Everything about that day seemed intended to increase her misery. Though she had known beforehand that Frederick was leaving, the sight of trunks being loaded into a waiting carriage made her so gloomy she had to escape. She took refuge in the garden. She did not want to say goodbye. She knew—given the state she was in—that she would cry.

But she was not destined to be left to her solitude. Very soon, a quick step crunched on the gravel behind her.

"I see that my departure means nothing to you," said Frederick joining her on the path. "Clearly you prefer walking in the garden to bidding me farewell."

"I dislike goodbyes, especially when I know we will not meet for a long time," said Georgiana.

"We will see each other sometime soon, I am sure. Now that the war is over, travel is much easier," said Frederick cheerfully.

Georgiana nodded and kept her gaze on the tips of her blue slippers.

"I hope all this unhappiness is not occasioned by my departure?" said Frederick with some concern.

Georgiana looked up quickly. "Oh, no. *No!*" She liked Frederick a great deal, but she had certainly not developed an attachment to him.

"Good," said Frederick, tossing her a relieved smile. When she did not smile back, he continued, "Is there something troubling you?"

"Nothing you need to worry about," she replied.

He offered her his arm and began to stroll down the path with her.

"I will not interfere in your affairs, of course. But I do have something of my own to confide in you. Mind, you must tell no one at all of this, not even Robert."

Surprised by his earnest tone, she promised readily, wondering what he could possibly tell her that was so secret.

"It is about my sister. I cannot leave without assuring myself that someone at least is aware of her situation. I feel that I can trust you, and since you are close to her in age, perhaps you will be able to help her."

For a moment he hesitated.

"Pray do not tell me if you think it would upset my cousin," said Georgiana.

Frederick smiled. "You have just proved to me that I was right to trust you." He lowered his voice. "We were not sent here by chance. I fear my sister is in disgrace, for she formed a very improper attachment, and Mama deemed it best that she be removed from temptation as soon as possible."

Georgiana gave a little gasp.

Frederick nodded, as if she had actually said something. "I see you realise the gravity of the situation. But I beg of you, not a word to anyone. I mentioned it only because I hope you will help me keep an eye on her, for she has taken the enforced separation very badly, and I would not wish her to do anything foolish."

Georgiana thought of the cheerful young lady who was so full of vibrant energy. She could not imagine anyone less likely to be suffering from a broken heart than Clarissa.

"I will look after her," said Georgiana.

Frederick took her hand and bowed over it.

"Thank you, Cousin. I am in your debt. I did not like to leave without assuring myself that someone would watch out for her. Goodbye for now."

He turned and left. A few minutes later, the doors of the carriage shut. The rattle of the carriage as it moved away slowly faded into silence.

It saddened her to say goodbye to Frederick, but he had distracted her with his new revelation. She pondered Clarissa's behaviour, turning over in her mind specific moments with her cousin. She found nothing that would provide any clue to Clarissa's state of mind. She could only conclude that Frederick had exaggerated his sister's distress. The other alternative was that, after a long time at sea, and some time already in England, Clarissa no longer felt the separation so strongly.

Nevertheless, her sympathy went out to her cousin, for she knew what it was like to love someone unsuitable and to be forced to relinquish him.

It was in that moment that Georgiana decided to aid and support her cousin no matter what the consequences. Later, she would come to remember this moment with irony, but for now, her mind was quite made up.

❧

Georgiana discovered one more new thing about her cousin before the day was over. As she was leaving the drawing room to fetch some thread, Clarissa stopped her.

"I have just found out that Mrs Jenkinson has a piano in her room. I do not like to practise in the drawing room, especially since there always seems to be somebody there. But in Mrs Jenkinson's room, we are left to our own devices. Shall we go there?"

Georgiana, who also disliked practising when there were people around, readily followed her.

Clarissa lifted the piano cover and, running her fingers expertly up and down the keys, launched into a humorous, light capriccio piece. It displayed Clarissa's virtuosity very well and lifted some of the heaviness from Georgiana's spirit.

"That was beautifully played," said Georgiana, applauding wholeheartedly. "I am not familiar with the piece, and I see that you have not brought your music sheets. Is it by an American composer?"

Clarissa smiled a little secret smile. "I suppose you could say so. I will tell you the name of the composer, but you must not reveal it to anyone. It is by a Miss Clarissa Darcy."

Georgiana regarded her with astonishment. "The whole of it? Did you not have any assistance from your music master?"

"None." Clarissa beamed.

"But it is beautiful! No wonder you played it so well."

Clarissa's eyes blazed with pride. "Thank you. I have revealed the truth to very few people—just a couple of friends, Frederick, and my younger brother and sister. Even my mother does not know. I am glad you like it, since I consider you a good judge."

They heard the sound of heavy footsteps coming down the hallway towards them. Clarissa jumped up, an unusually flustered look on her face. Georgiana laughed as Clarissa scrambled onto the settee and picked up a book of poems.

Dawson, Lady Catherine's maid, entered, and, casting a suspicious look at Clarissa, began to bustle around the room.

"Her ladyship was just now asking what the two young ladies were up to," she said. "I believe you are wanted in the living room."

"Tell Lady Catherine we will join her there very soon," said Clarissa.

Dawson puffed up a pillow, straightened out a table cloth, cast another searching glance at Clarissa, then left the room.

"Lady Catherine sent her to spy on us! Imagine that! Are we to have no peace anywhere in the house? I thought at least here we would not be disturbed," said Clarissa.

"Apparently not," said Georgiana, who was not at all surprised. "But I don't know why you are behaving in such a furtive manner. It is perfectly acceptable for you to play the piano. You do not have to pretend to read. On the contrary, according to Anne, Lady Catherine would object more strongly if she knew you were reading."

Clarissa smiled wryly. "I did not think of what I was doing—I just knew I did not want anyone to find out my secret. If I stay long enough in this house, I will be jumping at shadows. For now though, since Lady Catherine does not wish it, and Dawson has no doubt gone to report us, I intend to read," she said defiantly. She took up the book she had grabbed earlier, and, tucking her feet under her, she gave every appearance of preparing to read for some time.

Georgiana, who did not wish to read, strayed over to the piano and began to sing the Duchess of Devonshire's *I Have a Silent Sorrow*. She did not know why—sometimes she thought whimsically that since the Duchess was her namesake, there was some connection between them—but the song had always fortified her when she was gloomy.

It was the wrong choice. Her fingers hammered at the piano, and her voice yelped. So when Clarissa winced yet again at a discordant note, she put down the piano cover and picked up a book lying on the table. It was *Waverley*, a novel which had taken London by storm. Confident that a good novel was just the thing to distract her from her worries, she settled down to read. But this enterprise proved even less successful than the other.

Her mind seemed capable of holding only one thing, a single phrase—*dull as ditchwater*.

There was no escaping it. He had injured her with his words. He had humiliated her. He had pierced her pride. But she felt it clearly; he had said nothing but the truth.

She *had* become too dull. After Wickham's betrayal, she had spent a great deal of time alone. She had promised herself never to make the same mistake again. So she had withdrawn into herself and devoted all her energy to her music. She had put her childish gaiety—for that was how she saw it—fully and firmly behind her.

Her brother had been kind and he had tried his best to cheer her up, but he was a young man, with his own interests and pursuits. And then he had fallen in love and devoted himself to Elizabeth and his marriage, and now he had a son.

Somehow, she had fallen into a rut. She had not even known that she was in one until now. When had anyone last praised her about anything but her music? True, music was an important part of any young lady's education, but surely there should be something more than that to recommend a young lady to society?

She had allowed herself to become dull. Mr Channing's words had hurt her all the more *because* they were true. It was more than time to put Wickham behind her. She would be starting her Season in the next few weeks, and she did not want to be declared the dullard of the season.

She had to do something.

Georgiana observed Clarissa's stylish form as she sat on the sofa, absorbed in her reading. Her dress was white muslin, with folded bands at the hem and a high collar, nothing elaborate at all. But the eye was drawn to the exquisite shawl—shimmering blue with gold embroidery and tassels at the corners—draped elegantly over her shoulders, and the white satin bandeau trimmed with shimmering blue flowers.

Her own clothes, in contrast, were very plain—her white dress complemented by a pale yellow silk shawl, and a hat of matching yellow silk with a straw brim. They were well made. They were fashionable. But they were—dull.

At that moment, Clarissa looked up and smiled. It was a smile that suggested shared secrets and common interests.

"Do you suppose we ought to join Lady Catherine now?" she said.

An impulse came to Georgiana, blindingly obvious the moment it occurred to her.

She would ask for her cousin's help. Who better to ask? Clarissa was even capable of drawing someone as morose as Anne out of her shell. Why not her? They would be ordering a new set of clothing for her in readiness for the season. She would depend on Clarissa's advice entirely in selecting her clothes. She would take lessons from Clarissa about how to behave, and she would learn to be lively. She would transform into a charming, buoyant young lady.

No sooner had she resolved on this course of action than she acted on it.

"Wait. I have something particular I wish to ask you, Clarissa," said Georgiana. She wondered even as she spoke whether Clarissa would laugh. It would be too humiliating if Clarissa were to laugh.

"I am waiting," said Clarissa agreeably.

Georgiana took a deep breath. "I would like you to help me with my launch into society. My sister Elizabeth will make an excellent chaperone, I am sure. But I would rather rely on *your* guidance in my choice of clothing, for I find your clothes very much to my taste. Also, I would like your help to tell me how to behave with a gentleman, for Elizabeth is quite charming, but she has a sharp tongue and is quite different from me, and I could never be like her, but I would like very much to be like you."

The sentence was so long that she grew breathless by the end and had to stop to take a deep breath. She looked in mute appeal at her cousin, praying that Clarissa would not say something cutting and destroy her hopes.

Clarissa, her eyes shining, took Georgiana's hand in hers. "You flatter me too much, Cousin. I am not at all remarkable. But I would gladly give you any assistance you would like."

Georgiana slumped back against her seat in relief. She squeezed Clarissa's hand in thanks, quite unable to utter another word.

Clarissa, who was never one to say something without acting immediately on it, sprang to her feet and began to pace the room restlessly.

"I have some ideas for clothing that would suit your colouring," she said enthusiastically. "I have sometimes wished to suggest some changes, but held back for fear of being thought impertinent. But I know just what would work for you."

She came and stopped before Georgiana, examining her closely. Then she resumed her pacing.

"I have a tendency to overdo things. Anyone who knows me will tell you that. So if you really wish me to help you, you must promise me that if I interfere too much you will tell me, very clearly. Do you promise me that?"

Georgiana would have promised anything at that point. "Of course I will tell you if you go too far," said Georgiana.

"Then let us begin this very minute," said Clarissa, and tugging her by the arm, she dragged her away.

Chapter 10

IT HAD BECOME ANNE'S HABIT TO JOIN THEM DAILY FOR A stroll around the grounds close to the house. Anne seemed to have reached some agreement with Mrs Jenkinson, for they usually met at the same time, and she no longer had to depend on furtive notes.

Though they could hardly be called close friends, the three young ladies had at least abandoned any appearance of formality and spoke very readily of many things—just as long as they did not touch upon Anne's situation directly. Any reference to that matter brought an immediate tension into the air that was very difficult to dispel.

By now spring was in full bloom, prepared, it seemed, to stay its course, with none of the surprises Nature likes to let loose on unwary mortals. Along the slope which led down from the house, white and yellow competed with green, as daisies and buttercups insinuated themselves in the midst of the verdure.

On one particular day, a pleasantly warm sunny day, Clarissa suddenly threw down her parasol.

"Oh, how I love daisies," she cried, and flopped down onto to the ground. "I cannot help it. I have longed to sit among them for days! You do not know how hard it has been to restrain myself."

Georgiana hovered above her. She wondered how wet the ground was, worried about grass stains, and considered whether they were within sight of the house.

"Come on, Georgiana," said Clarissa. "I thought you wanted to make some changes. Let us sit and make daisy chains, like little children. You too, Anne. How could the two of you possibly resist it?"

Anne hesitated. Then, pulling away one of her shawls, she arranged it carefully on the ground.

"You can sit next to me, Georgiana," she said. "That way we can protect our clothing. We need not be quite as reckless as Clarissa here."

Georgiana felt intensely annoyed with herself. Her condition must be dire if even Anne was willing to do something she hesitated about! If she did not start soon, how could she change enough before the beginning of the Season?

So, tossing all uncertainty behind her, she sat on the shawl offered by Anne.

It was strange how sitting on the ground gave one a different perspective. She ran her hands through the blades of grass, allowing the tips to tickle her palm. She followed the progress of a beetle as it laboured through the grass as if through a forest of tall trees and clambered over a bent blade with as much difficulty as a huge fallen trunk. She picked a buttercup and cradled it in her hand, admiring the soft yellow petals and wondering that something so diminutive could stand out so clearly from a distance.

Clarissa held up three daisies linked together. "Let's see who can make the longest chain," she challenged.

Soon the three young women were engaged in the sustained effort of making daisy chains. They made bracelets for their arms and crowns for their heads and necklaces to adorn their necks, and were quite a sight when, some time later, they walked back to the house, carrying the springtime inside with them.

❦

Henceforth, Anne's behaviour altered in small ways. She did not stray far from the protection of the house, nor did she honour the Darcy cousins with any special confidences, but she went out unaccompanied more and more often. She liked to walk in a small copse behind the house and was seen heading in that direction at least once or twice a day.

Georgiana felt that they had accomplished a great deal by helping her gain a little independence. Clarissa disagreed, however, for it was not so very remarkable that a twenty-nine-year-old woman should wish to walk in her very own park. She still did not go out alone on her little phaeton and ponies—Mrs Jenkinson was always with her.

When Georgiana reminded her that Anne was at least able now to escape the latter's surveillance, Clarissa shook her head. Her suspicions of Lady Catherine remained as strong as ever.

"How are we to know that this is not a trick on the part of Lady Catherine? She may well be relaxing her watch over Anne simply to give us the illusion of Anne's freedom. It is very likely that, the moment we leave, Anne will be back under the thumb of her keeper."

But Georgiana, who had known Anne longer than her cousin, could sense something different about her, a new sense of purpose that had not been there before.

"I think you are taking too pessimistic a view of things, Clarissa. I am sure that Anne is different, and if so, it is due to you, and I thank you for it. Have you not noticed there is more of a spring to her step and that she is less inclined to retreat to the corner of the room? Why yesterday she even sustained a short conversation with Fitzwilliam and Elizabeth."

"Yes, perhaps you are right. Still, she moves far too slowly for one who is so young, and she has not given up a single one of her shawls yet, nor her muff."

"But if she is ill, how can she do so? You are expecting far too much too quickly. The kind of changes you are looking for cannot be accomplished in a few weeks or even in a few months."

Clarissa frowned. "You may be right. I do not know what I expect to tell the truth. I am too carried away by my hopes for her."

Georgiana remembered Clarissa's characterization of herself as likely to overdo things.

"You must check yourself, otherwise you will go too far, and she will retreat back into her old habits," said Georgiana. "You should be content that you have brought about the beginnings of change at least. That alone should be enough."

Georgiana, however, was not so serene about the changes that she wished to happen to *her*. She could hardly wait to go to London now, for she was impatient to acquire a new and more vibrant wardrobe. She had acquired an aversion to all her old clothes and now wandered how she could possibly have agreed to wear them in the first place.

They were due to leave for London in ten days. Georgiana tried to convince her brother to leave a few days earlier, pointing out that they had very little time in which to prepare for her come-out, for it was the beginning of May, and the Season had already started. Darcy merely smiled and said he was glad she was finally showing some interest in the Season, but that removing themselves early would only create ill feeling with Lady Catherine, who would take it as a slight. She expected them to stay six weeks, and they would. He reminded her—again, as if anyone could possibly forget—that it was Lady Catherine who had made the effort to set aside her pride and to receive her new nephew into the family after their estrangement.

Appealing to Elizabeth did not avail her either, for her sister had some notion of the country air being better for a baby than that of London and preferred to keep him away from London as long as she possibly could. As if a few days more or less would matter!

So—deprived of the chance to acquire new clothing—she spent a great deal of time in her room, trying out different expressions in the mirror and struggling to acquire one similar to Clarissa's, which somehow managed to convey a sense of practised ennui with keen interest. It proved quite impossible to replicate.

She had moments of intense panic too. It would seem to her then, suddenly, that the Season was all too close and that she needed far more time—a whole other year, really—to prepare herself if she was to avoid presenting herself as a tedious nobody.

And throughout, no matter what her disposition was, she continued to hear those words in her head—*dull as ditchwater*—and to picture the brief flash of pity on Mr Gatley's face when he realised that she had overheard them.

⁂

The next afternoon all the ladies except Lady Catherine walked together to Hunsford parsonage to visit Charlotte Collins, wife of the worthy vicar and an old friend of Elizabeth's. Anne did not go with them all the way. She picked a bench in an elevated location that gave her a view of the parsonage in the distance and informed them that she would meet them again when their visit was over.

When they returned, however, Anne was not at their agreed meeting place. Surprised, they stood about, wondering if she could have returned to the house without them.

They had just concluded that this must be what had happened when Anne reappeared, breathing heavily as she struggled to climb to where they were standing.

"I am sorry," she said. "I grew tired of sitting and thought I would visit the small pond behind those trees over there. I used to wade in it when I was a child." She smiled as she met with incredulous looks from Caroline and Elizabeth. "Hard to believe, is it not, that I used to do such things? But I assure you, I did. Anyway, when it came time for me to return, I found I was too tired to hurry up the hill. You see the results."

"Then lean on me," said Elizabeth. "That will surely make it easier for you to walk back."

Anne objected that she only needed to catch her breath and then she would have no difficulty walking again. This proved to be true, for she kept up easily with them as they meandered slowly towards the house.

They arrived there just in time to see an unexpected rider dismount and enter the building.

"I wonder who it could be," said Clarissa.

"It looks like Colonel Fitzwilliam," remarked Elizabeth.

Anne confirmed that possibility. "My mother has been expecting him these three days," she said.

Georgiana was surprised that Lady Catherine had said nothing of the visit.

As they entered, they found Colonel Fitzwilliam speaking to Darcy, who had come out into the hallway to greet his cousin warmly.

"What news of Napoleon?" he was saying.

Lady Catherine's voice arose from the drawing room. "Let us wait to hear the news until my nephew has had a chance to sit," said Lady Catherine.

Elizabeth held out her hand and greeted him cordially as well. Robert Darcy stepped into the hallway at this point and came to stand at Caroline's side. Colonel Fitzwilliam bowed formally to them both, and they responded with equal politeness. Georgiana was surprised at the sudden tension between them, particularly when Robert was in general very friendly.

To Georgiana, however, he was his usual self, and she found herself more pleased to see him than she expected.

Clarissa, who was the only one who did not know him, eyed him curiously when he was introduced to her and asked him one or two questions, to which he responded pleasantly enough.

They all moved into the drawing room where, as expected, Lady Catherine was seated in her usual chair.

"So this is the famous Colonel," said Clarissa, nudging Georgiana in the ribs. "He is not very remarkable in looks, but he seems nice enough. I say you should marry him."

Georgiana frowned. "I have no intention of marrying him, thank you."

Clarissa grinned. "Why ever not? Think of all that money staying in the family. You must consider the future of the Darcys."

"Stop it, Clarissa," said Georgiana as Colonel Fitzwilliam turned his eyes in their direction. "He might hear you."

Lady Catherine ordered tea and refreshments, adding, with a quelling glance at Clarissa, that they also required a single cup of coffee.

"Miss Darcy is from America. She does not drink tea," she said in explanation to Colonel Fitzwilliam.

Colonel Fitzwilliam, who knew nothing about Clarissa, replied that one could not expect the whole world to like tea and that coffee had its advantages.

"It seems the whole town of Boston has reached that conclusion," said Lady Catherine. "They destroyed all their supplies of tea." She chuckled, clearly thinking this utterly absurd.

Georgiana could tell Clarissa was getting ready to dispute this statement. She pinched her cousin on the arm to distract her.

"I believe you misunderstood, Lady Catherine," said Robert calmly. "The Bostonians only object to tea provided by the *British*. We are perfectly happy to drink it if is supplied by our own ships."

Lady Catherine regarded him as though an insect had suddenly decided to stand up and speak.

"Well, there are no American ships now to bring you your supply *here*," she said. "But I suppose Mrs Darcy has cured you of these strange notions by now."

It was Caroline's turn now to look indignant.

"You must tell me the latest news of Napoleon, Fitzwilliam," said Darcy quickly, hoping to avert a skirmish.

Fortunately, Colonel Fitzwilliam answered readily. "News out of France is scarce, with much of it conjecture. Those fools Whitbread and Ridgely are agitating in parliament and are still determined to prevent us from going to war, but they won't succeed. Mr Whitbread, I heard, was hissed when he rose to speak. The general consensus is that a British army will have to be assembled—perhaps in Brussels—under the command of Wellington. My regiment may possibly be sent over, which is why I came here to see everyone before leaving."

Georgiana did not like the sound of those words. They held an ominous tone. She wanted to ask him if he really thought there was any danger of Napoleon invading Brussels, but Lady Catherine jutted in before her.

"We are very happy that you have done so, for I have been meaning to speak to you about something important before you leave. In fact, I was planning to send you a letter. But then you wrote to tell me you were coming, and I did not have to do it."

The tea things were brought in, and the conversation was postponed until everyone had been served.

"If you are planning to go off to war, then there is something urgent that needs to be resolved," continued her ladyship. "I have thought the matter over and reached a decision."

Colonel Fitzwilliam, who was used to his aunt's pronouncements, continued to sip his tea and gave her his polite attention, hoping to be able to return to the subject of Napoleon very quickly.

"I had originally thought Georgiana would make you a good wife. But I have since realised that she is too young and too raw to be suitable for you. Besides, you are one of her guardians, and that creates some awkwardness. Someone closer to your age will do better. I have, therefore, decided, after a great deal of thought, that I will bestow Anne's hand on you in marriage. I think it would be best for everyone if we settle everything now, before you leave. I can arrange matters with Mr Collins. You need not wait for the bans to be called."

Colonel Fitzwilliam choked on his tea. In the midst of concern over his welfare, pats on the back, and offered handkerchiefs, nobody thought to look at Anne.

With the crisis over, however, all eyes turned to Anne, who had stood up, and, with a white face, wrapped her shawls about her, and, for once brushing aside the hovering Mrs Jenkinson, left the room with small quick steps, murmuring something about being suddenly taken ill.

General dismay greeted Anne's reaction to Lady Catherine's announcement. Clarissa rose to follow her out of the room, but her ladyship stopped her in her tracks.

"You may remain here, Clarissa," said Lady Catherine.

Their eyes met. Georgiana tensed, preparing herself for an outburst.

"Clarissa," said Robert gently. He winked at her and smiled faintly.

She nodded as though he had said something and sat down.

Lady Catherine was the only one not perturbed by her daughter's sudden departure. A look of immense satisfaction had settled on her face.

"You must not mind Anne, Fitzwilliam," she said, turning to the Colonel. "Her nerves are easily shattered. My announcement gave her so much pleasure, she was completely overwhelmed. You know she is very fond of you."

Georgiana wished she could think of some way she could help Anne. On the one hand, she was more than glad that Lady Catherine no longer considered *her* a candidate. On the other, she had the same response as Clarissa. She wanted to go to Anne and talk to her and to convince her to stand up against her mother. But what was the likelihood of that happening? Besides, what could she offer to do? Beyond asking Anne to come and live with them—which was quite impractical, especially when Georgiana would be caught up in the events of the Season—she did not see any way out.

Colonel Fitzwilliam gave no further indication that evening whether he welcomed the arrangement or opposed it, and Lady

Catherine did not raise the subject again. But after dinner the gentlemen did not join the ladies in the drawing room, clearly preferring to stick to their port.

She could only hope that Colonel Fitzwilliam was strong enough to stand up to his aunt, and that Anne's fortune would not prove to be too great of a temptation.

Chapter 11

THE NEXT MORNING ANNE DID NOT SEND THEM A NOTE, NOR did she join them on their accustomed walk through the grounds. This inevitably gave rise to the darkest kind of conjecture from Clarissa.

"She is back in her prison. She has been forbidden from meeting us," said Clarissa dramatically. "Lady Catherine intends to force Miss de Bourgh into this marriage, and she will brook no opposition."

Georgiana worried over this. "Perhaps. It is too early to say. Possibly Anne is simply ill," she said. "Or very likely she is staying away because she does not want to encounter Colonel Fitzwilliam. She was quite mortified yesterday at Lady Catherine's announcement, particularly since the Colonel did not take it very gracefully. Why did she have to announce it so publicly?"

"To force the Colonel's hand, of course," said Clarissa. "Anyway, if she only wanted to avoid Colonel Fitzwilliam, she could still meet with *us*. I think it most likely that Lady Catherine has locked Anne in her room. She has put her on bread and water until she gives in."

Georgiana frowned at her cousin. "This is no time for flights of fantasy. We are facing a serious problem here."

"Flights of fantasy? Do you not believe Lady Catherine will force Anne into this marriage?"

Georgiana knew Lady Catherine had set her mind on the marriage. "She may not force her—at least, not in the way you think. But she will certainly make her life very difficult if she tries to refuse."

She hesitated, knowing Clarissa would object to what she had to say.

"I spent the whole of last night considering Anne's problem. I hardly slept a wink for thinking about it. At the end, I concluded that it is not such a great sacrifice for Anne to marry Colonel Fitzwilliam, if he is willing to marry her, that is. My cousin is a very pleasant gentleman. He will make her life as comfortable as he can. It would certainly be far better for her than staying under her mother's thumb."

Georgiana expected outrage at her statement. Clarissa, however, pressed her lips together for several moments and considered it.

"That would all be very well," said Clarissa slowly, "if I could be sure it would be a regular marriage. But I would not count too much on it. Colonel Fitzwilliam has no residence of his own, and he is a soldier. Anne can hardly follow the drum! And Rosings Park is Anne's inheritance. Lady Catherine will arrange for him to be established at Rosings once the two are married, which would mean they would *both* be under her thumb." She shuddered delicately. "He would be a fool to agree."

"One cannot choose, when one has little money to live on," said Georgiana. "And the prospect of a huge fortune such as Anne's is enough to tempt any man, let alone someone who is a younger son and has no resources of his own."

Georgiana's spirits were depressed by her own words. The constraints of a gentleman such as her cousin weighed heavily upon her. With no options for work but the Church or the military, money had to be the decisive factor in his marriage. He would be a fool *not* to agree to such an opportunity as marriage to Anne, however much unhappiness it would entail. A gentleman with limited funds cannot afford to consider niceties such as happiness.

"It is too bright a day to be gloomy," said Clarissa. "Let us go riding and enjoy the outdoors while the sun shines."

They set out for a long ride. It was indeed a beautiful day. Puffs of white clouds dotted a blue sky, and the scents of cut grass, earth, and blossoms intermingled in the air around them. The moment they left the shadow of Rosings, their youthful spirits returned. They raced each other across a meadow, the wind playing havoc with the pins that held their hair. The groom that accompanied them was forced to exert himself to keep up with them.

"Shall we go into the village?" said Clarissa, as they reached the borders of Lady Catherine's property.

"No, we cannot." Georgiana was intensely conscious of her windswept hair. "That would not do at all."

"I *need* to see people. I need a change. No one has come to call on us for more than a week."

Despite herself, Georgiana had to laugh. "Considering that we were just discussing a new addition to our party—Colonel Fitzwilliam—I don't see how you can say that. We can return to Rosings, tidy ourselves up, and walk into the village afterwards if you wish."

"If you promise me that you will not give in to Lady Catherine if she tries to keep you from doing so."

"I promise," said Georgiana, and hoped that she would be able to keep the promise.

"Very well," said Clarissa.

They were on the verge of returning when they were hailed, and Mr Channing and Mr Gatley came riding towards them.

"Well met indeed!" said Mr Channing. "We have been wracking our brains to think of a way to call on you. Mama tells me Lady Catherine does not approve of gentlemen callers, especially as we do not usually call on her. And Darcy has been very disobliging, for he has not invited us once since our last card party."

Clarissa chuckled. "He is probably worried that Lady Catherine will take over the game again."

At Channing's approach, Georgiana's mouth went dry. She had imagined his words had cured her of her interest in him. She had resolved that, the next time she saw him, she would feel nothing but dislike towards him. She would be a fool to react in any other way. Yet the moment he appeared, her resolutions fell by the wayside. His eyes of intense blue only had to alight on her, and she was doomed. She gravitated towards him like a moth to a candelabra.

She would simply have to prove to him that she was not as dull as she thought. Not today, of course. Today she would have to be content to remain in the background. She needed time. But she would prove it to him.

"I wondered what had kept you away," Clarissa was saying. "I was afraid we had made no impression at all on anyone in the neighborhood."

Channing responded to her remark by urging his horse forward so that they rode neck to neck. Inevitably, Georgiana and Mr Gatley took their place behind them.

Georgiana resigned herself to talking to Gatley, though her ears strained to hear Channing's exchange with her cousin. "Thank you for your flowers, Mr Gatley."

"Think nothing of them."

He had used a polite but unfortunate expression. That was precisely it. She thought nothing of them.

Which did not mean she should not be gracious. Gatley had been civil to her, at every point. Certainly it did not mean—just because she found his cousin infinitely more appealing than him—that she could not be pleasant to him as well. She determined to make every effort to sustain a conversation with him.

"Have you always lived in this area, Mr Gatley?" she said, drawing on her training in the arts of drawing-room conversation.

"I was born and raised here. But after attending school, I joined the army and fought in the Peninsula, despite opposition from my parents. I am not an only son, though my brother was still very young, so they could not prevent me. I was discharged two years ago when my father died, and I returned to take over management of the estate."

"Your absence explains why I was not introduced to you before."

"You would have met me before if you had not been estranged from your aunt."

Georgiana was at first startled that he had referred to her brother's quarrel with Lady Catherine so directly. Then she appreciated the directness. It felt more natural than the significant silence she had met with so far from others.

"It is the nature of families to quarrel," she said, smiling a little.

"Lady Catherine cannot be an easy person to have as a relation," he remarked.

"True, though I am accustomed to her ways and have learned to accept her restrictions while I am here." She thought of Anne, who lived with those restrictions all her life. "But then, I am only here for a short time. I can imagine it must be more difficult if one had to deal with her all year long."

Ahead of them, Channing leaned over and whispered something into Clarissa's ear, provoking a peal of laughter.

"Your cousin must find it difficult," said Gatley.

She wondered if he had followed her thoughts about Anne, then realised he was speaking of Clarissa.

"I think Clarissa is quite capable of holding her own against Lady Catherine," she said wryly.

"And you are not?" said Gatley.

Georgiana considered this. "I try to avoid conflict," said Georgiana. "So far, I have not been forced to confront her. She paid me little attention when I was younger—I belonged in the nursery—and it is only now that she has begun to notice me at all. I do not know what I would do if I was forced to go against her wishes."

"Perhaps you are stronger than you think," said Gatley.

The words awoke some hope in her. She intended to be persistent, at least, until she met her objectives. "Perhaps. I hope in any case that such a situation would not occur."

They rode quietly together for a while.

"Is there any sight more agreeable than horse-chestnut trees in bloom?" said Gatley, as they passed by one of the large trees.

"I believe you suggested that lemon trees were more agreeable," said Georgiana with a little smile.

"I spoke of the *aroma* of lemons," he said with a twitch of his mouth, "not of the view."

"I am glad to hear that you are at least constant in what you like," remarked Georgiana.

He cast her a sidelong glance but did not reply.

By now Rosings had come into view. It was time for the gentlemen to turn back.

"I will be looking out for you every day from now on," said Channing to Clarissa, as he took his leave. "I know now where you like to ride."

"You will be doomed to disappointment then," said Clarissa, "for we hardly ever ride in this direction."

"I shall live in hope," he replied.

Clarissa laughed.

"Until we meet again then," said Gatley in a friendly manner, smiling widely.

The smile illuminated his face. If he would only smile more often, he would be almost handsome, for his features were well-proportioned. For a few seconds, Georgiana wondered at the difference a smile could make to someone's appearance.

But then his cousin laughed, and Georgiana made the mistake of looking at him. Azure eyes captured and held her, and Gatley was nothing beside him.

❧

Something was wrong. Even from a distance, Georgiana was sure of it. Figures milled about Rosings like blue ants—the colour of Lady Catherine's livery. Georgiana could discern no order in the chaos, though as she approached, she could make out Lady Catherine at the entrance, issuing commands.

"I wonder who could have arrived?" said Clarissa, squinting a little as she tried to make out what was going on.

"No one. Something bad has happened," said Georgiana, her heart clenching. "Let us make haste."

They spurred their mounts onwards. As they approached, Lady Catherine came hurrying towards them.

"Where have you been?" she said. "We have searched every-where for you."

Clarissa began to answer. "As you can see, Lady Catherine…"

"Silence!" said Lady Catherine, taking hold of the horse's reigns. "I have no patience for your impertinence right now. I have one concern only. Tell me at once. Where is Anne?"

Clarissa's expression suggested that Lady Catherine had taken leave of her senses. But Georgiana knew her aunt better. Despite her penchant for drama, she did not remember ever seeing Lady Catherine so distraught.

Not waiting for a footman to help her down, Georgiana slid to the ground and went to her aunt, partly to prevent Clarissa's horse from reacting to Lady Catherine's harsh grip and partly to draw her attention away from Clarissa.

"Anne did not ride out with us, Lady Catherine. She does not ride."

"None of your impudence, young lady! This is hardly the time to make light of things. She does indeed ride, though she has not done so for years. No doubt you have browbeaten her into going riding, and she has suffered a fall. I can think of no other explanation."

Georgiana looked to her brother, who was just now emerging from the house, accompanied by Robert and Colonel Fitzwilliam. They were clearly going riding.

"Can you tell me…?"

"Anne is missing," interrupted Darcy. "She is nowhere to be found. We can only hope it is nothing, but she has been missing for hours."

Horses were brought forward by the groom, and the gentlemen mounted swiftly.

"You will look everywhere, will you not?" said Lady Catherine. "She may have fallen and sprained an ankle or hurt herself some-where on the grounds and be unable to return to the house."

"Rest assured that we will search every corner of the park," said Darcy. "Do not worry, Aunt," he added, gently. "We will find her."

And with that, the gentlemen set off.

Clarissa meanwhile had dismounted. "Is there a horse missing from the stables?" said Clarissa, as if only now responding to Lady Catherine's question.

Lady Catherine threw Clarissa a look of utter contempt.

"If she had taken a horse, she would have taken a groom. She is not as lost as all that to propriety," replied her ladyship, unaware that she was contradicting her earlier assertion that Anne had gone riding.

"She usually walks with us in the morning, but she did not join us today," said Georgiana, wanting to be as helpful as possible. Clarissa gave her a reproachful look. Georgiana's admission was a betrayal of Anne's trust.

"I am well aware that she did not," said her ladyship. "I am also aware that you and this insolent upstart here have done everything possible to encourage her to escape the protection of Mrs Jenkinson."

Clarissa's eyes blazed. However, with an enormous effort at self-control, she bit back an angry retort, then turned and stalked away.

"Allow me to inform you, Miss Clarissa Darcy," said Lady Catherine to her retreating back, "that if anything befalls my daughter, I will hold you to blame."

Lady Catherine, having given vent to her spleen, drew herself up and marched into the house with her maid Dawson close at hand.

Mrs Jenkinson, for once, was nowhere to be found.

❦

Georgiana entered the house slowly. She skirted around the drawing room and headed upstairs to the small parlour, where she hoped she would not encounter Lady Catherine. She found Elizabeth there, trying to soothe little William, who was teething, while Caroline was busy writing a letter.

"I see Lady Catherine has given Clarissa a set-down," said Elizabeth, who was standing near the window and must have heard the exchange.

Clarissa stormed into the room at that moment. Georgiana guessed that she had been sitting at the top of the stairs, waiting for her to come in.

"What on earth happened?" said Clarissa. "Has the bird flown? Has Anne escaped her prison? Heaven forbid!" She gave a hard, angry laugh.

"I can perfectly understand why Lady Catherine is distraught," said Caroline, putting down her quill and blotting the ink before folding the letter. "But I do not understand why you are so bitter about it. The most likely situation is that Anne is very upset by her mother's high handed management of her marriage and needed time alone to reflect on things. It is all a fuss about nothing."

"I cannot agree," said Elizabeth, gently rubbing William's back and walking him up and down. "If that was the case, she would have taken refuge with Georgiana and Clarissa, where she would have found a ready ear and a great deal of sympathy. I think there *is* something worrying in her absence."

"Can someone tell me what has happened exactly?" said Clarissa. "If we must be accused of aiding and abetting Anne in her crime, then at least we should know the details. Then perhaps we would stand a chance of defending ourselves."

"You must make allowances for Lady Catherine's anxiety, Clarissa. I am sure she did not mean what she said," said Elizabeth.

Clarissa snorted.

"In any case," said Caroline with a sigh, "there is really hardly anything to recount. Last night Anne retired very early, almost immediately after she left the drawing room. She told Mrs Jenkinson that she was developing a fever and asked for a sleeping concoction to be brought up, which she drank. That, at least, was what the maid who gave her the concoction informed Lady Catherine yesterday."

"You see," said Clarissa, breaking into the narrative and looking significantly at Georgiana, "I told you every move of hers was reported."

"Do you want me to answer your question or not?" said Caroline.

"I do. I am sorry I interrupted."

"Apparently, her usual practise in the morning is to rise very early and to ring for tea, but this morning she did not," said Caroline. "Mrs Jenkinson ordered the maid not to wake her, thinking that since she had taken the sleeping infusion, she would still be drowsing. However, around eleven o'clock, when Anne had not yet made an appearance, she began to worry that her mistress was seriously ill. When she entered her chamber, however, she found the bed was already made and Anne was not in her room.

"She thought nothing of it at first. Perhaps Anne had given her the slip, as she had apparently been doing for some time. So she assumed Anne was with you. But later, when none of the servants could tell her where Anne was, she grew puzzled. She then enquired about you, and discovered that you had gone riding and that only two horses had been taken, so she could not have gone with you. She raised the alarm with Dawson, hoping she at least had seen the young mistress, but when Dawson could not account for her, they both went to Lady Catherine."

Caroline spread her hands on the table before her and raised her eyebrow. "That is as much as we know, and I do not think there is any point in speculating until we know more about the matter. Let us play a game of whist to pass the time until the gentlemen return."

No one wanted to play whist, however, and Caroline soon returned to her letter writing. Elizabeth, who had succeeded in putting Lewis to sleep, went upstairs to take him to the nursery.

They would have done better to follow Caroline's advice and play cards, for now the young ladies had nothing to do but stare out of the window. The minutes stretched into hours, and the silence deepened.

Georgiana's eyes began to blur from the effort of trying to make out three distant figures on the horizon.

Finally, however, her efforts were rewarded.

"There they are!" she cried, bringing Caroline to her feet. Clarissa rushed to the window to confirm it.

"Yes, there they are!" said Clarissa with intense relief.

But their happiness soon diminished as the figures came closer. They watched until the men's features became apparent, and they could see the sheen covering the horses.

"They have not found Anne," said Georgiana.

Chapter 12

THE THREE WOMEN HURRIED DOWNSTAIRS TO DISCOVER WHAT had happened. The gentlemen passed through the doorway and took off their overcoats silently.

"No news?" said Caroline to Robert, who was the first to enter.

He shook his head. "No trace at all," he replied.

There was no chance to ask more questions. The gentlemen strode immediately to the drawing room, where Lady Catherine waited with Dawson.

"Have you found her?" she said, though it was abundantly clear from their expressions that they had not.

"I suggest we send for help," said Darcy. "We need as many people on horseback as possible to conduct a search."

"And have the whole neighborhood abuzz with the news?" said Lady Catherine bitingly. "Certainly not!"

"Lady Catherine," said Robert, "if Miss de Bourgh is injured, then we need to find her by nightfall, before the chill comes in. She has a weak constitution—"

"Yes, yes," interrupted her ladyship. "I know what she has."

"With your permission, Aunt, I will send for some of the neighbours, and we will organize a search party," said Darcy.

"Then do so," said Lady Catherine. "You may count me as one of the party."

Mr Darcy hesitated, then nodded. "You should not go alone, however." He turned to Caroline. "Caroline, if you would be so kind as to accompany Lady Catherine?"

"Of course," said Caroline.

"May we search as well?" said Georgiana.

"No," replied Darcy.

"We need as many people as possible, Fitz," said Robert.

Darcy examined Georgiana. "Very well, you and Clarissa can search, but you must both stay under the supervision of Elizabeth. Where is she, by the way?"

"I am here," she said, stepping into the room.

"We will," said Georgiana. To prove it, she linked her arm in Clarissa's and took her over to where Elizabeth was standing.

"Three ladies must search together, while each man searches alone," muttered Clarissa. "Where is the wisdom in that?"

"He means to keep you safe," said Elizabeth.

"What could be safer than Rosings Park?" said Clarissa.

"Patience!" said Elizabeth with a smile. "At least you have a chance to participate."

Cold meats and pies were brought in while word was sent out to various neighbors. Lady Catherine meanwhile studied the map of the park with Darcy and the colonel, and the search area was split into different sectors.

By and by, a number of gentlemen gathered in the front of the house. Georgiana immediately located Channing, who waved at her and Clarissa and grinned.

Mr Gatley was part of the search party as well. The moment he arrived, he immediately came over to Georgiana's side.

"I was very sorry to hear the news about your cousin, Miss Darcy," he said. "There is no need to worry yet, however. No doubt she has just taken a fall and will be found easily enough."

Georgiana nodded. "That is what we hope."

He bowed and returned to the rest of the group, where Lady Catherine was now issuing instructions.

Channing caught Clarissa's attention and wriggled his brows most comically while Lady Catherine spoke.

Clarissa smothered a giggle. "He really ought not to," she said to Georgiana. "This is serious business."

"We cannot expect a stranger to feel the same anxiety over Anne's disappearance as we do, I suppose," said Georgiana.

Just as the search party prepared to set out, Mr Collins scurried forward to join them. He dismounted and ran hastily to Lady Catherine.

"My sincerest apologies for my delay, your ladyship," he said, gazing up at her. "If I could but explain…"

"Never mind, Mr Collins," said Lady Catherine, curtly. "We are preparing to leave. My daughter's fate depends on us."

She made to move on, but he stepped in front of her horse. "You cannot imagine the depth of my sorrow at such a tragic occasion, your ladyship," he said, speaking rapidly, "I am sure as a mother— and an excellent mother, if her ladyship will permit me to say so—your grief—severe as it must be—can have no bounds. For if a tragic event should have occurred—but we must not speak of such things—for it is by no means certain—you may count on me to assist your ladyship in any way I can. Your ladyship will find me willing to go to any lengths in this painful task of seeking Miss de Bourgh, for I assure you—"

"I am certain you will do your best, Mr Collins," said Lady

Catherine, "Now return to your mount, and Mr Darcy will give you instructions."

Torn between apologies, lest he had incurred her ladyship's displeasure, and anxiety that Mr Darcy would leave without giving him instructions, Mr Collins stumbled away.

Lady Catherine, who was supposed to set out herself, lingered behind to speak to the ladies.

"What did Mr Collins mean? What tragic event? " said Lady Catherine.

"I am sure I cannot imagine," said Elizabeth quickly.

Lady Catherine fixed her eyes on Elizabeth. "You are not such a fool as all that. If you know what he means, you must tell me immediately."

"I do not think you should take Mr Collins at his word," said Elizabeth. "He is prone to exaggeration at the best of times. Let us be on our way, Lady Catherine. We cannot afford to delay."

"Nevertheless, you must have some idea what he meant."

When Elizabeth did not answer, Lady Catherine turned to Caroline. "Well, have you nothing to say either? Have all the Darcy men married dunces?"

"You must ask Mr Collins yourself when he returns," said Caroline calmly. "I cannot presume to comprehend what he is thinking. Shall we leave?"

Lady Catherine, seeing she was to receive no answer, urged her horse to a trot.

Georgiana and her companions moved off in a different direction, towards the copse of birch trees that was their search area.

They peered through the tree branches and brushes aside the brambles with crops or sticks, their search yielding nothing. They were hoping to glimpse something that would mark

Anne's presence—a shawl perhaps or the muff that Anne always carried—but none of them materialized. They searched carefully, hardly speaking, moving until they encountered the group from the next sector covered. They exchanged serious greetings, while each group reported the same: they had found nothing.

Just to make sure, they returned and searched again.

With each minute that passed, Georgiana's heart constricted further. At the beginning the whole thing had seemed very unlikely. She had not really taken it seriously. In fact, Georgiana had half believed it was a way for Lady Catherine to rein Anne back in under her wing. She had even thought—to her shame—that Lady Catherine was hoping that by lengthening Anne's leash, some accident would befall her. Then her ladyship would be fully justified to bring her daughter back under her iron rule again.

But as Anne's disappearance became more and more impossible to explain, Georgiana now began to worry in earnest. There was guilt at the heart of her worry, and a horrible suspicion that they had in some ways contributed to her disappearance. She was terrified that the role they had played in encouraging their cousin to become independent would have serious consequences. For it was true that Anne was frail and unaccustomed to depending on her own resources. If some accident had befallen her, she might not know what to do. Nor did she have the strength to survive long without help.

After another look through the copse and the adjoining area, it became abundantly clear that they would not find Anne there. Clarissa suggested that they return.

"Let us look one more time," said Elizabeth.

"Perhaps we *should* return to the house," suggested Georgiana. "Maybe someone has found her already."

Elizabeth, however, insisted on one more look, just in case. When it wielded nothing, she turned back to the house, shoulders slumped in defeat.

They arrived there to discover that several of the searchers had already returned, but no one had any news.

"I'm afraid," said Clarissa to Georgiana. "We know she could not have gotten very far, since she tires quickly, yet no one has found her. I cannot help agreeing with Mr Collins. I can think of no other explanation for her disappearance."

Georgiana stared at her cousin.

"But what did Mr Collins mean?"

"Remember the other day, when we went to see Charlotte? When we found her missing? She came from the direction of the pond."

It was too terrible to contemplate.

"Surely you are not implying…"

Clarissa nodded as though she had spoken it. "It is possible."

"Do not say such a thing, Clarissa. Why would she do such a thing? Mr Collins could not possibly have intended that."

Oh, if that happened. To think it would all be their fault; that they had driven her to such desperate measures by harping on her situation. How would she ever be able to live with herself?

"Intended what?" asked Elizabeth, who had come up behind them.

"I—," said Georgiana, in considerable distress.

Clarissa flushed and looked down at her feet. "'Tis only what I thought Mr Collins was implying. I would never have come up with it myself," she said defensively. "I thought he meant that she had drowned herself."

"Hush!" said Elizabeth, looking round at the drawing room uneasily. "Do not repeat such a thing to anybody. I cannot for a moment imagine that is what Mr Collins had in mind. I know you are fond of Gothic novels, Clarissa, but we are *not* characters in a novel."

"Then *what* did he have in mind?" retorted Clarissa defiantly. "If you will not tell me what he meant, you cannot blame me if I am forced to speculate."

Elizabeth looked kindly at the young woman. "If you knew Mr Collins as I do, you would know he probably meant nothing by it at all." A small smile appeared at the corner of her mouth. "In fact, you had better think about it as little as possible."

Clarissa's expression remained mutinous. Elizabeth, however, smiled even more widely. "I should not tell you this, if you have not yet discovered it, but Mr Collins is among the silliest men of my acquaintance, and it is very likely, if you were to ask him what he meant, he would not remember saying anything at all."

Clarissa was only partly mollified. "You cannot throw me off the scent so easily," she said. "It is true that Mr Collins, as you say, is addle-brained, but you have not given me a convincing account of Anne's disappearance."

"You may count on it," said Elizabeth confidently, "nothing more alarming has happened than that Anne has taken a fall and, out of reach of any kind of assistance, she has not been able to return home. I am sure one of the search parties will return with some such news soon enough. Meanwhile, something warm to drink may do us good and prevent us from speculating too wildly."

She said this in a tone that was light and could not cause offence, and the two young ladies—in the manner of very young people who prefer to dismiss unpleasant things that do not agree with their view of the world—were able to chase away their fears when faced with a more sensible view of the matter.

Nothing in Elizabeth's manner revealed that she was herself very anxious for her husband's cousin. She did not consider that Anne would have done it deliberately, but it was possible that Anne *could* have fallen into the pond or the stream that ran through Rosings. Encumbered by her clothing and the multitude of shawls around her, she may have been unable to swim.

∗

None of the returning parties had anything new to report. As dusk fell, the search was called off with an agreement to resume it the next day as early as possible.

Darcy comforted his aunt the best way he could, by telling her that even if the night was cold, Anne was equipped with enough shawls to keep her warm, and that her daughter was sensible enough to drag herself to some kind of shelter, even if she was injured. Elizabeth and Caroline assured her of the same thing.

Georgiana and Clarissa were sent upstairs—to be out of Lady Catherine's way, presumably. They were only too glad to be removed from her presence, and Clarissa spent the rest of the evening teaching Georgiana how to make a Grand Entrance into a room full of strangers.

It was not that they were not worried about Anne. It was that they did not want to think about her. Far better to remain optimistic and to wait and see what tomorrow would bring.

∗

The next day, a number of the gentlemen appeared in long boots and fishing clothes. Georgiana registered their clothing with dismay. It was clear now that Mr Collins was not the only one who had considered the possibility of drowning. They departed to search all the ponds on the grounds and to inquire downstream whether she had been found, while others continued the search for her beyond the boundaries of Rosings Park. A halfhearted search of the grounds was also conducted, with Lady Catherine leading, but the area had been combed thoroughly the day before, and no one deemed it likely that the search would yield any result.

Georgiana, meanwhile, could no longer dismiss the possibility that something terrible had happened. Her unruly thoughts had become a reality, and for the whole day she was haunted by the image of Anne being carried back, dripping with water. She could not bear it.

She was profoundly relieved when those wearing the long boots returned empty handed.

❧

The third day the search broadened to include the village. Again, not the slightest trace of Anne was found.

Finally, with everyone who had participated in the search gathered in Lady Catherine's living room, Darcy delivered his verdict.

"We have done what we can in the immediate area. We would like to thank you all for the assistance you have given us, but we will have to begin searching farther afield now. To do so, we will have to make an entirely different assumption about Anne's disappearance. She was not so strong as to venture very far on her own. We therefore have to conclude," and here he looked at Lady Catherine, "that Anne has been abducted for ransom."

Lady Catherine nodded.

"That is the conclusion I reached myself. I am willing to pay the ransom, of course, as long as they do not hurt her."

"It is not the custom of abductors to harm their victims," said Gatley, "since their only goal is to obtain as much money as possible. If she is harmed, they will not receive the money."

"We will continue to search for her with the hope that some clue will help us reach her abductors. But now it is a waiting game," said Colonel Fitzwilliam. "We must wait for a note from them, which should be delivered soon."

But two days passed and no note came.

⁂

Six days had passed since Anne's disappearance, and they were no closer to knowing what had happened to her. Colonel Fitzwilliam could no longer stay away from his regiment and was forced to leave. The Darcys' plans to remove to London were postponed.

Lady Catherine had taken to her rooms and rarely came downstairs. But that particular afternoon, they were all gathered together for tea in the drawing room. Caroline and Elizabeth had both persuaded Lady Catherine to come down, saying it was not good for Lady Catherine to shut herself up alone.

They were soon to regret this kindly intervention.

The gathering was doomed from the start. When nerves are strung so tight, the smallest matter is likely to cause the strings to overextend.

In this case, it was Clarissa who stretched the string to breaking point.

For once, she did not intentionally provoke Lady Catherine. She did not knock over Lady Catherine's tea caddy intentionally. But the fact was, she had no business passing by the tea tray at that particular moment. She was not helping with passing the tea cups, and she was excluded from the tea circle, for she had her own coffee.

But she rose—as she later explained to Georgiana—because she thought she saw something from the window—something white moving between the trees. She rushed to look out, hoping it was a clue to Anne's disappearance. On the way, she passed the table holding the tortoiseshell tea caddy and the water urn. Somehow, her dress caught on the caddy, and it toppled to the ground.

Lady Catherine always locked the caddy, as one generally did with such a precious commodity as tea. But she was planning to brew another batch, and so she had left it open for the moment, with the latch loosely fastened.

As the caddy toppled to the ground, the latch came undone, and the tea scattered all over the floor.

"Clumsy, clumsy child!" exclaimed Lady Catherine. "My Souchong tea all over the carpet! Do you realise how precious this tea is? No, you would not, of course, for was it not your fellow citizens from Boston who cast shiploads of tea into the ocean?" She tugged at the bell pull vigorously.

She directed the footman who appeared directly to his knees. "Rescue what you can of it," she ordered. "We cannot allow it to go to waste."

Lady Catherine sat back in her chair and closed her eyes, as if the incident marked the end of her patience. Clarissa took the opportunity to move noiselessly past her. But, as if sensing her, Lady Catherine's eyes flew open. A vindictive look came into them.

"Do not think I am finished with you, young miss," she said. "You have played enough games with me." She turned to the footman. "Get up," she said. "You may leave now."

The footman, who had been carefully collecting the leaves and placing them on the tray, rose and walked away.

"*You* may pick up the leaves," she said to Clarissa.

A wave of general protest at this extraordinary demand rippled through the room.

"Do you think I do not know that you knocked over the tea deliberately? I have seen your sly looks when you thought I was not looking. You have intended to do this for days now. Pick the leaves up."

Clarissa put her hands behind her back and, standing very tall, replied in a clear, defiant voice.

"I will not pick the tea leaves up, Lady Catherine. I apologise for knocking the caddy over, but it was an accident, and I will not pick it up."

"I have had quite enough of your brazenness," said Lady Catherine. "And I have had enough of your meddling. Because of you, my daughter is missing. It was you who urged her to take walks alone, and you who pressed her to escape the watchful eye of Mrs Jenkinson, even knowing full well that she might easily trip and fall. Behold the consequences! Because she was unprotected, she became an easy target. Had Mrs Jenkinson been there, Anne would never have been abducted. It is you, and you alone, who is responsible for everything that has happened. You have polluted the hallways of my residence and caused untold harm to my only child. I have been more than patient. Yet even now you defy me." Lady Catherine straightened up in the manner of a judge who is about to pronounce judgment. "You are no longer welcome in this house. You must leave immediately."

At her words, Robert Darcy came to his feet immediately, anger written all over his face.

"Now you are going too far, Lady Catherine. You forget that she is my sister."

"I forget nothing, Mr Robert Darcy. And I meant every word I said."

"Enough, Aunt," said Darcy, springing to his feet as well. "You are overwrought and do not know what you are saying. We will make allowances, given the unfortunate events that have recently transpired. But you cannot speak to my cousin in this manner."

"I will speak as I wish under my own roof!" replied Lady Catherine. "I do not need my sister's child to tell me how or how not to conduct myself. I hope you will not be foolish enough to continue in your defence of a young girl who has had only one goal since she arrived, and that is to turn my own daughter against me."

Darcy's face darkened. "Come, Lady Catherine," he said, maintaining control over his temper with difficulty. "Surely you do not mean to suggest that a mere child of seventeen could have such an influence over a lady of twenty-nine? If Anne is really so easy to persuade, then you can hardly blame Clarissa for it. It is patently absurd to suggest such a thing."

Lady Catherine stared coldly at Darcy.

"I am not accustomed to being addressed in this manner. I resent it exceedingly," she said. "You will cease your support of this unruly child at once."

"I have no intention of doing so," said Darcy, "Once again, Lady Catherine, these are exceptional circumstances. I am sure that in the normal course of things, you would realise that a mountain is being made out of a molehill. I suggest that we wait until tomorrow. By then, the whole thing will have blown over."

"I have given you my warning, Darcy," said Lady Catherine relentlessly. "As long as you continue to support the person who is responsible for my current unhappiness, then you leave me no choice in the matter. Do you withdraw your support?"

"No," said Darcy.

Her ladyship paused to take a deep breath, then announced, "You will see that I am perfectly capable of being reasonable. I will not require you to leave tonight. You will all arrange to leave Rosings by tomorrow morning."

Chapter 13

CLARISSA AND GEORGIANA TRIED NOT TO MAKE THEIR PLEASURE at leaving Rosings too apparent. For Georgiana, perhaps, the task was a little easier, for she was more accustomed to restraining herself. In vain, however, did she remonstrate with Clarissa, who ran excitedly down the stairs of the house and danced a jig as soon as they were outdoors, though they could have been easily seen through the tall windows.

"I know, I know, Georgiana, I ought not to be happy. Not when I caused a rift between my family and Lady Catherine. I feel terrible about *that*. And I feel even worse about Anne's situation. My feelings are no reflection on *her*, I assure you. I'm consumed with worry about her. But I shall be *so* glad to go away. Anywhere in the world would be better."

She twirled round, stretching her arms out above her and looking up at the sky.

"I will be so glad to leave! You have no idea how much I have loathed living in this house, where I have been trapped since I arrived from Boston. If only I had never come! I have been on the verge of melancholy since the day I arrived. I certainly would have understood Anne if she had decided to drown herself in a pond. I was quite ready to do it myself."

Georgiana was shocked by Clarissa's statement. Even the fact that she could think that way horrified her. "You must never say things like that! You know you cannot possibly mean them."

"But I do mean them. Not the part about the pond, perhaps, but about the melancholy." She paused and stared into the distance. "You really do not know how it has been for me. At least at the beginning, I had Frederick here, and I could talk to him. But now he has gone, and I do not know when I will see him again. I really miss him."

Georgiana understood Clarissa's sentiments very well, for she had missed her brother for years, longing for the holidays to come so she could be reunited with him.

"It will become easier, with the passage of time," said Georgiana. She hesitated, then added shyly, "And I hope you will come to see me as a sister one day, as I already see you."

With that Clarissa threw her arms around Georgiana, and, embracing her tightly, said she need not fear, for she already thought of her as not only a sister but a friend.

※

The young ladies would not have felt quite so guilty about being happy to leave if they had heard Elizabeth speak to Darcy. Elizabeth was another person who was only too glad to be expelled from Lady Catherine's presence. For, as she told her husband later, she had had the most difficult time reining in her temper on several occasions.

"You have not heard half the things she said to me," said Elizabeth, all the petty moments surfacing now that she was free to express them. "Would you believe that she told me the boy was ill-favoured because he did not resemble the Darcy side of the family?"

Darcy's indignation at his aunt's behaviour rose rapidly to new heights.

"And listen to this," said Elizabeth, her eyes dancing now in anticipation of Darcy's reaction. "She told me that the name Lewis was not worthy of the dignity of an old family like the Darcys!"

"What?" said Darcy. "When I especially chose this name to honour Sir Lewis with an eye to appease my aunt?"

"I know. Really, Darcy, we are well out of here. I am glad, in a way, that this incident with Clarissa occurred. It was unfortunate for Clarissa, of course, but it was time we left, and you could never have left Rosings as long as Anne's fate was undetermined."

"Of course not," said Darcy. "But I cannot be happy about this schism. I am very reluctant to leave my aunt to her own devices under the circumstances."

"It is for the better," said Elizabeth firmly. "In London you can engage the services of someone who can make discreet enquiries. You cannot engage the services of the Bow Street Runners without evoking a scandal, but some quiet questions in the right places from someone with experience in matters of this kind may well help us uncover the truth."

"You may be right," replied Darcy. "In any case, I can help you settle in London, and if nothing else can be unearthed, I will return here. My aunt will not turn me away, I am sure, particularly if I am here to help. With Robert and Caroline in London as well, you will not miss my company overmuch."

At this Elizabeth protested, stating archly that she would miss his company very much, but she understood well enough that he preferred Lady Catherine's company to her own.

⁂

The Darcys departed for London the next day without much ado. Lady Catherine did not emerge from her chamber at the last moment—as the young ladies had feared—miraculously contrite and begging them to stay.

"Though I had half hoped she would," whispered Clarissa, as their carriage rumbled down the long entrance and she knew they were safely away. "I would have felt better about the whole thing then."

As they passed the Hunsford parsonage, they caught a glimpse of Mr Collins, his nose pressed to the window.

"If it were not so early," said Elizabeth, with a half smile, "he would be running to Rosings by now to find out the reason for our early departure."

"Oh, he is quite capable of setting out for Rosings without even noticing the time," said Darcy.

Georgiana's pleasure in leaving Rosings would have been much stronger if it were not for two factors. The first was her anxiety over her cousin. She tried not to think of Anne locked up in some darkened room, left to her own devices, deprived of all forms of comfort. How would someone as delicate as she survive if treated brutally? Would her abductors realise that she was sickly and that she needed to be kept warm? Would they even care? Suppose she were to die as a result of their neglect?

The second was the knowledge that her fate and her cousin's hung in the balance. For what everyone knew, but no one mentioned, was that it would be impossible for the young ladies to fling themselves into the social activity in London until Anne was found. For Georgiana, whose Season had already been delayed one year because of the baby, the thought that it could be delayed once again weighed heavily on her spirits.

All this she expressed in a half-whisper to Clarissa, since Darcy and Elizabeth had long since drifted into their own private conversation.

"I have prayed and prayed that she is safe," said Georgiana. "And I do hope Lady Catherine was wrong, and that it is not our fault that she was abducted."

"I am trying my best not to think about it all the time," said Clarissa, "but my mind seems to be coming up with more and more gruesome possibilities. As for feeling guilty—how could I not feel responsible? Even if Lady Catherine had not made a point of it, I would have felt very uncomfortable about our role in this whole calamity. Of course, Lady Catherine made sure to put the blame squarely on us."

The two ladies were silent, each struggling in her own way to deal with her qualms of conscience.

"But sometimes I wonder if your brother was right. If Anne—who is much older than us—chose to follow our advice, are we really so much at fault? Are we really responsible for the actions of a woman over ten years our senior?"

Despite her protestations, however, she sank into a gloomy silence, and sat staring absently out of the window. Georgiana too sank into gloom. Whatever way one viewed it, Anne's disappearance was nothing short of a nightmare.

Even Anne's situation, however, was not enough to quell their spirits as the carriage rolled into London, and the hustle and bustle of Town overwhelmed their senses. A more extreme contrast to

Rosings could not be found. The motley cries—newspaper boys, knife grinders, chimney sweeps—the streams of conveyances— carts overloaded with vegetables jostling for position with shining yellow barouches—the hoards of people—the costermongers, the bands of charity school children, the porters, the fashionable ladies, the merchants. They had entered a different land.

Once in London, they separated. Georgiana went to her home in Berkeley Square, while Clarissa lodged with Robert and Caroline in Grosvenor Street.

"'Tis the first time I will be alone with Caroline and Robert since I arrived here," said Clarissa. "I hope it will go well and that you and I will not be prevented from visiting each other by our separate lives."

There was no need for her to fear a separation. It was not long before they were thrown constantly together again.

For despite the uncertainty surrounding Anne, a decision was made by the guardians to start with some of the preparations, which at the very least should include acquiring an appropriate wardrobe. No one said anything directly to either of the young ladies. But the rounds of shopping began. For a young lady who wishes to attract a husband must be in possession of everything fashion dictates she should have.

Caroline, whose taste in clothing was well established, soon took over the task of escorting the young ladies to the modiste, for Elizabeth quickly tired of the task, and with the excuse of keeping an eye on baby Lewis, laughingly absolved herself of all responsibility.

"For you must know that I scarcely know one end of a pattern from the other and have barely the patience to let *myself* be fitted for a gown, let alone spend hours surrounded by chattering debutantes who can never make up their minds about anything."

"Oh, I do not mean you," she remarked as almost identical expressions of dismay appeared on their faces. "*You* are very decided on what you want and are far quicker at choosing than any young ladies I have met. But we are never alone, not at this time of the year. I do not enjoy finding myself with debutantes who giggle and gossip and disparage everyone around them, while you are busy being fitted. In any case, I am sure you are in far better hands with Caroline, who has always had superior taste."

Elizabeth would have been surprised to know that it was not Caroline, in fact, who guided Georgiana's taste, but Clarissa, and that it was she who approved or disapproved Georgiana's choices.

Nevertheless, in the midst of shopping expeditions and an endless succession of fittings, Georgiana found a grey shadow inside her, a constant reminder that something was wrong. It was there even when she laughed and wondered at the new self that was emerging in the mirror. But most of all, it emerged at night, when she was haunted with all kinds of fears about her cousin Anne's fate.

❦

News came one morning, when Mr Darcy, who made it his habit while in Town to go over his business in the mornings with his secretary, was looking over some accounts that had been presented to him. The morning caller—a non-descript gentleman of average height and ordinary clothing—called at an unusually early time of the day, which immediately aroused Elizabeth's suspicion. He remained closeted with Mr Darcy for such a long time that Elizabeth had to prevent herself any number of times from inventing an excuse to scratch at the door and enter. A few minutes later, Georgiana, who had heard the visitor arrive, came down to enquire if there was any news. The two women stood waiting impatiently in the hallway for the visitor to leave.

After what seemed like hours, Mr Darcy emerged and accompanied the caller to the door.

"You will send me news by express if you hear anything at all, no matter how trivial," he said.

From his tone, Georgiana quickly surmised that the news was not all bad. Elizabeth let out a breath she did not know she was holding.

As the door closed behind their visitor, Mr Darcy turned and frowned at them.

"Surely you have not been waiting all this time in the hallway?" he said. "I hope you, at least, Georgiana, did not stoop to eavesdropping. I would not put it beyond Elizabeth however."

Elizabeth answered his frown with one of her own. Georgiana came to Elizabeth's defence and reproached her brother with mock severity for impeaching them without any proof.

Darcy gestured to them to enter the library.

"Well, are you going to tell us, or do you propose to keep us in suspense all morning?" said Elizabeth.

"The news is good," he said, shutting the door firmly behind him. "At least, we know that until a few days ago she was alive and well, and we know that she was not abducted."

Georgiana wanted to cheer. She had never heard better news in her life.

"So she has been found?" asked Elizabeth.

"We have not been so fortunate. But we have managed to follow a trail of hers. She travelled north toward York, where she stayed a few days, apparently with friends, for there was no news of her at any of the inns. She was then seen travelling further north in the company of a young gentleman and a servant. Her trail now has been lost, but we are hoping to pick it up again soon. It may well be that she is heading for the border."

"An elopement?" said Georgiana in shock.

"I am glad that she is alive at least and not in any immediate danger," said Elizabeth. "Did your sources say whether she was travelling of her own volition, or was she being forced?"

"Everything indicates that she is travelling of her own volition, though it is too soon to be sure."

"Why, then, did she not leave a note informing us of her intentions?" said Georgiana.

"I can only surmise that she does not wish to be found," said Darcy grimly.

There was, however, still the possibility that she was being coerced into marriage by some ruthless fortune seeker and that she was in need of rescue. Through some contacts of Colonel Fitzwilliam, men were dispatched quickly north to watch North Road and to intercept Anne if she tried to reach the border.

A rider was also sent out with an express to deliver to Lady Catherine. The rider returned the next day, however, with Darcy's letter unopened.

Georgiana had not seen her brother so borne down by emotion since the unfortunate incident with Wickham four years ago.

"Is there no end to my aunt's folly? Does she not wish to hear news of her daughter? Does she think pride more important than her daughter's safety? At times like this, I cannot believe that Lady Catherine could bear any relation to my mother, who was so gentle—"

Elizabeth interrupted this futile torrent of words by laying her hand on his arm. He stopped and turned to her, as he always did, with a half smile. They moved away together, leaving Georgiana alone in the hallway.

❦

The news of Anne's sighting brought Georgiana enormous relief. The grey shadow that had dogged her as she went about her preparations dissipated, along with the nagging guilt she felt about continuing with her life as if Anne had never existed. Anne was safe. That alone was enough to bring more of a spring into Georgiana's step. She could set aside nightmarish images of Anne's death. She was alive and in no physical danger.

With the issue of Anne's safety now resolved, they could finally start to plan for the Season.

Both Darcy families gathered in Berkley Square to discuss the matter. The situation was very delicate, argued Caroline, who was generally Elizabeth's guide in matters of etiquette. However one looked at it, they needed to tread carefully. It was only too easy to draw the disapproval of society, who would relish the smallest whiff of scandal related to Lady Catherine, who had always put on airs and consequently alienated a great number of people in London society.

Clearly it would be too heartless for the young women to be launched into full-scale festivities when no one knew yet exactly what had happened to Anne. It was one thing to know definitively that she had eloped of her own volition, another entirely to have the issue still unresolved. From this perspective, it would be wiser to keep the young ladies' activities limited, in case something unexpected occurred and they were forced to withdraw.

The other aspect that had to be considered was the elopement itself. If Anne had indeed eloped, then what would happen when the news broke out? Unless there was a serious attempt made to keep it quiet, then it would sooner or later become the subject of scurrilous gossip. How would it then affect the young debutantes' chances for marriage? This seemed yet another reason to limit the scope of their introduction until matters were clearer. The fewer the people were who knew the young ladies, the less impact the widespread knowledge of an elopement could have on them.

Caroline's arguments were repeated in different forms by everyone else, and the conclusion was the same. The young cousins were to have a launch, but a very circumscribed one. Mrs Darcy's plans for a large ball were abandoned, and a small musical soiree was proposed instead, providing a chance for each of the two ladies to exhibit their musical abilities.

As no strenuous objections were made by anyone to these plans, the soiree was resolved upon and preparations began.

❦

Three days after this momentous decision, Elizabeth and Georgiana were in the parlour reading. It was a stormy day and any errands that needed to be done had to be postponed. The parlour was completely still, apart from the occasional sound of a page turning or the noise of the wind agitating at the windows.

The quiet was disrupted when Darcy strode into the room, waving in his hand a letter.

"Oh, what is it?" cried Elizabeth, jumping up hastily. "Not bad news about Anne, I hope?"

Darcy smiled reassuringly. "No. Set your mind at ease. It is nothing like that. No. I have had the great honour of receiving a letter from Mr Collins."

Elizabeth's lips twisted as she heard the name. "My worthy

cousin? Come tell us what he has to say, for whatever it is, it has you in a rare state."

"You will see why, in a minute. I will not attempt to read the whole letter to you, for he has written four full pages, crossed! *He* does not have to pay for them. But you will quickly understand the general direction of the letter from a few paragraphs."

I will endeavour in every way I can to persuade her ladyship—for I flatter myself that I have some little influence on her—to practise the forgiveness and compassion that is so much her nature, in spite of the gross provocation practised towards her, even after her ladyship condescended—after much persuasion, I might add from my side—to extend the olive branch to you and invite you to Rosings Park. Nothing can mitigate the grievous wrong that has been done to her in inciting her only daughter and heiress to folly, and, in retrospect, one can only wish that this young person had never been invited so graciously by Lady Catherine, for to trespass on her ladyship's hospitality while at the same time plotting to do her harm quite escapes comprehension, even if one were to allow that her Foreign upbringing is partly responsible for such wicked inclinations. For a young foolish person to so heartlessly bring tragedy to the family—but I will speak no more on this matter. Suffice it to say, I will not endeavour—nor should I—to soften her ladyship's heart towards her, for estrangement from such a superior person is the least punishment she deserves.

I will do my best to move her ladyship to bring to mind the family ties that join you, Mr Darcy, to her, for such ties must not be unbound, but rather strengthened, provided you are prepared to sever all connections with such a person. Should I receive your promise to undertake such a thing, I will do everything in my power to convince Lady Catherine to return you to her bosom and to embrace you once again as family. Meanwhile, I beg leave to be of service in any way I can by passing on to Lady Catherine any information pertaining to her daughter, over whom she suffers untold pangs of anxiety, and I have great fears of her falling into a slow decline...

"The letter continues in this manner for some time." He started to crumple it in his fist then thought better of it. "He has become too puffed up with his own consequence, simply because of his association with my aunt. To venture to suggest to me, her nephew, what course of action would benefit me in being reintroduced into Lady Catherine's presence! That is quite beyond anything."

"I am not surprised," said Elizabeth, "for when it comes to Lady Catherine, he has always been like this. But to cast such aspersions on Clarissa and to suggest that you cut your connection to her, that is going too far. She may be guilty of interfering in the relationship between mother and daughter, but that is hardly a criminal act."

Georgiana's blood ran cold, for she, like Clarissa, was guilty of intervention. She *had* incited Anne to rebellion. Once again the seriousness of her actions returned to her, and she sat, frozen in her seat, wondering how something so very innocent had had such terrible consequences.

"I suppose there is something useful to his letter," said Elizabeth, surprising Georgiana out of her reverie.

"I would be grateful if you could explain your meaning, Elizabeth, for I see nothing useful in it at all."

"You now know how to communicate with Lady Catherine."

Darcy stared at her, then began to laugh. "You are perfectly correct, of course. It seems that I must answer this letter after all. It would be quite impolite not to."

⁂

Everything was ready for Georgiana's launch. The invitations had been sent and accepted, the food was planned, and the music chosen and rehearsed. Nothing remained but to wait for the crucial evening and to hope no news of Anne would result in any last-minute changes. Clarissa in particular was so impatient to begin she could scarcely control her high spirits.

"I feel like a nervous filly that has not been exercised for too long. You do not know, Georgiana, how much I need to go out into society. I have been held back far too long. If I do not start to dance and flirt very soon, I am afraid I will get into mischief, and I will have to be sent away."

"You are not thinking of something shocking, are you?" she said anxiously. "Not now. Not when *everyone* is in London."

Clarissa raised her brows and surveyed her cousin, then sighed. "No I would not. I would not want to hurt *you*, after all." She lowered her voice to a whisper. "I am not planning anything so very shocking. But I have heard that Mr Channing is in town, and I want him to call on us. He lacks encouragement. If we do not meet him soon, I will have no choice but to write to him."

Georgiana, who had suspected as much, pressed her lips together. She too would like to see Mr Channing, though she did not think a letter, or indeed half a dozen letters, were likely to bring him to her—at least, not until her new plan had been carried out.

"It is not at all the thing to correspond with single young gentlemen," said Georgiana.

"Do you never have the temptation to do something improper?"

"I do, very often," said Georgiana with a smile. "But I quickly control it." She had learned her lesson young. One should only play with fire if there was no chance of being burnt. She herself had been burnt too badly to wish to repeat it. "Do not fret so much, Clarissa. We will soon have the chance to meet more young gentlemen than we could ever wish for. Meanwhile," she said, tossing her head playfully, "you will need to continue with your lessons, for although I am making headway, I am still not fully comfortable in the venerable Art of Flirtation."

"Really, there is nothing to it," said Clarissa. "As long as you remember to look mysterious and unassailable, the men will flock to you."

Despite these words, however, Clarissa had a great deal to say about that Art. Georgiana jokingly told her that she should open a school to teach young debutantes the skills needed to successfully attract the male species.

"It would be far more useful than a finishing school," said Georgiana. "You would earn the undying gratitude of all the matrons in London."

Georgiana herself was beginning to enjoy her cousin's instruction. She particularly enjoyed the names Clarissa had invented for the different Arts. She was making definite headway. By now she had practised fluttering her eyelashes and pouting in front of the mirror so many times her face quite ached with the effort.

In fact, she was becoming so accustomed to it that, without thinking, she reacted to one of Robert's remarks by pouting prettily.

"Oh, cousin Robert," she said teasingly, "surely you cannot mean that ladies are only interested in clothes. That is hardly kind to our sex in general."

Robert threw her a shrewd glance and replied rather blandly that he was not given to blanket statements about ladies in general, since he was surrounded by ladies that were far more intelligent than he. The ladies jokingly disclaimed such a thing, and a lively discussion ensued.

But her conduct had not escaped her brother's notice. As she went upstairs to her chamber after the guests departed, Darcy called to her.

"A word with you, Georgiana," he said.

She followed him into the now empty drawing room with sinking spirits.

"I have detected some changes lately in you, Georgiana, and I do not know what to make of them."

She waited.

"I know you are spending a great deal of time with your cousin. Do not mistake me. I like Clarissa well enough. She is a lively young lady and full of spirits, and despite Lady Catherine's conviction, I do not think there is any harm in her. She sometimes risks going too far, but I think she has too much sense to get herself into real trouble."

He studied Georgiana gravely. "Nevertheless, I do not think it is wise of you to emulate her. Her character is different from yours. Nature has made you quieter and more sedate. Those are not bad traits in a young lady—in fact, society as a whole would regard it as very becoming. Why would you then wish to change who you are?"

He seemed to expect some reaction, but she had none.

"I have seen it in young gentlemen, particularly, who are sent to school and choose to emulate an older boy they admire. In the end, they succeed in neither becoming the other boy nor remaining themselves. They are but an imperfect imitation, and they lose who they are in the process."

Again he waited for her reaction.

"I like you very much as you are, little sister," he said with a smile.

His manner was affectionate, but his use of the words *little sister* provoked a sense of rebellion in her. He wanted her to remain forever like this, his little sister, and he did not want her to grow up.

She said nothing of this to him, of course. Instead, she bowed her head and allowed him to kiss her on the brow as he usually did.

"I will remember your words, Brother," she said, quite in the manner that she used to. But how differently she intended them now! She *would* remember his words, but only as a spur for her to change and grow. He would learn soon enough that she was no longer a ten-year-old desperate for a kind word from him and happy when he suddenly noticed her existence.

She had her own ideas about who she wanted to be.

Chapter 14

GEORGIANA KNEW SHE OUGHT TO BE FEELING NERVOUS AND shy on her debut night. She was supposed to float into a ballroom in her white gown and to draw all eyes towards her. Instead, she had to come downstairs just as the guests were arriving to signal to Clarissa from outside the drawing room—discreetly—that she needed her flower back. Clarissa had tried the flower on, and she had disappeared downstairs with the flower still pinned to her head—the only flower that matched with the green sash of Georgiana's dress. It was really most aggravating.

There was something very mundane too about going into one's own drawing room on one's debut night. And when one literally bumped into Mr Odysseus Moffet in the hallway without having completed the last touches on one's hair—well, one could be forgiven for not taking matters very seriously.

Though Mr Moffet clearly did. His eyes widened at the reduced amount of material covering her front and bowed a deeper bow than he had ever given her before.

"Miss Darcy," he said, "it is an honour to be present at what must be the most important evening of your life. Barring, of course, your wedding—" He checked himself as he realised that it would be highly indelicate to mention her wedding night, especially to a debutante about to make her entrée into Society. "It is an honour to be present," he concluded lamely.

Georgiana, who had been to dances when she was *fifteen*— fifteen seemed such a long way away at the moment—remembered Clarissa's instructions. She put out a limp hand to Mr Moffet and looked up soulfully into his eyes. It was really too ridiculous. Surely not even Mr Moffet would fall for such a contrived move!

But he grasped her hand and gazed back at her as though she had given him a precious gift. She tugged at her hand but found it gripped too tightly for her to retrieve it.

"Mr Moffet," she said, pulling away both her hand and her gaze. "If you could excuse me?"

Mr Moffet finally realised that he needed to let go.

"You *will* allow me to turn the pages for you, will you not, Miss Darcy?"

"Most certainly, Mr Moffet," she replied.

She would have turned and gone up the stairs, but the butler announced Mr Channing, and of course it was impossible for her to turn—or leave. Not when this would be her chance to test whether Clarissa's teachings were effective.

She waited with apparent calm for him to approach, standing in what Clarissa called the Imperial Pose, the slightest hint of amusement on her face.

Channing's gaze grazed over her, dawdling just a few seconds longer than politeness would allow. A heady rush coursed through her. This was what it was like to be admired. This was what it was like to claim a man's attention. This was what it was like *not* to be dull Miss Darcy.

She *liked* it.

Then several people arrived at once, among them Mr Gatley. What they said hardly registered in that swift racing of the blood that now gripped her.

Mr Channing moved on, into the drawing room, beyond her reach. She assessed whether it would be entirely appropriate for her to follow, given that it was an informal soiree, and that Clarissa was already there. She could claim him, then, and he would continue to admire her, and she would be vindicated.

Mr Gatley's voice drew her back into the world of the mundane. She held the Imperial Pose and nodded graciously. She reached out her limp hand to Mr Gatley.

He took it and bowed over it, but did not gaze into her eyes.

"I see that Clarissa has chosen your gown," he remarked, his dark eyes taking in her appearance with a tinge of amusement.

The Imperial Pose wavered a little.

"I have no idea what you mean," replied Georgiana.

"A certain change in style—she has chosen well however."

Well, she could not expect everyone to be impressed by the Imperial Pose. She descended from the lofty position.

"I am glad it wins your approval," she said, but she could not resist trying that little flutter of eyelashes Clarissa had taught her, just to see how he would react. He raised a brow.

"Something caught in your eye?" he said, with a glint in his own.

It was useless. Mr Gatley did not understand these things. No wonder ladies stayed away from him. Now Mr Channing, on the other hand—

Another gentleman came forward to claim her attention.

"Good evening, Mr Turner," she said in her regular tone to her brother's friend, because she did not care to draw *his* interest. She had known him forever.

He was the last of the arrivals. Of course it was all wrong, standing in the hallway receiving everyone. One was supposed to make a Grand Entrance. Clarissa had made her practise this entrance so many times, drilling into her the dramatic effect she needed to achieve, and now there was no point in even having one.

Well, she would have to make her Entrance later, during the musical part of the evening. Georgiana was to play the piano forte, and Clarissa had agreed to play the harp, which she did not like, but which—she had been told—showed a young lady's bare arms to advantage.

"Such an insipid instrument," Clarissa had said. "I wish I never learned how to play it." But play it she would, at least tonight, and it would mark her entrée into London society.

Georgiana entered the drawing room without the flower on her hair.

"What did you do with the flower?" said Caroline, the moment she set eyes on her. They had picked out that particular flower together and declared it quite perfect to bring out the hazel tinge of Georgiana's eyes.

"Ask Clarissa," she replied.

It was typical of Clarissa's sense of mischief to deprive her of the flower just when she could do nothing about it. But *she* had made her own plans as well. She had tiptoed into the dining hall when everyone was upstairs changing and moved the name places around so that Clarissa would have Mr Gatley for dinner and she would have Mr Channing. She was looking forward to seeing Clarissa's reaction.

She should have known, of course, that Clarissa was too clever for her. For when it was time to be seated, there was Gatley's name, written in crisp gold letters, placed perfectly correctly next to her own.

She could do nothing at this point but send Clarissa a look that promised retaliation. Clarissa, however, did not see her. She was too involved in laughing at something Channing said.

"Anything wrong, Miss Darcy?" Gatley's sharp gaze missed nothing. He had followed the way she had glanced immediately at the place name. He was perfectly capable of putting two and two together.

It could hardly be flattering for him to know that she had tried to rid herself of his company. Her conscience came to life and started berating her. He could not help it that he was not as entertaining as Channing. He was a perfectly affable gentleman—quite agreeable, in fact. She could at least be polite, which was something she *did* know how to do.

She turned to answer him, one of her best smiles on her face. Not one of the ones Clarissa had taught her, but one of her very own.

"Nothing of importance, Mr Gatley. It is merely a game Clarissa and I are playing. But tell me, are you now in London for the Season?"

❧

Georgiana's chance for a Grand Entrance was somewhat ruined again by Mr Moffet, who rose to his feet the moment she appeared in the doorway and rushed to the piano forte to fulfill his promise to turn the pages. Channing, who was not aware of a previous arrangement—and was conveniently situated close to the piano forte—reached the piano sooner.

"Miss Darcy has kindly allowed me to perform this service for her," said Mr Moffet with the satisfied look of a cat that has already caught the mouse.

Channing gave a lazy smile that held a hint of steel.

"Are you quite certain?" he said.

Mr Moffet frowned as he moved from absolute certainty into flustered doubt.

"As a matter of fact…" he scrambled to recall the conversation in the hallway. Had she really said yes, or had he imagined it? "I believe she did," he said tamely.

"We shall ask her, shall we?"

Georgiana was now cast into a dilemma. She knew whom she would rather have standing next to her, but she had already promised Mr Moffet the honour. She was frustrated with both of them for destroying her Grand Entrance, for no one in the audience had spared her a glance. She sighed as she moved towards the piano forte. It was flattering to have gentlemen argue over her. It certainly was a pleasant change from being ignored. But she did not like the choice she would have to make.

Keeping in mind Clarissa's instructions, she fixed a firm, playful smile on her face, and, touching Mr Moffet's shoulder with the corner of her fan, she bent forward and murmured. "*You* were my first choice, of course."

Mr Moffet preened up and smiled, his confidence restored.

"You have put me in a painful situation, gentlemen," she said. "While I would be honoured to have either of you turn the pages while I am playing, I fear it is too distracting to have both of you do so. And since it would be unfair to choose among the two of you, I am afraid my choice has to lie elsewhere."

Channing was still smiling that lazy smile. She wished more than anything that she could choose him, but it was impossible.

"I must ask you, Mr Gatley, if you could possibly help me out?"

She chose Gatley because she could rely on him utterly to step out with no nonsense and simply do what must be done. Channing's reaction to her statement, however, was unexpected. The lazy smile wavered, and his face hardened for just the briefest moment.

"Your wish is my command, Miss Darcy," he said, his bow a study in elegance, his eyes seeking hers.

"All yours, Cousin," he said to Gatley, brushing by him.

Gatley smiled tightly, aware of the audience before them.

Now it was Clarissa's turn to make a Grand Entrance. Georgiana watched her in envy. She did things just right—the pause, the sense of expectation, the hush that fell on the room as she took her first step forward. Georgiana wondered if she would ever learn to do this. Perhaps she lacked some essential sense of the dramatic or the ability to discern the right moment.

Clarissa walked across the room to the harp, all eyes upon her.

"You should have known Mr Moffet was likely to steal your thunder," murmured Gatley from behind her. "You should not have entered until he took his position at the piano."

Georgiana did not need someone murmuring instructions over her shoulder.

"It is too late now to repair it," said Georgiana.

"There will be a next time. One can always learn from one's mistakes."

Clarissa, whose timing was impeccable, shot her a reproachful look from under her eyelashes as she settled behind the harp. Georgiana immediately swallowed down her retort and looked sombre, her hands hovering over the keyboard in preparation.

In the complete silence that followed—clearly Gatley was not going to whisper anymore—Clarissa raised her slender arms. Georgiana almost grinned at Clarissa's self-conscious manner. She herself could not imagine why the sight of a lady's arms could be in any way appealing.

Clarissa gave a signal—a quick nod of the head—and the musicale began.

For once, Georgiana did not lose herself in the music, though she played well enough. Gatley's coat brushed against her arm each time he leaned forward to turn over the page, and it distracted her. It was quite impossible to concentrate.

She would have to remember not to ask him to turn the pages again.

❧

Channing was there when she finished. He offered her his arm and they moved together toward the refreshment table.

"May I congratulate you on the success of your first recital?" he said. "I do not believe I have ever heard the piano forte played so well."

"You have heard me play before, Mr Channing," she said, then bit her tongue as she remembered Clarissa's warnings not to point out an error in a gentleman's reasoning. She could not withdraw her words, but she added a teasing smile to it, hoping it would undo the damage.

"I have indeed. But you were then only a young girl just out of the schoolroom. Now you are a beautiful young lady on the verge of"—he hesitated fractionally—"conquest."

Georgiana thrilled to hear such words on his lips. Did he really think her beautiful? Was it possible that a few changes in her appearance could produce such results? Did he really see her so differently now? A pleasant warmth stole over her, and she basked in the praise. She longed for this moment to last forever.

To her chagrin, Mr Moffet came up to her just then, thrusting a plateful of food before her triumphantly, and the mood shattered.

"Miss Darcy, I have brought you your food. First, I chose one sample from each dish, then I reconsidered. It occurred to me that after such a laborious performance, you must be in need of sustenance to bring up your spirits. So I returned and picked out a second portion from each. I hope that is to your liking?"

She really could do nothing but accept the plate, not after he had gone to so much trouble on her behalf, which meant, of course, that she was obliged to sit with him. Regretfully, she released Channing's arm.

"*A bientôt,*" murmured Channing. "You will have to compensate for abandoning me not once but twice tonight."

"I will do my best," she replied, so taken with his words that she forgot to flutter her eyelashes.

⁂

Two days later Georgiana's pride was further satisfied when a gleaming high perch phaeton came to a halt in front of their townhouse. Georgiana, who was sitting close to the window, gazed at it with awe.

"I will venture to guess the owner of such a set-up," said Elizabeth, eyeing the gleaming vehicle with some amusement. "It could only belong to our Mr Channing."

Georgiana's cheeks sizzled at the mention of his name. "Surely not *our* Mr Channing?" she said, trying to cover up her reaction.

There was only time for Elizabeth to give an enigmatic smile before that very gentleman was announced.

Channing was in high spirits. He complimented Elizabeth most charmingly on the success of the musicale and admired her skills as a hostess most agreeably.

"A party does not have to be a crush to be a success," he added.

"A few well-selected guests can create a far better evening than a ballroom full of strangers. Do you not agree, Miss Darcy?"

Georgiana thought of Mr Moffet and wondered if he would qualify as a well-selected guest in Mr Channing's opinion. She answered with a twinkle in her eye that there were definite advantages to smaller events where everyone knew everybody else.

But Channing was positively bursting with excitement to tell his news and had grown impatient with small talk.

"You are the first of my acquaintance to set eyes on it," he declared. "Tell me what you think of it. Is it not heavenly? See how high the perch is set above the ground? I do believe it is the highest vehicle I have ever seen—the most amazing contraption! I can scarcely believe that it manages to stay upright. But I can assure you it does. I gave it a run in the Park, and though I drove fast, it remained steady as the mail-coach."

The ladies duly admired the phaeton. Georgiana pronounced it the epitome of elegance, while Elizabeth owned that the finish was very fine. Channing, encouraged by their admiration, launched into a witty account of his dealings with the carriage maker.

By the time he was finished, the allotted time for calling on young ladies was over.

"I would be honoured if you would drive out in Hyde Park with me on the phaeton," said Channing. "For it needs only a beautiful young lady to complement it. If you will allow me two or three days until I feel entirely certain of its safety, I will send a note round to specify the day."

Georgiana could hardly believe her ears—that Mr Channing should speak so flatteringly of her. But Clarissa had warned her against seeming too eager, so she dimpled and responded that she would be happy to receive his note.

"I cannot promise that I will be available however," she said, severely, "for I am often engaged these days. There are so many events to attend, I hardly have a moment for myself."

"You must do everything in your power to put aside some time for me, Miss Darcy. And I will enlist Mrs Darcy's support. You will lend me a hand in this, will you not?"

Elizabeth, appealed to in this manner, smiled and said she would see what could be done.

Channing had to be satisfied with this. He bowed, urging her to keep her promise to him. "For you did promise to make it up to me, you know, when you turned me away twice."

"Of course," she said, giving him her hand, "but I did not say when."

A startled expression passed across his handsome visage, to be quickly replaced by pique.

"Then I shall have to haunt you until you do," he said, and walked away.

Georgiana's triumph was now complete.

Chapter 15

GEORGIANA RECEIVED A NOTE THE VERY NEXT DAY, ATTACHED to an enormous bouquet of flowers. In it, Channing requested her presence for a drive around the Park on Tuesday afternoon.

Georgiana thus had three days in which to worry about whether the weather would be good enough for him to be able to honour his appointment.

Tuesday afternoon arrived, and with it came a serene blue sky. Georgiana could now allow herself to give in to the delicious stir of anticipation. A whole hour of having Channing to herself! An hour with no interventions or distractions. She could scarcely believe it. Surrounded as she was always by watchful eyes, Georgiana was beginning to understand the behaviour of those scandalous young ladies who evaded their chaperones to be with their admirers. For one could hardly ever speak more than two words to a gentleman without being interrupted.

In Hyde Park, of course, they would also be surrounded, their every gesture noted by observers whose sole purpose in being there was to gather every morsel of gossip they could find. But perched on top of a phaeton—which surely must be the very top of the world—she and Channing would be alone, and they would finally have an opportunity to know each other better.

Georgiana descended to the drawing room much too early, dressed in her favourite pelisse, her hair painstakingly styled, and her favourite bonnet perched on her head. It was silly to have nothing to do but wait, for now she was bound to fiddle with her hair and undo the carefully coiled curls, or crumble her dress by fidgeting.

But then the knocker sounded. Georgiana struggled to control her expression of delight. It was bound to be Channing, arriving early like her. How fortunate that she was already dressed and ready for him. As footsteps approached she steeled herself to wear a polite expression of interest. It would not do to reveal too much eagerness. Clarissa had drummed at least that much into her.

The door opened. But instead of Channing's tall figure, Georgiana beheld that of Clarissa.

Georgiana could barely conceal her dismay, for she did not wish to see Clarissa, not now. She almost shooed her away.

"How well you look, Georgiana!" said the familiar voice. "You are already wearing your pelisse—are you not too warm? Do you intend to take a drive in the Park? Who is your admirer? Come, you must tell me all about it."

For a long moment, Georgiana considered hiding the truth from Clarissa and finding some way to rid herself of her overly curious cousin. But she knew fooling her would not be easy, and besides, it would prove exceedingly awkward if Channing were to mention their outing to her. So she resigned herself to telling the truth. Hopefully, she would convince Clarissa to leave before Channing arrived.

"You are quite right, Clarissa. I am indeed engaged to drive in the Park. But my admirer, as you call it, is none other than our friend Channing. So, you see, there is nothing of particular interest to tell."

Georgiana knew her smile was too bright and her voice was brittle, and that instead of avoiding suspicion, she had in fact attracted it. She was not surprised when Clarissa regarded her closely.

"Channing? Really? Has he asked you to ride with him? Does he plan to take the family barouche or the phaeton?"

"The phaeton."

"Well, that certainly is a mark of favour. For he was telling me only yesterday that his phaeton is strung so high and is so delicate a contraption that it needs all his skill to drive it, and that he can only allow young ladies whose nerves are steady as a rock to sit at his side."

"He did not say this to me," said Georgiana, treasuring her cousin's words, "but it must, as you say, be a sign of favour to be invited if that is what he said."

Clarissa continued to regard her cousin with her tilted gaze. "He invited me as well, you know, or he would not have told me that. I am to drive with him tomorrow."

Georgiana did not know how to answer. Something was wound up inside her, like a spring ready to go, but the sensation was so unaccustomed that she could not fathom it.

"Perhaps we can both join him today," said Clarissa brightly. "Do you not think that would be amusing? Will he not be surprised to see us both here waiting for him?"

The spring coiled tighter.

"I hardly think that would be a good idea, Clarissa," replied Georgiana, looking towards the window. "Surely if he is worried that driving the curricle with one lady may be difficult, think how much more difficult it would be with two. Besides, if you are planning to drive with him tomorrow, why would you want to drive with him today as well? He will surely invite me to come along with you tomorrow, in that case."

Even as she spoke, she realised it was not such a bad idea after all. For one never knew with Clarissa. The very idea of her younger cousin driving alone with Channing troubled her. Perhaps she ought to sacrifice her own time with Channing to prevent such a situation. In any case—or so she reasoned—it would be almost impossible to be rid of Clarissa. And there were decided advantages to her spending two days in a row with Channing rather than only one.

Georgiana's goal, therefore, quickly changed from making every effort to prevent Clarissa from driving with them, to making sure that the two of them would join him on both drives.

Neither young lady thought it important to consult Channing himself to discover his own wishes.

"The more the merrier, I suppose," said Clarissa with a quick laugh.

Having reached an agreement, with each lady convinced that she had outmanoeuvred the other admirably, they chatted contentedly about any number of insignificant things while awaiting the arrival of the young gentleman himself.

The long-awaited rap of the knocker finally reached them. Georgiana controlled the urge to spring to her feet. She compelled herself to sit composedly, her hands in her lap, as befitted a well-bred young lady.

Hibbert the butler appeared, and with him a gentleman. But the name that fell upon their ears was not Channing. Instead, Hibbert announced a name that could not have been more unwelcome at that moment. It was Gatley.

She received him just as she ought, her manner courteous and friendly, but inwardly she wished him anywhere but there, wondering why he constantly appeared at the most inopportune moments.

"I hope I have not arrived at an inconvenient time," he said, echoing her thoughts, "but I was passing this way and thought I might invite Miss Darcy to ride in the Park. But now that I see both of you are here, I will quite happily extend my invitation to Miss Clarissa Darcy as well."

"It is really most kind of you, sir," said Georgiana, "but I am afraid we have another engagement. Your cousin has very generously invited us to drive with him this very afternoon."

"Indeed?" said Gatley. He considered this with a perplexed expression, then added, "Are you sure it was today?"

"Quite sure," said Georgiana, making an effort to answer civilly. "Is today not Tuesday?"

She went out to the hallway, and brought the card that was pinned to the bouquet. "It says here: *Tuesday at half past five?* And here is his name, clearly written."

Gatley took the card and examined it blandly. "Yes, this is my cousin's writing, unquestionably. I must have been mistaken."

Georgiana decided she would ignore his comment. He was trying to provoke her curiosity, but she had no intention of indulging him. Clarissa, however, fell easily into the trap.

"Whatever do you mean, Mr Gatley? Why *should* you be mistaken?"

"Only that I saw Channing drive by me not twenty minutes ago in his new phaeton with a young lady by his side, heading in the direction of the Park. But I must be quite wrong in my deduction. Perhaps he was simply returning the young lady home before coming here to call on you and Miss Darcy."

He was bent on trouble. Georgiana could see no other reason for Gatley's words but the intention of discrediting his cousin.

"Mr Channing is entitled to drive whomever he wishes around

town, Mr Gatley," she replied firmly, refusing to rise to the bait. "I do not think he needs to account to us for his every move."

"He certainly does not," said Clarissa, smiling. "Mr Channing is universally liked, and it is only natural that he should be seen about town with more than one young lady at his side."

Georgiana did not find Clarissa's words particularly cheering.

"I hope I do not impose if I wait here for a few more minutes," said Mr Gatley.

"Not at all," replied Georgiana. She would not make any effort to converse however. She was quite put out with him for casting aspersions on Mr Channing. He was proving to be just as Channing had described him—someone who believed he had the moral right to control people's lives. Worse, he was proving to be a gossipmonger intent on spreading rumours. One would not have thought it.

A strained silence followed. Georgiana was too well bred to allow it to stretch for long, even if she was vexed with him. Her instincts as a hostess finally came to the fore.

"Shall I ring for refreshments, Mr Gatley?" she said.

"Very kind of you, Miss Darcy, but you need not trouble yourself, for we will be quickly forced to abandon them. My cousin should be here any moment."

His statement held a certain sharpness—an unmistakable note of irony—that Georgiana did not like. A quick perusal of him revealed nothing in his face, however, and she decided she had imagined it. She made a remark about Napoleon, which could always be counted on to provide a lengthy topic of conversation, and it was some time before the subject was exhausted.

The clock chimed the three quarter hour. Georgiana relentlessly subdued the doubts that rose up in her. London streets were busy and full of a myriad obstructions. Besides, fashionable gentlemen were not so very nice in their notions of time. One was almost obliged to be fashionably late in London, and a quarter of an hour did not even begin to qualify for that—not for someone like Channing.

The door opened. But again, the young ladies were doomed to be disappointed, for it was only Darcy and Elizabeth.

"Gatley," said Darcy. "Hibbert told me that you were here."

"Mr Darcy, Mrs Darcy," said Gatley. "A pleasure to see you. I came to accompany the young ladies to the Park, only to discover they were otherwise engaged."

"Really?" said Darcy, casting an amused glance in Georgiana's direction. "I see no evidence of that. It *appears* to me they are perfectly at leisure."

"If you must know," said Elizabeth, smiling too, "they are waiting for Mr Channing."

Darcy looked at the clock significantly. It was by now almost six.

"Is it no longer fashionable for ladies to make an appearance at a half hour past five, or have things changed recently?" he said.

Georgiana disliked being teased, and that her dear brother of all people should undertake to do so—she could not bear it. She would not expose herself to any more disparaging remarks. She stood up decisively.

"It does appear, Mr Gatley, that you were correct in your surmise that I had the wrong day. Thank you, but I am delighted to accept your offer of a drive in Hyde Park."

She did not look at Clarissa. If Clarissa wished to wait for Channing, then she could. *She* certainly did not care if Clarissa accompanied her and Mr Gatley or not.

"It is too late to go for a drive now," said Clarissa. "If you would be kind enough to drop me off at Grosvenor Street, I will accompany you that far."

Georgiana regretted her impulse as soon as Clarissa descended from the landau, for even with a groom present, she was conscious that she was alone with a gentleman she knew very little—and one, moreover, that she was not sure she liked at all. She could not even practise her Arts on him, for he was completely impervious to them. She was at a loss as to why he had called to take her for a drive, for he certainly betrayed no interest in her. Perhaps he had heard something from his cousin and had come to rescue her from embarrassment.

His interference, kindly meant though it may be, was humiliating. She had not asked him to mediate between her and Channing. It would have been far better if he had left her to suffer her disappointment alone. Then at least there would have been no witnesses.

But perhaps he had other reasons. Georgiana had caught glimpses of some sort of rivalry between the two. And there may be other reasons, unknown to her. Curiosity propelled her to probe his motives. She did not, however, set out to question him the way the old Georgiana may have done—in a more direct, though infinitely more naïve way. Instead, she gave him a sly smile, as though to coax some admission of partiality for her out of him.

"You really have been most gentlemanly, Mr Gatley, to offer to replace your cousin in this manner," she said, casting him a sidelong glance. "You have been quite the knight in shining armour, for without you, I would still be waiting at home for your cousin."

Mr Gatley slowed the horses to a trot as he negotiated through a particularly busy knot of traffic. Nothing in his appearance indicated that he had heard her, and since she could hardly repeat the question—for he might have heard her—she sat impatiently by his side, waiting for the road to open up before them.

"Perhaps we may run into Mr Channing in the Park," she said, eventually, for lack of anything else to say.

"Is that what you wish?" asked Gatley, driving through a narrow gap between a cart full of vegetables and a small gig that sped past them too quickly.

Georgiana regretted her words immediately. It was her turn to pretend she had not heard. She gave her full attention to a young lad who was sweeping the road, but when he stopped and whistled at her she turned her head quickly, only to find Gatley's dark eyes brimming with amusement.

"You cannot quite make up your mind, can you?" said Gatley. "One moment you play the coquette, and the next you blush like a young girl fresh from the schoolroom."

Needless to say, this remark did not endear him to her. Nor did she know how to answer him. She was out of her depth in this unexpected conversation.

"You play a dangerous game," he said in an almost offhand manner. "For you do not know the rules, and you do not know how far you can go without harming either yourself or someone else. Your cousin, perhaps, can play with less risk. She has some inherent sense of what to do."

Georgiana was beginning to grow tired of being told that Clarissa played the game—whatever it was—better than her.

"I do not know by what authority you speak to me in this manner," she replied coldly. "You are little more than a stranger."

"True enough," he said.

They had now entered the Park. Georgiana quickly realised how little chance she would have had of conducting any kind of meaningful conversation with Channing, for almost as soon as they entered the Park they had to stop and exchange greetings and introductions with any number of persons.

"You are correct in maintaining that I have no right, and I apologise if you think my remarks too presumptuous," said Gatley, during a quiet moment. He seemed to know a vast number of people. "But you will admit that I know my own cousin better than you know him. I will say no more—only that you must not take everything he says or does too seriously. Other than that, I promise to remain silent on the subject for the rest of the drive. Indeed, it is far too pleasant an evening to dwell on unpleasant subjects. Let us enjoy the drive at least, and I am even willing to promise that I will never ask you to drive in Hyde Park with me again. Will that satisfy you?"

An odd trick of light from the descending sun turned his eyes suddenly from dark brown to liquid gold. She became aware for the first time that his features—the sharp contour of his jaw, the gently arching outline of his nose, the dark lashes that bordered his eyes—were actually very handsome. Why had she never noticed before? He caught her staring. For an instant, their gaze met and tangled. Her breath caught. His eyes were warm and rich and golden—a reflection of the sun.

She pulled away from that steady gaze and composed herself, making herself breathe more deeply. She hoped he did not think she was staring for any particular reason. It was just because of the way the sun had fallen on his face, nothing more. She deliberately turned her attention to a high phaeton coming their way.

As ill luck would have it, the driver turned out to be Channing, accompanied—she guessed—by the same young lady Gatley had mentioned.

If she thought Channing would be discomfited at being caught out in this manner, she was quickly proven wrong, for as soon as he spotted her he drew back his horses and came to a halt by the side of the landau.

"Well met, Cousin!" he said cheerfully. "I see you have stolen the beautiful Miss Darcy all to yourself."

He leaned down far enough over the edge of the high perch for her to fear that he would unbalance it, and addressed himself to her in a half whisper. "You must endure his company as best as you can, for I am sure you must find it deucedly sombre. Has he been lecturing you on your behaviour?"

He was entirely correct, of course. Gatley *had* lectured her on her behaviour. And he *was* a great deal too serious. But Georgiana was so exasperated by Channing's sublime forgetfulness that she came immediately to Gatley's defence. "On the contrary, Mr Channing," she said, "your cousin has been everything that is amiable. I could not have wished for a more agreeable companion."

At that moment Gatley chose to set the landau in motion again, and they had soon left Channing behind them.

"Touché. I believe you ruffled his feathers a little," said Gatley, his lips twitching. "Under normal circumstances, I would thank you for your kind defence. But I am certain that your flattering remark was more a reflection on my cousin's behaviour than my own."

Georgiana was finding Gatley altogether too clever for his own good. His comment piqued her, and all charitable thoughts of him came to an immediate demise.

"Have you and your cousin always been rivals like this?" she enquired, startling herself with her audacity, yet determined not to let him have the last word. The question was rhetorical and she did not expect an answer. She meant it as a challenge.

The question clearly startled him. His quick frown revealed his displeasure, and almost instinctively she began to formulate an apology. He did not give her the chance to utter it, however.

"Rivals?" he said. "I had never thought of it that way." He stared at the ears of the grey horse ahead, reflecting. "Perhaps there is some truth in it, though why, heaven only knows. Percy's father was very harsh, and mine was—I am tempted to say the opposite. My father was always kind and forgiving, whereas his father was, to put it mildly, vindictive and bitter. Whenever he came home from India, Percy escaped him by coming to stay with us. He was afraid of him." He paused, remembering. "I suppose in many ways he envies the closeness of our family. He grieved for my father a long time when he died. But does he see me as a rival? I do not think so."

Georgiana had not meant that Channing saw Gatley as a rival. She had meant something else entirely. Given Channing's attractive personality, she had thought rather that Gatley would wish he had Channing's ease in social situations and would be envious of Channing's success with the ladies in particular. But she should have known that Gatley had too high a sense of his own worth to see it any other way. She smiled to herself. It is a truism that people see the world from their own vantage point, moving through life with blinkers on their eyes. How true this was in Gatley's case!

"Have I amused you?" asked Gatley, puzzled.

"Yes, I suppose you have," said Georgiana, "but please do not ask me to explain why."

He examined her closely. Normally, such scrutiny would have intimidated her, but now, his bafflement made her laugh even more.

For the rest of the drive they exchanged little more than banalities. But her amusement lasted until she reached home, so that when Elizabeth asked her if her drive had gone well, she was able to answer, quite truthfully, that she had enjoyed it very much.

Chapter 16

THERE MUST BE A MOMENT IN A YOUNG LADY'S LIFE WHEN HER family no longer appears a sanctuary, but rather a prison—even if woven with the silken threads of concern—obstructing her chance of going out into the world. Georgiana had reached that moment.

"I hear that you enjoyed your drive with Mr Gatley yesterday," said Darcy the next day, at a quiet family dinner that was rare these days—for they were either invited somewhere or dinner was in some way interrupted by cries of appeal from the nursery. "Do you not find Gatley an intriguing companion?"

Georgiana did not like to have her words misconstrued. She had enjoyed the drive, but not for the reasons they had assumed. Darcy had that approving, paternalistic expression he had acquired after little Lewis was born. She was tempted to tell him that she was not a baby—and that she did not like being viewed the same way.

"Hardly," she said pertly. "The drive only confirmed to me that Mr Gatley is as conceited and blind to his own faults as Mr Collins."

She derived some satisfaction from seeing the indulgent expression disappear. But the satisfaction was short lasting. Even as she spoke, she was conscious that she was being very unfair to Mr

Gatley. One could not compare the two men at all. But having made the statement, she prepared herself to defend it.

"Do you not think that is a little harsh?" said Elizabeth, blinking at the look of defiance Georgiana sent her brother.

Darcy put down his fork and wiped his mouth. This, she knew, was a prelude to a dressing-down, and she had no intention of hearing one tonight.

"I hope you will excuse me," she said, scraping her chair against the floor as she rose, and effectively interrupting as her brother started to speak. "I have a little headache. I think I will retire early."

"Yes, of course," said Elizabeth good-naturedly. "A good night's sleep is the best cure for the headache."

"Very wise words," muttered Georgiana, as she strode past, "though how I could be expected to get to sleep when I have a headache, I am sure I do not know."

Elizabeth gave no sign of having heard, but Darcy seized a corner of Georgiana's paisley shawl as she passed him.

"You will apologise to Elizabeth, Georgiana. She meant well by her comment, and you answered rudely."

Georgiana left the shawl in her brother's hand and continued on her way. She reached her chamber and threw herself on the bed.

It was always about Elizabeth, was it not? Or about the squawking child upstairs, she added mentally as high-pitched squeals reached her from the nursery, even through the closed door. It was always about *them*.

And to think she was glad when her brother married! To think that at one time she could never have imagined leaving home. She used to think she would never marry. That she would stay with Darcy, and run the house for him, and be perfectly contented with her music and the garden and the humdrum everyday activities that made up her life.

Now she felt so hemmed in—so *constricted*—she could hardly wait to leave.

And this was where the reality of her situation chaffed at her even more. For if she wanted to leave—which she did, urgently at this point—there was only one way open to her and that was marriage. Unless she, like Anne, simply disappeared. For a moment she toyed with the idea. How much more comfortable it would be to live one's life away from the prying eyes of society, in complete obscurity, free of the constant interference of one's relations.

But then common sense came to the fore. It was nonsense, of course, to envy Anne. They knew nothing about her fate. For all they knew, she was married by now, forced into it by some ruthless villain who had abducted her by force. Or perhaps she had been so desperate to escape her mother that she had run straight into the clutches of a debauched fortune hunter. As always when she thought of Anne, a sharp jab of guilt pierced through her. If only she and Clarissa had not encouraged her to walk out alone! And if only they knew what had happened to her.

She was not so very desperate. She would not make that mistake. She had had a brush with it—had been almost tempted—but then she had been only fifteen, and even then she had hesitated, at least enough to confide the scheme to her brother. Besides, she could not compare her home to Rosings, however much she may dislike the changes that had occurred since her brother's marriage.

Besides, she would have to leave soon enough. For that was what the Season was about, was it not? About finding an acceptable gentleman, marrying, and setting up her own establishment? About starting a new life with a stranger?

The truth was, Georgiana could not make up her mind whether she looked forward to the possibility, or whether she really hated it.

One of the advantages of youth is that one thinks nothing of a disagreement, however unpleasant it may have been at the time. By the morning, Georgiana, with that ability to put the disagreeable behind her, hardly remembered her brief flare of temper from the night before. But if she had expected the storm to blow over by itself, she was very much mistaken. The moment she reached the breakfast room, a maid brought her the message that her brother was awaiting for her in the library.

She sighed, and, aware of the confrontation to come, she took as much time over breakfast as she could. She considered ignoring the summons. But what good would that do? It was bound to happen sooner or later.

She entered the book room and found him seated behind the great mahogany desk, looking very much the head of the Darcy family. His brows were drawn in thick lines over his eyes, his mouth tightened into thin disapproval. At first she was struck by apprehension. Her brother had never dealt with her in this manner before. She quaked under the severity of his glance.

But then she rallied forces. Why should her brother make her quake? She was no longer a child, to be afraid of his opinion. If he was to stop thinking of her as a child, she would have to stand her ground, perhaps even counter his attack with one of her own.

She prepared herself for battle.

When he finally spoke, however, his words completely disarmed her.

"Georgie," he said, using his term of good-humoured affection for her, his expression softening. "I have the distinct impression that you are not as happy and as carefree as you used to be. I know that making the transition into adulthood is not easy. And without a father or a mother to guide you, it must be doubly so. You must especially feel the lack of a mother. As a brother who is more than ten years older than you, I can hardly expect to be the recipient of confidences—quite the opposite, I suppose—but I would be honoured if you could confide in me and tell me what is troubling you."

Georgiana almost ran to him and threw herself into his arms. But, an iron force—not fully her own—interceded, and she controlled the impulse. It would hardly serve the purpose, to run to him like a child.

He waited long enough to ensure that she was not planning to take the opportunity he had offered.

"You may as well sit," he said with a sigh. "This will take some time."

She took a seat, as far away from the desk as possible.

Having told her to sit, he stood up himself and walked to the window.

"I can guess part of the reason for your unhappiness. For years you have had me to yourself. Since our father's death when you were ten, I was not only your brother, but father, mother, and sister to you too—an impossible task, as you can imagine, particularly for a young man only twenty at that time. I did not spend as much time as I ought with you perhaps—for I too had my life to live—but when I was with you, you could be sure of my undivided attention. Now, however, you have not only one but two other persons who share my affection."

He paused to give her a chance to speak, but she said nothing.

"At first, you were happy to receive Elizabeth into our midst, and you saw her as a welcome sister. But now, as I form my own family, you fear that you will be excluded."

This was so close to the truth that Georgiana wanted to cry out that it was true. She was an intruder in this happy household, where she no longer felt she belonged.

But again, that iron force prevented her, reminding her that she was an adult now and that she should depend on no one.

"I am sure that you need no reassurance that you occupy the same place in my heart as you always have. But my duty now extends to my wife and my child as well. That is not something that will change."

Georgiana forced herself to remain distant. She would not respond. She would not complain. She needed to remain strong.

"You must find your own peace in the situation. I cannot help you find it, though I know that eventually you will. In any case, you will soon have a family of your own to care for. That is the purpose of bringing you to London, is it not?" He paused. The words lingered between them, part of the new barrier that had sprung up when before there was none.

Darcy waited for her to say something. She did not know what he expected of her. To plead with him perhaps? Well, she had no intention of doing so.

When it was clear he would receive no answer, his expression turned stern again.

"Meanwhile, however, you are still a member of this household, and as such, I insist that you treat Elizabeth with every respect due to my wife, for I will not tolerate any slights to her."

If Georgiana's heart had begun to soften at the earlier part of her brother's speech, his unequivocal manner now hardened it completely. She took exception to his words, all the more since she had done nothing seriously disrespectful. She had just muttered a few words, nothing more. She had thought her brother's protectiveness towards his wife in other instances amusing, but when it was directed against her! His words stung more than she could have thought.

"Elizabeth shall have my respect, as you have it as well," she replied. "But remember that, though you may force me to give Elizabeth the respect she craves so much, you cannot force me to like her."

And with that, she turned her back on her brother and strode out of the room.

❦

Needless to say, the encounter with her brother provoked in her an urgent need to leave the house. Without a word to either Darcy or Elizabeth, she called for the carriage.

Her destination was Grosvenor Square. It was only there, she was convinced, that she could find the understanding she craved. She thanked the lucky fate that had brought her cousin to England. Who would she have talked to otherwise?

She arrived to find her cousin's household still awaking. Forced to kick her heels downstairs as she waited for Clarissa to drink her chocolate and dress, she squirmed with impatience. After that, she had to partake of breakfast, for Clarissa refused to go out without eating, and she was compelled to make polite conversation with Caroline, who was blissfully unaware of the depth of turmoil she was going through.

It seemed like several excruciating hours before they were finally able to set out, with the excuse of needing to make some small purchases.

"Now we can be very snug, and you shall tell me what has happened to make your face as long as a lamppost," said Clarissa when the carriage started moving.

Georgiana, who had held back everything for the longest time imaginable, immediately poured the whole sorry tale into her friend's ears.

But instead of the understanding she expected, Clarissa was more inclined to dismiss the whole matter offhand.

"Too much is being made out of nothing," said Clarissa at the end of the story. "'Tis but a tiny storm in a tiny teacup."

Georgiana frowned deeply at her cousin.

"Do not fly into a rage at *me*, Miss Darcy," said Clarissa, laughing. "You can have no quarrel with *me*. I will admit that, having grown up elsewhere, I do not fully understand all the rules of behaviour that are so important here. Why even yesterday Caroline—who has been such a help to me—pointed out that driving with Channing alone in the Park could be tantamount to a declaration of engagement and advised me to call off the drive. Is that not the drollest thing?"

Georgiana saw it was useless to make Clarissa understand her distress. In any case, she was only too ready to be distracted with the mention of Channing.

"I do think Caroline is making too fine a point of it," said Georgiana. "One drive in an open carriage cannot hold any significance. It would be different if you did it repeatedly. Besides, you will not be going alone. I am to accompany you. Or have you forgotten?"

It became apparent that Clarissa *had* forgotten, or at least that she had chosen not to remember. For how could it have slipped her mind, when they had spoken of it only yesterday? Was it possible that Clarissa was planning to drive out with Channing *without* her?

"Of course! Then there is no need to worry at all," said Clarissa brightly. "If you were to come with us, then all would be well. I would hate to become the object of conversation for every rumour-monger in Hyde Park."

Georgiana wondered why Clarissa should care about such a thing, when she was so careless of appearances generally, but she said nothing. She was still rattled by the idea that Clarissa might be deliberately trying to exclude her.

At that moment Clarissa noticed a striped turban with gold tassels in the window of a milliners' shop. "Oh, look! Is it not in the manner of Byron? Quickly, tell the driver to stop. I simply must have it!" With barely enough patience to allow the footman to let down the steps, she half-tumbled out of the carriage.

Georgiana hesitated, for the milliner was not a fashionable one, nor were they on a fashionable street.

"You cannot wish me to go inside by myself," said Clarissa impatiently.

"We can send a footman," she answered, but Clarissa was already stepping through the doorway.

Georgiana resigned herself and descended slowly—and with dignity—from the carriage. By the time she had entered the shop, Clarissa was already trying on the hat.

"What do you think?" she said, putting it on and considering her image in the mirror. "Does it suit me?"

Georgiana admitted that it did.

"You do not consider it *tawdry*, do you?"

Georgiana assured her that it was not, for it was really quite elegant, in the fashion of the oriental. *She* would never wear it, but then she was not Clarissa.

"Then I shall buy it."

Clarissa glanced idly around the shop at the other hats on display, then let out a little cry.

"And I have found just the bonnet for you. It is exactly like a French bonnet I saw on one of the fashion plates. It matches your pelisse admirably, and it will look perfect on you."

The hat was not one Georgiana would ever have considered wearing. She was rather particular when it came to hats and hated fuss and ostentation of any kind. This one was striped in white and maroon, with a very high crown and a broad brim. The brim was overhung with lace. The side of the hat was decorated with berries, and a white ostrich feather completed the picture.

"Are you sure?" she said, eyeing the contrivance uncertainly.

"It is very striking."

Which was precisely what Georgiana feared. But she *had* asked Clarissa to choose her clothes for her. So, somehow, Clarissa persuaded her to purchase it and to wear it immediately, and it seemed easier to give in than to protest.

It was pouring when they left the shop. The clatter of pattens mingled with the splatter of the rain as it struck the cobbled road. Their plans for more shopping disappeared under the torrent, and they were compelled to turn back home.

They had no sooner driven a few yards, however, when Clarissa ordered the driver to stop.

"Look! It is Mr Channing and Mr Gatley," she said, her eyes sparkling. "Let us see how they approve of our new purchases."

She hailed them, and with a quick wave of the hand, invited them into the carriage.

"Much as you may wish to be soaked," she said through the window, keeping her turban safely under cover, "you can hardly say no if we rescue you from the rain. Those umbrellas cannot protect you. We can easily drop you wherever you wish."

"I am much obliged to you," said Channing, climbing readily into the carriage.

"Do you have a maid?" asked Gatley, hesitating outside, rain dripping down the sides of his umbrella.

"No, but we have two footmen," replied Clarissa. "They are currently being rained upon outside, so I hope we can start moving as soon as possible to save them from their misery."

He still hesitated, but with his cousin already inside he could hardly refuse.

Georgiana moved up the seat to make room for Gatley. The smell of damp clothing filled the carriage.

"I hope you will not catch a chill," she said, eyeing their wet clothes with concern.

"Thanks to you," said Mr Channing, "we will be home in no time. A glass of brandy is all I need."

"We have bought ourselves new hats," said Clarissa, glancing sideways at her reflection in the window. "You must tell us what you think. You must be perfectly candid, mind."

"I congratulate you on your choices, for you look very dashing indeed," said Mr Channing. "You too, Miss Darcy. Your hat is charming, but of course, so is its wearer."

His eyes lingered on her face. She had intended to give him a dazzling smile, but her smile wavered under his intense scrutiny. He continued to gaze at her until Clarissa thanked him very prettily, and he turned to respond to her.

Still, Clarissa could not be satisfied when the other gentleman in the carriage had not yet expressed an opinion.

"Mr Gatley, *you* have said nothing."

"I think your turban very pretty. It suits your character well, and it is exactly what I would have expected you to wear. I cannot make a judgement on Miss Darcy's hat, however, for it is too modern for someone as old-fashioned as I am."

Considering the exquisite and expensive tailoring of his navy waistcoat, matched with a cravat that was a masterpiece of white perfection, one could be forgiven for thinking him more concerned with fashion than he admitted.

Georgiana understood his comment as a rebuff and turned her face to hide the conflicting feelings which were surely branded on her face. On the one hand, she was chastised, for she knew she should not have allowed Clarissa to convince her to buy the hat. She should have trusted her own judgement. On the other hand, she—very naturally—resented the slight.

"Look at what you have done now, Mr Gatley," said Clarissa. "You have made my cousin sad."

"Come, Gatley, must you be so thoughtless?" said Channing. "Surely you can do better than that."

"I am not as skilled at flattering ladies as others of my acquaintance are," he said, his colour heightened. "I never study my compliments. When I pay tribute to someone, it is because I mean it."

Georgiana, further annoyed now by Clarissa's interference, deemed it time to speak, if only to show how very little Mr Gatley's opinion mattered to her.

"Some gentlemen seek to stand out from the crowd by professing to be harsher than others, and so lay claim to the higher moral ground. That is how they assert their own superiority," she said, in a light, dismissive tone. "In such cases, I believe it is far better not to give their remarks too much importance by taking them seriously."

"How so, Miss Darcy?" cried Gatley. "When I am endeavouring to be as sincere as possible?"

"By George!" said Channing, bursting into laughter. "I think she has your measure, Gatley!" He turned to Georgiana confidingly. "You have put him out of countenance completely, for he is quite accustomed to having others yield at once to his moral tone."

Gatley did indeed look quite put out. She was not happy about it, but she felt her position was justified. Perhaps he had not intended to wound her through stating his opinion, but he had made her appear foolish in front of her friends. He had been frank, but frankness taken too far could cross over into rudeness. There are many ways of saying the same thing, and the most direct is not always the best.

With Clarissa and Channing both laughing with her, Georgiana was able to perceive the whole matter as nothing more than a joke and to cast all misgivings aside.

They had arrived by then at Mr Channing's residence.

"I am afraid, Miss Clarissa, our drive in the Park this afternoon will have to be put off," he said regretfully, as he descended from the carriage. "But I promise I will make up for it to you. I shall plan an outing for us all, how about that? Would it not be amusing to get out of London for the day?"

The young ladies agreed enthusiastically. Gatley also expressed his agreement—not enthusiastically, it might be said, but positively enough.

"Then it is settled," said Channing.

* * *

For the few minutes that he was left alone with the ladies, Gatley endeavoured to engage them in light conversation. Miss Darcy answered rather sullenly, still displeased with his comment about her hat. Since he did not wish to return to that topic again, he was glad when his home came into sight, and he was able to leave the whole thing behind him.

Though truth be told, he was grateful for the ride. The sudden downpour had come so quickly his clothes had turned sodden even before he had been able to raise his umbrella. He and Channing would have had to return home in any case before they reached their club, if only to change their clothes.

He had been glad, however, to leave the close confinement of the carriage. There was something about the Darcy cousins that made him on edge. The American one, Miss Clarissa, was sharp and merry on the outside but with a hollow centre to her that he distrusted. Darcy's sister, however—well, he could only say that there was more to her than met the eye. She was changing quickly. She was copying her cousin, of course. But there were other changes too. Already she was not the same young lady he had seen at Rosings.

Take today, for example. She had spoken to him in a manner that both irked and intrigued him. Who would have thought her capable of such perception? He had not liked what she said—not when it was at his expense—but he had to admit that there was a grain of truth in it. She ought not to have spoken that way, of course. But then, he should have been more gracious in his comment on her hat. He had not liked being pushed to give an opinion by Miss Clarissa. He had thought her question brash and had countered it by deliberately saying exactly what he thought. The result, however, had been at Miss Darcy's expense.

Well, she had not let it pass, which was undoubtedly to her credit. She looked demure, with those soft round eyes that filled her face and frothy hair encircling it. But there was a barbed edge to her, and he had not yet determined if he liked it or not. And then, too, he was all too aware that she was trying to impersonate Miss Clarissa, which was not a point in her favour at all.

His valet helped him put his coat, which was really much too tight. He did not like the current fashion that demanded that his clothes fit him like a glove.

At least, he reflected, he did not have to wear stays.

He checked himself in the mirror. He was particular about his cravats. He liked the simplest knots, partly because they were the most elegant and partly because they were the hardest to get right.

"Did you get caught in the rain?" called out his mother, as he passed the parlour door.

He paused in the doorway. "We were soaked very quickly. I had to come back to change."

She regarded him with a steady gaze. "The carriage you stepped out of resembled that of the Darcys. I thought I caught a glimpse of Miss Darcy through the window."

It was a question.

"Yes," he replied. He said nothing further. He did not owe her any explanations.

She looked as though she was about to say something, but she held back.

Only after he had already left the house did he feel curious about what she had wished to say.

Chapter 17

A NEW HAT IS NO GUARANTEE OF HAPPINESS. AT LEAST, IT was not with Georgiana, who returned home to find that, in spite of her purchase, nothing there had changed. The hat did not make her more agreeable to her brother, who merely looked severe when he met her in the hallway and refrained from greeting her.

A young lady shunned by her family is an unhappy one indeed, particularly when she has been the recipient of a snub by a young gentleman. Georgiana was therefore in a very uncharitable frame of mind when she entered the parlour to find Elizabeth engaged in a *tête-à-tête* with Caroline.

They stopped speaking immediately when they saw her and looked at her with identical polite smiles.

"A charming hat," said Caroline, "very *à la mode*."

Georgiana raised her brow and glanced towards Elizabeth, who said nothing.

"Clarissa suggested it," said Georgiana, taking the hat off and tossing it into a corner.

"Clarissa has natural taste in matters of clothing," said Caroline, "though perhaps a trifle eccentric for someone her age." She spoke affectionately. "You are lucky to have Clarissa to advise you. Do you not agree, Elizabeth?"

"Very lucky," said Elizabeth.

Georgiana tried to remember the last time Elizabeth had said something like that about *her*.

"Everyone likes my cousin," said Georgiana brightly. "I am very lucky." Though at this moment she did not feel lucky at all.

"Clarissa is very like Robert," said Caroline. "Everyone likes Robert." Her face positively glowed at his mention.

"They do have a natural exuberance that makes them very desirable company," agreed Elizabeth. "It is a Darcy trait."

Georgiana could think of *one* Darcy who was not gifted with that trait. Someone who was more likely to be associated with dullness than with exuberance. Really, she was beginning to tire of hearing Clarissa praised.

"I must have stepped in a puddle," she said, rising to her feet, "my hem is wet. I need to go upstairs to change." Perhaps she should raise her skirt as Clarissa had done on that first day. She could be sure of their attention then.

But there were no gentlemen in the room, and no one to be shocked.

Caroline nodded. Elizabeth said nothing. Even before she had quit the room, they were back to their half-whispered exchange.

She almost collided into the housekeeper, Mrs Busby, who was on her way to the parlour to consult with her mistress about the menus.

Georgiana rarely indulged in impulsive acts. She generally thought twice about everything. She had never been one of those children who were ever getting up to mischief and thinking up pranks. But she was peeved, and the appearance of Mrs Busby, who had once been *her* housekeeper, not Elizabeth's, only increased her ire.

A wicked idea sprang to Georgiana's mind, and she did not hesitate.

"You need not trouble Mrs Darcy," said Georgiana. "She is engaged in a most particular conversation with Mrs Caroline Darcy and would not wish you to disturb her. I would be happy to consult with you on tomorrow's menu."

The housekeeper had known Georgiana far longer than she had known Elizabeth, and, sensing the young lady's feeling of displacement, did not see any harm in indulging her young mistress this one time.

It took a few minutes of close consultation for everything to be planned.

"Make sure you tell Cook that it is a special meal for Mr Darcy," said Georgiana. "I would like to surprise him."

⁂

Georgiana took her place at dinner the next evening with every expectation of deriving great enjoyment from it. Her good humour had been fully restored. She only wished that Clarissa could have been here to laugh with her, but she would have to content herself with her little victory alone.

Mr Darcy took one spoon of the turtle soup, choked over it, and glared at the hapless footman.

"Am I right in assuming this is turtle soup?" he said.

Darcy peered at Elizabeth, who looked at the soup in confusion.

"I know that you dislike turtle soup, Elizabeth. You need not have ordered it especially for me, for I can easily order it at my club without any inconvenience to you."

Georgiana waited with bated breath for Elizabeth's response.

"I do not dislike turtle soup so very much," murmured Elizabeth.

"It is just not one of my favourites, that is all. Cook makes a good turtle soup. She should be given the opportunity to show it off once in a while."

Darcy smiled at Elizabeth tenderly.

"It is very kind of you to place cook's feelings before your own, Elizabeth," he said, eating the soup with relish. "I admit I am fond of Cook's soup. It is far superior to that available at the club." A moment later, however, he frowned. "But what about you? You are not eating. You should have requested something else for yourself if you meant to indulge me."

"It is hardly a tragedy for me to miss out on my soup, Fitzwilliam."

"No, of course not," he said, "but I cannot eat so heartily when you have nothing to eat yourself."

He turned to the footman. "You may bring in the next course for Mrs Darcy."

The next course was duly brought in, and here Elizabeth was unable to conceal her reaction. She stared at the serving dish in dismay. The oysters were arranged lovingly on the plate. They sat on the plate like an accusation.

Elizabeth did not eat oysters. They made her break out in a rash.

Darcy took in the scene with a glance.

"You do not eat oysters either," he said, "though they *are* a particular favourite of mine." He wiped his mouth and put down his napkin. "What the devil is happening? Has Cook gone mad?" He turned to the footman. "What is the next course?" he asked. "Devilled eggs, by any chance?"

"I believe so, sir," said the unhappy footman.

"Another of my favourite dishes which Mrs Darcy does not eat," he said. "Request Cook to come up immediately! What is the meaning of this? She had better provide a very good explanation."

Georgiana began to tremble. She had not imagined for a moment that someone else would be blamed for her mischief. She had assumed that her brother would know immediately that she alone could have planned this. Now the situation had become decidedly awkward, and she had no choice but to confess.

"Fitzwilliam," she said plaintively. "It was not Cook's fault."

Darcy's thunderous look turned upon his sister.

"You!" he said. "You are the one who came up with this outrageous scheme? To what purpose, may I ask? Merely to see Mrs Darcy suffer?"

"I did not…"

"Has it come to this? Does it give you pleasure, Georgiana, to make your sister unhappy? Or did you hope that, to protect you, she would eat the oysters and suffer an attack?"

His withering glance made her shrivel up inside. She had never been the object of his contempt before, never in her whole life. No matter how angry he had been at her in the past, he had never looked at her in this manner. Misery washed over her in waves. *Has it come to this?* It was the same question she longed to ask him, but could not.

"Come, come, Fitzwilliam," said Elizabeth, laughing. "You cannot mean to take all this so seriously? It is only a prank, and a small one at that. At least she did not tie my sash to the chair, or put a toad into my pocket."

If Elizabeth had intended to lighten the atmosphere, her words resulted in the opposite.

"A prank, Elizabeth? A prank? Is she some eight-year-old encountering her governess for the first time? You speak of toads and sashes and pranks as if that were something quite in the ordinary. But I can assure you, it was not something my father would have tolerated even when Georgiana was a child, let alone now, when she has entered Society and is on the verge of *marriage*, in God's name!"

But Elizabeth, if anything, seemed all the more amused by his indignation.

"Are you trying to tell me you never engaged in any pranks when you were her age, at University? That you were a model of propriety and never thought it funny to trick the Masters and run circles round the Deans? Pray do not tell me so, for I shall find it very unnatural indeed!"

He opened his mouth to protest, but she forestalled him.

"If you try to hoodwink me, I will ask Bingley. I am sure he has a few stories to tell me that will cast an entirely different view on your character."

Darcy's protests died down, and he grinned ruefully at Elizabeth.

"Very well," he admitted. "I confess myself guilty of the occasional prank. Now are you satisfied?"

He was rewarded with a smile.

But his eyes fell again on the oysters.

"Though how you could think..." he began, glaring at his sister.

"Ask Cook to send up some bread and cheese for me," said Elizabeth to the footman. "I shall content myself with that, for I am sure you have done an excellent job of selecting all the foods that I dislike most," she continued when the footman had left, addressing herself to Georgiana. "I own myself flattered that you are so aware of my taste in food. I *had* wondered why Mrs Busby didn't speak to me today. Will you have some oysters, Fitzwilliam? I really would much rather put them closer to you."

Her eyes danced mischievously. It was by now readily apparent that she had not taken the least offence.

Meanwhile, Georgiana sat in her chair, unable to move, a veritable picture of misery. Her attempt to enrage Elizabeth had not only failed, but had been turned against her, and had only served to confirm to her brother Elizabeth's superiority.

❦

The evening was not over by far. She had planned the dinner badly—or at least, she had not predicted the outcome well enough. For now they had to appear at an informal dance, and much as she would have liked to cry off, she knew Channing would be attending, and she did not wish to miss the opportunity to see him.

As she dressed, she dreaded the carriage ride. She was sure Darcy would take the opportunity to lecture her in some way. She donned her gown like armour, and instead of admiring herself in the mirror—as her maid Rosie advised her to do, declaring she had never seen her look so handsome—she thought only of ways to counter Darcy's attack. She descended the stairs with a frown on her face, ready for a skirmish.

"This golden colour becomes you, Georgiana," said Darcy. "You should wear it more often. It brings out the colour of your eyes."

Elizabeth too admired her clothing and remarked that she was really very glad she had left the selection of Georgiana's gowns to Caroline, for her taste was far better. Darcy immediately denied it, and a playful argument ensued during which Georgiana was entirely forgotten.

She could not sulk, of course, not when going to a dance, especially when she knew Mr Channing was to be in attendance. She was aware that all the work she had done—everything she had achieved, through Clarissa's help—could be undone very easily. For she could not deceive herself for a moment into believing she had captured Mr Channing's heart. She had attracted his attention—if his intense glance this afternoon was any indication—but she had some way to go before she could have a real place in his affections. She could not even begin to be complacent.

Clarissa was there before her. Which was another complication she was growing tired of; for just as Channing rarely showed up without his cousin, it seemed equally rare to see Channing without Clarissa. Of course, she knew it could not be helped. They attended the same occasions and knew the same set of people, and they could not expand their circle of acquaintances very much yet because of their limited appearances.

She could not understand why Clarissa hovered around Channing. Her cousin gave no serious sign of attachment, yet she pursued him the instant he appeared on the scene as though her life depended upon it. And perhaps it did. For whenever she tried to approach the topic of Channing to her cousin, Clarissa turned uncharacteristically reticent. Which did not bode well, to Georgiana's mind. For surely if the younger woman had nothing to hide—no deep attachment, no dreams for the future—she would have simply answered Georgiana's questions without hesitation.

Guilt reared its ugly head—and the possibility that, in winning Channing for herself, she might be causing harm to her cousin. Yet why should *she* feel guilty? Georgiana had never made a secret of wishing to attract Channing's notice. She had told Clarissa of her intentions from the start. And Clarissa had agreed to help her.

As she considered this, all feelings of guilt ebbed away. One could argue that, if they *were* competing for the same gentleman, it was entirely Clarissa's fault. She knew Georgiana had an interest in

Channing. The shoe, one could say, was on the other foot. Clarissa was trying to steal Channing from *her*. It was blatantly unfair of Clarissa to compete with her.

Well, Georgiana had no intention of withdrawing her suit. Time alone would tell who was going to be the winner.

With that in mind, Georgiana headed straight for the little group that was gathered in the corner. Clarissa was there, as were Channing and Mr Moffet. She discovered, to her surprise, that they were talking about novels.

"I like *Waverley* very much indeed," Clarissa was saying, "though if the mysterious writer of the novel *is* Sir Walter Scott, he has no business writing novels, when he is already a famous poet."

"One would think you would have preferred him not to write the novel. Do you prefer poetry then, over novels? That is quite singular, surely, for a young lady."

"As a young lady, I am willing to read anything that is good."

"Not a political work, I would wager," said Mr Moffet.

Both gentlemen laughed, Mr Moffet's perfect lips curling with pleasure at his own wit.

"I would not qualify *Waverley* as a political work," said Clarissa with a deliberate smile, though Georgiana had seen the quick flash in her eyes.

"We were not speaking of *Waverley*," said Mr Moffet with kindly condescension.

Georgiana, realising that Clarissa was preparing to say something unpleasant, quickly asserted that she thought *Waverley*'s reputation very well deserved, for she had never read a better book.

"There you see," said Mr Channing. "All young ladies love novels."

"Surely gentlemen admire novels as well," said Clarissa. "The Prince Regent is known to do so. It is rumoured that he honoured the unknown author of *Pride and Prejudice* with an invitation to Carlton House."

Mr Channing's thoughts had shifted to something else.

"Speaking of invitations," he said, "I am only a humble country gentleman and cannot invite anyone to Carlton House, but I would like to issue an invitation to these particular young ladies—and gentleman too. Moffet, you may bring your sister along as well."

"Cease all this dilly-dallying, Channing," said Moffet, "and come to the point."

"I recall that when they were in Kent, the Miss Darcys were invited to visit some ruins—an invitation which never materialised, unfortunately."

Mr Moffet looked sullen at this reminder. "Hardly fair, Channing, when you know very well…"

"Never mind that," said Channing, breaking in, "I am in the position to remedy the situation. I recently visited a friend in Farnham, and I remember him saying that he lived close to Waverley Abbey, from whence the hero of our much admired novel hailed. Since the ladies have expressed such a lively interest in *Waverley*, what say you that we form an expedition there? The area is reputed to be the prettiest in Surrey, and we could picnic there and explore the ruins. Is that not a fabulous idea?"

General enthusiasm greeted his suggestion, and with parents, chaperones, and matrons in attendance, permission was quickly requested and just as quickly received.

"Are you satisfied with my plan, Miss Darcy? Have I not endeavoured to win your favour?" said Channing, approaching her as a set was about to begin. "Surely now you will keep *your* promise and not turn me down for this dance."

Georgiana, who could not possibly have turned him down,

remembered just in time to restrain her eagerness and give off an air of general indifference.

"I will not turn you down this time, Mr Channing," she said, turning up her nose, "but you must not think that I am as easily pleased as *that*."

He grinned. "Then I see I shall have to endeavour to do something else to please you," he said. "But you will have to tell me what it is—for I am completely at a loss."

Georgiana laughed, for he was really quite silly. But she was making inroads into his affection, and that was all that mattered.

Chapter 18

Two days after the dance, news of Anne arrived which threw everything they had learned earlier into doubt.

The men who had been sent to watch the London-Edinburgh road returned, having waited in vain for anyone of Anne's description to appear. All traces of her had vanished after she left York. It seemed they had been mistaken in thinking she planned an elopement.

The search had now turned to other directions.

Elizabeth shook her head when she heard the news, and said that it should have been obvious to them all. Why should Anne need to flee to the border, when she was already of age? The idea of her fleeing northwards had misled them, and no one had stopped to wonder why she would be eloping. She could marry anywhere she wished, as long as she could procure a licence.

"Which leaves us with no clues at all," said Darcy. "We cannot even be sure that the lady who was seen in York was Anne. We have lost a great deal of time following the wrong trail. We can no longer be complacent. I shall have to employ a number of men to work on this."

Things once again looked decidedly grim. For if the man on the case had been mistaken, then they were back to the beginning, and who was to know what had really happened?

Apart from the anxiety suffered by everyone over Anne, the bad news had another impact. For two days, all the young ladies' activities for the Season were cancelled. But again it was Caroline who provided the most sensible view of the situation.

"It is too late now for Georgiana and Clarissa to withdraw from the London scene. To do so would give rise to unnecessary speculation. For what reason could we possibly give for it? There could be no convincing way to explain it at this point, and society will be only too glad to supply reasons of its own."

No one could deny the wisdom of this, not even Darcy, whose mouth tightened, but who could find no argument to oppose it.

And so it was, that despite Anne's unknown fate, the round of entertainments continued, including the promised outing to the old Abbey.

❧

Georgiana had high expectations of the expedition. She resolved to find an opportunity to spend time alone with Channing, even if both Clarissa and Mr Gatley were in the party. She lay awake in bed after she had put out her candle, and thought of ways she could draw him away from the others. If she did not succeed, then she would only have herself to blame.

But already things were not going well. First, the trip was postponed because a strong storm had been unleashed during the night and going on a picnic was out of the question. Then, on the night before they were supposed to go, Elizabeth developed a cold. Darcy hesitated to send Georgiana without Elizabeth as chaperone. But after many assurances that she would be adequately watched over, he relented, on condition that she would travel with the Gatleys. Accordingly, a note was sent to them, and Gatley's carriage made its due appearance the next morning.

Georgiana, who was apprehensive about spending more than three hours in a carriage with Gatley, soon put all her misgivings aside. Mrs Gatley immediately engaged her in conversation, enquiring about her impressions of London society so far and recounting some anecdotes from her own first Season, many of which involved Georgiana's mother as well.

"Ah, what a long time ago all that was," said Mrs Gatley nostalgically. "And now to think it is your turn to go through it all."

"Would you do anything differently if you could live through it again?" said Georgiana.

Mrs Gatley thought about this for a little while. "No, for how could I? With two children I am very proud of—my daughter married well with a family of her own—and a husband I never regretted marrying for an instant, for he was the kindest man one could ever find—no, I have nothing to regret." She considered this for a few minutes. "My only suggestion to you is: do not take everything too seriously. Life has a way of becoming serious afterwards. You might as well enjoy yourself while you may."

"I am not sure that is the best advice for a debutante, Mother," said Gatley. "You know only too well that any sign of flightiness in a young lady would be condemned by Society."

"Not at all," said Mrs Gatley, "you have the wrong bull by the horns, Henry. There is nothing more charming than a young lady who is enjoying life."

Gatley countered her, and the discussion went on for some time. Georgiana watched them and smiled. She hesitated to give an opinion, thinking that surely she could have little to say, when she herself was a debutante. For what could she know what Society's perceptions were?

"I hope we are not boring you, dear," said Mrs Gatley. "You

have not voiced your opinion yet. Do you not think Henry takes himself far too seriously?"

Now on *that* she had a definite opinion. "From what I have observed of him, it is indeed the case," she said. "But I can agree with neither of you about what a young debutante should do." She hoped she would give offence to neither. "I think one should not prescribe anything for a young debutante, for each young lady is different, and should choose her own path. What good is it to ask a young woman who is grave and serious to be full of laughter? Or to ask the opposite of one who does nothing but laugh. And coming out *is* a very serious matter. It should not be undertaken lightly. Perhaps, in looking back, you may see things differently, but I cannot imagine that there can be a more serious moment in a young woman's life than the time she must select the gentleman she will live with for the rest of her life."

She spoke with some passion, and was both surprised and pleased with herself by the end of it.

"Brava, Miss Darcy!" said Mrs Gatley. "You have put us to shame. Has she not, Henry?"

Gatley was smiling. "One can hardly disagree with such earnest conviction," he said. "I concede readily that Miss Darcy has the right of it." His voice held enough warmth in it to signify his approval, and Georgiana found herself smiling back at him.

The conversation soon turned to their destination and what to expect.

"I have heard it said that the area near Farnham is among the prettiest in England," said Mrs Gatley, as they admired the view from Hogs-Back.

"A fitting setting for the hero of *Waverley*," said Gatley. "I have taken the liberty of bringing the book with me. I thought perhaps we could take turns reading from it. Then perhaps we will be more educated when we visit the ruins."

Georgiana, who had brought a copy herself, produced her own, and Mr Gatley laughed.

"Had I known that you owned a copy, I would not have exerted such pains to find a copy myself," said Mr Gatley.

"I never thought to mention it," said Georgiana.

"Of course not," said Mrs Gatley, leaning over and patting her hand. "Why would you? Well then, who is going to read first?"

"Mr Gatley," said Georgiana.

"Miss Darcy," said Gatley, at the same moment.

Mrs Gatley looked from one to the other. "Well, I see neither of you have chosen me."

Georgiana, embarrassed, began to stammer an apology, but Mrs Gatley dismissed it with a wave of her hand and a smile. "Oh, I am not the least offended. I would much rather listen to the two of you read. Why don't you start, Gatley, and Miss Darcy can continue when your reading becomes too monotonous. For have you noticed that even the best reader begins to lose expression after reading several pages?"

Georgiana had noticed the same, and she agreed heartily with Mrs Gatley. "If we are to switch very often, then you must also participate, and that way we can have more variety and more time to rest our voices."

Mrs Gatley accepted and urged her son to start.

Mr Gatley was a good reader. He had a rich, deep voice and a fine sense of the dramatic. At first she did not look at him, but simply enjoyed the strong tenor of his reading. Then, as he continued, she turned in his direction and began to watch the play of emotions across his face as he read. His face was expressive, his eyes dark and lustrous. Channing had said he could be agreeable, once he set his mind to it. It was clear that he had set his mind to it on this occasion at least, for he showed none of the haughty attitude he had displayed on other occasions. He read with anima-tion, and afterwards, when they put down the novel and engaged in conversation, she thought that he really could be quite appealing, once he had decided to.

Their reading was interrupted when Channing's carriage—not the phaeton, fortunately—edged past them, forcing their coachman to swerve to avoid having its wheels caught. Channing was in the box, holding the reins, squeezed with his coachman on one side and Clarissa on the other. Clarissa was clutching her hat, which was in danger of being blown away, and her face held an expres-sion both alarmed and thrilled. Channing shouted for them—slow coaches all—to move out of his way.

Henceforth, Georgiana found no pleasure in the reading, and all her thoughts were occupied with the picture of Channing with Clarissa by his side.

❦

The moment Georgiana reached her destination, she was ready to spring out of the carriage to find him. She wanted to tumble out and run over to where Channing's carriage stood. She restrained herself, however, bearing in mind Clarissa's advice about the Grand Entrance.

As it is, her Grand Entrance—or exit from the carriage, in this case—was completely wasted. Clarissa, who had travelled the whole way with the Channings, jumped down from the carriage with Channing's assistance. They waved to Georgiana and the Gatleys in a friendly manner but were soon moving across the meadow in the direction of the ruins, with Clarissa tugging impatiently at his arm. Miss Moffet came forth and claimed Gatley's arm in the familiar mode of old childhood friends.

Georgiana was thus left to follow with Mr Moffet, who immediately came forward to take her arm, and they sallied forth to meet the hired guide who was awaiting them. The three matrons—Mrs Gatley, Mrs Channing, and Mrs Moffet made up a solid wall behind them.

The ruins were located on a picturesque turn of the river Wey. A lush old yew tree watched over the ruins. Butterflies flittered around purple foxgloves and white ragged robins, and bumblebees hummed in contentment. The guide explained about the Cistercian monks who had lived there and the refractory that had housed them, and about the slow decline in their numbers over time. Everyone exclaimed over the vaulted crypt, with its arches and elegant columns, even Georgiana, for whom ruins generally held little appeal. The rest of the ruins, however, looked much like any others, and it required too much of an effort at reconstruction to bring them to life.

Clarissa was in raptures about everything, exclaiming over every stone, sighing over the crumbling walls, and peering with fascination through the hollowed windows.

"To think that this lonely spot was once visited by kings! To think of the pomp and ceremony, where now ivy clambers up the walls and only devastation remains. Imagine the glorious church, with its rich ornaments and its imposing presence. Yet this is all that is left."

"Do you really think it was richly ornamented?" said Georgiana doubtfully, looking at the drab dark stone. "The walls seem quite plain."

"I am inclined to agree with Miss Darcy," said Gatley, passing his palm across the rough surface. "The plainness of the flint work suggests this was a humble type of abbey, not something elaborate at all."

"You heard the guide say that it was visited by both King John *and* Henry III, Mr Gatley. Why would two powerful Kings come all the way here if it was nothing but a humble Abbey?"

"Your vision of kings, I suspect," said Gatley, "coincides very closely with the three wise men of the East, in their turbans and shimmering robes."

Clarissa shook her head. "I am sure the old Kings of England were just as fond of riches and ornament as those of the East. No, I have quite made up my mind. There was power here. I can feel it all around us."

A sheep just then emerged from the vaulted crypt and put an end to Clarissa's flight of fancy by bleating loudly. Everyone laughed and the discussion shifted to other things.

❦

A picnic was soon served, during which Clarissa returned persistently to the pathos of the ruins, with their air of decadence and neglect.

"If only I could write poetry," said Clarissa wistfully. "For there must be some way to capture this landscape on paper."

"Leave poetry to men," said Channing, chuckling. "Surely watercolours would be far more appropriate. There is nothing more charming than the sight of a young lady sketching or painting."

"Oh, I am not at all good at painting or sketching. I do not have the patience for it. I find it quite dull," declared Clarissa loudly.

"I am sure Miss Darcy is proficient at painting," said Mr Moffet. Everyone turned to look at her.

"I hope you brought your sketchpad," said Channing.

"I did," she was happy to reply, glad to have Channing's attention.

"I will sketch the scene for you," she offered Clarissa. "Then you will have a memento of your visit to reflect upon at leisure."

"Perhaps you could also sketch Miss Clarissa into the scene for me," said Channing, "Then, I too would have a keepsake to reflect upon at leisure."

So much for gaining Mr Channing's attention.

⁂

Georgiana soon discovered that she had gained nothing by offering to sketch and lost a great deal. For she was now forced to sit still and watch everyone else play hide and seek. Even Mr Gatley participated. He ran around and laughed and was as silly as the rest of them, while she was condemned to contemplate the melancholy scene of the crumbled ruins, which she had not even cared about in the first place.

Soon Mrs Gatley, announcing that she was quite tired of sitting after the long carriage ride rose to her feet and suggested to Mrs Channing that a game of hide and seek would surely do them good.

Her sister puckered her lips and looked uncertain. "Do you think so?"

"Of course."

Mrs Channing, though not convinced, rose and did as she was told, following Mrs Gatley reluctantly.

Only Georgiana and Mrs Moffet were left sitting. The others laughed and shouted and played at hiding.

Her frustration reached such a peak that she felt quite prepared to tear up the sketching pad. Fortunately, before she could put into practise such a detrimental plan—for she would certainly lose face—she hit upon the idea of sketching the young people themselves as they skipped around. It gave her an excuse, at least, to watch Channing more closely.

Sketching their happy faces did not make her feel better. Clarissa was right; there was nothing in the world as dull as sketching.

For good measure, she added some sheep.

Meanwhile, Mrs Moffet, who had been more firm than Mrs Channing in refusing to join in the game, brought her chair closer to Georgiana's.

A particularly difficult patch of embroidery seemed to require all her attention. She was working on a scene with a swan, and seemed to have reached a part that needed delicate work. She said nothing for several moments.

"You must be very fond of the Odyssey," remarked Georgiana by and by, feeling that she should make an effort to be polite.

Mrs Moffet denied having read the Odyssey or anything of the classics.

"Indeed," she said with a laugh, "I have no inclination towards reading at all.

"But one hears these things bandied about everywhere, and the moment dear Odysseus was born, I knew he had the look of a hero, and nothing would satisfy me but to call him by a hero's name. For I have always disliked my own name, you know. Jane is such a trivial name, and I cannot think that anyone called Jane could possibly be anyone of importance. But with a name like Odysseus, there can be no limit."

"Foul!" came a cry from Mr Channing, interrupting Mrs Moffet's explanation. "You are cheating, Mr Moffet! You are not supposed to look while you are counting! What shall we do with him? Shall we dunk him in the river?" He looked at Clarissa.

"By all means," said Clarissa. "Serves him right for cheating!"

Georgiana wanted to protest that Mr Channing too had cheated, for she had seen him, and that it was hardly fair to punish only Mr Moffet. But Mrs Moffet had grown so alarmed by this time that she rushed forward to defend her son, beating down the hands of Mr Channing with her parasol and chastising him loudly.

"You should be ashamed of yourself. Have you not outgrown this by now? I remember all too well the time you pushed Moffey into the river because his father bought him a mare, and he would not let you ride it. You will not dunk my son or anyone else in the river"—and here she stared significantly at Mr Channing— "simply for opening his eyes while counting. Why, he might catch his death."

Channing protested that he did not really mean to do it, only to discourage Moffet from cheating again.

Meanwhile, Mr Moffet, his neck cloth awry and his hair as ruffled as his pride, glared at Channing.

"Oh come, Moffey," said Channing with the familiarity of a childhood friend. "Surely you don't mean to hold it against me. Where's your sporting nature?"

Mrs Moffet, reassured that her son was not to be mauled or thrown into the river in the near future, returned to her seat, looking satisfied. As if she had never been interrupted, she picked up the threads of her conversation with Georgiana.

"I chose the name Athena for the same reason, you know," said Mrs Moffet. "Is it not the best name a girl can have?"

"Athena has a noble ring to it," replied Georgiana.

"Yes, it does indeed," replied Mrs Moffet. "The name of a goddess will give her a great advantage in life, mark my words."

Mrs Moffet's mission in life was to improve the situation of her children, for she was convinced that her own lot in life would have been much better if only her parents had tried harder to provide her with the advantages needed for success.

"Not that I have anything to complain of in Mr Moffet. He is a perfectly respectable gentleman and has proved to be a very obliging father, and we rub along well enough. But even he agrees with me that one must not become complacent, and must always strive to improve oneself and do everything one can to assure that one's children's lot is better than one's own."

Georgiana wondered how much Mr Moffet agreed with his wife, since he had remained in the country, steadfastly refusing to go up to Town.

"Is he not very handsome? Mr Channing was always jealous of him, for my son is certainly the handsomer of the two," asked Mrs Moffet proudly, putting down her embroidery and following her son with her eyes. "The girl who catches my Odysseus's fancy will quickly realise how lucky she is to have him."

Just then Miss Moffet let out a scream and ran towards them, with Channing in hot pursuit. She took refuge behind Georgiana's chair, and Georgiana, faced with Channing in front of her and Athena behind, her, covered her sketchbook to prevent her sketch from tearing. A playful dodging game ensued, in which Athena proved very skilful at evading Channing. Georgiana meanwhile did not know where to look, for Channing was far too close to her. Fortunately, the game came to an end when Channing lunged at Athena and caught her by her dress.

"You should not have tried to escape me," he said, grinning. "You knew I would win at the end."

"But I *did* get away. Admit it," said Athena. "You have to acknowledge that I had you for a moment."

"Only for a moment," replied Channing.

They returned to the others, and the game—whatever it had become, for it was no longer hide and seek—resumed.

"You know, I am quite determined to have Mr Channing for Athena," said Mrs Moffet suddenly.

Georgiana stiffened. "I do not know why you are telling me this, Mrs Moffet. It is up to Mr Channing to choose the object of his interest, surely."

"True enough," said Mrs Moffet quite good-naturedly. "But I think your cousin would not make him a good wife, and neither would you."

"I do not know what you mean," said Georgiana faintly.

"You will come to understand it well enough," said Mrs Moffet. "He is not for you. He will suit my daughter far better. They have known each other for years, and she has his measure. *You* are too clever for him."

Not knowing what to make of this remark, and whether to take it as praise or discouragement, she did not reply. She hoped Mrs Moffet would enlighten her further. But Mrs Moffet had resumed her embroidery and had become quite absorbed by it. She brought it closer to her face and examined it carefully for flaws.

Georgiana could not shake off the feeling that Mrs Moffet had given her a warning to stay away.

※

Presently, tired of their games, everybody began to drift in their direction, since drinks had been set up next to them on a table for those who were thirsty.

Clarissa came over to see how the sketch was progressing.

"I like it," she said. "Though I wish you had focussed on the ruins more. You have spent more time drawing us."

"Did you draw me?" asked Channing, coming over. "Let me see."

Georgiana waited for his verdict.

"Very nice, you have captured me quite well," said Channing. "Shall this be my copy?"

"I cannot give you the original," she replied. "I promised the sketch for Clarissa."

Channing seemed put out that she could deny him. He turned deliberately to Miss Moffet, who was standing next to him, and invited her to take a stroll with him.

Georgiana could not help feeling that he had done it almost as a punishment.

"You should not look so stricken," whispered Clarissa, leaning over. "You are supposed to conceal your feelings, Georgiana. What did I teach you?"

The reminder served its purpose. Georgiana sprung to her feet and headed towards Gatley.

"I am thoroughly tired of being seated," she said gaily. "I hope you will keep me company in a walk."

Mr Gatley, raising an eyebrow, answered politely that he would be more than glad to accompany her.

Georgiana caught Channing looking in her direction. She was so anxious to prove to him that she was indifferent to his slight that she turned quite flirtatiously to Gatley.

"I am still a little irked with you, Mr Gatley, you know."

"Indeed?" he replied. "I was not aware of having offended you."

"You may profess ignorance, but you surely remember our last encounter. I did not want to mention it in front of your mother, but I have not quite forgotten it."

It was quickly apparent that he had no idea to what she referred.

"Surely you remember that I was quite cast down by your comment about my hat."

Gatley threw a quick glance at the wide-brimmed leghorn bonnet she wore.

"Yes, I do remember," he replied with a half-smile. "And now you are wearing one that is quite different. You see I am not quite as forgetful as all that."

"No, I did not think you *could* be. But tell me then: Do you like this one better?"

"You must allow that I am not a good judge of ladies' fashions, particularly when it comes to hats. I am sure your hat is very fashionable, for I have seen enough to know that enormous bonnets laden with fruits, flowers, and enormous feathers are quite the rage at the moment."

"That is what is called damning with faint praise," remarked Georgiana, though secretly she agreed many of the hats were quite monstrous.

"I prefer to remain neutral on the subject of female fashion."

"I can only conclude, in that case, that you believe a female should not follow fashion at all."

"That is not my meaning. One cannot be introduced into society in anything but the latest fashion. But from those fashions, a lady has some choice."

"Hardly, when the fashions are dictated by others."

"I shall try to explain what I mean. Do you think a dress looks as well on a modiste's mannequin—no matter how perfectly proportioned the mannequin—as it looks on a real young lady, despite her imperfections?"

"No, of course not."

"That is what I wish to say about your manner of dressing. You have tried to adopt a certain style which may look well on others, but since it is a style not your own, it lacks conviction."

"You are suggesting, then, that I am as lifeless as a mannequin?" she cried.

"I am suggesting only that a style that is your own—no matter how simple—may sit better on you than the most elaborate costume, however expensive and fashionable it may be."

Since to Georgiana the word *simple* at the moment was very high on her list of detestable words in the English language, one could not expect her to be gratified by this statement.

"Then you would condemn me to be dowdy, since that apparently seems to be my style."

Gatley stopped abruptly. Georgiana feared that she had pushed him so far. But he merely pointed his walking stick at a swan that was just then traversing the water. The water parted before it on both sides, and it glided majestically through, buoyant as air.

"You see the swan, how simple, and how graceful its contours are. She is perfect as she is. Beyond those white feathers of hers, she needs no more ornamentation. Would you agree?"

"Naturally," said Georgiana.

"Think then how different she would be if she happened upon a peacock, and struck with envy at its vibrant colours, determined to cover herself in colourful feathers as well. How would the swan then appear?"

Georgiana was heartily tired of this conversation by now.

"I believe you are about to tell me," she remarked.

"Yes, I will tell you. She will be ridiculous. She will neither be a swan, nor a peacock, nor anything else at all but a swan pretending to be a peacock."

"Very well, Mr Gatley," she said, still trying to be playful, though she was sorely tempted to send him to the devil. "I will not ask your opinion about my hat another time if I am to be compared first to a mannequin, then to a swan masquerading as a peacock. It seems I am to be a figure of fun."

"You wilfully misunderstand me, Miss Darcy. You know very well that my intention is to compliment you. But I can see that you will not be content unless I am more direct." He smiled. "I will paraphrase. What I meant to say is that you are quite beautiful yourself and require no decoration. Now are you satisfied?"

Georgiana wished she could be satisfied. But Mr Gatley had placed so many qualifications on his praise, and had spoken in such a manner, that he had cast doubt on the very words he was expressing.

She put up her chin in mock haughtiness. "I will accept your compliment, Mr Gatley," she said with a little smile. But she could not resist teasing him. "It is far better, at any rate, than your moral tale about the swan."

Mr Gatley did not rise to the bait. His lips twitched in amusement, but he gave no answer.

Chapter 19

IN THE SECOND WEEK OF JUNE, AS THE SEASON REACHED ITS height, an astonishing piece of news reached them.

"I can scarcely credit it! Anne, of all people!" said Darcy, striding into the drawing room with a missive in his hand.

"Another letter from Mr Collins?" enquired Elizabeth.

"No. It is from my informants. We have definite and confirmed news of Anne."

Anne's trail had been picked up once again, and it led to—Liverpool! Nothing could have been more startling. Her name, or one very similar—an Annette Burrows, who answered to her description exactly—appeared on the passenger list of a vessel that had sailed to Philadelphia nine days since. The same Annette Burrows had stayed at an inn close to the harbour, waiting for the ship to sail, for a few days, and had been seen by several witnesses who all described her in much the same way, including the numerous shawls she wore.

Darcy paced the room as he read them the letter he had received. "I realise now that she has played us all for fools. Clearly she planned to go to Liverpool all along. She knew that none of the packet boats can predict their sailing schedule and that there are often delays because of merchandise or weather. I can only conclude that her appearance in York was a deliberate attempt to mislead us, so she would have the time to wait for the vessel to sail without being caught. It is very likely she booked her passage beforehand."

Georgiana struggled to reconcile her image of Anne with the person who had planned such an elaborate trick. She had already realised in Rosings that Anne was far more intelligent than she had supposed. She had certainly fooled everyone, including her mother, with her appearance of docility. Now it appeared she had fooled them even further.

"But what would she do in the United States?" said Georgiana. "How will she manage, once she is there?"

"I am sure if she was able to cook up the whole ruse, she is perfectly capable of managing once she is there," said Elizabeth, "though I must own myself very surprised that she was capable of such a thing."

"How could she have done this to us?" said Darcy.

"She did not do it to us," said Elizabeth, "she did it to herself, and for herself. You do not enter the picture."

"But to be so inconsiderate—"

"You have given *her* little consideration over the years," said Elizabeth. "It does not surprise me that she would not consider *you* when she is making a bid for freedom."

❧❧❧

A curious part of the human psyche is that the moment a person presumed to be in danger is discovered to be safe, everyone's anxiety turns into anger. That, at least, was Georgiana's experience. For now that she knew Anne had been safe all along, she became incensed at the callous way her cousin had led them by the nose.

The more she thought about it, the angrier she became. How could she have put them all through such turmoil, when she was in fact perfectly comfortable, and when *she* had know her plans all along? Georgiana and Clarissa had almost been forced to cancel their Season, while she was mocking them, probably congratulating herself on how clever she was.

The anger soon burned itself out, however, particularly when Clarissa reminded Georgiana that Anne, after all, had had no choice. What else could she have done? She could hardly have informed them of her intentions beforehand, knowing that of course everyone would have intervened to prevent her. Yes, she had inconvenienced them a little, but it had not been that bad. It was more a question of the anxiety and uncertainty that they had experienced on her behalf. But that, surely, was nothing compared to Anne's own uncertainty and fear that she might have been followed and caught.

In any case, the definite knowledge that Anne was safe had a very positive effect and lifted the dark cloud that had hung over the young ladies' entrée into Society. There was even talk of Elizabeth giving a ball. The number of activities the young ladies were allowed to attend now increased twofold, and they were introduced to so many new faces that Georgiana stopped being able to distinguish one person from the other. The entrance hall was filled with flowers, and Georgiana could begin to feel that she might be a success after all. Her new expanded list of invitations did not bring her into contact with Channing for some time—and she began to convince herself that she had quite forgotten about him.

Then suddenly one night, she spotted the familiar flock of gold hair, and everything came back to her with a vengeance.

He had only to lift a hand in greeting, and she was lost.

Not for nothing, however, had she been attending one social event after the other. She had become far more accomplished by now at hiding her feelings. So when he made his way across the room towards her, she was able to retain the Imperial Pose and to receive him with an air of arrogant superiority.

"Mr Channing, how nice to see you," she said, her heart thudding. "I see you are alone, without your cousin. Where is Mr Gatley?"

Channing did not look pleased. "I could ask the same of you. Where is Miss Clarissa?"

Georgiana realised she had started on the wrong foot. She tried to set things right by referring to their last meeting.

"I am very grateful to you for arranging the excursion to Waverley Abbey. I enjoyed it a great deal. I have since had the pleasure of re-reading the novel."

Channing shuddered dramatically. "Rather you than me," he said. "I can think of nothing more tedious."

She was surprised. "But it was you who suggested the trip. I had thought you liked *Waverley*!"

"You cannot really think I would have read it, Miss Darcy. There are so many other things I prefer to do," he said. "Dancing, for example. You still owe me a favour, do you not? Will you put my name down for a dance?"

Georgiana, who was beginning to be vexed by his offhand dismissal of her interests, forgot everything in the joy of finally being invited to dance with him.

❧

The next morning the townhouse at Berkeley Square received a caller. Gatley stopped by to let them know that he was arranging a trip to Richmond, and he wanted to be sure of Georgiana's interest before going ahead with the arrangements. Georgiana agreed readily enough, especially after she heard that Channing was to be one of the party.

Everything went as planned—except that Channing unexpectedly brought with him two friends of his; Miss Emily Parvis and Mr Walter Parvis. Georgiana did not particularly like Mr Parvis, but Clarissa had met him before and appeared to be quite friendly with him.

It took forever to find a place that was dry enough for the older ladies to set up their chairs. It had rained the day before, so the grass was quite wet. The right spot, moreover, had to give the chaperones a clear view of the river, the bridge, *and* the embankment. But at last, everything was set up, and those who wished to hire the rowboats could finally go on their way. Both Elizabeth and Caroline expressed their readiness to join them on the river, but Mrs Gatley refused and said she would stay with her sister and Mrs Moffet.

"It is too damp," she said. "I prefer to sit here and watch you row around in circles."

This occasioned some protests, all the gentlemen immediately affirming their prowess at rowing. Mrs Gatley replied in an imperious tone that they had yet to prove themselves. Whereupon the young men set out, all eager to demonstrate their abilities.

They hired three boats. An argument ensued, during which both Mr Moffet and Mr Parvis wanted to row. The agreement was only settled after Channing convinced his friend to come in the boat with him, and they could take it in turns to row. "For I plan to have the prettiest girls with me," said Channing.

Mr Moffet, very pleased with the outcome, carried the oars proudly, in the manner of one holding a trophy.

"I have not been on a boat for a long time," remarked Elizabeth with an uneasy little laugh, as she stood at the edge of the water. "I do hope I will not fall in."

This fearfulness was so unlike Elizabeth that Georgiana shot her a questioning glance.

"I fell into the water once," explained Elizabeth, "and I was soaked through. Since then I have avoided boats entirely. But it would be quite silly to avoid them forever, just because of one fall."

"If you have already fallen in once, then you have nothing to fear," said Caroline, "for it is very unlikely that such a thing would occur twice in one's lifetime."

"*I* have never fallen from a boat," said Channing, "and I have been on a river endless times. All you need is a skilled oarsman, Mrs Darcy, I assure you, and there would be no chance at all of the boat tipping."

One would have thought that after such a remark, he would offer his services. Instead, he turned away and reached a hand out to help Clarissa climb in.

Georgiana, who was standing expectantly right next to his boat, felt the slight like a physical blow. He did not even glance towards her.

How long could she continue to delude herself? It was all so utterly useless. All her efforts to change and become different were completely futile. No one with a modicum of sense could avoid the obvious conclusion. Channing preferred Clarissa over herself—had done so from the beginning—and nothing she did or said would change that.

Tears of frustration rose up in her eyes as Gatley, inevitably, extended his hand to her with a smile. She did not take it, still somehow hoping that Channing would invite her to join him. But Miss Moffet stepped daintily into Channing's boat and took her seat there, followed by Mr Parvis. While she hesitated, Elizabeth joined Mr Moffet, after he assured her that he was a superb rower and that she could trust him not to let her fall. Miss Parvis then joined Elizabeth and Moffet.

Georgiana could not refuse to ride with Gatley, not without openly snubbing him, could she?

"Come, Georgiana," said Caroline, seeing her hesitate and misunderstanding her reasons. "There is nothing to it." As if to illustrate it, Caroline took Gatley's hand and stepped in.

With no choice in the matter, Georgiana stepped forward to join her.

Meanwhile, the others had cast off.

She had never been in a boat before. She did not like the way the boat moved and swayed about. She could understand now why Elizabeth was nervous. It had looked much easier when everyone else had climbed in.

Gatley gave her an encouraging smile.

"It is not as difficult as you think, Miss Darcy. Give me your hand, and I will help you in," he said.

She felt remarkably silly. She was the only one left behind and everyone watched her. The other two boats were already in the river, and were starting to pull away. Gingerly, she took a step forward and lifted her foot to place it inside the boat. Gatley's firm hand helped her balance, and though the boat shifted a little, she grew more confident.

"Steady now," said Gatley.

Everything would have gone well were it not for the fact that the bank was very wet from last night's rain. The wash from some passing boat shifted the boat a little, and Georgiana's left foot, which she had set down on the boat, did not land solidly. Instead, it pushed the boat away from her and away from the shore. Meanwhile, her right foot, struggling to take root in the wet bank, encountered only mud and silt. She lost her balance and slid forward towards the water. It was only Gatley's hand that prevented her from falling to the ground. She flailed and tried to right herself, but her right foot stomped up to her knee in the water, and the cold river seeping into her clothing.

From the other boat, a roar of laughter rose up.

"Miss Darcy!" cried Channing. "Now you have done it! You have taken a bath already, and we have not even set out!"

From beside him, Clarissa let out a loud peel. "Feel free to take a swim, since you are already wet!" she cried. Soon Mr Moffet and Miss Moffet added their giggles to the laughter. Mr Parvis and his sister laughed. Even Elizabeth seemed infected by the hilarity of the situation.

Gatley's hand steadied her and pulled her into the boat.

With the help of Caroline, she was able to sit down, and to conceal the fire that burned on her cheeks by bowing her head and smoothing down her skirts.

"You did not hurt yourself, did you?" enquired Caroline. *She* had not laughed, at least.

"No. Mr Gatley held me up."

"You have not injured your ankle?" enquired the latter, pausing as he moved the oars into position.

"No, I received no injury." Which was true enough, for the only injury she had received was to her pride. *That* injury smarted and pained and lingered.

It was a warm spring day, but it was not yet summer. The dampness of her clothing soon seeped through. It clung to her skin, a cold insistent presence.

The others rowed ahead of them, and they talked loudly and

laughed and dipped their hands in the water. Georgiana gathered her damp clothes about her, and remained silent. By and by, as the others drew farther away, she could hear nothing but the gentle splashing of the oars in the water, the croak of a cormorant, the whish of the current as it passed them by. Caroline exchanged some polite conversation with Gatley, but had fallen silent, content to sit quietly in the boat, holding up her parasol against the sun.

"Oh, aren't they beautiful?" said Caroline suddenly, as a swan glided by, its head regal, its body graceful in the water. "So much prettier than geese."

Gatley, a quiet smile hovering on his lips, remarked that, amazingly, despite their delicate appearance, swans were unpleasant creatures, quite inclined to be aggressive and to bite. "Very much like geese, I would think."

Caroline laughed. "Yes, I know all about geese," she said enigmatically.

Georgiana was not interested in the swan nor in the information Gatley conveyed. It was of course a veiled reference to their former conversation, and at this moment it rankled, for it served as a reminder of her own stupid vanity. She really was like that swan he had talked about, the one that had strutted like a peacock.

She leaned over the side and stared into the dark depths of the river, struggling to restore her good humour. She could not sulk all day just because Channing had not paid her attention.

Her reflection quivered as another boat passed them. Georgiana bent closer to examine her eyes, for the murkiness of the water made them look hollow. An eel slipped through the water and she followed its path, fascinated by the supple movement.

The steady rhythm of the oars dipping in and out of the water stopped.

"Steady, Miss Darcy! If you lean over too far, we will tip," said Gatley.

She righted herself slowly and mumbled an apology.

"You are cold and wet," he remarked quietly.

She wished he would take up the oars again and keep rowing. She did not want his attention. But the oars stayed stubbornly still, and she was forced to look at him.

"I am wet, but I am not cold," she said.

"I can tell you are cold," he replied, "for you have goose bumps on your arms."

He reached a decision.

"I am sorry to cut the expedition short, Mrs Darcy," said Gatley. "I know you will be disappointed, but it is damp and cold on the river and hardly the place for someone with wet clothes."

Caroline nodded. "You are perfectly correct, Mr Gatley. But you need not cut *your* expedition short. If you would be good enough to row us to the shore, I will see to it that Miss Darcy returns home safely."

"It is too long a trip for you to travel unescorted," he replied. "I have been on the river so many times it holds little interest for me. I came for the company, not the river. I will be happy to escort you."

The sun suddenly appeared from behind a cloud. His dark eyes caught the light and glittered strangely. They tugged at something inside her, and Georgiana felt a tremor, as though a feather had trailed across her skin.

"We would be glad to have your company," said Caroline, giving Georgiana a gentle prod of the elbow in her ribs.

"I would be grateful, sir, for it is true that my clothing has become quite clammy and uncomfortable. I would like to go home."

As she stepped out of the boat, the sound of merriment and laughter floated down the river to her. Her throat constricted, but she promised herself that, whatever happened, she would not cry.

＊

Caroline insisted on inspecting Georgiana's stockings when they reached the carriage, requesting Gatley politely to wait outside for them. Drawing down the shades, Caroline took one look at them and told Georgiana to take them off.

"I cannot!" said Georgiana, horrified "How could I then sit here all the way to London without any stockings?"

"Mr Gatley is a gentleman. He will not inspect you to see if you are wearing stockings, and if he does, well, he will have a surprise, will he not?"

"My dress is not very long," said Georgiana, since the current fashion reached above the ankles.

"You will have your boots on,"

The effort of removing her stockings in the narrow space of a carriage, as well as Caroline's attempts to coax some laughter out of her, soon lightened her mood. It was as if the wet stockings themselves were responsible for her unhappiness, for the moment she peeled them off, she began to feel better.

"Now your boots," said Caroline.

Georgiana immediately regretted taking her half-boots off. For without the smooth surface of her stockings, with her feet damp, and the nankeen boots wet, it was impossible to put them back on.

"If only I had worn leather boots," she said. "If only I had thought more of the mud and less of elegance!"

"Try harder," said Caroline, squatting to the floor of the carriage. "I will steady them for you and pull them up. You push."

But the boot did not yield. Try as she would, it refused to accommodate her foot.

"It must have shrunk," said Georgiana.

"I have never heard of such a thing," said Caroline, "but I can think of no other explanation."

"What shall I do?" said Georgiana, staring in despair at the reluctant boots and at the shrivelled wet feet resting on the carriage floor.

"I cannot imagine," said Caroline.

Just then Gatley knocked at the carriage door.

"Are you ready to leave, ladies?"

Caroline and Georgiana exchanged glances and burst into suppressed laughter.

"What shall we do?" whispered Georgiana, aware of Mr Gatley on the other side of the door.

"You shall have to put the boots next to you on the seat," she said, "and cover yourself with the blanket. Quickly."

The stockings were still on the floor. Georgiana blushed to think of Mr Gatley setting eyes on such an intimate item of clothing.

"The stockings," she said, wrapped up in the blanket and unable to move.

Caroline scooped up the stockings.

"Just a moment, Mr Gatley," she replied. "We will be with you shortly."

She held out the stockings. "Here, stuff them in your reticule."

But Georgiana's reticule was quite useless for such a function. It was very pretty, made of knitted silk with elaborate beading, but it could hold nothing more than a small delicate kerchief and a few coins.

"Let us take one each," said Caroline, opening her own reticule.

This proved to be the best solution.

"You may come in, Mr Gatley," she said, pulling up the shades.

"We will have to hope we do not need a handkerchief on the way back," said Caroline, in a half-whisper. "I wish I had thought of it earlier."

"It is too late," said Georgiana, as Gatley stepped through the doorway and filled the carriage with his presence.

Chapter 20

Georgiana was more than annoyed at herself for interrupting the outing. She felt guilty for dragging Gatley away, when it was he, after all, who had arranged the whole trip to Richmond. Now, because of her silliness, he was obliged to drive back to London.

He took the seat next to Caroline, who sat directly opposite her. Georgiana was intensely aware of her naked feet touching the dusty floor of the carriage. Every jolt of the carriage, every quiver, passed through the soles of her feet. She was aware, too, of the side of his shiny leather boot, just inches from hers, and imagined what would happen if he accidentally stepped on her bare toes.

She caught a couple of the glances he sent her way too. There was something different about them, something she could not define, that made her question whether he suspected what lay beneath the blanket.

Meanwhile, he gave no sign at all of resenting his inconvenient return to London. He was in remarkably good spirits, his dark eyes lightened by humour. He entertained them at first with boating tales featuring some of his friends, then with stories about his first attempt to row a boat.

For some reason—Georgiana was sure it had something to do with her need to hide her feet—the carriage seemed smaller than usual. She did not recall having such a sense of his closeness to her when she had travelled with them to the ruins. It was the exact same carriage. Why then did she see him in more detail—from the tiny scar at the corner of his upper lip to the thick lashes that lined his eyes?

A sneeze interrupted these unfamiliar thoughts. Caroline, who had not gotten wet at all, was sneezing. Unthinking, hand on her mouth, she groped with the other hand for her reticule and opened it.

A glimpse of her own white stocking met Georgiana's eyes. How was she to stop Caroline from bringing the stocking to her nose?

Caroline sneezed again.

The stocking, long and silken, and not at all like a handkerchief, appeared in her hand.

She raised it to her nose.

Georgiana had no choice. She had to stop Caroline most urgently. Any verbal statement would attract the attention of Mr Gatley, who was looking out of the window.

She kicked Caroline hard in the shin.

Caroline stopped pulling out the stocking, frowned, then, realising what she was doing, crumpled the stocking quickly into a ball and stuffed it back into her reticule.

Caroline's hand stilled in the act of tying the reticule. She looked pointedly at the ground.

It was Georgiana's turn to frown. Then horror coursed through her as she spotted a row of dainty pink toes peeping from under the blanket. She pulled her foot back to safety, keeping a close eye on Gatley, who was still looking outside.

It was only when they reached the familiar townhouses of London that she sat up in her seat in a panic. They had a far bigger obstacle ahead of her to deal with. How in heaven's name could she step out of the carriage in her bare feet?

She threw a desperate look at Caroline. Oddly enough, the same thought seemed to occur to Caroline at the same moment, for her eyes widened. Luckily, Caroline's usual good sense in emergencies came to the fore.

"Mr Gatley, I wonder if we could drop you off first at your address, before going round to Berkley Square?"

If Mr Gatley thought it a strange request, especially since they were riding in his own carriage, he was too much a gentleman to say so.

"Of course," he said. "I will instruct the driver."

They dropped him off at his townhouse.

Both Georgiana and Caroline breathed a sigh of relief as the door shut behind him and the carriage began to move away.

Georgiana stretched her leg out and wriggled her toes.

"You cannot imagine how cramped my legs feel, for I did not dare move them, in case the blanket slipped and revealed my feet again."

Caroline began to laugh once more.

"We still have one more obstacle to surmount," she said, "which is how to get you into the house again. You cannot be carried in, with bare feet."

In the end, they found a solution. They would send the footman to fetch Georgiana's maid Rosie and to request her to bring some clean stockings and open shoes to the carriage, and all would be well.

"What a to-do," said Caroline. "I cannot believe how complicated it all has been."

"Well, at least Mr Gatley never noticed," said Georgiana.

If Georgiana had been privy to Gatley's thoughts, she would not have been so complacent.

He whistled a merry tune as he ran up the steps to his home and handed his hat cheerfully to Gibbs, the butler, who promptly handed it to a footman. He headed immediately to the library, where Gibbs poured him a snifter of Madeira.

"Has anything untoward occurred, sir?" asked Gibbs. "You have returned early."

"Nothing untoward, no," he replied. "Something quite enchanting did occur however."

The old retainer stood waiting placidly to see if his employer would see fit to inform him.

Gatley laughed. How could he tell the butler about Miss Darcy and her little pink toes? She had tried so hard to hide them— little knowing that he had spotted them from the beginning. Her futile efforts made him shake with suppressed laughter, and he had been forced to look out of the window for the longest time until the fit had subsided. And then Mrs Caroline Darcy with the stocking! It had easily been the most amusing carriage rides he had ever been on.

Gibbs was still waiting.

"Miss Georgiana Darcy slipped in the mud and was obliged to return home. It was—amusing."

Gibbs did not answer, a sure sign that he disapproved.

"You would have laughed too, Gibbs, if you were there."

Gibbs said nothing, a definite indication that his disapproval had reached rare new heights.

"I can't explain it, Gibbs, I'm sorry. Not without relating the whole story. If you keep standing here, Gibbs, I will be tempted to tell you. So I think perhaps you ought to go and leave me to my reflections."

Oddly enough, the moment Gibbs closed the door behind him, Gatley lost the urge to laugh. He cast his memory back to that moment by the riverside, and Miss Darcy's humiliation as Channing opened his mouth to laugh and the others followed.

He did not like what was happening to his cousin. Channing was careless, of course, and his success with the ladies, happening to a weak mind, had made him arrogant. But he was not generally malicious. Yet lately he had seen some small signs of this—nothing very obvious, but a tendency that made him uneasy.

He would not like Channing to become anything like his father.

He would have to talk to him, of course, even though it was becoming harder now to do so. Channing, rather than turning to him for advice, seemed to be erecting a barrier between them. Perhaps it was just as well. Channing had depended on him too much in the past. Maybe it was time he went his own way. He was certainly more than old enough, at twenty-three. As long as he was not led astray by his new set of companions, people like Parvis who were callous and self-absorbed. Channing tended to be weak-willed and too easily led by others.

Like Miss Darcy. She too was easily led by others. If only she could realise that, by imitating her cousin Clarissa, she was doing herself a disservice and might even end by being hurt. If only she would listen to what he had to say.

❧

Georgiana's missing stocking did not go unremarked with her brother either. Darcy, hearing a carriage, was alarmed first by their early arrival, and then alarmed even further by the odd comings and goings of the servants. He came out quickly and peered into the carriage.

"Has anything happened?" he said, seeing Caroline in the carriage. "What has happened to Elizabeth?"

How characteristic of her brother to ask first about Elizabeth.

"There is nothing to worry about, Mr Darcy," said Caroline. "Elizabeth is perfectly safe and even now enjoying a boat ride on the river. The reason for our return is simple: Georgiana has had a soaking, and Mr Gatley was kind enough to cut short the excursion and bring her home."

Darcy opened the carriage door just as Georgiana was engaged in putting on a stocking. He raised his brows eloquently.

"We had to take them off in the carriage," explained Caroline. "We did everything in our power to hide the fact from Mr Gatley."

Georgiana looked so much like a guilty child trying to hide a stolen piece of cake that Darcy could not help laughing.

"You had better go inside, Georgie." Then, as she slipped on the slippers provided by Rosie, he remarked, with laughter in his voice, "I hope you are not imitating your cousin in this as well however. It will not do to show your calves to the gentlemen."

His laughter convinced Georgiana that her brother would make light of the incident and that she would not hear of it again.

He was more disturbed, however, than he let on.

Following a dinner together that very evening, Darcy did not stay behind to drink port as was his habit, but joined the ladies immediately in the drawing room.

"You must tell me all about the trip, Elizabeth," he said.

"There is not much to tell, except that I enjoyed it tremendously.

We rowed on the river, had our picnic, and made the best of a beautiful spring day."

"Did you not realise that Georgie had fallen?"

Elizabeth bit her lip. "I did realise that she had slipped, but since Mr Gatley held her steady, she came to no harm. I was very surprised to return from our rowing expedition to discover that she was gone."

Darcy put down his cup and looked intently at Elizabeth.

"One would hardly expect a chaperone not to realise that her charge had disappeared—even worse, that she had ridden all the way to London in the company of a single gentleman."

Elizabeth put down her cup likewise.

"I think it very reasonable for a chaperone to take her eyes away from her charge if she knows her charge is in capable hands. And she did not ride *alone* to London with a single gentleman. I did not know you objected to Caroline Darcy. In fact, to judge by the past, I had rather thought you approved of her."

They faced each other for a moment, eyes locked in some fierce silent communication incomprehensible to others.

Georgiana, unable to endure this silent battle, decided to interfere. "I have come to no harm, as you can see, and I was under the eye of Caroline every moment of the day, so I see no cause for you to disagree at all."

"Oh, but there is," said Elizabeth, "for as long as Fitzwilliam continues to treat you as a wayward child, we will never have any peace. I must say this, even if I risk wounding Georgiana in the process. Perhaps Georgiana was foolish enough—at the tender age of fifteen, when still very much a child—to be on the verge of elopement. But even *then*—and that was the remarkable part—*even then* she had the sense to tell you about it. Yet you have looked upon her ever since as if she was a piece of Wedgwood china likely to crack any moment."

She turned to Georgiana. "Some more tea, Georgiana?"

Georgiana shook her head. Elizabeth poured herself another cup, then continued to speak in a calm, even tone.

"Now, three years later, your attitude towards her has not changed a bit. Look at her, Fitzwilliam. She is a grown woman. She will soon be married and mistress of her own household. You cannot hide her in the cupboard because you are afraid she will be broken."

"You speak as if it is wrong to protect my sister," said Darcy.

"No, I speak as if it is wrong to distrust her."

The words rang out in the silence. Georgiana knew as soon as Elizabeth said them that they were true. They were the reason she did not—could not—feel comfortable with her brother anymore and why she constantly felt the urge to flee from his presence.

Darcy frowned and drained the last of his tea. Suddenly, he put down the teacup again on the table. It clattered loudly in protest.

"Do *you* think I distrust you, Georgiana?" he asked.

Again, she wished she could run to him and throw her arms around him as she had done when a child, but she could not. She was a woman now. She could not.

She nodded. "Yes," she said almost in a whisper.

Darcy's answer was to rise quickly and stride to the door. He quit the room, leaving Elizabeth and Georgiana behind to exchange glances.

"We have upset him," said Georgiana, in a hushed voice.

To her surprise, Elizabeth began to laugh. "Yes, we have upset him, and it is a very good thing indeed."

Georgiana did not speak again to her brother that night. She retired early, caught in a storm of churning emotions. All her certainties—the things that had anchored her for years—had been wrenched from her, and she was completely adrift, for there was not a single point of navigation she could use to guide herself. Clarissa had been her guide, but she realised belatedly that Clarissa was very far from being a beacon. After what happened today, she was repulsed by her, by her mocking laughter, by the way she threw herself at Channing, by her irresponsible and indifferent manner. Perhaps she was making too much of it, but she had always disliked mockery, and she had somehow never imagined she would be the target of her cousin's derision.

And then, of course, there was Channing. She knew what he thought of her, exactly. His harsh judgement of her that day of that first dance had not essentially changed. Perhaps he occasionally thought her worthy of interest, but it was only a momentary thing, quickly forgotten when something—or someone—more appealing came along. A ruthless cold wind swept through her as she acknowledged this reality. All the new clothes and the Grand Entrances in the world were not going to help her.

Who then could she turn to? Her brother Fitzwilliam—always her anchor—had himself taken a different direction, and she could not follow him.

She was lost—alone in a tumultuous storm that washed over her in unruly waves, and she had no idea what to do.

Chapter 21

ALL NIGHT, LIKE A CLARION CALL IN THE DARKNESS, CLARISSA'S laugh rang out in Georgiana's mind.

For the fact was, she would not have minded Channing's mocking face so much if it were not for that laugh. Channing had humiliated her. But Clarissa had hurt her more because she had betrayed her. She could not blame Channing. He had slighted her from the start, and she had been foolish enough to persist on her senseless mission of gaining his affection. As if by willing it, she could turn herself into a different kind of person—one who would immediately capture his heart. She could only blame herself if he brushed her aside. She had set herself an impossible task and had failed at it. Even Mrs Moffet had tried to warn her. Yet despite everything, she had taken every tiny hint of encouragement on his part—nothing more than small pebbles cast her way—and built whole castles out of them. Well, she had received her just deserts. So be it.

But with Clarissa matters were different. Georgiana had never fully trusted Channing, even while she tried to gain his affection, because she knew the truth already, somewhere inside her. But she had trusted Clarissa. She had trusted her, in fact, more than she had trusted anyone in her life, more even than her brother, which was saying a great deal. She had entrusted in her the hopes of becoming someone different, a more glamorous young lady, one who did not shy away from attention. She had never tried to dream before, but meeting with Clarissa had given her the hope that it was possible, that she *could* go beyond herself and achieve what she wished.

The indiscriminate storm that howled inside her settled and shifted, blowing Georgiana inevitably in one direction. She directed her anger towards Clarissa. Because Clarissa had ultimately chosen to mock her ambitions.

She had believed that she knew Clarissa, but she did not; she really knew very little about her. She thought back with irony on that day when she had first heard from Frederick about Clarissa's plight and her resolve to stand by Clarissa's side. Now she felt that she had been deceived in her cousin's character from the beginning and that she had allowed herself to be ruled by her without even waiting to ascertain her true nature. She had been willing to see in her a fellow spirit, yet what had Clarissa really revealed to her about who she was? Only the little tricks she had taught her about how to deal with men, which she had learned in turn from someone else. They told her nothing about the real Clarissa.

Yet, how could she give up her cousin's friendship? The cousin with whom she was sharing her first London Season? It would be awkward, to say the least, and give rise to a great deal of speculation. What excuse could she possibly give for giving Clarissa the cut? It would give rise to rumours and innuendoes that she could do very well without. It was bad enough that Anne's disappearance was like the sword of Damocles, hanging by a thin thread over their heads.

Which left her with only one choice. She would have to confront

Clarissa and demand an explanation for her behaviour. She would hold her accountable. She would make sure Clarissa realised how much unhappiness she was causing. Georgiana would go to Grosvenor Street early the next morning and meet her head-on.

No sooner had she made her decision and resolved to put it into action, than she was able to turn over on her side and fall asleep.

❦

She had intended to remain calm. To approach the matter calmly and rationally, and to simply ask her cousin, in a cool and haughty manner, about the meaning of her behaviour. She would walk into Robert Darcy's townhouse, ask the butler to summon Clarissa, and wait for her in the drawing room. A large, impersonal space would be best, she decided, rather than the parlour, which was too intimate for such an occasion.

She would come to the point at once and ask Clarissa if she intended to marry Mr Channing. She would of course show no emotion, whatever Clarissa answered. She would nod solemnly and then move on to the crux of the matter, which was, naturally, Georgiana's concern about her cousin's increasing wildness.

She wanted to conduct herself like her brother, to raise her brow as he did, and to quietly but firmly tell her cousin what she believed was wrong with her behaviour.

Only it did not happen that way.

Instead, the footman had hardly opened the door when Clarissa bounced out, and they collided at the bottom of the stairs.

"Goodness!" said Clarissa breathlessly. "I did not expect you today. I was setting out for the lending library—what on earth is the matter, Georgiana? You look quite as severe as Mr Gatley." The very name seemed to throw her into peals of laughter.

"I do not think Mr Gatley as funny as all that," said Georgiana.

"What? Do not tell me you have conceived a *tendre* for him?"

Georgiana made a significant gesture towards the footman hovering behind them. "Perhaps we could discuss this somewhere else?"

Clarissa hesitated, but there must have been something in Georgiana's manner that commanded her attention, for she started up the stairs with a sigh.

"I would like to talk to you in the drawing room." It seemed silly, now that she said it, but she clung to the idea firmly. In reality, she did not know what she would say to Clarissa, only she felt that there was something irrevocable in this moment—something very formal—that it was a turning point in their connection and that the intimacy of the parlour was not what she wanted.

The moment the door shut behind them and Georgiana had chosen a seat—an upright chair that had no arms and was quite uncomfortable—the words fell from her mouth of their own accord.

"If you are under any illusion that carrying on so openly with Mr Channing will make you more attractive in the marriage mart, I must tell you that you are very much mistaken. The only thing that will happen is that you will be thought one of thousands of giddy, senseless girls who have succumbed to a gentleman's charms and thrown away their reputations in the process."

Taken by surprise by this sudden, vehement attack in one not generally given to anger, Clarissa sprung up. Colour flooded into her cheeks, and anger sparked from her eyes.

"I thought *you*, at least, would not speak to me in this manner. I thought you, at least, would not judge me. But it appears I am quite mistaken in my assessment of you."

"I could say the same of you," said Georgiana. "When I first met you, I thought you one of the most confident, courageous, and intelligent young women I had met. I admired you so much I thought you worthy of imitation. I admired you for your fearless way of speaking. I thought so well of you I even allowed you to choose my clothing for me." She paused to find the right words. "But I have slowly come to discover the truth. Your confidence is not confidence at all—it is simply brashness. Your courage stems from indifference. Your outspokenness comes from a disregard for others and what they think. I was utterly deceived by you." Her disillusionment, her crushed hopes, her sense of betrayal surged relentlessly through her. "You do not understand," she said, embarrassed as salt tears burned her eyes.

Oh, she was doing things all wrong. She had not intended to cry at all.

"I *trusted* you," she said, those words summing it all up. She stood up, planning to leave, but the tears she had been holding back flooded her eyes, and she slumped back down onto her seat and sank her face into her hands.

Clarissa, who had been first angry, then flattered, and then bewildered, rushed over immediately to her cousin and, wringing her hands in consternation, stood by her, trying to determine what to do. She crouched down next to her and tried to look into her face, which was covered by her hands.

"No, Georgiana, no. You must not! *Please* stop. I really cannot bear to know you are so upset. If it is because of me, then I *must* know what I have done."

Georgiana looked at Clarissa with red-brimmed eyes.

"If you do not know what you have done, what use is it for me to explain?"

Clarissa rose and marched up and down the room several times. This went on for several minutes. Georgiana watched her, her tears dry.

At some point Clarissa came to some conclusion. She came back to where Georgiana sat and threw herself limply into an armchair next to her.

"Very well. I will confess I have behaved badly. It would be useless to say it was unintentional because I knew very well that I was behaving badly, but I could not help myself."

She let her arms fall loosely over the side of armchair and slid down until she was half reclining, like a puppet whose strings had been released.

Georgiana did not know what to do. The energy that had fuelled her anger had drained away. She could scarcely recollect the source of her anger. She had a shadowy recollection of slipping in the river and of being mocked, but she no longer knew why it had upset her so.

"There are many things you do not know about me," said Clarissa suddenly, "and in that sense I think you are right. I *have* deceived you, in more ways than one. If you will allow me the chance, I will explain to you how and why. But I will understand if you do not wish to listen."

Georgiana examined her cousin warily. She did not want to listen. She did not want to be taken in once more by Clarissa, who was clever with words.

But she could not deny her cousin the right to defend herself.

"I will listen," she said guardedly.

"I know my brother Frederick must have told you why I came to appear so suddenly in England. No, you need not deny it," she said, as Georgiana began to protest. "I know my brother well enough.

He will have told you that my mother sent me here to keep me out of trouble. And that I formed an inappropriate attachment. Bad enough to bundle me onto practically the first ship out of Boston once the peace was declared. She might even have sent me away even if peace was not declared, and left me to my chances with the pirates. She probably thought the pirates would get the worse end of the deal." She paused and smiled, an ironic, bitter smile.

"My attachment to Mr Parker—that is his name—was just the last straw. I had been causing trouble for her for a while, and she did not know what to do about it. She could not wait for the war to end to pack me off to my brother and have *him* deal with the problem."

"Are your mother's notions very strict?" asked Georgiana, puzzling this over. It would take someone like Lady Catherine to think Clarissa so completely unmanageable.

"Strict?" said Clarissa with a laugh. "You have no idea. Most people have forgotten that we were first settled by the Puritans. In Boston now, we are very different from those early settlers. But my mother, you have to understand, is a Wigglesworth." She seemed to expect a reaction, but to Georgiana the name meant nothing.

Clarissa assumed a voice of ghostly horror. "You know— Michael Wigglesworth, *The Day of Doom?*"

Even this dramatic rendition did not provoke any reaction. "Come, you *must* have heard of it."

Georgiana had not.

"Well, there you are. It goes to show how different you and I are. For many years, most children in Massachusetts were required to memorize Wigglesworth's verse along with the catechism. It is a ghoulish warning against sinfulness. Anyway, the illustrious Mr Wigglesworth was a distant cousin. My mother read *The Day of*

Doom to us as children—more because the author was a relative than for the doctrine.

"I am afraid I do not fit in very well with my mother's notions. She sent me here because she hopes perhaps the more rigid rules of English society would help to tame me. She decided I was a lost cause. She did not realise that it is much easier to break the rules when one is surrounded by strangers. One does not know any of them, so one cannot really care for their opinion." She stared glumly at the floor.

"I understand some of what you are telling me," said Georgiana. "But I did not come to talk to you because I wanted to know why you were breaking the rules. It is a matter of indifference to me why you do so. You may have some very clever explanations, but they do not interest me." Georgiana took a deep breath. How could she communicate her meaning to Clarissa? "I came here because I hold you accountable. I do not believe—no matter what your troubles may have been in Boston—that you have the right to treat me as you have done. *I* am not a stranger. *I* did not consider you a lost cause. I appreciated you because you were different. I looked up to you and wanted to learn from you. And all I received from you was scorn."

Clarissa bounced up and came towards her so suddenly that Georgiana was startled. Her cousin cast herself on the floor in front of her. "Do you know what it is like to be in a country where you know no one? You will tell me that I am being ridiculous, for I am here with Robert, so I am hardly alone. But my brother is a stranger to me now. He is married, he has been here some time and has already changed so much I scarcely know him."

This was something Georgiana understood. *This* she could sympathise with.

"Every face I see is new. I was torn from the place where everything was familiar and placed among people who most often than not make assumptions about who you are simply because you belong to a different country."

Georgiana tried to imagine what it would mean to leaving everything she knew behind.

"It feels lonely," said Clarissa, as if that summed up everything. "And on top of it all, I have waited and waited for him to come to me, but he never came. He promised he would follow. I have waited, every day. But he never did."

Suddenly Georgiana understood everything. All that bright, bubbling laughter, all the mischief and the defiance, while beneath the surface lurked uncertainty, torment, and dejection.

"Yes," she whispered. "Yes, I know."

Georgiana threw her arms around Clarissa, who began, quietly, to cry.

It was not long before every secret was revealed. Clarissa spoke about Mr Parker, the man she had left behind, of the dreams they had dreamed together, of her loss.

Georgiana spoke of Wickham. She spoke of her confusion when he had proposed for them to elope together, of her very difficult decision to inform her brother. What had she hoped for by doing so? She had foolishly hoped that her brother—since he had grown up with Wickham as one of his closest companions—would give them his blessing on the marriage. She had not imagined that Wickham would be sent away. Nor had she imagined that Wickham did not care for her at all.

It had taken a while for her to accept the truth. She had slowly come to terms that it was her money he wanted, not her. As news of his distressing behaviour reached her from more than one quarter, she began to shudder at her narrow escape.

And then he had died suddenly. She had been given no chance to mourn him, for no one had expected her to. What was he to her, after all? No one had given a moment's consideration to how his death had affected her. There was little enough for her to mourn, but still she felt sorrow over what could have been.

And as Georgiana spoke to her cousin, she was able, for the first time, to smile at her youthful folly and put it completely behind her.

❧

The young ladies were laughing together when the door opened and Robert entered the room.

"You have been closeted in the room for more than two hours," he said. "I cannot imagine what you two could have to talk about for so long."

Georgiana, her eyes clear and sparkling, replied, "Oh, I cannot say. This and that."

"You do not fool me," said Robert, "for what other topic of conversation do young ladies have? You have been whispering about young gentlemen, of course."

"Brother Robert," said Clarissa, "in general, you are quite correct. Gentlemen are an infinitely fascinating topic of conversation, particularly if they are handsome and charming. But in this instance you are entirely wrong, for we have been speaking about something far more important. We have been speaking about ourselves."

Robert did not know what to make of this speech, so, after exchanging a few more general remarks with them and teasing

Georgiana in a good natured way about the stocking episode, which Caroline had recounted to him, he excused himself and, quitting the room, left them once again to their own devices.

Georgiana did not stay very long after that. They had said everything they wished to say, and they each needed time to reflect on the unexpected revelations that had been made.

But as Georgiana reached the doorway, Clarissa called her back.

"Wait. There is still something I wanted to say."

Georgiana waited, hoping it was not some huge new revelation, for she had had enough for one day.

"I did not intend to hurt you by trying to capture Channing's attention. As you now know, I care nothing for him. My heart is still in Boston, and I still hope—though I am not so foolish as to set too much store by it—that Mr Parker will find the courage to come here and find me. Maybe not yet, but some time in the near future. Channing means nothing to me at all. I wanted to prove something to myself, though I cannot imagine what. I will not stand in your way if you care for him. Let him not come between us."

Georgiana was moved by her friend's gesture. Her road was now free. If Clarissa made no attempt to engage his interest, he would turn to her. She was certain of it. She waited for some emotion to surface—triumph, excitement, pleasure—anything. But there was nothing.

"You know, it is really quite strange, but now that you say I can have him, I realise that I do not want him either."

Clarissa laughed in relief. "Then let him not come between us," she said, "for I would not have liked to discover you were genuinely attached to him."

And with that resolved, Georgiana was able to go away feeling very pleased indeed.

Chapter 22

GEORGIANA WOKE UP THE NEXT MORNING FEELING AIRY AND light. She took a deep breath and smiled. The iron fist that had been squeezing her for some time had gone away. For the first time for a while, she was not gripped by uncertainties the moment she opened her eyes. Anne was safe; Georgiana no longer wished to prove herself to Channing. And there was no longer any reason to be upset at Clarissa. She had not really been really aware of it, but the rivalry between them had nagged at her for some time. Now they had put it behind them.

Georgiana spent a leisurely morning at home. She trimmed one of her hats, and settled down to a basketful of much neglected sewing which needed to be done. She was just thinking that it had been a long time since she was so contented, when she heard quick steps coming down the hallway and a moment later Clarissa hurried into the room, quite out of breath.

"I hope you do not mind, Georgiana, but I agreed to go with Mr Channing, Mr Parvis, and Miss Parvis to see the exhibition at the East India Company. Mr Parvis's father works in the company, and so Mr Parvis has access to parts of the exhibition which are not available to the general public. You know how fond I am of artefacts from the East. I was going to go alone, but then last night it occurred to me that it might be improper, even if it is a working day and the offices are all busy, and I am taking Hatty, my maid. Still, I think it would be better if you came with us."

Georgiana would have preferred to remain peacefully at home.

"I thought you said you would not be seeing Channing any more," she replied.

"Just this one time, and I am not going to see Channing. I am going to see the exhibit," said Clarissa. "Please can you come?" she said imploringly.

Georgiana hesitated. But after their conversation she had become too aware of her friend's unhappiness to deny her the opportunity to find some distraction.

"I will come with you. But it would be better still if Elizabeth could join us. Let me ask her."

"Make haste, then. They will be calling for me in Grosvenor Street, and I do not want to be late."

But when they asked Elizabeth, she was too distracted. Little Lewis had had a fall, and his lip was bleeding. It was all Nurse and she could do to keep him still as they held the cloth to his mouth. He screamed and wriggled so much that Elizabeth was alarmed that he had received some other injury. She barely looked up when the girls said goodbye.

The cousins hurried to Grosvenor Street, only to find that they had plenty of time before Channing was due to call.

A carriage finally came to a halt in front of the door, but instead of Mr Channing, the butler announced Mr and Miss Parvis.

"Where is Mr Channing?" said Georgiana, when the greetings were done.

"He will be joining us at East India House shortly. There is not enough room for all of us in the carriage, so we agreed to meet there."

Georgiana had never been to East India House. Everything about it exuded an air of grandeur. It was a vast building, meant to impress—with its huge columns, and the statues of Britannia, Europe, and Asia that presided over Leadenhall Street. Inside, it was equally awe-inspiring, though Georgiana secretly liked the Court Room best, since its light airiness formed a contrast to the more gloomy aspects of the building. Tea was brought to them by a clerk, and they partook of refreshments and cake.

"Is your father to join us?" said Georgiana, as the tea things were cleared and the guide Parvis had hired appeared before them.

"Yes, most certainly. He is in a meeting with the board of Directors, but he has promised to make an appearance as soon as it is adjourned."

"Does your father know Warren Hastings?" asked Clarissa curiously. "I read all about his trial. My father saved all the newspapers cuttings related to the case."

"Oh, did he indeed? Whatever for? What a lot of old nonsense. Nothing to it, you know," said Parvis. "Some private jealousies and toes that were trod on—you know the sort of thing."

By now they had entered the library. Georgiana was immediately struck by the grandeur of the dome and the plaster rosettes all around. Clarissa exclaimed over the elaborate calligraphy and magnificent colours of the Persian manuscripts. Georgiana admired the collection of shells.

They moved to the next room. Here they stared at the Indian idols which were set up in various corners of the room and the Hindu and Goorkha swords. Hatty, Clarissa's maid, let out a scream when the figure of an English soldier being attacked by a tiger came to life. The tiger roared, and the soldier, who was on the ground, cried out in distress and flailed about.

"Oh, look, Miss, at those monstrous claws on the beast!" she exclaimed.

The guide explained to her—in a contemptuous, condescending tone—that the effect was produced by turning a handle. She amused herself for the next few minutes with turning the handle and reproducing the movements and the sounds.

Meanwhile, Clarissa wandered off to admire some of the coins and other treasures scattered about the room. Mr Parvis, observing Clarissa's pleasure, took her arm and drew her ahead, leaving Georgiana to walk with his sister. Georgiana made a half-hearted effort to speak to Miss Parvis, but she quickly realised that beyond talk of hats and bonnets and dresses, Miss Parvis had little to say.

Georgiana was therefore at leisure to notice that however much Clarissa was absorbed by her view of the exhibits, Mr Parvis was not. He seemed more intent on finding excuses to come closer to her and to conceal them both from the others. Clarissa discovered a number of paintings portraying scenes in India, and she pored over them, with Mr Parvis pointing out scenes that were particularly noteworthy. Georgiana was uncomfortable with the situation, for they were alone with someone who was practically a stranger, and who was paying Clarissa marked attention. She was not unduly alarmed however. She expected either Mr Channing or Mr Parvis's father to appear any moment.

Meanwhile, the guide took her to the Babylonian exhibits and began to explain to her something of their history. She listened politely, for the history of ancient cultures had never appealed to her, in spite of the current vogue for antiquity, but she tried to remember as much as possible, feeling that she ought at least to educate herself. The next exhibit they moved to was charming. It was a garden, with figures of birds and animals made of gold, and trees with leaves of silver and a pond made from mother-of-pearl.

The guide once again launched into a long explanation.

It was some time later that Miss Parvis, plainly bored, complained that she for one would be happy never to view the collection again.

"Parvis always loves to bring everyone here, especially young ladies he admires, and what must I do but come along too. You cannot imagine how dreary I have come to find this room. But tell me, do you think this colour suits me? I believe lemon is quite the fashion this season."

Georgiana became aware that the quiet murmurs of Mr Parvis and Clarissa as they looked over the paintings had ceased and that they were no longer in the room.

"Let us catch up with them," she said to the guide, calling Hatty to her side.

They entered the next room in time to see Clarissa looking very flustered. Mr Parvis, clearly in a temper, called Miss Parvis to join him. Flashing a quick smile at the two young ladies, she hurried to catch up with her brother as he exited through a doorway.

Their guide cleared his throat.

"Perhaps you would care to continue the tour another time?" he said.

Georgiana nodded. The guide held out his hand, clearly expecting payment. Georgiana had no idea how much to give him. She had not brought much money with her, not thinking she would need it. She dropped a sixpence in his hand.

"My dear young lady, it would hardly be worth my time to explain things in such detail for such a small amount."

Clarissa dug in her reticule and tossed a half crown into his hand. "I trust this will be enough," she said. "Come, Georgiana!"

"That was much too generous," said Georgiana.

"It was the only coin I had," said Clarissa.

"We need to catch up with Mr Parvis immediately. He is quite capable of setting off and leaving us behind. Do you know he tried to slip his hand around my waist?"

Georgiana was not surprised. She had half expected something of the sort and was very angry with Channing for not coming. She wished now she had instructed Hatty to stay close to Clarissa every minute.

"What did you do to make him so angry?"

"I slapped him," said Clarissa.

"Well, he deserved it," said Georgiana. "His behaviour has been very reprehensible."

"I'm glad you said so, for I was afraid from his reaction that English ladies never slap gentlemen. But how else could they put a stop to things if they have gone too far?"

"We had better hurry and catch up with him. You can explain the whole debacle later."

But when they reached the entrance, neither Mr Parvis nor his carriage were anywhere in sight.

❦

"How could he have done this!" cried Georgiana. "Can he be so utterly reprehensible as to abandon us alone in the City, simply because you would not let him handle you?"

"Well, since he is nowhere in sight, I can only conclude that he *is* utterly reprehensible." Clarissa sighed. "We shall have to make our way home ourselves."

The day, which had been bright when they left home, had changed completely. A light fog had descended upon the world, swathing the buildings around them. The street, which during business hours was teeming with merchants, prosperous Cits, and clerks going about their business, now looked almost empty. A forlorn-looking carriage cluttered by in the milky light. Leadenhall Street had seemed earlier a well maintained, momentous sort of street. But its usual inhabitants had migrated elsewhere, replaced by ethereal figures.

A shadow flitted in a doorway. Georgiana saw it only with the corner of her eye. But when she looked again, there was nothing. She was allowing her imagination to run riot. She really ought not to read any of those Gothic romances Clarissa loved so much. There was nothing at all sinister in a little bit of fog. London had its fogs. It was part of the weather, that was all.

A hackney cab rumbled by. They gestured for it to stop, but it was already taken.

They waited for a few minutes, but the business hours were over, and there was hardly any reason for the hackneys to come this way.

Again, she felt rather than saw that shadow. Not just one, several of them.

"Did you see that?" she said, peering through the veil of fog.

"I thought I saw something," said Clarissa, drawing her pelisse closer.

"I hope we find a hackney soon," said Georgiana. The awareness of being watched by invisible eyes unnerved her.

"We'd do better to go inside again, Miss," said Hatty. "We shouldn't stand here, at any rate. We're making targets of ourselves."

"You're quite right," said Clarissa. "We could ask that friendly guide to procure a carriage for us. We paid him enough, at any rate."

Georgiana readily agreed. They hurried in quick steps towards the heavy shelter of the building.

"Not so fast, young ladies," said a voice. A murky figure emerged from the fog.

He reeked of gin. Georgiana stepped backwards, only to find her way blocked by one of the columns.

Around them, dark shadows broke the milky fog like a circle of statues.

"Such pretty dainty things," said one of the men, pulling Georgiana's reticule from her hand.

Georgiana tried to grip the reticule, but he wrenched it easily out of her grasp. He held it up above her head, out of her reach. "Maybe if you give me a kiss I might give it back to you."

General laughter greeted this.

A hand reached out and grabbed Clarissa's reticule. It joined Georgiana's, suspended in the air.

"How about that cross there. Now ain't that pretty too?"

Hands rough as plaster slipped round her neck.

Georgiana stood as still as she could. He could take the pendant. She would not resist. There were stories bandied around—stories of cutthroats who thought nothing of killing you for a coin, let alone a gold cross.

She did not look at her cousin. She just hoped Clarissa would not decide on any sudden heroics. Hatty too. They were searching her for valuables.

They could just as easily take the pendant, then kill her.

She refused to think about it.

A carriage careened through the street and headed straight for them. The horse stopped just in time right in front of them. A door swung open and a gentleman jumped out.

"Leave the ladies alone!" The familiar voice held an unmistakable threat. An officer's voice, accustomed to obedience.

He could have saved his breath. The shadows had dissolved into milky opaqueness as soon as the carriage approached, taking their booty with them.

Georgiana stood in the fog, looking up at Gatley, who was pointing a musket at them.

"You can put that down now," said Georgiana in a colourless voice deprived of all emotion.

Gatley's mouth was tight—a white line in an ashen face. Or was it the fog? Georgiana could not be sure.

"Good afternoon," he said icily. "I hope you have not suffered any loss beyond the reticules?"

"No," replied Georgiana. She returned to animation again, as if coming out of a trance.

His face was so familiar, so handsome in that moment she could have thrown her arms around him. "You appeared at just the right moment. Oh, I don't know how to thank you!" Her hand trembled as she held it out to him. He took it briefly. "How fortunate for us that you had business here!"

"Fortune has had nothing to do with it," he said briefly.

Clarissa had not moved yet. She looked dazed, almost as if she was sleepwalking. Georgiana stepped back and took her cousin's arm.

"Help me," said Georgiana to Hatty, who also had a similar glazed look.

The command restored a sense of normalcy to Hatty, who took her mistress's other arm and put it around her shoulders. "You can lean on me if you want, Miss. We wouldn't want you fainting on us, now, would we?"

Together they helped Clarissa into the carriage.

Gatley stepped aside as they went by, then followed them in and shut the door behind him.

"I knew about your plans for a visit. Channing told me. But when my aunt came to visit us she told me he had received word of an important mill—a boxing match—and had gone in pursuit. I then realised that you had come here escorted only by Mr Parvis and his sister. I rode over immediately to ensure that all was well—I do not have too high an opinion of Mr Parvis." He looked grimly out of the window. "Still, even I did not imagine he would be so lacking in conduct as to abandon you on the street."

"Then we are even more indebted to you," said Georgiana, "if it was not chance that brought you here."

He did not seem to have heard her. Certainly, he did not acknowledge her words. That white line around his lips was still there. It was not just from the fog.

He turned to Clarissa, who sat quite still in the corner.

"It is quite beyond belief that you could behave so irresponsibly," he said to her. "You are a stranger to our country. You do not know our customs. You should be guided by people who know better than you what is acceptable and what is not. You skirt the edge of propriety without wondering if you are putting others in danger as well as yourself. What would have occurred if I had not happened along? Have you considered that?"

Gatley's dark eyes were hard as agate. Georgiana waited for Clarissa to rebuff him, or to make a dismissive comment, or to laugh his anger away, but she seemed to have shrunk into herself. She looked like a child, her eyes large and black, her face sallow. She did not utter a word.

Her spirit twisted inside her to see Clarissa like this. Truth be told, she herself was still trembling. She did not know why she trembled. She did not know if it was from fear or from anger.

Gatley's words brought out the anger. She was used to kindness from him. His harshness now, when what she needed most was gentleness, kindled the spark that the trembling had kept under control. The anger that flared was the anger that should have been directed at the ruffians who had cornered them. Now it found a direction. Gatley had no right to reprimand either her cousin or her in this manner.

And to think that she had greeted him as a saviour! She had been ready to think the world of him in that instant.

But now she could see that Channing—whatever his faults may be, and they were a multitude—had spoken the truth about his cousin. Gatley had assisted them, but for what purpose? Out of the kindness of his heart?

The answer was clearly no. Self-righteousness motivated him—to be able to lecture and moralize and browbeat them into accepting what he considered right. And he was taking full advantage of the fact that they had no choice but to ride with him to impress upon them that they were at fault.

It was *not* their fault that they had been accosted. When they had set out, it was with the confidence that they would be properly escorted. How could they possibly have imagined that they would be abandoned? How could they be faulted in that?

"And you, Miss Darcy," he said, turning those dark eyes like a hammer to nail her to the seat. "*You* have no excuse of not knowing where to go and where not to go in London. You, at least, were aware that the City is no place for well-bred ladies. Yet you are so easily persuaded, so easily under your cousin's thumb, that you will follow her to ruin rather than go against her will."

She had heard enough.

"Stop the carriage instantly," she said. "Stop it now! For I will not endure another moment here with you. What right do you have to castigate us? What right to intimidate us? Do you think that because we were treated uncivilly by those men, you have the right to abandon all civility toward us? That because we were insulted by others, you may insult us yourself?"

The whiteness around his mouth disappeared as he turned pale. She was too far gone, her anger and frustration too acute, to care about his reaction. She shook, and her words tumbled out as if she had held them back for ever.

"You speak as though I knew what would befall us if we came to see the exhibit, as if, by coming here, we had been asking for something like this to happen. As if I would deliberately seek out such treatment! The whole of society conspires to keep us ignorant and to set us rules and guidelines without ever explaining the consequences if we break the rules. How could I have known that a visit to an East India House exhibit would put us in a position of needing rescue? We were to have been escorted by two gentlemen, as well as another young lady, and Clarissa's maid. If there is anyone to blame, blame your cousin for not escorting us and for introducing us to someone who does not have a gentlemanly bone in his body. Blame yourself. You knew about Parvis's character, yet you allowed him to join us on our boat trip, a trip you yourself organised, and you said nothing about him. Castigate them. Castigate yourself. Do not seek to castigate us."

She glared at him. She was still not finished.

"You have rescued us, yes, and I will always be grateful for that. But if you mean us to see you as a knight errant, then you will be very disappointed. A knight errant would provide comfort and support to the ladies he rescued, not do everything he could to increase their misery. It is clear that nobody has taught you that one of the principles of chivalry is to behave as a gentleman."

She was striking back, hammer to hammer, and she was not finished yet.

"As for you accusing me of being under my cousin's thumb, then it is a case of the frying pan calling the kettle blackened, for I have never met a man more under the thumb of another than you. Why your cousin cannot move anywhere without you following him around, like a little puppy—" She halted, knowing that she was going too far, that her words had lost their truthful ring.

"You have made your feelings on the matter abundantly clear, Madam. You need not speak any farther. I apologise deeply for any offence I may have caused you, and for what you consider my want of conduct. You shall have your wish. I will not force you to endure my company a moment longer. I will instruct my coachman to drive you to your residence."

And with that, he signalled the coachman to stop, and bowing briefly, he took his leave.

"Wait!" cried Georgiana, but he had already gone.

Plagued by conflicting emotions—consternation at her own words, stubborn conviction that he deserved every word, frustration at having been deprived of the object of her wrath, and stinging shards of fear from her encounter in the street—she sat staring unseeing from the window, oblivious to her cousin's presence.

By and by, she became conscious of the space around her and turned to see Clarissa observing her quietly.

"Oh, Clarissa!" she said, "What did I do?"

A ghost of a smile hovered on Clarissa's lips. "You did nothing at all, beyond losing your temper, and telling him exactly what you thought."

"But what a terrible thing to do! And now we have deprived him of his carriage as well, after he rescued us and provided his assistance."

"You need not attach too much importance to that part, for he is a man and will be able to find his way back. For a moment, in fact, I was worried that you would carry through your threat to leave the carriage. Now *that* would have been a problem, for who knows how quickly we could have found a hackney to take us home, and we may well have fallen into the same problem as befell us before, for I have no idea where we are."

Georgiana looked out of the window and actually looked at the neighbourhood through which they were driving. "Goodness! Thank Heavens he had the presence of mind to leave the carriage himself. Yes, we *would* have been in a rare pickle," she said, and began to laugh.

⁂

The moment he stepped out of the carriage, he realised he had made a mistake. He had allowed his temper to get the better of him, and the result was that he now was without a carriage, in a part of Town he did not know at all. He was able to protect himself, of course, at least against a single assailant. But chances were, the way things were happening today, he would be more likely to be confronted by a group of cutthroats.

Though to be fair, not everything had gone wrong. He had not had to fight with the ruffians in Leadenhall Street. When he had seen Miss Darcy with her back against the pillar, glaring defiantly at the men around her, his blood had roared, and he had leapt without thought to her defence. Luckily the men had dispersed, frightened away by his sudden appearance. Which was providential for all of

THE DARCY COUSINS

them. Ever since the government had taken stricter measures to regulate the City and to enforce tougher measures against crime, criminals had grown more desperate and more prone to use violence against their victims.

He looked around him uneasily, every sense alert. The fog swirled around him. It was not thick, but it limited his visibility, so that he could not trust the edges of his vision, where everything seemed just a little hazy and distorted.

It would take a stroke of luck to find a hackney.

As if conjured up by his thoughts, a hackney emerged out of the mist. He waved at it. To his complete surprise, it stopped. He was so taken by surprise, he almost expected the door to swing open by magic. But it did not. He opencd the door himself, checked the inside to make sure it would not spring any surprises, and entered.

He sat back in the seat. The tension of the last hour washed away, and he felt drained of all energy.

How could he have made such a mess of things? It was as if he had deliberately set out to anger Miss Darcy. In fact, he had done everything he possibly could to provoke her. He could not explain it, except that he himself had been so shaken by the incident that he could not think straight at all.

He had noted her trembling hand, and he had responded by lashing out at Clarissa Darcy, putting the blame squarely on her shoulders. Except that Miss Darcy was right. Miss Clarissa was not to blame any more than she was.

The fact was, somewhere, in the back of his mind, he had chosen to lash out at Miss Clarissa because he had expected her to retaliate. He had expected her to fight back, tooth and claw. She sat in the corner instead, saying nothing, *accepting* his blame.

285

And Miss Darcy had retaliated instead. She had protected her cousin and defended herself.

It was all so topsy-turvy, so contrary to his assessment of the situation, that he had trouble grappling with the new image of Miss Darcy that was emerging. She was not the timid little squirrel he had imagined her. She was fierce and protective, and she had turned against him like a lynx—he had come across one in Portugal, as she fought to protect her cubs—when he had tried to hurt her own.

He grinned to himself. She had been fierce and magnificent in that moment. She had been…beautiful.

Except that she had accused him of appalling things, things that wounded him to the core and snuffed out that grin from his face very quickly. But she had been justified—on the whole.

At this moment he could not think of a single thing he could possibly do to make her forgive him.

Chapter 23

THE CARRIAGE DROPPED OFF GEORGIANA IN BERKELEY SQUARE and continued on its way to Robert's house. Georgiana tried to creep up the stairs, hoping her return would pass unnoticed, but she had hardly gone a few steps when Elizabeth's face peered down at her from the banisters above.

"Oh, you have returned. As it turned out, I could easily have gone with you, since Lewis fell asleep after you left and slept most of the time. I missed my chance. Tell me about it. Was it as thrilling as Clarissa expected?"

Georgiana briefly considered not telling Elizabeth anything. She really did not want to go over the whole thing with anyone else. Now that she had arrived home, she felt completely drained of energy. The last thing she wanted to do was provide a coherent explanation to someone else. She needed to piece things together for herself first.

But Elizabeth was smiling expectantly, and besides, she and Darcy would be bound to hear, sooner or later. She may as well tell the whole sorry story and finish with it.

"I suppose it probably *was* what Clarissa expected," she replied. "But the visit did not go well at all. In fact, it was very nearly a disaster."

For the first time, she considered what could really have happened on Leadenhall Street. A cold shiver swept through her. It all could have been so much worse. Gatley's arrival had indeed been providential.

As Georgiana related the events of the afternoon to Elizabeth, it was as if she was telling a tale that had occurred a long time ago. She could scarcely believe that it was only a few minutes since Gatley's carriage had deposited her here.

"And so Mr Gatley came to our rescue," she ended.

She told her nothing about the quarrel in the carriage.

Elizabeth gave a horrified gasp. The colour drained from her cheeks.

"This is all my fault!" she cried, jumping up and moving around in quick agitated steps. "This is worse than I could ever have imagined! Not in my wildest dreams. I should never have let you go alone. I should have come with you."

"I do not see how your presence would have mattered," said Georgiana desolately.

"I would not have allowed Mr Parvis such liberties. He would have found it difficult to take advantage of the situation with me there."

"Perhaps, but he took advantage of my preoccupation—and Hatty's—to separate Clarissa from us, so he may have done exactly the same if you had been there."

"I doubt it. He would have been more circumspect."

Georgiana was doubtful. Mr Parvis was so brazen, so certain of his position as the son of an administrator in the East India Company, she did not think he felt accountable to anyone.

But Elizabeth was too torn by remorse and recriminations. Nothing that Georgiana said could convince her that she was not to blame.

"What if Mr Gatley had not run across his aunt and had not known there was something amiss? Imagine what would have come to pass! My neglect could have led to appalling consequences."

"Nothing happened, Elizabeth," said Georgiana, "and that is the end of it."

The story was revealed to Darcy later in the evening, as they gathered in the drawing room before making their way to a ball at the Keelings's. Elizabeth was distraught and blamed herself for being such a dreadful chaperone.

Darcy apparently agreed.

"This is not the first time such a thing has occurred, Elizabeth" said Darcy sternly. "I know you are young yourself, and I know how badly the mantle of matron and chaperone sits on you, but I had thought you more responsible than that. You know that the City is no place for young ladies, yet you let them go, escorted by no one other than a maid who is scarcely older than they are. What did you think the young maid could have done to protect them, pray?"

"It is not as if she sent us alone," said Georgiana, staunchly defending her sister. "Mr Parvis and Mr Channing were to be with us, and two footmen, and Miss Parvis, and Hatty—surely that should have been enough protection. None of us thought of danger. We thought only of propriety, and Elizabeth was satisfied that the proprieties were met."

Darcy considered her words for some time, then nodded his head. "I suppose you are right. You were not to know that Mr Channing would not show up—though *that* is not without precedent. I do recall another such occasion very well. And you could not have envisioned that Mr Parvis would first insult Clarissa and then abandon you to your fate. Perhaps Clarissa overreacted by striking him, but no gentleman would behave as he did, no matter what the provocation." He rose and paced the room angrily.

"By God!" he said, turning round suddenly. "I am half decided to call him out for this."

Georgiana gasped.

"No, no, you must not, Brother!" cried Georgiana. "Do not even say it in jest!"

Darcy had not said it in jest. But her words struck home, and the pallor of his sister's face brought a white tinge to his.

"No, of course not. I did not mean it," he said, sitting down and putting his hands to his face.

For several minutes, a deep silence settled over the room. Wickham's ghost inhabited the space between them, and his death was in everyone's mind. He had been wounded in a duel after running off with another man's wife.

Finally Darcy put down his hands. He rose and, striding over to Georgiana, he sat next to her. He took her hands in his own.

"I cannot bear to think that you could have been harmed. But you need not be afraid that I will fight a duel over it." He squeezed her hands in reassurance. "You cannot expect me to do nothing, of course. I will arrange a meeting with Parvis's father. I will make sure his father knows about it, and I will insist that he takes measures to prevent such a thing happening again."

❧

The discussion brought the events of the day home to her, and she felt too fatigued to want to go to a ball. Both Fitzwilliam and Elizabeth wanted to stay with her and keep her company, but she insisted that all she wanted to do was rest in her room.

They refused to go.

In the end they had a quiet evening at home. They played crib-bage, then Fitzwilliam and Elizabeth sang for her, and they had a cold supper together. When they were certain she did not suffer any ill-effects from her adventure, only then was she able to go up to her room.

But despite all their efforts, she could not sleep a wink. At first, it is because she imagined the wraith-like figures stepping through the fog. They surrounded her, closed in slowly. Dread petrified her...

She willed herself to push aside those shadows. They had not harmed her. Perhaps they had not intended to harm her at all, only to take what they could and leave. She focused instead on Gatley.

She would never forget that first moment, when his familiar features had appeared before her, sharp and clear despite the fog. She had been flooded with such powerful emotions—a mix of joy, relief, and affection—she was amazed that she had not thrown herself into his arms.

What had she done instead? She had unleashed her tongue at him, accusing him of so many things she could hardly remember. He had behaved badly, there was no doubt of it. She would not find ways to justify his conduct. But to accuse him of not being a gentleman, after what he did for them! To insult his very honour! What had come over her?

She recalled his words; his pitiless condemnation of Clarissa, his unrelenting criticism of them both.

She did not regret what she said. He deserved everything that she told him.

Yet how could she quarrel with the very person who had come to their rescue? He had guessed they would be in trouble, and he had ridden headlong to their aid. And what did he receive in return? A tongue-lashing delivered by a harpy.

The night passed. Inside her, a tempest raged. Different waves of feeling battered at her. Her fear of the murky figures alternated with a subdued, simmering anger towards them. She resented Gatley's words, but her resentment battled with her embarrassment at repaying his rescue with accusations and insults. Still, she clung to the fierce certainty that she was right.

At the end, the tempest left her hollow. All that remained was a vague sense of regret because she did not think Gatley could possibly forgive her.

❧

The next day, sluggish from lack of sleep, Georgiana confided to Elizabeth some of what had happened in the carriage.

"You cannot blame him, surely, for being angry," said Elizabeth. "Think of his position. Think of what would have happened if he had not appeared at that moment. He was not expecting to see you in the street surrounded by thieves. He was taken by surprise. You could not expect him to be perfectly calm and polite afterwards."

"It still did not entitle him to treat us like wayward children."

"You know as well as I do that people can say things they regret in the heat of the moment."

Georgiana allowed it to be so. Her own words came back to her, and she blushed as she recalled them. She supposed she owed him an apology. Perhaps she ought to have made allowance for the fact that the incident had caught him off-guard, as it had done with them. He had come out of the carriage prepared to fight.

Nevertheless, she still felt strongly that he had been remarkably boorish and had displayed an amazing lack of delicacy.

She certainly did not want to apologise.

Later in the morning an enormous and very handsome bouquet of flowers arrived for her. The note attached to it was very simple.

With my humblest apologies.
Gatley

The apology dissolved the last traces of her resentment. He was contrite. He had not let his pride stand in the way. His anger had stemmed from an impulse to protect them from harm, however inappropriately he had phrased it. She was still angry, but the good he had done far outweighed the impact of his unfortunate behaviour. She was willing to forgive—more, she was willing to apologise in turn.

Fitzwilliam, passing her as she pondered his note, smiled at her in a friendly fashion.

"I think we need to thank this hero of yours," he said. "I would like to invite Mr Gatley and his mother for a special dinner. What do you think?"

Georgiana was more than pleased to have a private occasion in which to present her apologies and to speak with him away from prying eyes.

"I would be very happy to express my thanks in this way," she said.

"Good. Then if is agreeable to you, you can be in charge of planning the dinner. But you must promise me you will not have anything on the menu that Elizabeth cannot eat."

Georgiana flushed at this reminder of her petty vengeance but agreed happily enough.

Georgiana spent a disproportionately long time planning the menu for the dinner. She drove Cook to distraction by planning a dinner, not for two guests, but for thirty. And then she could not quite make up her mind on the main course.

"If you don't decide what you want, Miss Georgiana, I will have to decide everything myself, see if I don't."

Georgiana, knowing she was being unnecessarily fussy, gave Cook a rueful smile.

"I want to get it just right, you see," she said to Cook, who had been a familiar part of her life since she was a child.

"Then you'd better leave the kitchen so we can get on with it," grumbled Cook.

Cook was not the only one who was complaining by the night of the dinner. Georgiana's maid was quite at her wit's end trying to keep up with Georgiana's constantly changing opinions over what she planned to wear.

"If you don't mind, Miss," said Maid, "it might be best if I chose for you. I have an eye for these things, you know. You need not worry. You'll dazzle Mr Gatley, that you will."

Georgiana's cheeks turned pink. "I do not wish to dazzle Mr Gatley. I cannot imagine why you would think such a thing."

Maid turned away quickly to hide a smile, but not quickly enough.

"You are smirking, Maid," said Georgiana. "I saw you."

"Heaven forbid, Miss Georgiana," said Maid, hurrying to choose her a dress. "When have you ever found me guilty of such a thing?"

A last moment panic ensued when Georgiana turned her room topsy-turvy to find a chain she particularly wanted to wear—only to find she was already wearing it. But then finally everything was ready, and she prepared to make her Grand Entrance.

Her eyes flew immediately to Gatley the moment she entered the room. He was, as always, immaculately dressed, his cravat perfectly tied, and his tailored dark blue coat fitted without a crease over his broad shoulders. He looked cautious, his expression non-committal. Her heart sank. Perhaps she had misunderstood his note. Perhaps it was nothing more than a formal apology for an offence caused and did not stem from any sincere impulse. Or maybe he had thought better of it since. Perhaps he was still angry at her for slighting his honour.

Well, she owed him an apology, and she would deliver it, come what may.

It did not prove as easy to speak to him in private as she imagined. With so few people present, snatching a moment of privacy would be very tricky indeed. And then she had her duty as a hostess to consider, since in many ways this was her invitation.

She made every effort to welcome Mrs Gatley in as friendly a manner as possible. As usual, she immediately fell into conversation with her, and before long she was drawn out to tell her side of the events on Leadenhall Street.

"I have heard a brief outline of the events from Gatley, but he was rather reticent about providing details, so I must rely on you, Miss Darcy, to explain the circumstances."

This was not surprising, since Gatley had not asked for an account and had reached his own conclusions. Georgiana was not very comfortable relating what had happened, but she could not refuse to talk about it without appearing churlish. So she told the story, conscious every moment of Gatley's presence in the room.

Mrs Gatley proved to be a sympathetic listener. She quickly understood Georgiana's discomfort and contrived to put her at ease with her questions.

"Did they carry any weapons?" she asked, when Georgiana tried to describe the men who had attacked them.

"I did not see any—but they could have been hidden."

"Perhaps they meant only to toy with you and not to do any serious harm."

Georgiana found the statement comforting.

Gatley listened without comment. Georgiana wondered if he was passing judgment on her even now.

"Well, the ordeal is over now," said Mrs Gatley. "You should not dwell on it. It is best to put it all behind you."

"Except that we have Gatley to thank," said Darcy. "Do you not think Gatley here has the look of a hero? Are you not going to thank him, Georgiana?"

Georgiana wished Darcy did not still behave as if she was a child who needed to be reminded of her manners.

"I would indeed like to thank Mr Gatley for his timely rescue," she said. "I cannot imagine what would have happened if you had not reached us just then."

Gatley inclined his head formally. "I did nothing at all. Any carriage that would have happened by would have scattered the villains."

"That does not diminish the fact that you deliberately set out to make sure we were safe, Mr Gatley," she responded.

Gatley bowed. "Then I shall say it was an honour, Miss Georgiana."

There was a reluctance about him that she did not quite fathom.

The doors to the dining room were opened, and the butler announced that dinner was served.

As they moved towards the door, Georgiana grasped the opportunity of being able to speak to Gatley alone.

"I would like to apologise, Mr Gatley," said Georgiana. "I should not have spoken to you I the way I did in the carriage."

"I deserved every word," said Gatley earnestly. "You were right. My behaviour was appalling. I am embarrassed even to think of it." He looked so genuinely contrite Georgiana's heart went out to him. "I really was not much of a knight errant, was I? *You* should not apologise. But I hope this means you have accepted my apology."

Georgiana nodded. "Of course."

He smiled at her, and she glowed in the warmth of the smile. The world around her sparkled and winked at her.

"The Season has done wonders for you," remarked Gatley's mother after they were seated. "You look quite radiant tonight. You are clearly one of those young ladies who flourish once introduced into society. I remember very well our conversation on our way to Waverley Abbey. I believe you have found just the right approach."

Elizabeth immediately wanted to know about their conversation, and soon a lively discussion ensued about the expectations placed by society on young debutantes, in which Georgiana did not hesitate for a moment to express her opinion.

No dinner in those days could be considered complete without a mention of Napoleon, for the whole world was talking about him. London was packed with people hoping for a glimpse of him when he was brought to England.

"I do not know why so many people assume he will be brought to the Tower," said Mrs Gatley.

"I suppose they think he deserves to be treated as Royalty. He *was* an Emperor, after all."

"As if that signifies," said Darcy, "since it was a title he himself invented."

"Still, he was a man of genius and a great Commander. It took many armies to defeat him," said Gatley, "and he was able to instil strong loyalty in many people."

"I think the mark of a great ruler," said Georgiana, "is not his ability to make war but to achieve peace."

"Well spoken!" cried Mrs Gatley. "I think men are a great deal too likely to admire warfare, as if there is any merit in it."

"Now you have done it, Miss Darcy," said Gatley. "We will never hear the end of it, for my mother is a supporter of Mr Whitbread."

"*There* you have a great leader," said Mrs Gatley. She gave a mournful sigh. "But look what came of him—such an ignoble end for one who had so much courage."

There was a solemn gloom as everyone contemplated the sad wastefulness of Mr Whitbread's death. It was incomprehensible to Georgiana that he would want to take his own life, when he had so much to offer.

"Would you have us overruled by Napoleon, then? If we had listened to Mr Whitbread, then we would even now be under the rule of the Emperor."

"Pah!" said Mrs Gatley. "He would never have invaded England."

"You are quite mistaken about that, Mrs Gatley," said Darcy. "For there is evidence of several plans to invade England. They were foiled by spies, fortunately."

"What did I tell you?" said Mrs Gatley. "It is the spies who saved England, not the armies."

A lively discussion ensued, and dinner passed quickly.

Georgiana, who participated as vigorously as the rest, intercepted several glances from Gatley and was very well satisfied.

⁓⁂⁓

The dinner was approaching the end. The cover was removed, and the desserts brought in. The pastry chef had truly outdone himself, particularly in the large centrepiece that was carried in ceremoniously by two footmen.

Gatley took one look at the enormous pastry that sat before him and exploded into a loud guffaw.

Everyone at the table stared at him in bewilderment. Everyone, that is, except for Georgiana, who hid her smile under her napkin, and tried to look innocent.

Darcy raised his eyebrow. "I am glad to see you in such good spirits, Gatley." His eyes went quickly to Georgiana. "Georgiana, of course, planned today's menu. She enjoys the occasional—ah—prank."

Gatley knew the polite response would be to compliment Georgiana on the excellence of her choice and deny that there was any prank involved. However, at the moment, he did not trust himself to speak. The swan, with its shiny white icing and elegant contours was very beautiful indeed. The pastry chef had gone to great lengths to produce it.

It was the odd arrangement of peacock feathers on its head that was the problem.

"Well, I think she has chosen very well," remarked Mrs Gatley, trying her best to be tactful. "I have rarely had such an excellent combination of dishes. The peacock feathers seem a little odd, perhaps, but they are very pretty."

At this, even Georgiana had to laugh.

❧❀❧

The warm glow did not desert Georgiana even when she went to bed. She could not help feeling that Mrs Gatley approved of her and seemed in many ways to encourage a connection between Georgiana and her son.

Georgiana did not know what to make of this. It was all too new and strange. Just a few months ago, she would never have thought it possible. Now—well, it was far too early. And besides, nothing had occurred between her and Gatley at all that would indicate that he was thinking of such a possibility. Certainly he seemed to admire her, but she had thought the same of Channing, and she had been very much mistaken.

She pushed aside these thoughts. She did not have to make any decisions now, nor did she want to second guess Gatley regarding *his* feelings. She would take her time and let matters unfold as they would.

Chapter 24

"I SPOKE TO MR ALBERT PARVIS," SAID DARCY A FEW DAYS LATER, peering into the upstairs parlour and finding Georgiana sewing quietly. "He was incensed to find out that his son was using his father's position in the company to attract the attentions of respectable young ladies. He was even more alarmed to realise his daughter was one of the party. He apologised profusely for what happened, and promised me that his son's actions would not pass unnoticed. I left the meeting quite certain that his son and daughter will feel the repercussions."

The repercussions soon became general knowledge, though the reason for them was not disclosed. It was soon universally known that Mr Parvis and his sister had been sent from London to rusticate in the country and would not be back again that Season. Darcy received a painstaking—though blatantly insincere—apology, penned by Mr Parvis, which he passed on to the young ladies. Georgiana was glad to be rid of him and hoped she would not have to encounter him again during the next Season.

It was not long before they received another apology. Gatley called on each of the Miss Darcys, with his cousin in tow. Channing entered the house in Berkley Square with bowed head and a sheepish appearance, not at all his usual carefree self.

"I hope you will believe me when I say I never expected this to happen," he said to Georgiana. "I thought I was doing Miss Clarissa a favour. I know she has a passion for oriental artefacts. I believed I was providing her with a guide who knew the collection better than anyone else. I never thought for a moment that he would possibly behave so badly. Granted, I did not know Parvis well, and so I was wrong to have entrusted him with your care, but you can be sure that I would never have deliberately put you in such a position."

He was so repentant and seemed so genuinely distressed that Georgiana assured him that she did not hold the incident against him.

"Fortunately," she said, "and thanks to your cousin's intervention, all is well that ends well. Let us put the whole thing behind us and hope that nothing of this kind will occur in the future."

Channing assured her that he had learned his lesson well. Soon afterwards he departed with his cousin, some of his old devil-may-care attitude restored.

Georgiana wished they could have stayed, for she had been so involved with Channing's apology that she had hardly spoken to Gatley, though not a moment had passed when she had not longed to go over and be at his side.

Meanwhile London was abuzz with activity. The decorations and victory celebrations added to the usual air of frantic activity. The Season passed its zenith and began to wane, but the crowds gave no sign of diminishing. News of Napoleon's surrender reached England, and everyone waited to hear Napoleon's fate. Rumours grew that he was to be confined in the Tower of London.

The rounds of parties and routs continued, indifferent to the outcome. As they followed each other relentlessly, the boundary between one event and the other began to blur in Georgiana's mind, except for those in which she was able to spend time with Gatley.

Then word arrived that Napoleon was being held in a ship off the coast of England: the HMS *Bellerophon*. It was not long before the location of the ship became widely known and flocks of people headed in the direction of Plymouth.

The young ladies, naturally, wanted to have the privilege of seeing the imprisoned Emperor but could convince no one to take them. The Darcy gentlemen both disapproved of his treatment and considered that keeping him on board a ship for all and sundry to come and gape at him eroded any dignity he still had.

Certainly Napoleon played to the crowd, for it was rumoured that he made a regular appearance on deck every day at half past six. Not contented, however, with his official appearance, hundreds of ships sailed by the *Bellerophon* daily hoping to see more of the famous figure. It was even said that he stood long enough on deck for artists to produce paintings of him.

Since neither Caroline nor Elizabeth showed the least interest in a sighting either, Georgiana and Clarissa resigned themselves to missing the grandest event of the century, though not without numerous complaints.

One such complaint was addressed to Gatley, with very fortunate results. It appeared that Mrs Gatley at least was not immune to the Napoleon vogue and was, in fact, very eager to set eyes on him herself. There was no time to be lost. There was already discussion about moving him to an unknown location, and any delay could jeopardize their chances.

Reaching the coast, however, proved to be a considerable struggle, with every conceivable mode of transportation being used to convey people towards the sea. And when they arrived there, they feared it was all for nought, for there was no boat to be had anywhere.

"Let us stay on the beach," said Gatley. "Perhaps something will turn up unexpectedly."

As luck would have it, they encountered a single-toothed old fisherman who had just come in early for the day.

The old fisherman, however, was not at all eager to set out again. He muttered that his missus was expecting him, and that he'd already been out and come back and why should he set out again? Even Gatley's very excessive offer—at least worth a week's fishing—did not tempt him. He was determined to be stubborn. He had come in early because he wanted to go home.

In the end it was Clarissa—coaxing most insistently—who got him to agree.

"You're just like my granddaughter," he said. "She has that same wild look about her. And she won't stop asking."

At the end he agreed to take them out, but as he went about his work, he grumbled about all the people who had come to see Napoleon. "They're obstructing us poor folks," he said. "How are we supposed to get out and fish when the sea's full of boats?"

The boat stank of fish. Gatley concealed his amusement as Georgiana came on board. The stench must have reached her even before she came aboard, yet she stepped in as if she was walking into a perfumed garden. Not for the first time, he admired her self-possession. She revealed nothing at all, not even the faintest twitch of her nose.

Clarissa, however, was not so circumspect. "Ugh! I had no idea fish could smell so foul."

His mother, too, expressed herself candidly. "Could we have not rented something a little better smelling?"

"I do not know what you are referring to, Mother. What could be better than the salt tang of the sea, the restorative essence of seaweed, and the healthy fragrance of sea-creatures from the depth of the ocean?"

"I can think of a lot of things," replied his mother. "Still, I suppose we must sacrifice if we are to see Napoleon himself."

There were no seats in the boat. They were obliged to stand. Gatley drew closer to Georgiana, and the two of them stood side to side, the wind blowing into their faces.

Georgiana loved the feel of the wind on her face. She made a half-hearted attempt to shelter herself against the sun, then put down her parasol as the wind threatened to tear it from her grip. It was the first time she had been to the coast in many years—not since the disaster at Ramsgate.

She waited for the usual dull ache which she always felt when she thought of that place, but there was nothing. She was so astonished she did not even notice they had started to move, and she had to cling to the side to steady herself.

The ache was gone. Exhilarated, she watched the shore recede behind them.

"I love the sea!" she exclaimed and laughed, and the others, capturing her mood, laughed as well as the boat set out and the waves splashed against the sides, spraying them with droplets of sea foam.

"This is far better than rowing on the river," she said, turning to Gatley. Their gazes connected.

"Although I think it very likely that you will soak your stockings again." His eyes were brimming with secret amusement.

Odious man! He had noticed the stockings after all. She should have been shocked, but instead she grinned back at him.

"I have leather boots, this time," she replied.

She thought he said "too bad," in an undertone, but she could not be sure, for they had reached a large gathering. There must have been hundreds of boats there, all jostling for position.

They slowed down as the fisherman tried to squeeze through the crowd. Some skilful manoeuvring brought them in closer, at least as close as they could possibly get.

The name of the ship loomed in front of them: BELLEROPHON.

Mrs Gatley peered through the telescope they had bought at an exorbitant price from an enterprising vendor on the beach.

"I see someone with a commanding presence—oh, no, he is dressed in a British naval uniform. Perhaps he is Captain Maitland." She moved the telescope to the right. "Someone is coming on deck. I can't see him properly…"

"The Emperor himself…"

"'Tis Boney…"

Awed whispers, raucous shouts, hissing, and cheering came from various boats.

"Why are they cheering?" asked Georgiana, wondering who would want to cheer such a monster.

"He has his followers, even here," replied Gatley. "There are many who see him as a hero."

"He *is* a hero." said Clarissa. "In Boston there are many who see him as a champion of democracy and freedom."

Gatley raised his brows. "He had his chance as ruler, and if he did practise democracy and freedom, it must have been of a very strange kind. He certainly did not deal with his opposition very fairly."

"I can see him now," said Mrs Gatley, urgently, interrupting the argument and peering intently through the telescope.

Everyone wanted a turn at the telescope now. It passed from

hand to hand, each one worried that Napoleon would disappear before they had a chance to behold him. But at the end everyone was able to observe him perfectly well.

Napoleon Bonaparte, who never lost an opportunity to play to the crowd, appeared on the deck looking every bit the Emperor. Every eye was upon him.

Georgiana had expected to be disappointed. But instead, she was full of awe.

"So that is what a Grand Entrance is supposed to be about," she said to Clarissa later. "I wish you had told me. I was doing it all wrong."

Clarissa laughed. "You no longer need to know about Grand Entrances, Georgiana. Your season is over, and you have found your match."

Georgiana, who still had had no definite indication of affection from Gatley, shook her head. "Do not reach conclusions too quickly, Clarissa. Nothing is certain yet. I am not even sure of my own feelings, let alone Gatley's."

It was possible that he cared for her. Certainly, he was showing her a great deal of attention. But she had been mistaken before, and she would not make the same mistake again.

That night, as Georgiana fell asleep, in those magical moments between waking and sleeping, her mind was filled with many things: the gentle water lapping at the sides of the boat, the stench of fish, Napoleon imprisoned in a ship, and Gatley, his dark eyes regarding her tenderly. A sense of peace came over her and she sank into it, surrendering to that quiet joy.

All was well. Nothing bad could happen anymore.

A few days later, as Georgiana and Clarissa were trimming their hats at Robert Darcy's home, a letter was brought in addressed to Clarissa. Clarissa opened the letter, looked over it quickly, then folded it and set it aside.

This did not escape Robert, who interrupted a consultation he was having with Caroline concerning the estate, to quiz his sister.

"You have received a letter, I see," he said. "I wonder who could have sent you one? And why you hide it so guiltily? Do you think she has a secret beau, Caroline?"

"Hush," said Caroline. "You know it would be most improper for her to receive a letter from a gentleman. You should not jest about such matters. You do know, Clarissa, that to receive such a letter, and to answer it, would be tantamount to an engagement? I only say this because you may not know it."

"Yes, I do know it," said Clarissa. "It is not from a gentleman." She sought wildly in her mind for a way to divert their attention. "It is from an old school friend of mine in Boston, who has been sent here to visit her relations."

"Really?" said Robert with interest. "Do I know her family?"

Clarissa, caught in her own trap, decided evasion was the best answer. "You need not pretend you know all my school friends. You never showed any interest in such details. You were always too busy with the business."

One of the most powerful tools of manipulation devised by the human race is guilt. It can always be relied upon to divert unwanted attention from oneself. This moment was no exception. Qualms of conscience immediately descended upon Robert, and he put his hand to his neck to loosen his cravat.

"Did I really neglect you so much?" he asked.

Clarissa, feeling the stirrings of that same sentiment, laughed.

"No, no, you need not worry. One cannot expect a gentleman to stay at home and attend to his sisters, after all."

Leaving him to ponder that, she rose from the table and signalled to Georgiana.

"Shall we go upstairs?" said Clarissa.

Georgiana, who was in the middle of some rather delicate ruffing, was reluctant to put it down. But a warning glance from her cousin prompted her to rise quickly.

"There must be something in that letter," said Robert. "I would dearly like to know what this old school friend of yours has to say."

"I am sure you would be very bored by it—I never knew you were interested in gossip."

Robert raised an eyebrow. "It depends on the gossip."

Caroline threw her a shrewd glance. "As long as it not from a gentleman, I am sure it will not be of any interest to us," she said calmly. "Cease this game of cat and mouse, Robert. Girls will be girls, after all."

Clarissa took this opportunity to leave the room, dragging Georgiana behind her. She practically ran up the stairs. Georgiana followed, trying to puzzle out who could have sent the letter. An idea sudden sprang to her mind.

"Do not tell me you have heard from Mr Parker?" she said, in an excited whisper.

"I wish," said Clarissa, her face crumpling. "Now *that* would be news worth having!"

"Then what—" Clarissa pulled her into the room and shut the door, leaning heavily against it.

"You will never guess who sent it."

"Of course I will never guess," said Georgiana, who was tired of all this suspense. "Can you not tell me without making a big show of it?"

Clarissa, who would have enjoyed tormenting her cousin, gave in reluctantly.

"If you insist, I suppose I must tell you." She took out the letter and held it out to Georgiana. "It is from your cousin."

"Colonel Fitzwilliam?"

"No, of course not!" Unable to keep the secret to herself any longer, she handed over the letter. "'Tis from Anne. Anne de Bourgh."

Georgiana stared at the letter, stunned.

"What does she say? Quick, let us read it."

"You may read it aloud," replied Clarissa. "It is addressed to the two of us."

Georgiana unfolded the letter nervously.

Dear Cousins,

I am sending you this letter to inform you that I have taken up a teaching position in a school, under the name of Mrs Williams. You may wonder that I took such a drastic step and that I should have aspired to such a lowly situation. I can assure you, however, that I have never been happier in my life.

I have wanted to write to you for some time now, to thank you for your kindness during your visit to Rosings. It meant a great deal to me to have you to talk to.

I beg of you to keep this letter a secret and to conceal the information from everyone else. You know the consequences very well if anyone were to discover where I am. However, if you could find some way to visit me some day at a future date, I would be glad to receive you. I am at Mrs Saunders's Academy for Girls in Richmond.

Annabelle Williams

"Is that all she has to say?" said Georgiana, tossing the letter down in disgust. "When everyone has been consumed with anxiety about her? And she wishes us to keep it a secret? Does she not intend to inform even her mother?"

Clarissa nodded. "That was exactly what I thought when you first started reading the letter. But if you think about it, what choice does she have? If she informed Lady Catherine, do you think her ladyship would allow her only child—an heiress to a large fortune—to teach in a school? You know she would not."

"We have to tell my brother at least. He needs to know the truth, after all the effort he has been through to discover her whereabouts."

"It is better for him to think she is in Philadelphia. Then he will think her out of his reach," said Clarissa. "Besides, she has written to us in confidence. We cannot betray that confidence. It is a matter of honour."

"Honour is for gentlemen," said Georgiana, "not for us."

Clarissa threw her a disdainful look. "Perhaps, but I would not betray one of your secrets, not for anything. We may not use such grandiose names, but we have our own form of honour nevertheless."

"But to keep my brother in the dark—"

"I wish to God I had not shown you the letter, Georgiana! I did not think that you would give preference to your brother over a young woman who has asked for our help."

Georgiana closed her eyes. She too wished she had not seen the letter. She would have preferred not to have the burden of this knowledge, for what good was it to know the truth?

The more she thought of it, the more she grew disturbed by the whole situation. Why would Anne wish to become a teacher, when she had a fortune at her disposal? It did not make sense. And why had she booked a passage to Philadelphia, when she was not planning to go there at all?

Something was not right. Someone else was involved. Someone who had pretended to be Anne and booked the passage on the packet boat. Even now, for all they knew, Anne was being held under duress—perhaps even forced to get married. The letter was yet another ruse to convince them Anne was safe.

Georgiana had to know the truth. If she was really at this girls' Academy, then good. But suppose she was not? They had to go and see her.

Surprisingly, her cousin was not convinced of this at all.

"You are going too far now, Georgiana. Your suppositions make no sense at all. You must admit that imagination is not your strong point. You have conjured up a convoluted story that will convince no one. Not even *I* think that she is being held under duress. I think she has provided us with a perfectly rational explanation."

"There is nothing rational about an heiress wishing to teach a school full of spoilt girls who have nothing in their heads but to make trouble. *You* have not been to a school here. I have. I know what they are like."

"I have been to a school in Boston. I imagine all schools for young ladies are very much the same. Tell me. Why would she not wish to teach? It is a noble profession."

"Perhaps. I do not mean to cast any aspersions on teaching. I just cannot imagine someone as delicately reared as Anne *choosing* to be at the beck and call of a mean, selfish brood of young ladies."

"*You* were at such a school, and I am sure you were not mean or selfish. In any case, it is unlikely she would be teaching the daughters of the affluent members of society. There would always be the risk of discovery in that. She must have chosen a charity school, and she may feel she is doing some good in the world by helping girls less fortunate than she is. It is not impossible." She looked at Georgiana's miserable face. "Not all people are content to be idle, Georgiana. My father left a life of idleness behind him when he went to the United States, and I can assure you he never regretted it."

Georgiana pondered over this for some time.

"I cannot help feeling uneasy."

"I have heard nothing else since I read you the letter, Georgiana. I do not know how you can be harping on the same thing all the time when you have far more interesting things happening to you. I have noticed Mr Gatley paying court to you. What do you intend to do about it? Do you plan to accept him if he proposes?"

The blood rushed to Georgiana's face. It was true that Mr Gatley had been particularly attentive.

"He has not proposed, so I do not wish to think about it yet," she replied, embarrassed. "But you need not think to distract me that way. It does not mean I should not be concerned about Anne."

"Very well, then," said Clarissa. "I can see that you will not be contented until you have discovered the truth about her. In that case, I have an idea. We will go to see her in Richmond. It will kill two birds with one stone. You can spend time with Mr Gatley, and at the same time, you can assure yourself of Anne's safety."

"But we cannot tell Mr Gatley about Anne."

"No, obviously not," replied Clarissa.

A few minutes of concentrated effort produced a plan. They would tell Mr Gatley that Clarissa had received a letter from a school friend of hers from Boston who had married an Englishman beneath her station and that she would like to see her, to be sure that she was faring well.

"It is close enough to the truth, isn't it?"

Georgiana hesitated.

"I do not like this whole idea, Clarissa. We will have to lie, not only to our families, but to Mr Gatley as well. And what will Mr Gatley think?"

"He will not approve, but he will do it for your sake."

"But how will we contrive it?"

"Leave it to me. I will think of something."

One can always find plenty of reasons to do something one should not do. Georgiana, who knew very well that they were embarking on a foolhardy endeavour, soon convinced herself that there really was no harm in it at all. What could possibly go wrong, after all?

❦

Thus they found themselves once again setting out without a chaperone. They could not bring a maid, for fear that she should reveal something about Anne's whereabouts. There could not be the smallest hint of a whisper to indicate that Anne was still in England. The presence of a groom, then, had to be sufficient.

So there they were, in carriage, in the company of a single gentleman. Mr Gatley had not quite approved of the arrangement and deemed it more proper to ride on top with the coachman. He had been led to believe that Clarissa was visiting an old school friend of hers who had married unwisely and of whom her family disapproved. Georgiana hoped the clear weather would hold and that he would not be obliged to ride outside in the rain.

It was a short trip in any case. By the end of the day, they would be back—having spoken to Anne and assured themselves of her safety—and no one would be any wiser.

But fate has a way of intervening just when one least wishes it. In their case, fate took the form of a large but hidden pothole in the road.

The carriage lurched suddenly as the wheels teetered over the edge of gaping nothingness and slid into it. Clarissa was thrown roughly against Georgiana. For a few tense moments they were certain they would overturn.

They did not.

The carriage righted itself. The ladies disentangled themselves from each other, straightened the objects that had tumbled about with them, and returned to their places. They laughed in relief. But instead of continuing along the way, the carriage remained obstinately still.

"What has happened?" said Clarissa, opening the door.

She instantly slammed the door shut again.

"What is it?" said Georgiana, alarmed.

"Don't look," said Clarissa, pushing her back into the carriage.

Georgiana turned deathly white. "Have we—? Did we run over someone?"

Clarissa cast her head back against the squabs and shut her eyes.

"Answer me!" repeated Georgiana.

Clarissa, who had now recovered from the initial shock, jumped up again. "We have to help him!" she said, urgently.

"Help whom?"

Clarissa was already out of the door.

Georgiana's heart thudded violently as she realised the truth. She stumbled out of the carriage, terrified to have her worst fears confirmed.

Gatley was lying in a muddy patch by the wayside. There was blood on his head, and he was unnaturally still.

She stood, staring helplessly at him.

"Is he—?"

The coachman and the groom were leaning over him. They looked up when they heard her.

"No need to worry, Miss Darcy," said the coachman. "He's alive. Though he's had a right knock on the head. Head wounds always look worse than they really are though."

Georgiana, weak with relief, drew closer. She crouched down next to him. Slowly, she ran her hand across his cheek. He was so unlike himself, so unmoving and pale.

Clarissa crouched next to her, and put her arm around her shoulder.

"If you don't mind, we'll carry him and lay him in the carriage," said the coachman.

His words brought to her the awareness that she ought to be in control of the situation. She stood up decisively. He was alive, and he needed help. That was the important thing now.

"Yes, yes," she said. "We should get him home as quickly as possible."

"If you don't mind, Miss Darcy, it might be better not to rattle him too much."

"Of course not," said Georgiana, pursing her lips together in thought. "I remember passing an inn not too long ago. It cannot be more than a few minutes down the road. We can take him there, and we can send for a physician."

"Yes, miss, The King's Arms," said the coachman.

Gatley did not recover consciousness, despite the inevitable commotion involved in being picked up by the groom and the coachman and deposited on the seat inside. In the shadows of the carriage, his pallor was all the more apparent. He was so inert, Georgiana put her ear to his chest half a dozen times to assure herself he was still breathing.

At The King's Arms, which she discovered with some relief to be a reputable-looking place, she requested a bedchamber and a private parlour. The innkeeper, a red-faced man called Ned, took in the situation at a glance and sent for a physician immediately.

The physician, Mr Blaine, had little to say. He bandaged the head wound and assured the young ladies when he returned to the private parlour that the wound itself was not worrisome.

"But we do not know what impact the blow may have had inside. Head wounds are not always predictable," said Mr Blaine. "I shall return later to ascertain whether he has recovered consciousness. I have instructed the coachman to send for me immediately under certain circumstances—particularly if there is bleeding from the nose or ears. We shall have to wait and see."

Georgiana thanked the physician and instructed him to leave his particulars with the footman, who would arrange for payment later.

As soon as he departed, Georgiana turned to Clarissa, her brows knitted with worry.

"We cannot stay here, Clarissa. We need to leave as soon as possible." She twisted her fingers together. "I am consumed with worry, knowing we are alone at a public inn so close to London. Any of our acquaintances could run into us here."

"Leave?" said Clarissa. "How could you think of such a thing? Will you abandon him to total strangers?"

"He would not be alone. The coachman—Oskins, he said his name was—will remain with him. He seems very loyal to Mr Gatley. And the physician will attend to him later."

"And how did you intend to return without the coachman?"

"We could leave the groom behind…" But even as she said it she knew they would not do such a thing.

She exhaled loudly. "If we must stay, then, you must promise me that you will not under any circumstances undertake to nurse him."

Clarissa made an impatient gesture of protest, but Georgiana persisted.

"It will be bad enough if someone were to discover us alone in this hostel with a gentleman who is not related to us. It would be infinitely worse, however, for us to be discovered alone in this gentleman's bed chamber."

"But he is injured. He is in no condition to make advances to us of any sort. What could be more absurd?"

"Society does not care a fig for that. All they would care about is the delicious flavour of scandal." She gave a humourless smile. "If you broke this rule, not even your exotic status as an American would save you."

"What foolish, foolish rules these are! Who then is to take care of him? Are we to entrust his care to a stranger?"

Georgiana sat silently looking at her hands. "I am sorry to say this, Clarissa, but I think we had better send for our brothers," said Georgiana. "We may be obliged to spend the night."

She expected Clarissa to argue, but her cousin gave a resigned shrug.

"How do you mean to explain our being here?"

"We will have time to think of something," said Georgiana.

"However much it goes against the grain for me," said Clarissa, slowly, "I admit that we have no choice. Even *I* know that our situation here is impossible."

A message was sent out. But try as they would, they could come up with no foolproof explanation of why they were there.

When Darcy and Robert arrived, there was going to be trouble.

Chapter 25

GATLEY AWOKE WITH A TERRIBLE HEADACHE. HE STARED around him in astonishment, trying to regain his bearings. The room was small, equipped simply with a large chest, a cupboard, an armchair, and the large canopied bed he was lying in. For a moment he remembered…nothing. His only certainty was that he had never been in this chamber before.

He sat up slowly. The blood in his head beat a quick rhythm, like a drum. Or were there drums outside? He put a hand to his head. His fingers found the rough linen of a bandage.

He must have been wounded in the fighting. But if so, why was he then in a room and not in a tent? What on earth was going on? Was he so badly wounded that they had taken him to England? That was not very likely.

He sat up very carefully. Head wounds could be tricky, as he knew from some of the men who had been injured before him. They were unpredictable. One could seem perfectly well, then be suddenly struck with dizziness and fall to the ground. He had no intention of compounding his injury by falling. He swung his legs down from the edge of the bed and looked out of the narrow window. The scene that met his eyes did not look like Portugal or Spain. It was like England.

He stood up carefully. His window overlooked a courtyard that was most definitely English, to judge by the timbering and gables.

A carriage thundered into the courtyard. Two gentlemen—not soldiers—descended and headed swiftly towards the inn. Mr Darcy and Mr Robert Darcy.

The names brought back everything. He remembered the carriage teetering as they struck a pothole. There had been an accident. His memory did not supply him with more information. What had happened? Why were the Darcy gentlemen looking so grim? Had something happened to Miss Darcy? Was Miss Clarissa injured?

He swung round quickly. Stars flashed in front of him. He clung to the bed post until the stars stopped twirling.

"Steady now," he said to himself.

He had to know. Sharp talons of anxiety gripped him and dug into him.

He made his way down the stairs slowly. Every now and then the stars reappeared and he had to stop and lean against the wall. Finally, he found himself in front of a closed door and recognised Darcy's voice.

He strained every muscle in his body to listen. Miss Darcy's voice reached him. He closed his eyes and leaned against the door as relief washed over him.

She was safe.

Then he felt tremendously guilty for thinking only of her. There were others who could have been harmed—Miss Clarissa or the coachman or the groom. But the talons that had torn at him lifted.

"It is not what you think," said Miss Clarissa's voice.

Miss Clarissa was safe too. Again, the relief weakened him, and he sagged further against the door.

He had not been listening to what they were saying until now. He had only listened for their voices. But now the voices resolved themselves into words, then into meaning.

"And you—you would do better not to say anything," said Darcy. "How can your sense of propriety be so twisted that you can sneak off to an assignation in a public inn! Have you no sense of behaviour at all? Robert—is it possible that your sister can be so completely without propriety?" Robert seemed to have nothing to say about the matter. "One can make allowance for your ignorance of our customs, Madam, but this is beyond enough. To set up a secret meeting with Mr Channing, and to arrange for Mr Gatley to bring you here—"

He saw stars again. But these stars were different. They came along with the roaring in his ears as the blood rushed up to his head.

He had heard quite enough. He stood upright, his strength returning to him with his anger. How dare they involve him in this sordid affair! How dare Georgiana use him in this way? And Channing too! The drumming in his head turned into heavy hammering.

He most definitely had something to say.

⁂

The door flew open. Gatley stood in the doorway, looking ghastly under the white bandage but otherwise unharmed.

Georgiana's delight at seeing him safe overcame all else, and she jumped up with a cry of delight.

"You are recovered, Mr Gatley! Oh, I am so very glad."

"Good evening to you all. Miss Darcy, Miss Clarissa, Mr Darcy, Mr Robert Darcy." His face was tight and pinched, his eyes drawn.

Georgiana reflected that he still looked very ill, though there was something in his eyes that made her uneasy.

"I hope you did not sustain a serious injury," replied Darcy coldly.

"I am quite recovered, as you can see," said Gatley in clipped tones.

"Then perhaps I should ask you to give an accounting of your behaviour? Is this something you agreed upon with the young ladies' knowledge, or did you and your cousin set up this assignation without their knowledge?"

"I could ask you out for such a question," said Gatley, cold as ice.

"I accept. Name your seconds," replied Darcy in clipped tone.

"Stop!" said Georgiana.

"Do not interfere in matters that do not concern ladies," said Darcy.

"I will, and I shall interfere," said Georgiana. "Before you decide to pull down those swords from over the fireplace there, may I have a word with you in private, Brother?"

"You may not. I have nothing to say to you."

"Then may I speak with Mr Gatley?"

"Certainly not alone," replied Mr Darcy. "Have you not broken enough rules already?"

"Fitz," said Robert, "perhaps there is another explanation…"

"Kindly stay out of this, Robert."

"I *will* speak with Mr Gatley," said Georgiana, desperation lending her strength. "Really, Brother, I never thought you could be so *foolish*. Would I have sent for you if I had planned a secret assignation in an inn?" Satisfied that she had scored a point and that it had thrown him off for at least a few minutes, she left the room and reappeared a few minutes later with a chambermaid.

"Amy here will be present when I talk to Mr Gatley." She nodded at him. "May I speak to you?"

324

It was very clear that Mr Gatley had no desire to talk to her at all. She waited, her hands twisting together behind her back.

"Well?"

He gave a curt nod and followed her to a small side room, a storage room in some disarray, full of barrels and boxes and all kinds of discarded objects. She waited for Amy to enter, then shut the door.

"I do not believe we have anything to say to one another," said Gatley, not giving her the chance to say a word. "You have deceived me, Miss Darcy, and manipulated me. There can be nothing you can say to me that will change that. What explanation could you possibly have for misleading me—nay, deliberately deceiving me? When I specifically asked you if you had your family's approval? And to think that you have taken advantage of me in this matter— to do what? To set up an assignation with my cousin and his friends? In spite of what you have seen of them? What is it about my cousin that is so alluring?" He stopped and leaned on the wall, burying his head under his arms, too overcome to continue. Georgiana, still unable to believe the stream of accusations he was throwing at her, observed him coldly. If that was what he believed, then she hoped he would suffer miserably.

By and by he stood up straight again. "And to think that you made me a part of it! What did he do? Did he ask you to bring me along? Did you intend to laugh with him about how gullible I am?"

Georgiana, who had brought Gatley here to try and reason with him, stared at him impassively.

"To put me in such a situation that I appear to have conspired with Channing to bring you here!"

He turned away towards the doorway, then swung round to throw one last accusation at her.

"By God! And I thought I could trust you! But I should have known that you were too much under your cousin's sway, too weak and too lacking in spirit to oppose her."

Earlier, when she had demanded this interview, her only concern had been a desperate attempt to put a halt to his quarrel with her brother before it went too far, for once a duel had been set up, there could be no backing out of it. She had not planned anything. She had no idea what she would say to him, nor did she have any excuse to give him. The only possible way out of the mess was to tell him about Anne, and she could not. She was honour bound not to tell him, and she could not betray her cousin, even for the sake of his pride. Anne's whole life was in her hands.

But she could not stand by and allow him to spew out all these accusations without responding at all. At least she would disprove his last sentence.

She went and stood against the door. She would not let him leave until she had had *her* say.

"I cannot tell you my reason for being here," she said icily. "It is perfectly innocent, even if you will not believe that. But it is a secret nevertheless, and it must remain a secret. I can only ask you to trust me when I tell you that nothing improper was intended. Beyond that, I will leave it to you to search deep enough inside yourself to recognise whether I could possibly be guilty of the things you accuse me of."

Gatley was not so enraged as to be incapable of considering her words.

"I can believe, possibly, that you are not guilty of anything improper yourself," he said, "but can you say the same of your cousin? I have seen the way she flirts with my cousin. It does not take much skill to realise there is something between them. And I am convinced that your affection for your cousin blinds you to her faults. You allow yourself to be guided entirely by her. We have previous proof of this. I have allowed for your inexperience in the past, and excused your behaviour by accepting that your motivation—your affection for her—is at least pure. But I am afraid that this time you have gone too far. There can be no excuse now."

Georgiana felt as though an iron hand had fallen upon her and was squeezing her ribs, stifling the very breath from her lungs.

"You have accused me, tried me, judged me, and found me guilty, all in the space of a few minutes. Is this then your opinion of me? Is this your reaction when the finger of blame is pointed at me? Is this, then, the value of your friendship? If others cast stones at me, you join them in casting stones?" The iron hand tightened. She could hardly breathe. "You and your cousin both passed judgement on me when we first met, and nothing I have said or done since then has made the least bit of difference. Fortunately, I care nothing for the opinion of Mr Channing. Nor do I care for yours. Go, then," she said, moving away from the door to let him past. "You are absolutely right. We have nothing we can say to each other."

She clasped her hands together tightly behind her back, willing him to leave at once, before she said something she would come to regret. She had hoped somehow to appeal to his sense of fairness at least. But she should have known better. For what was it that Channing had said of him when they had first met? He had said his cousin was too apt to judge others and find them lacking. Well, here was the proof.

Gatley gave the tiniest bow, and sweeping past her, opened the door, and was gone.

As if her confrontation with Gatley was not enough, she returned to the private parlour to find Darcy waiting for her.

"So, Georgiana. What do you have to say for yourself?"

The icy calm that had sustained her through her encounter with Mr Gatley now abandoned her. She crossed the room and threw herself into the armchair that stood by the fire, exhausted beyond caring. Too much had happened that day.

"Well?" said Darcy.

"Ease off, for heaven's sake, Darcy," said Robert. "They have been through an accident. We can deal with this issue later, when tempers have calmed down a little."

"Thank you, Robert, but I do not need your advice on how to deal with my sister."

"And I would thank you, Darcy, not to deal with mine."

The two men's eyes locked. Neither of them was prepared to back down. Any moment now, Georgiana was convinced, they too would challenge each other to a duel.

"Devil take it!" said Georgiana, jumping up, her patience in shreds. The two men were so taken aback they turned immediately towards her. "If you will kindly sit down, both of you, then I will tell you what is going on."

"No, Georgiana!" exclaimed Clarissa.

"We have no choice but to reveal the truth," said Georgiana. "Do you want them to kill each other?"

Clarissa slumped down onto her chair, and leaning her elbows on the table in front of her, propped up her head in her hands as if her head had become too heavy.

The gentlemen had at first been reluctant to follow Georgiana's demand. Now they were too intrigued to consider refusing.

Georgiana, with all eyes on her now, wondered if she was doing the right thing. She held the fate of another woman's future in her hands. What if her brother decided to drag Anne back to Rosings? Could she really be the one responsible for such a terrible thing?

She swallowed, licked her lips, and uttered a small prayer that she was not about to do the most terrible thing in her life.

"I—" She stopped. She could not do it. She shook her head.

"I am sorry. Clarissa is right. I cannot tell you the truth. You may judge me as you see fit, and I will take the consequences, but I cannot say anything."

A sigh of relief reached her from the table—Clarissa, at least, applauded her decision. That would have to be enough.

"You are playing games, Georgiana," said Darcy, his temper snapping. "Very well, if you will not tell the truth, then I will deal with the matter as I see fit."

Georgiana bowed her head. "That is what I thought." *She* knew that she had done no wrong. *She* knew that she was not guilty of misconduct. That was good enough.

"Very well, so be it," said Darcy, thwarted enough to become unwise. "I will have to demand that you remove from London and go to Pemberley immediately. Your Season will have to be curtailed until next year."

Georgiana nodded. What did it matter in any case? This Season had brought her nothing but misery. She had nothing to keep her in London.

"But why should Georgiana be punished?" said Clarissa "None of it was her fault at all."

"If you are so concerned about Georgiana, perhaps *you* are ready to tell us what has transpired?" said Darcy in clipped tones. "You would not wish her to be punished for something that *you* were guilty of, would you?"

"Back off, Darcy," said Robert. "I cannot prevent you from talking to your sister like that, but I will not allow you to do so with mine."

Darcy turned his back and stalked to the window.

"Clarissa?" said Robert kindly. "It seems to me that this is all about some small thing that has been blown out of proportion. Are you sure that your secret is so dire that you cannot tell it? I know that you have a tendency to exaggerate and to prefer the dramatic over the mundane. Perhaps your secret is not so very important. Surely it cannot hold anyone's life in the balance."

Clarissa looked helplessly at Georgiana.

"It is not my secret to tell," she replied.

Darcy swirled round. "All this talk is getting us nowhere. It is not Georgiana's secret to tell, nor is it your secret to tell. Whose secret is it then? By God! Have we not had enough of mysteries, with Anne's disappearance, and now—" He stopped, and something flashed into his face. "Does this have anything to do with Anne?"

The mingled expressions of horror, guilt, and relief on their faces were enough to tell him he had found his answer.

"Good heavens, is that all? Why did you not say so?" said Robert, and he began to laugh.

"It is no laughing matter," said Georgiana. "It is Anne's life we are talking about."

"But what could it possibly have to do with Anne?" said Darcy. "She is in America."

Georgiana sighed and exchanged glances with Clarissa, who shrugged helplessly.

"Since you have guessed that it is about Anne, you will soon guess the rest. But I will reveal nothing unless I have your word of honour—both of you—that you will not attempt to force Anne to return home."

"Do you think me such a tyrant, Georgiana?" said Darcy.

Georgiana lifted her brow cynically.

"Your word, Brother."

"You have it."

"And you, Robert."

"Of course."

"And that you will tell no one at all of this—not even Elizabeth or Caroline."

"You are making me quite nervous with this talk," said Robert with an uneasy laugh. "You cannot really expect me to keep secrets from Caroline."

"This is not your secret to share or not to share. I need your word of honour, cousin Robert, or I cannot speak."

"You have it, Georgie. I give my word of honour not to speak of it to anyone."

Georgiana nodded. "Fitzwilliam?"

"I cannot say I am happy with it, but I give you my word of honour."

"Then I will tell you where we were going when we met with the accident. We were going to visit cousin Anne."

"All this time, we have been searching...!" exclaimed Darcy.

"No!" said Clarissa. "Why is everyone so very ready to jump to false conclusions? We did not know until recently."

Robert nodded. "I knew there was something fishy about that letter you received."

Georgiana, satisfied now that she would be heard, launched into an explanation of what they had learned from Anne's letter.

By the end, both Robert and Darcy looked grave.

"I cannot say I approve your conduct," said Darcy. "But I agree that your options were limited."

"In all fairness, I can understand how the whole situation came about. But the question is, what do we do now?"

"We must go and see Anne."

"But you cannot!" said Clarissa. "Oh, how could you shame me so? What will she think of me?"

"She will think badly of you and will know better than to trust you again," said Darcy. "But that is of little import, compared to the need to verify that she is safe."

Clarissa was not happy with this remark, but no one could deny the truth of it. It was decided, therefore, that they would spend the night at the inn—after sending home the news that the young ladies had suffered little more from the accident than a shake-up—and on the morrow would set out early to satisfy themselves as to Anne's safety.

❧

Georgiana was so angry at Mr Gatley that it did not even occur to her to wonder where he was. It was Darcy who rose abruptly and strode to the door.

"We have forgotten Mr Gatley! We must tell him that there has been a misunderstanding. I will explain to him what happened."

"He will be sharpening his dagger upstairs, no doubt," said Robert. "Be careful."

Clarissa giggled.

Darcy was not amused. "Must you turn every situation into a joke?" he said.

"Not every situation. Some are funnier than others," replied Robert.

"I'm sorry to say this, Fitzwilliam, but you cannot tell him the truth," said Georgiana heavily. "We cannot reveal anything at all about Anne. You gave your word."

"Then what do you propose to do? We cannot let him leave without an explanation. Georgiana, the things I accused him of were very grave—grave enough for him to challenge me to a duel. His name must be cleared."

Georgiana reflected that in turn, Mr Gatley had levelled some very grave accusations at *her*, and he had made no effort to clear *her* name. Let him think himself wronged. Let him ponder what it meant to be found guilty and judged without the smallest evidence. *She* did not care to relieve him of that burden, when he had not given a moment's consideration to *her*.

Whatever happened, she would make sure no one entrusted him with Anne's secret. She knew now she could not count on him. Very likely he would condemn Anne for hiding from her mother, and go straight to Lady Catherine to inform her. How could she believe in him when he had turned against her at the blink of an eye?

"You can inform him that you realised that the young ladies were telling the truth," said Robert, "and that I suddenly remembered the school friend that Clarissa had talked about. We could say that she had eloped with a British naval officer and that there was a large scandal attached to her, which was why Clarissa was visiting her in secret. I am sure there are any number of stories we could tell. None of them would reflect well on Clarissa, but they would be better than your wild accusations of secret assignations and some such."

Darcy gave a rueful sigh. "Anything would be better than that. And to think that I accused Mr Gatley—who is one of the most honourable men I know of—of being involved! I do not know how I will ever be able to look him in the eye again."

He sat down again. "Let us come up with a likely narrative then, which we can present to Gatley as soon as possible."

Georgiana, who had no interest in reconciliation, replied that any narrative was acceptable to her, as long as she was not expected to deliver it.

No sooner said than done. A story was agreed upon, and Mr Darcy set out to present it and to express his sincerest apologies.

A few minutes later, however, he returned. Gatley had already left.

※

Gatley did not know which was worse, the headache that clunked and squeaked inside his head like the springs of the carriage beneath him or the bitter bile that churned inside him, turning him physically sick. A part of him—the sensible part—told him he was not yet well enough to ride home. He really should not have left in such a hurry. The other part threw caution to the wind as the carriage tore down the road, wanting to put as much distance between himself and that cursed inn as possible.

They had played him for a fool—in more ways than one. To think that Darcy—who should have known better—had seen fit to reprimand him! And to be humiliated in that manner in public! To have his honour questioned! He had been prepared to fight a duel, for heaven's sake. It may yet come to that. A gentleman could not allow his honour to be brought into question so openly without consequences.

And then to find that no explanation was provided. When Miss Darcy had asked to speak to him, he had hoped that she would explain matters to him, that there was some reasonable way to account for what happened. Then he would at least be willing to swallow his pride at the insult and accept that the circumstances required prudence. For her, he would have been willing to do so.

But no! No explanation was forthcoming. No account was to be provided.

He had been met with evasion and duplicity. And when he had insisted on discovering the truth, what had he encountered? More accusations and scorn. And nothing but coldness from a young lady he had come to admire. He had been fooled by that innocent-looking face, but he should have known better.

Yet how could he have guessed that they would go so far as to set up an assignation in an inn and that he should have been duped into taking them there? And who would she be meeting with, pray, but his own cousin? He had seen her making eyes at no one else. He would never have thought things had progressed so far though. But Darcy himself had said so, and Darcy would not make accusations like this without good reason.

After this, his cousin would have to marry Clarissa, of course. His cousin had been nothing but trouble throughout this Season; broken promises and irresponsible behaviour galore. The three of them—Miss Darcy, Miss Clarissa, and Channing—had been the bane of his existence since he had come to London. It was always one or the other that was in trouble. Somehow, every time, he was expected to step in and rescue them from their own folly. As if they were mere children falling in scrapes!

They had to comprehend that they were adults and that no one was there to save them if they broke the rules. Well, now Channing had been hoist by his own petard. As had Clarissa. Darcy would never accept anything less than marriage.

Of course, he might never live to see the wedding. One of them would be hurt, at the very least, perhaps even killed, if there was a duel, and he did not think he could possibly kill Darcy. Not even after what his friend had said of him, though he deserved it.

He thought regretfully of Miss Darcy, and his heart—along with his head—throbbed with pain. He had made allowances before. He had apologised before and had meant every word of it. But one could not keep bending over backwards. There was such a thing as dignity and pride and honour.

This time she had gone too far, and there was no going back.

Chapter 26

IT WAS FAIRLY EASY TO FIND THE ACADEMY. AN ELDERLY MAID admitted the Darcys and preceded them through a long corridor to a back room that obviously served both as an office and a small classroom.

A tall lady of middle years was alone in the room, standing near a small chalkboard. She had sharp dark eyes, dark hair with strands of grey, and an air of quiet authority. She was dusting chalk from her hands when they entered, but as soon as they were announced, she looked up and went pale.

"Mr Darcy. Miss Darcy," she said. She acknowledged the other two by inclining her head.

Mr Darcy bowed to her tensely. "Mrs Saunders. I suppose I should have expected this."

Georgiana had some vague remembrance of a very kind lady who had been Anne's governess. "Mrs Saunders," she said. "I remember you."

"So you should, Miss Darcy. I picked you up and dusted your clothes a few times when you fell," said Mrs Saunders. She had already recovered from her shock at seeing them. She began to move to the door. "I suppose you are here to see Mrs Williams. I will fetch her for you." At the door she hesitated and half-turned. "I hope you are not here to take her away. She will not go with you, you know."

They waited for some time for Anne to appear. Tension filled the room. Darcy stood very tall, his face severe. Robert leaned against the wall, alert but ready to be amiable. The two young ladies watched the door anxiously.

No one recognised the young lady who entered the room. It would be an exaggeration to say that she walked in with a quick step, for she entered quite slowly. But her tread was firm, and her back straight. She had cropped the hair around her face and her hair hung down in loose ringlets. Her cheeks were rounded, and at present held a sharp tinge of scarlet.

"I wrote to you in the strictest confidence," she said severely, looking from Clarissa to Georgiana as if they were errant children.

Georgiana, addressed in this fashion, recovered from her astonishment at the change in her cousin and smiled happily at her.

"Oh, Anne! It is good to see you looking so well!" Impulsively, she went to her and threw her arms around her.

Anne, who had come prepared to fight, was placed at a disadvantage by this welcome.

"Thank you," she said, patting Georgiana on the back awkwardly.

"Well then," said Darcy, who was also thrown off balance by the startling change in her appearance. "I suppose we do not need to worry that you have been ill-treated."

"Ill-treated?" said Anne with a smile. "No, not at all. I have never been happier."

There was a moment of silence in which everyone digested this new information. It was Anne who finally broke the silence.

"I am sorry that I had to leave without a word to anyone. I hope it did not cause too much of an uproar."

"Miss de Bourgh—Mrs Williams—You can have no idea of the uproar your disappearance caused!" said Robert, who was leaning on the wall, watching the scene with an amused air.

"Mr Collins was convinced you had thrown yourself in the lake," said Georgiana, not at all amused, "and your mother was sure you had been kidnapped for ransom."

Anne put her hands to her face. "I never thought—it never occurred to me that such interpretations would have been placed on my behaviour. I thought it would have been clear to everyone—especially you, my young cousins—that I was unhappy and needed to leave. *You* understood that, surely?"

"I understood you were unhappy, but I never imagined that you had the—" Clarissa was about to say the strength, but realised it would hardly be tactful.

For a moment Anne looked liked the person they had known—frail and uncertain. She gave a small bitter laugh. "Courage? You could not imagine that I had the courage to leave, could you? But that was precisely why I had to leave. Because I had become nothing—just Anne, the weak, helpless cousin, Anne whom no one thought worthy of consideration, Anne who sat in the corner and kept quiet."

Georgiana wanted to disagree. She wanted to say it was untrue. But the truth stared her in the face, and to deny it would be a lie.

"Lady Catherine cast us out of her house and accused us of being responsible for your disappearance," said Clarissa.

Anne wrinkled her brow in puzzlement. "In what way responsible?"

"Well, we *did* encourage you to escape from Mrs Jenkinson," replied Clarissa staunchly, though why she would take Lady Catherine's part she could not imagine. "We *did* convince you to go on walks and to spend some time alone. Perhaps if we had not appeared on the scene, you may not have been encouraged to leave."

Anne stared at Clarissa in astonishment, and then began to laugh. "Oh, Clarissa, you cannot really believe that! Surely you cannot think the few exchanges we had were responsible for my disappearance." She shook her head at the absurdity.

"If I told you for how long I have planned this! How I have saved every penny I could without rousing the suspicions of either Mrs Jenkinson or Lady Catherine. How Mrs Saunders and I have made plans to open this school together for years, and how carefully I planned my route so I would not rouse suspicion. Clarissa, do not think me ungrateful for your attempts to help me, but really it is quite ridiculous to think you could have had anything to do with my disappearance. Your presence only provided me with the excuse I needed to cast off Mrs Jenkinson, and the distraction of so many people being around provided me with the opportunity to leave undetected. I have waited for such a distraction for *months*. It was very inconvenient for me, when my mother cast off Darcy because of his marriage. All my plans had to be delayed."

"In that case," said Darcy, who had come prepared for something entirely different and still have not quite recovered his bearings, "it would be quite useless to try to convince you to return home."

"Quite. You understand me, Cousin. I have no intention of returning, not when I had to work so hard to leave. And especially now that I know how much trouble you all went through because of my escape."

"Do you really think life as a teacher has more to offer you than life in the luxury of Rosings?" said Darcy persistently.

"Yes, for at least I will be serving some useful purpose."

"The novelty will fade," said Darcy gently, "and you will have burned your bridges. You will awaken one day to find yourself confined to a life of drudgery. You will come to regret abandoning the life you could have had."

"I cannot imagine such a thing. Here at least I feel strong. There I was wasting away. There I was nobody."

No one could argue with that, for it was true that at Rosings, Anne had been little more than a cipher.

"Then come with us," urged Darcy. "I will shield you from your mother, and I will ensure that you may have the chance to meet someone you may care for and marry. We will introduce you to people in London. I will make sure you are independent of your mother's control."

She shook her head.

"I will be merely replacing her control of me with that of a husband. No. Here I am completely independent, and need only be accountable to myself. I have made my decision, and I will abide with it, for better or for worse. I cannot imagine that I will ever have cause to regret it."

Her eyes sparkled with an intense light, and with her red cheeks aglow, Georgiana thought she had never looked so well nor so strong. Gone was the sickly-looking, thin spectre. Here was a woman that was now fully alive.

"You realise that by continuing on this stubborn course of action, you will be forfeiting your right to your property. The property is not entailed, and Lady Catherine will likely pass it on to someone else," said Darcy.

"When has the possession of such property benefitted me? When has it brought me any happiness?" cried Anne. "I have known nothing but sickness and misery in Rosings. I hope never to set eyes on it again."

"Very likely your mother will pass it on to Colonel Fitzwilliam."

"Perhaps, or perhaps to his younger brother, Arthur. She has always had a soft spot for him, even though he is a rascal and ran away to join the navy when he was seventeen. I wish both my cousins well. I am content where I am."

"Anne," said Darcy gently. "I know you are happy now. But think of it. The years will pass. You will spend your life serving others, teaching young ladies to make their way in society, while you remain trapped here, scarcely able to step outside the school for fear of being seen. You will live your life in drudgery, eking out a meagre existence, growing old to live in genteel poverty. Is that what you wish for yourself? Is that how you see your life? The novelty will wear off soon enough, and you will come to regret relinquishing everything you had for a humdrum existence."

If he had expected to influence Anne by his words, he quickly discovered otherwise.

She smiled. "I know all this. I have thought about it. I have planned this for so long—it has taken me years to put my plans into fruition. I have set aside enough money to buy a small house nearby, and I have enough money in bonds—under another name—to provide me with a small income on which to live, so I need not be dependent on the school. You need not worry for my security, cousin Darcy."

"I see you have indeed thought of everything," said Darcy.

At this Georgiana, who could stand it no longer, broke in. "Come live with us, Anne. You need not go back to Lady Catherine. You can stay with us. We will help you."

Anne smiled again. "Thank you, cousin Georgiana. You have a kind heart, and if things were different, I would have taken up your offer. But I do not need anyone's help. I am happy where I am."

It was clear that nothing would sway her.

"But you can't possibly be satisfied with teaching. Why, you are hardly more than a governess!" said Georgiana.

"Some people may look down on a governess, but I am not one of those people."

"Yes, but—"

"Enough, Georgiana," interrupted Darcy. "I have done what I could to persuade her, but I can see it is useless. There is no point in adding your arguments to mine."

"Why did she write to us then?" said Clarissa. "There must have been a reason."

"I wrote to you because I wanted to assure you I was safe, and because I did not mind if you knew my little secret. I trusted you."

Clarissa, with a little start of guilt, began to explain why they had been forced to reveal her whereabouts. Anne waved her explanation away, and Clarissa drifted into silence.

"I am not blaming you, Clarissa. I am sure you have good reasons. I had hoped, in the years to come, that you would visit me, and provide me with news of the family. I did not want to be cut off completely. Now I hope all of you will do so. You are always welcome."

Darcy nodded. "We will respect your wishes not to tell Lady Catherine of this visit," said Darcy. "If at any time you change your mind, you are very welcome to come to us, and we will do what we can to support you."

Georgiana thought there were tears in Anne's eyes, but she could not be sure.

"You are very kind, Darcy," said Anne. "I will bear that in mind, for one can never tell when circumstances may change."

Darcy stepped forward and took her hand. "I hope you know what you are doing, Anne."

"I believe I do," she replied.

Just then the door opened and Mrs Saunders entered. "Do you need my assistance?" she said. She scrutinized Anne's face.

"All is well, Mrs Saunders," she said, smiling. "Can we offer you all some refreshments?"

"No, thank you," said Robert, pushing away from the wall and starting to move. "We must be on our way. We left home in a rather tearing hurry. How on earth I am to explain this whole thing to Caroline without telling her the truth, I have no idea."

Georgiana gave Anne a quick embrace. "I am glad you have found what you are looking for, Cousin," she said, and then it was time to leave.

❧

"I cannot feel easy about this," said Darcy, as they settled in the carriage. "I cannot help but feel that I should have done something before. I should have stood up against my aunt and urged her to allow her daughter to live a more normal life."

"You are not to blame," said Georgiana. "We all thought her sickly and weak, and assumed that she could not go about by herself."

"That is exactly what I blame myself for. Why did I never doubt that? Why could I not have made more of an effort to invite her to spend time with us alone in Pemberley?"

In the silence that followed, Georgiana tried hard to remember Anne as a young girl and found only the same image that she had described to Clarissa. Anne had been too old for her, and Fitzwilliam had been too young to understand things at the time.

"We are all to blame, in our own ways," said Robert. "None of us took the trouble to discover the real Anne, and now it is too late. But we need not speak of it as if it is a tragedy. It is not as if we have lost her. She was just as lost to us before, when we scarcely acknowledged her existence. At least now *she* is happy."

"If I could persuade her to return home—"

"You cannot wish that for her, Fitz," said Georgiana, "for no matter how changed Lady Catherine may be, she will never change so much that she will cease to control Anne."

"But to think that my own cousin—" Darcy did not complete the sentence. He sat staring out of the window, sunk into gloom.

✦

They had set out from the King's Arms without eating. By now they were all too hungry and thirsty to postpone luncheon. Accordingly, they stopped to eat at The White Swan, a small riverside inn at the border of Richmond Green.

The innkeeper bowed politely and welcomed them, but told them that, regrettably, the private parlour was already occupied. However, if it pleased them, he would set up luncheon in a quiet corner of the taproom which was separated from the rest, and where they would not be disturbed.

The door of the private parlour opened at that moment, and a familiar voice reached them.

"What do you mean, no eel pie? I must speak to the landlord at once. Why, this is an outrage! We expressly stopped here because we were told that you are famous for your eel pie. In fact, we were told you were known as the Eel-pie Inn."

"I'm very sorry, sir," said the beleaguered servant, "it looks like there's been a misunderstanding. It's the White Cross that's known as the Eel-pie. You can see it from here—over on the island. It's very famous for its pies, Sir."

Mr Moffet emerged from the room, looking decidedly peevish. His eyes alighted on them at that moment, and the sullen look disappeared immediately. "Miss Darcy!" he exclaimed. "What an unexpected pleasure!" He bowed formally to the whole party. "We have just now arrived. You must join us for luncheon. It will be a squeeze, but I think we can endeavour to fit everybody."

Darcy did not appear overjoyed at the idea. But he could hardly refuse, when their only other option was to eat in the taproom.

❦

The Darcy party entered the parlour to find Mrs Moffet sewing industriously. Georgiana noticed that it was the same piece of embroidery—a cushion—that she had been working on during the picnic. She had only paid attention then because the drawing depicted a swan standing in the grass, with a background of pine trees, which was unusual. Mrs Moffet appeared to have stalled on the neck, for the head was still a blank.

Georgiana asked her if she was working on a set, for surely it could not be the same one.

"I see you have caught me out, Miss Darcy," said Mrs Moffet with a quick glance to make sure no one overheard. "I will tell you a secret, but you must promise not to reveal it to another soul." Her cheeks were suffused with pink.

"Of course not, Mrs Moffet," said Georgiana.

"I believe you will not, for you seem to be a very nice kind of young lady." She dropped her voice to a whisper. "The fact is, I never really learned the art of embroidery. My mother never knew how either. Yet it is such a genteel occupation," she said leaning closer to Georgiana. "I practise it for the sake of my daughter, because no-one will believe that she is accomplished in embroidery unless they saw me embroidering as well. Athena, of course, is very accomplished at it, since I expressly hired a seamstress that could teach her. But my stitches are so very bad, you know—so horridly cramped and uneven—that I am always forced to undo them whenever I go home, and I never seem to progress any farther."

"Are you sure you are not too much of a perfectionist, Mrs Moffet?" said Georgiana. "It seems to me the part you have finished is very well done indeed."

"Oh, that is Athena's work," said Mrs Moffet. "It *is* very fine, is it not? It was she who did the work you see, and I am trying my best to finish it, but it is taking so very long." Mrs Moffet regarded the swan's neck sorrowfully. "I wish I could go faster," she added with a sigh.

"You must not capture all Miss Darcy's attention, Mama," said Mr Moffet, who had just finished ordering their food with Darcy and Robert. "There are others who wish to speak to her, you know."

Mrs Moffet laughed. "Very well," she said, "I will not stand in your way." And in a quick whisper she added, "I think my son is quite taken with you, Miss Darcy. You are a lucky lady indeed!"

⁂

The luncheon that was served was tasty enough, even if it did not include eel pie. Georgiana, however, found that she was not very hungry. Her stomach churned, and she could not get the scene in the storeroom at the inn out of her mind. She was forced to pay attention to Mr Moffet, who was certainly making every effort to capture her interest. She listened to him with half an ear.

"You are not quite yourself today, Miss Darcy," he said, finally, showing more insight than she would have expected.

"I am sorry, Mr Moffet. I do not feel quite well."

"Perhaps a little fresh air might do you some good," said Mrs

Moffet. "Why don't I take the young ladies for a little walk outside while the gentlemen have their port?"

Miss Moffet jumped up readily enough, and Georgiana and Clarissa had little choice but to join her.

"The view is most agreeable by the river," said Mrs Moffet. "It was such a pity, Miss Darcy, that you were forced to go home that day, for the others had the most wonderful time."

Georgiana did not wish to be reminded of that day, for it brought home most miserably the image of Gatley as he had been then. He had seemed so kind and so caring. Who would have thought that he was so ready to betray her?

They set out to walk, and Miss Moffet chattered for a while about her experiences of the Season, and her latest dress, and how successful it had all been. She kept up a continuous stream of chatter for a few minutes, and Georgiana made every effort to respond. She could not help feeling that Miss Moffet wanted to say something else entirely.

"This may have come as a surprise to you," said Miss Moffet, her voice changing suddenly as she abandoned the chatter. "But I have reason to believe Mr Channing is planning to ask me to marry him. I would not blame you at all if you do not believe me, for I know Channing has been a most shocking flirt. Those who do not know him may misinterpret his flirtations as a sign of interest. In fact, I have often warned him about it. But he insists that he means no harm by it." She sighed. "Men, you know."

She seemed to assume they understood what she meant, but she made no attempt to explain. In the silence that followed, Georgiana wondered if she should explain that she was no longer interested in Channing but could think of no tactful way of saying it.

"I have known Channing for the longest time," said Miss Moffet, breaking into the silence. "We have grown up together. I know he means nothing by it, for even when he singles out anyone particular for his attention, it does not last long. He will marry me, you know."

"Of course he will marry you, my dear," said Mrs Moffet. "I already told Miss Darcy so."

"I wish you luck, Miss Moffet, if that is the case," said Georgiana.

"And I as well," said Clarissa warmly. "As long as he can make you happy."

"I am glad you understand, for I would not wish you to be hurt by him. He can be quite careless at times."

"Thank you for the warning," said Georgiana. A thought occurred to her, and she suddenly wanted an answer. "You say you have known Mr Channing a long time. How about Mr Gatley? Have you known him as well?"

"Yes," said Miss Moffet. "I have known him almost as long. They used to be boys together. Channing was forever getting into trouble, and Gatley was forever saving him." She frowned at the memory. "He felt sorry for Channing, you see. Channing's father was never there, and when he did come from India, he made it clear he far preferred Gatley over Channing—his own son! It was not Gatley's fault, of course, but it was an uncomfortable situation to be in, especially since Channing was quite jealous. And—I hate to say this, for he will be my father if I marry Percy Channing—but the older Mr Channing is quite a brute. I hope he does not decide to come back." She paused, reflecting on this. "I will certainly make sure we do not live under the same roof."

"You most certainly will not!" said Mrs Moffet. "Your father and I will see to it, I can assure you."

"Anyway, all this was a very long time ago," said Miss Moffet, "and now it is quite the other way. Channing is the favourite of society and adored by all the ladies, while Gatley is—well, you know Gatley. He makes little effort to draw attention to himself. Channing says he could have all the ladies too, if he took the trouble, but he is too conscious of his own worth to do so. Channing does not need to make the effort. He attracts all the ladies to him; he cannot help it."

Her tone was laced with pride, as if it was something that reflected well on her.

Georgiana could not help but feel sorry for her and was fervently glad that at least *she* no longer cared anything for Channing.

Not that she had fared much better with Gatley. Clearly they were both a lost cause. She had never met with a more self-righteous person than Mr Gatley. And at this point, she hoped never to set eyes on him again.

Chapter 27

THE SEASON WAS REALLY DRAWING TO ITS CONCLUSION NOW. Napoleon was exiled to St Helena, and the celebrations of Wellington's victory were long over. The young debutantes' fates had been decided; they were either to marry, in which case they were successful, or they were to return next Season to a more desperate round of balls and soirees.

August the twelfth came and went, and London emptied out as hunting parties and house parties were arranged or as members of Society returned thankfully to the quiet of their country estates.

The two Darcy families also prepared to remove north to Derbyshire, with the as yet unmarried debutantes in tow.

"We have not even received any proposals," said Clarissa. "We really are the most unmitigated failures."

Georgiana felt very much a failure. Her spirits were most depressed, for she had invested a great deal of hope not in one young gentleman but in two. Three, if one considered Wickham as well.

Perhaps she was not meant to marry. Not every woman in England married. There were many who did not. It seemed she was destined to be one of them.

"I shall be very glad to leave," she replied. "I have come to dislike London."

Clarissa considered this. "I do not dislike London. But I must admit, the Season did not quite live up to my expectations. There was something—hollow about it."

There was certainly something hollow about it. Georgiana had never felt so empty and drained of all energy as she felt now. She would be glad to go back home to Pemberley. Perhaps, with any luck, she would convince her brother to forgo the idea of a Season for her altogether.

❧

The knocker on the front door rapped harshly, then rapped again and again, so insistently that Georgiana was tempted to open it herself.

"Whoever could be knocking in that insistent fashion?" said Elizabeth, going to the window. "I do hope Hibbert will answer soon, or the knocker will break," said Elizabeth.

The rapping ceased, though it was doubtful that the reason was a broken knocker. The appearance of Hibbert, the Butler, confirmed that the knocker was still intact. Hibbert struggled to maintain his dignity while a familiar form did everything he could to push past him.

"Mr Collins," intoned Hibbert, conveying the full force of his disapproval in the two words.

"I am very sorry to intrude on you in this manner, cousin Elizabeth, Miss Darcy. I specifically asked to speak to Mr Darcy," he said, "but I was shown in here instead."

"Mr Darcy is busy with his man of affairs. He will join us presently. Would you like some tea?"

It was readily apparent that Mr Collins would *not* have liked tea, as he had something of importance to impart. But he was in the impossible situation of having to wait for Mr Darcy. So he smiled as agreeably as his impatience would allow him and remarked that refreshments would be very welcome, as he had been on the road for a long time.

"I hope you left everyone well, Mr Collins. Charlotte and the little one are in good health?" enquired Elizabeth, after the tea things had been brought in.

"Yes, yes," he replied, rubbing his hands together, "It is exceedingly kind of you to enquire. My dear Charlotte does well, and she sends her greetings."

"And Lady Catherine?" said Georgiana, handing him a cup. "Did you also leave her well?"

The impact of these words upon Mr Collins was profound. His teacup clattered in its saucer, splattering tea onto his hand. He plonked everything down onto the table, took out a large handkerchief, and proceeded to wipe his fingers fretfully.

"You have guessed everything, Miss Darcy. I knew I could not hide the news for very long. This is precisely what brought me to London in such haste, and may I add, at great expense—but I do not count that, when it concerns my saintly benefactress, for considering what she has done for me—her kind attentions, her invitations to Rosings, her condescension, the improvements she made to my humble home—I could not have wished for a more generous and affable patroness—"

He would have continued his effusions for a while longer had Elizabeth not interrupted him.

"But tell us, Mr Collins, you really must—has something happened to Lady Catherine?"

Mr Collins did not appreciate the interruption. For a moment he wondered whether his clerical office allowed him to reprimand her for her discourtesy and considered what could be his best course of action. Fortunately the entrance of Mr Darcy saved him from making a decision which could have only earned him a problem.

A sombre bow provided the prelude for his words. "My humble apologies, Mr Darcy, for intruding on you in this unexpected manner. Were it not for the grim nature of my errand, I would never have presumed to arrive without prior notice."

"Everything is well at Rosings, I trust?"

"Alas," said Mr Collins, quite overcome, "I have bad tidings to impart—I can assure you that nothing would have made me so uncivil as to intrude on your presence without notice—but when even dear Charlotte advised me to make haste—"

His apologies continued at such length that Mr Darcy was obliged to interrupt.

"Yes, yes, that is all very well," said Mr Darcy, "but I hope you will come to the point. Is my aunt taken ill?"

Accepting the interruption from Mr Darcy—who was after all the nephew of Lady Catherine—Mr Collins wrung his hands in distress.

"You cannot imagine what she has had to endure, all these weeks, waiting for news of *That Person*."

"You mean Miss de Bourgh," said Darcy coldly.

"That is precisely the difficulty, Mr Darcy. For Lady Catherine has recently received information regarding That Person. She has sailed to America." He waited for a reaction, but when there was none he continued. "I have never in my life heard anything more shocking. Lady Catherine has taken it ill, very ill indeed. It is obvious now that That Person left of her free will, and that she has no intention of returning to the bosom of her family. Lady Catherine was quite prostrate with the news. She wrote immediately to her solicitor and arranged to disown her. Her ladyship will do everything in her power to sever any connection with such a wicked, disobedient girl, and has decreed that That Person's name may no longer be mentioned. You understand now why I cannot call her by her name, for it would go expressly against my exalted patroness's wishes."

"I am sorry to hear that Lady Catherine has been the recipient of such bad news," said Mr Darcy, "and I thank you for bringing it to me, but it was hardly necessary for you to post down to London to inform me in person. An express would have sufficed."

Mr Collins bowed deeply at this and expressed his humble gratitude that he was able to be of service to such an illustrious person as Mr Darcy.

"However, the reason for my precipitous journey to London was not to impart this news," he said. "Something of far greater import has brought me here."

Elizabeth by now was quite prepared to leave the room, so great was her frustration at having to wait so long to learn the reason for his visit. She could only conclude that it could not be anything of importance and that it was most likely a request for funding from Mr Darcy or some such matter.

"I hope you will not take it amiss if I speak freely," said Mr Collins, "for I would not cause offence to a nephew of Lady Catherine for the world."

Darcy commanded him to speak as freely as possible.

"I could not wait a moment longer to inform you of her circumstances, you understand. I told you earlier that the news she received laid her prostrate. However, it would be more correct to say that the shock of the news—terrible as it was—has so changed her that she is but a shadow of herself. Which is why I am here. It is not in my place to make suggestions to such an elevated personage as yourself, but I am quite anxious"—here he paused to clear his throat, overwhelmed with emotion—"quite anxious, nay, even *afraid*, for her ladyship's health and would suggest that your presence is most urgently needed in Rosings."

"Why the devil did you not tell me so earlier?" exclaimed Darcy.

Mr Collins perceived that he had caused offence but was quite at a loss to understand how. He was not a perceptive man, but he concluded from Darcy's language, uttered in front of the ladies, that he was somehow out of patience. He proceeded immediately to make amends, by apologising so profusely that Mr Darcy was forced to leave the room.

"Cousin Elizabeth," he said, as a blinding insight provided the explanation for Mr Darcy's odd behaviour, "I believe that your noble husband is so overset by the news of Lady Catherine's poor health that he was compelled to leave the room. Who can blame him, when one reflects on the excellence, the generosity, and the kindness that are so much a part of her ladyship's character? You would be well advised to follow him, to provide him with the kind of comfort only wives can provide."

Elizabeth's expression of surprise made him realise that she had perhaps misunderstood him. "I was not referring, of course, to one's *wifely duties*," he said, whispering the last two words, and casting a sideways look at Georgiana. "I was referring rather to a wife's obligation to provide support to her husband in the tempestuous moments of life."

Elizabeth, making a strenuous effort to appear anxious, rose immediately.

"Indeed, Mr Collins, you have put in me in mind of my duty, and I am afraid I *must* leave you, for, of course, my first duty must be to Mr Darcy."

And with that she quit the room, abandoning Georgiana to her fate.

Georgiana, however, was not about to be left behind.

"I am afraid, Mr Collins," she said, rising quickly to her feet, "that I too must leave you. In her rush to provide comfort to Mr Darcy, Mrs Darcy forgot that it is not entirely proper for me to remain alone with you."

"Your sense of propriety does you credit, Miss Darcy, however, as a member of the clergy—"

But Georgiana was not destined to hear what he said, for she had already left the room.

❧

The Season was over. Gatley had had quite enough of London and was more than ready to forgo the dubious pleasure of balls and routs and picnics and other such things, and to return to the quiet of the countryside. He had always disliked London at this time of the year, but this year it seemed worse than usual. With the weather turning damper, hinting of autumn already, a heavy oppressive air hung over town. Everyone talked of the striking orange sunsets, and there was talk of Turner frantically painting one landscape after another to try to capture it. But, notwithstanding the sunsets, London towards the end of August seemed like a fairground when the fair was over.

Normally, he would return home to Hunsford. But Kent did not hold its usual appeal. He had a sudden urge to travel north. His explanation for this break with his customary habits was that he had been neglecting a piece of property left to him by a distant relative near Kenelworth, in Warwickshire. At certain rare moments of reflection, he admitted it was likely he did not want to go to Kent because he wished to avoid any reminders of the Darcys. He would be certain to remember them each time he passed by Rosings. He had had quite enough of them this year.

He had received a note from Fitzwilliam Darcy the day after Gatley had left that wretched inn in Richmond. Darcy had wished to meet with him in order to clear the misunderstanding that had occurred. He had even hinted at an apology. Gatley's answer, invented at the spur of the moment, had been that he had urgent business to attend to in the north and that he would be out of town for some time.

And so he set out on an entirely unexpected trip to Warwickshire, and by the time he had reached Kenelworth, he had quite convinced himself that he had been a most neglectful landowner, and it was high time he attended to the property, met with his steward there, and made sure that his tenants were well taken care of. There was nothing worse than an absent landlord.

And from this far away, the whole quarrel in London took on a different perspective. Darcy's note was by now quite pointless. He needed no apology from Darcy. Darcy had slighted his honour, true. But Darcy was an old friend and understood him well enough not to mistake his motives. He had simply been in the grip of an uncontrollable anger, which was perfectly understandable, given the reasons for that anger.

With Miss Darcy, the situation was quite different.

Which is where things had become more complicated. For no matter how much he tried, he could not determine who was most at fault. His mind swung like a pendulum. One day, he would be filled with outrage that she had been so capable of abusing his trust that she had embroiled him in such an underhanded scheme.

The next day, however, he would awake with the conviction that he should have listened to her. He had judged her without looking at the facts, and he began to wonder if had missed some crucial piece of information. On those days, he had to restrain himself from saddling the fastest horse in his stables and riding to see her, in order to discover what that missing piece was and to give her the chance to explain.

But he was absolutely determined not to give in to the temptation. Because he knew if he did, he would forgive her. Precisely what it was that he had to forgive had become more and more blurred in his mind. There was a strong sense of betrayal, of being used, by her, by her cousin, and by Channing. He had not heard from his cousin since, nor had Gatley attempted any contact. Channing had stepped on his toes one time too many, and he had decided that he would have nothing more to do with him. Not that Channing had even noticed.

Nevertheless, he awaited almost daily the news of an engagement. For surely, if Channing had been planning a clandestine meeting with Clarissa, there would have to be an engagement. Darcy would see to it.

Meanwhile, he had received Miss Darcy's news regularly. His mother—while she was still in London—seemed to make it rather a point to write to him in excruciating detail how Miss Darcy had looked at the latest ball, what witty remarks she had made, and who she had danced with. And he had no choice but to read the letters.

His mother clearly favoured Miss Darcy, undoubtedly because she had been friends with Lady Anne, Darcy's mother. But she did not know the full truth about her, and he was too much of a gentleman to disillusion her.

Georgiana was sitting on a stone bench in the garden, viewing the sunset. It had become almost a habit of hers, on sunny days, to watch the colours spread across the sky. They were really quite remarkable. She had not seen anything like it—at least nothing that she remembered.

"You should paint them," said Clarissa, coming to join her.

Georgiana shuddered. "I never want to sketch or paint anything again."

"You cannot mean that," said Clarissa. "You cannot give up painting just because of a silly picnic."

"I suppose not," said Georgiana. She had taken that sketch out more than once and looked at it carefully. It was really quite ironic that no one had ever thought to claim it after all.

"Move up," said Clarissa. She sat next to her on the bench. The two of them observed the unfamiliar brazen sunset, each preoccupied with her own thoughts.

"I—I have heard bad news," said Clarissa.

Georgiana sat up in alarm. "What news? Is it about anyone I know?"

"You need not be alarmed. It is bad news for me. Just today I received a letter from my mother—"

"Everyone is well, I hope?" interrupted Georgian, filled with dread.

"Yes, yes. It is nothing to do with my family. It is news of Mr Parker."

"Mr Parker?"

Clarissa smiled bitterly. "Yes, the man who was to follow me here and to marry me. Mama writes that Mr Parker has announced his engagement to a young lady from Peabody, the daughter of a very rich sea merchant there. They are to be married in October."

Georgiana put her arm around her cousin's shoulder. "Oh, Clarissa! What terrible news! And all this time you have been waiting for him."

Clarissa drew away and stood up. "I suppose I felt deep inside me that he would not come, for I am not at all surprised. But I did wait and hope, and now it is all over."

Her voice was quiet. She stood very still, the sunset painting her face a garish orange.

Georgiana too stood still. She knew what it all meant. Pride, dreams, affections—all cut down, all betrayed, all at an end.

"I am sorry," she whispered, and she did not know if she was talking to herself or to her cousin.

<hr/>

"I have placed myself in an awkward situation," said Darcy at breakfast the next day, holding up a letter that had just arrived. "I have committed us to go to Ansdell Manor, the home of the Gatleys in Hunsford."

Georgiana's throat constricted as she heard the name, and the toast she had brought to her mouth toppled back onto her plate. She tried to cover her reaction with a cough, hoping no one would notice.

"Something wrong, Georgie?" said Darcy. "It looks like the toast went the wrong way."

"Nothing at all. I simply swallowed too quickly."

"Drink some tea. It will wash it down," said Elizabeth.

"I am perfectly well," said Georgiana, vexed by receiving so much attention when she had tried *not* to draw attention.

"In that case, I can explain my problem," said Darcy. "Since Mr Collins came to visit, I have felt troubled about my aunt's situation, even though I cannot credit Mr Collins with common sense when it comes to his patroness. Still, if he says my aunt is suffering, there must be some modicum of truth in it, however apt to exaggeration he may be. Since we are on the verge of going north to Pemberley, and will be there for several months, I thought it better to take the opportunity of going to see Lady Catherine before we travel.

"I cannot stay at my aunt's house—for obvious reasons—so I wrote to Gatley to see if I could put up in his house—Ansdell Hall—for a few days. It seemed to me the best solution. Imagine my consternation when I received a letter this morning from Mrs Gatley."

He held up the letter.

"She says that her son is not at Ansdell—he has gone to take care of some property in the north and then has some business in London afterwards—but that, if we can spare the time before going back to Pemberley, she would love to have company herself. I could avail myself of the plentiful hunting opportunities in the area, and I would not be alone, since Channing has just arranged a hunting party. We are consequently all invited to Kent to stay for as long as we would like to."

A bitter conflict immediately seized Georgiana's mind.

She wanted to go badly. The idea of being in his house—of being in the very same edifice where he lived—both repelled her and thrilled her. To haunt his garden, to breathe the very air of the rooms he inhabited, to know even where his bedchamber was situated—the very suggestion filled her with longing.

But what would be the point? It could bring nothing but torment to her. What purpose could be served by going there, whether he was present or not? She wanted to run in the opposite direction, to go as far from there as could possibly be.

No. She should not go, no matter how much she would like to. She had to stand firm. She needed to put this whole episode behind her and to recover her equilibrium again. She had recovered from her interest in Mr Channing. Clarissa was slowly recovering from her interest in Mr Parker. There was every indication that she too would recover from her strange obsession with Mr Gatley as well. But this would not happen if she went to his house, where everything around her would evoke him. She needed to forget, not to remember.

"It is very kind of Mrs Gatley to invite us," said Georgiana. "But surely we do not all have to go there. Lady Catherine would most likely see only you, Fitzwilliam, if she agreed to see anyone at all. She would certainly not wish to see me. Have you forgotten that, according to her, I am one of the perpetrators? I would by far prefer to set out for Pemberley."

Pemberley was her refuge. It was her source of comfort. The quiet of Pemberley, with its familiar hallways, the pictures of her ancestors, her childhood memories—it was the haven she had always returned to. When her father had died, after that incident with Wickham, even after Wickham's death, its green parks, its rolling hills, its serene lake—these had enabled her to find the peace and acceptance she needed. She was sure it would do the same now.

Darcy and Elizabeth exchanged glances. Something unspoken passed between them. Georgiana watched and waited.

"We shall all go to Pemberley soon enough," said Darcy finally. "I suppose you are worried that there is nothing for you but boredom at Hunsford, after the excitement of London. Have no fear. We will ask Clarissa to come with us, as well, instead of travelling north with Robert and Caroline next week. With Clarissa in

Hunsford and Mr Channing and the Moffets and a number of young gentlemen who are there for the hunting party, I am sure we can contrive to amuse you for one or two weeks."

"And Mrs Gatley is a very pleasant lady," added Elizabeth. "I was under the impression you liked her."

"Of course I do," said Georgiana.

She could not argue against it, for she had no real excuse not to go. She knew her brother would enjoy tramping through the countryside in search of game. She would have to argue against herself as well.

It was all too much effort. She resigned herself.

But she had never gone anywhere so unwillingly.

※

Georgiana did not know why, but as soon as she set eyes on Mrs Gatley's kindly face, a strong sensation of emptiness came over her. She felt as though life no longer meant anything at all. It was all grimness and doom.

As if she could sense her reaction, Mrs Gatley slipped her arm into Georgiana's and walked with her into the drawing room.

"You look tired, child. Has the Season been too much for you?"

It had, but not in the way Mrs Gatley meant.

"In some ways," replied Georgiana with a wan smile.

"I remember so well the Season I came out. Your mother Lady Anne was my good friend, as you know, and we were so excited, we could hardly wait. But after a while you discover that beyond the dances and the beaux and the dreams we weave, the first Season is about survival. Next year, when you return, you will have fewer expectations, and you will know better what you are looking for. Then you may find what is right for you."

But what if you find what you think is right, and it turns out to be wrong? She looked into Mrs Gatley's benevolent face and wondered if she could ask such a question.

As if she had in fact asked it, Mrs Gatley took her hand between two of her own.

"You young people are always impatient. Do not ask yourself too many questions just now. You will know what is right for you when the time is ripe. Things need time. You must let them develop at their own pace."

Georgiana shook her head. "I wish I could believe that. At the moment I do not believe that I will ever find the answers."

"If you ask too many questions, you will find no answers, only more questions. But time has a way of resolving things." Mrs Gatley's eyes crinkled at the corners. "I suppose you think I am speaking in riddles, and you are quite right. It is a habit one develops, as one grows older. I must not keep you however. I am sure you will want to go to your room and change."

Georgiana had the feeling that Mrs Gatley was telling her something very important. But, no matter how much she pondered, the meaning of those words remained just out of her reach.

She would have to wait and see.

Chapter 28

Mrs Gatley was out doing her rounds of the estate, distributing food and essentials to some of her less fortunate tenants, accompanied by Clarissa. Georgiana, who was under the weather, begged Mrs Gatley's indulgence and said she would join her next time.

It was pleasant to be able to sit in the parlour with no one but Elizabeth as a companion. Though as an hour went by, Georgiana began to feel less satisfied. She did not quite know what to do with herself. She tried to play the piano, but the pieces she played were so melancholic that she was in danger of falling into the doldrums. It was impossible to read, and she had no patience for sewing. And Elizabeth was not much of a companion, for she was busy rereading *Sense and Sensibility* and said nothing to her at all.

Georgiana was just beginning to grow very restless, and to wish that she had gone with Mrs Gatley, when their quiet was interrupted. The door opened and Channing, who had been playing billiards with Darcy, hovered in the doorway.

"May I beg your indulgence, Mrs Darcy, and ask to be allowed to speak to Miss Darcy in private?" said Channing, smiling at Elizabeth charmingly. "I have already spoken to Darcy."

The two ladies exchanged glances. Georgiana gave a small shake of her head. Elizabeth bit her upper lip uncertainly, then rose.

"Certainly, Mr Channing."

Georgiana tried to signal to her to stay, but Elizabeth ignored her. She quit the room, and the door shut behind her.

Georgiana, angry at being placed in such a situation, sat still in her chair, trying her best to put on the appearance of polite interest.

"Miss Darcy," said Channing, flashing her a boyish grin, "you have known me for some time now, and you can guess what I have to say to you."

"Pray, Mr Channing, you need say nothing further," she cut in.

He looked astonished.

"I do not understand, Miss Darcy. You have given me no opportunity to say anything at all."

"I can guess your intent, Mr Channing. I wish only to spare you the effort." She was surprised at herself. She did not know that she could be so firm. Even a few months ago, she would have held back and made herself listen to every word he had to say.

She recalled the day Channing had called her dull and insipid. How long ago it seemed! She tried to recapture her feelings on that occasion but nothing surfaced. If she had cared at that time for his opinion, she certainly did not now.

Yet, oddly enough, she felt grateful to him. In a way, he had spurred her to change, and she was glad of that. Perhaps she owed it to him to at least listen. One could call it a favour returned.

"But, Miss Darcy, you cannot be serious. I have come with all the best of intentions. I have called upon you to make you my wife." He came up to her and kneeled. "Nothing—nothing at all— would give me as much pleasure as hearing you say yes. I have come to respect and admire you as I have never respected and admired any woman before. From the start, you captivated me with your beauty. But now, as I have come to understand you better, I feel I would wish no one else to be the partner of my life."

He gazed soulfully into her eyes. She knew that soulful look. Clarissa had made her practise it in the mirror. She marvelled that she had at one time thought him attractive. There was too much self-assurance on his face, too much certainty of being admired. His vanity rendered his handsome features unappealing.

"I am honoured by your sentiment, if I could but believe it, but I am afraid I will have to say no."

His expression changed so quickly she almost laughed. "What do you mean, if you could just believe it?" he said, rising awkwardly from the kneeling position and dusting off his buff trousers. "Do you doubt my sincerity?"

"I do," she said. "I have watched you for several months fluttering like a moth, flying from one young lady to another. Really, Mr Channing, you cannot expect me to believe that you have suddenly settled on me."

"Whyever not?" said Channing ardently. "Is it the first time a young gentleman discovers the high value of one specific lady after admiring a number of others?"

"No. But you do not admire me, and you are not attached to me at all. I am afraid you cannot say anything that will convince me otherwise, Mr Channing, so you may as well give up."

"You mean it? You will not relent?" he said, still in that ardent tone.

"I will not relent."

"Very well," he said in a normal tone, without a trace of ardour. A sullen expression crossed his face. Then he grinned at her. "You are probably right. We would not suit. Our characters are too different." He sighed. "Mama wished me to propose to you. She did not want the opportunity to slip through my hands. You know how these things are."

She really ought to be angry at him, but his smile was so boyish she found herself laughing instead.

"Though it is true I have come to admire you, over time. You really are quite pretty, you know," he added.

Georgiana smiled. "Thank you. I will accept your sincerity in this, at least."

She rose and put out her hand. "Let us be friends at least," she said.

He took it, bowed deeply over it, and pressed a feather light kiss onto her fingertips.

"Of course we shall be friends. In fact, I would not be surprised if we will not soon be cousins."

He laughed at her bafflement and, with a quick determined step, left the room.

⁂

Georgiana waited until the door had shut behind him, then rushed to the hallway to waylay Elizabeth, who was skulking around suspiciously.

"You have been listening at the door," said Georgiana.

"I would never do such a thing," said Elizabeth.

"Even my brother is convinced you listen at doors," said Georgiana. "In any case, I did not appreciate being abandoned like that, Elizabeth," she said.

"I have started finally to appreciate my mother's finesse at such matters," said Elizabeth, laughing. "I am sorry, but I could not think what else to do. He would have proposed to you sooner or later. It seemed more sensible to have done with it earlier."

Georgiana acknowledged the truth of her statement.

"You did not accept him, did you? He looked very pleased with himself, but as he did not ask for congratulations, I did not know what to think."

Georgiana considered teasing Elizabeth by saying that yes, she had accepted him, but then decided against it.

"No, of course not. You could not think me so addle-headed, surely?"

Elizabeth looked relieved. "I had my doubts, at least when I saw him come out. I hoped you would have more sense than that." Elizabeth regarded her with a frown. "Though these days I cannot tell at all what you are about. You have grown much older suddenly."

"Is that a bad thing?" said Georgiana.

Elizabeth smiled. "Not at all. I am glad of it."

Darcy emerged from the billiard room and came to discover what had happened.

"Have you rid us of your suitor?" he said to his sister.

"Yes, Brother."

"Well, I am glad of it," he said, "though it did cross my mind that you might still harbour a fondness for him. I would not have cherished him as a brother."

"Certainly not!" replied Georgiana indignantly.

The doorbell sounded again, and the butler announced Mr Moffet, who wished to speak to Mr Darcy on a matter of particular importance.

Darcy raised his brow.

"I warn you, this is the last suitor of yours I will entertain today. If any more suitors come, I will have to turn them away."

Georgiana groaned.

She was more polite to Mr Moffet. He was at least more sincere than Channing, though she did not think his affections ran very deep.

"Miss Darcy," he said, "I know what I have to say will come as a surprise, and I have every hope that it will be a pleasant one. I am sure you cannot guess why I am here."

Georgiana considered telling him she knew exactly why he was there but refrained.

"I—" she began, but was interrupted immediately.

"You need not feel obliged to answer, Miss Darcy. I have certain things to say, and I mean to say them all. You deserve no less. If you will listen without interruption, you will soon discover what I am about."

Georgiana clasped her hands together, sat up straight in her chair, and prepared to listen. She hoped that whatever he had to say would not take a very long time.

"I know you do not expect flowery language—for you are not romantically inclined like your cousin. Not that I am condemning the Romantic, by any means, for my mother is quite fond of things Romantic. We have a garden set up in the Romantic way, you know, with a ruin—"

She really *had* to interrupt. At this rate, he would still be here in the evening. "You were kind enough to inform me about the garden some time ago," she said.

He laughed. "So I did! How kind of you to remember. Which just goes to show. Miss Darcy, you have a sensitivity of feeling, a delicacy, an understanding that exceeds any that I have encountered so far. And I can tell you that you are not the first young lady I have been acquainted with. You will understand when I say that young ladies tend to flock to me..."

This statement was followed by a recital of several stories concerning young ladies, whose names he was too much of a gentleman to reveal, who had set their sights at him. Then he enumerated at length the benefits for her of marrying him.

Half an hour later, Georgiana was finally put in the difficult situation of saying no to him. He left the room looking very vexed.

Georgiana wished now that she had not been foolish enough to listen to the whole declaration.

Two days later, Georgiana and Clarissa went out riding together. It was a sunny day, though a light September breeze nipped at them as they rode.

"Guess what happened this morning, when you went out walking with Mrs Gatley and Elizabeth?"

She immediately thought of Gatley. "Do tell me," said Georgiana, her heart giving a little flicker.

"Channing proposed to me!" said Clarissa slowly.

Georgiana twisted her head to look at her cousin. "Really! How droll!" She expected her cousin to laugh, but she did not. "You did not accept him, did you?"

There was a tense silence, in which Georgiana was gripped with apprehension. Suppose Clarissa *had* accepted him?

"No, but I was tempted. I did not refuse him though. I told him I needed more time to think about it," replied Clarissa.

"But why? When you know his heart is not in it? He proposed to me only two days ago. Clarissa, surely you are not serious. He does not care for you."

Clarissa shrugged. "I know. But then, none of our foolish ideas about love and affection have come to anything. Look at the two of us. What have our impractical notions brought us but unhappiness? I am resolved to be more sensible from now on."

She was silent. Georgiana heard the horse's hooves as they struck the ground, the distant mooing of cows, and the sudden cry of a hawk as it rose up through the air.

"Channing is not such a bad person, and I think I understand him," said Clarissa. "We will rub together well enough."

Georgiana shook her head. "He is not for you," she said, thinking of Mrs Moffet. "You do not know him as well as you think. You would grow tired of him in a week."

Clarissa did not reply.

They came to a high point on the road. The village of Hunsford lay before them, the small spire of the church visible against the sky.

"Let us ride past Rosings," said Clarissa on impulse. "I want to see the place where I spent those miserable first weeks when I first came to England."

"I had no idea then that you were so miserable," remarked Georgiana. "You certainly concealed it well."

"I fooled you, did I not?" said Clarissa with a grin. "But then, you did not know me at the time. So I suppose I was not so very clever."

Georgiana examined her cousin closely. She could tell nothing from her profile—she looked as she always did. Was there perhaps more of a stubborn edge to her jaw? It was impossible to say.

"And now?" said Georgiana, wanting to know. "Are you miserable now?"

Clarissa looked down at the mare's mane. It took her awhile to answer.

"I am not *happy*. The news about Parker still rankles. But I think I left him such a long time ago, that the news did not hit me as hard as I expected. Boston seems so far away, as does Parker, in many ways. It seems like another world, in some way less real than this one. I do not mean to say that I feel no pain. It is just that the pain is not overwhelming." She looked up and gave her cousin a twisted smile. "I plan to survive."

Georgiana nodded. "Yes. Though it is difficult to believe at first, one does survive. But you must promise meanwhile to do nothing foolish. Like marrying Channing, for example."

Clarissa nodded. "Very well. I will not marry Channing. Are you satisfied?"

It was Georgiana's turn to nod.

A small phaeton and ponies emerged from the side road, some way ahead of them. It passed through the center of the village and took the left fork—onto the road that led to Rosings.

"Oh, look!" cried Clarissa. "There is Anne's phaeton! With Mrs Jenkinson and—is that Anne? How can that be possible? Could she have decided to return?"

Georgiana peered at the distant carriage. It was too far away to identify the passengers, but there was no doubting the carriage. They had been seen in it often enough.

The very possibility that Anne could have given up her freedom and returned to her mother threw Georgiana into despondency. Of the three of them, she had thought at least Anne had found what she wished. How could things have gone so wrong for all of them?

"But why? It does not make sense."

"Let us catch up with her and ask her," said Clarissa.

"Oh, Clarissa, will you never learn? If she has returned to Rosings, we will have to leave her to her own devices."

"I have no intention of inciting her to rebellion," said Clarissa derisively. "I just want to discover what happened and why she decided to come back. I am motivated by curiosity alone, not by a desire for reform."

"Well, I am glad of that, at least," said Georgiana. "If you promise me you will not try to convince her to run away, I will allow you to come with me to meet her carriage."

"You can neither allow me nor prevent me," said Clarissa. "But you need not worry. I will not interfere. What would be the point, in any case? She would only come back again.

As they drew closer to the little phaeton, Georgiana observed Mrs Jenkinson wrapping a shawl solicitously around Anne's shoulders.

"How can she endure all those shawls in September?" she remarked. "You remember at the school? She did not have a single one."

"I suppose if you are sickly, you feel the cold more. You are not as resistant to sudden draughts," said Clarissa. "It was you who told me that. There is a nip in the air."

They had almost caught up with the carriage.

"Anne!" shouted Clarissa. "Wait for us!"

Georgiana expected the carriage to slow down or even stop, but it continued on its way, completely oblivious.

"Wait!" she cried.

"Anne!" they shouted together, hoping that by combining voices they could be heard more clearly.

Anne did not turn round. Mrs Jennings, however, looked back at them and sent them a look of such intense dislike that Georgiana reigned in her horse.

"Anne?" said Clarissa.

Georgiana wanted to cry. Could it be that Anne had reverted so much to her older self that she did not even want talk to them?

The carriage started to turn through the gate to move up the road that led to the entrance.

They could see Anne clearly now.

"Oh, Lord!" exclaimed Clarissa, falling back.

Georgiana too fell back. She could scarcely believe her eyes.

It was not Anne who was in the carriage, wrapped in shawls. It was Lady Catherine.

⁘

On Sunday, everyone but Georgiana set out to attend church. Georgiana stayed behind, pleading a digestive ailment. She did not know how they could all go to church so calmly when it was very likely there would be an exceedingly embarrassing scene. It was all very awkward indeed. For where were the Darcys going to sit? Would Lady Catherine allow them to sit in her pew, when she was not on talking terms with them? Or would they be forced to sit with Mrs Gatley? The whole congregation would be agog with curiosity.

This was her main reason, she told herself, for not wishing to go. She did not want to have to face the whispers and suggestions of the whole congregation. But there were other and, if one wished to be honest, more compelling reasons not to go. She could not bear to go back to the same church and revisit that first day when she had met Mr Gatley. She remembered only too well his eyes upon her then. She had suspected at the time that he was judgemental, and events had proved her right.

Once everyone left, she set herself the goal of reading ten pages. It was a worthy goal and soon achieved. Except that she turned page after page, without having grasped a word of the content. Finally, she threw down the book and decided that her best course was to take some air in the garden.

The last person in the world—the very last person in the world—she could have expected to see was Mr Gatley. Yet there he was, descending from his barouche and climbing the stairs to the house laboriously, his head down.

He had not seen her.

She froze like a hare caught in the glare of a lantern. Her mind told her she ought to run away, quickly, but her feet clung stubbornly to the hard marble surface they were standing on.

When she finally managed to tear one of them from the ground's pull, he looked up. It was too late.

A spark lit his eyes, and he took a quick step upwards, towards her.

"Miss Darcy."

"Mr Gatley."

Appropriate bows and curtsies followed.

"I did not expect to see you here," he stated.

"Nor I you," said Georgiana.

"It *is* my home, you know," he said gently.

"I know."

"I expected everyone would be at church," he said, as if that explained everything.

"I was not feeling well." This was her explanation.

"I have come down from Town," he said. "I came to pick up some papers."

"Ah," she answered.

He had not told her what she wanted to know.

"So you are not staying?" she asked, the words squeezing past her lips.

"No."

And that was that. That "no"—a single syllable—slammed the door on a brief hope that had foolishly sprung up inside her. Her lips trembled, and she controlled the betraying tremble by raising her hand to her mouth and pretending to yawn.

"Very well, Mr Gatley," she said finally, pleased that her voice did not tremble even though her lips did. "I will not delay you on your quest. I suppose you must ride back to London immediately."

"Yes, immediately."

She waved her hand in the direction of the garden. "I was going to take a walk," she said and set out quickly, just in case she said something very unwise, for she wanted to ask him to stay. But that would not do at all. It would be very foolish, extremely foolish, and it would earn her the rebuff that she deserved. For it was he, after all, who had wronged her, and if he had not discovered that by now—well, she was not about to enlighten him.

Only when she reached the safety of the garden—where she could retreat behind the hedges and become invisible—only then did she recall that she had not bid him goodbye.

⁂

Clarissa found her in the garden some time later, sitting on a wrought-iron bench and kicking up a cloud of dust with her feet.

"I have news," said Clarissa.

Georgiana looked up dully.

"Aren't you going to ask me what it is?" said Clarissa.

"Very well. What news do you have, Clarissa?"

"Lady Catherine was not in church! She did not show up! Which was excellent for us, of course, since it avoided a great deal of awkwardness. Even Robert was worried. I was very nervous all the way there, for I could see what a problem it would be if we did not sit with Lady Catherine. It would be announcing to the world that something was wrong. I wonder that Darcy chose to go to church at all. Perhaps he did it to make a point, so that Lady Catherine could understand more fully what she was doing. At the end, she did not come, so all was well."

Georgiana tried to evoke some interest in Clarissa's story, but her mind had become very listless.

"And the sermon was so dull I do not think a single person stayed awake," said Clarissa. "Without Lady Catherine to inspire him, Mr Collins has little to say for himself. I still do not understand how preachers can be appointed based on patronage and not on piety."

"It is a gentleman's occupation," said Georgiana indifferently. "It requires study and knowledge of the classical tongues. To be qualified, you have to know those at least." She was not interested in a discussion with Clarissa about English clergy, but she could tell from the militant look in Clarissa's eye that it was not a topic she was willing to abandon easily. "Can we have this discussion later? I prefer to enjoy some peace in the garden."

"Watch out, Georgiana. You are becoming quite dull again." She broke off and peered intently at Georgiana. "You look quite strange. Are you unwell?"

"That was precisely why I did not go to church," said Georgiana bitingly.

"No it was not," replied Clarissa. "You did not look like this when I left this morning. Something has happened since."

She continued to examine Georgiana intently. "You have seen Mr Gatley. Nothing else could have given you that look."

Georgiana groaned. "Just leave me alone."

"I will not leave you alone," said Clarissa. "At least not until you tell me what happened. I have to admit that *your* news is far superior to mine."

"You do not even know my news," said Georgiana, amused in spite of herself.

"Exactly. That is what makes it exciting."

She settled on a bench, patted the space next to her for Georgiana to sit down, and prepared to listen.

❧

Gatley cursed himself for being a fool.

He had intended to stay. That excuse of the papers—as if anyone could believe that he would ride all the way from London just to pick up some papers—was the best he could think of on the spur of the moment. It would take Miss Darcy no more than a few moments to realise that he could easily have sent for them rather than coming himself.

He had intended to stay. That is, until he saw her, standing at the top of the stairs, looking dazzlingly pretty in a simple muslin dress, and then his courage had failed him.

Not that he was a coward. But he knew that if he stayed, he would not be able to stick to his resolve, which was to set aside any lingering feelings he may have for her, as he had done so far very successfully, and to move on to a new phase of his life.

His coachman, Oskins, would think him quite mad. He had already made more than one veiled reference to how his master had never been the same since that blow on the head. Now he would have even more reason to think so. He had only last week returned to London from Warwickshire. He had informed the man that very morning that they would be staying several days in Kent.

Well, Oskins's opinion was not going to stand in his way.

He gave orders to leave. His servants—including his valet, who was not going to believe that Gatley had dragged him all the way from London for a mere hour's stay—barely had a few minutes to down some ale and food. Then it was straight back to London, without a word of explanation.

He would stop along the way and stay overnight at an inn. It would give everyone—the horses as well—a chance to recover.

As the carriage pulled out, he remembered that his mother would be returning from church about this time. He put his head out of the window and ordered Oskins to go full speed. The horses plunged forward, and the carriage hurtled down the road. He leaned back against the squabs, satisfied. The last thing he wanted to happen was to run into his mother. There would be no escape for him then.

He had to avoid Georgiana. She was wrong for him, wrong in every way.

If only she had not stood there at the top of the stairs, with something in her eyes that twisted his heart. If only he had had time to compose himself and to prepare himself for the encounter until they returned from church. Then he could have been spared this headlong flight back to London. For a flight by any other name was still a flight.

Well, done was done. The horses were thundering their way back, and his decision was made. He could not turn back again now.

Chapter 29

GATLEY SPENT THE WORST NIGHT OF HIS LIFE AT THE RED Lion. Not that there was anything wrong with the inn itself. As inns went, it was one of the better ones. But some mischievous sprite had stuffed his mattress with small sharp pebbles. He was quite sure of it. Though he could not for the life of him locate any of them.

He battled with the bed, which seemed to sink under him in all the wrong places and protrude in all the rest. He battled with the sheets, which had a will of their own. They slipped and slid away from him just when he was finally ready to drift off. And he battled with the fiends that told him he had to go back and seemed determined to pull him out of bed, right in the middle of the night, and force him to ride back to Hunsford, for what reason he could not imagine.

In the end, he told the fiends he would do what they wanted, just to silence them. By that time it was dawn, and, in that way fiends have of disappearing at the wrong moment, they slipped away, and he tumbled headlong into a deep sleep.

When he awoke, he realised immediately that it was very late. Some time last night, as he made his plans, he had decided that he was going to arrive early at Ansdell Manor, just after breakfast, and that he would ask Miss Darcy to join him in the garden, and he would have an earnest discussion with her.

He had no idea what he wished to say. He only knew he had to talk to her. It was his conscience, surely, that was keeping him awake. He had been much too candid in expressing his opinion, and he had not been nice—not at all. He owed it to himself, at the very least, to clear his conscience. Even if she was in the wrong. After all, she had helped him after the accident, according to Oskins, and had stayed with him, risking her brother's disapproval. She could always have left the inn and returned home, with no one any wiser about the whole thing. He owed her something for that. Yet he had not even thanked her. He would stop and get her some flowers along the way, and he would tell her that he should not have spoken to her that way, and everything would be resolved. He could then go his own way, without being pursued by fiends.

By the time he woke up, however, breakfast was long gone. The sun was already slanting towards the West, an ominous sign.

He dressed as quickly as his valet would allow and went downstairs to find the coachman. He was not looking forward to telling him that they would be driving back to Ansdell.

Oskins said nothing to him, of course, though Gatley was sure he had plenty to say to the others.

Half an hour later, when it seemed like they were positively crawling through the country, he leaned his head out and asked the coachman to put some life into the horses.

The wind blowing towards him brought him the sound of disgruntled curses, ending in Oskins' assessment of his master, which reached him very clearly.

"Love struck, that's what 'e is, the besotted fool. God help 'im!"

Gatley leaned back in his seat and considered this statement very, very seriously, all the way until they reached his country manor.

❧

Georgiana, who had withdrawn from company, preferring to be alone in the parlour, played the piano all morning. She played loudly and with emphasis, and in a heavy, grim manner. Elizabeth had been trying her best to ignore the wincing and the pained expressions on both Mrs Gatley's and Clarissa's faces, but as the relentless clamour continued on and on, she was forced finally to intervene.

"Georgiana is usually a very delicate player," she said, almost in apology, as she rose.

"She is playing with the delicacy of an elephant," remarked Clarissa.

"I think I need to talk to her," she said, and headed for the small parlour.

"You must not think I do not appreciate your playing, Georgiana," she said, pausing in the doorway. "But must you attack the piano so vigorously? We shall all be rendered quite deaf if this continues much longer. We can hear you quite emphatically from the saloon."

"I'm sorry, Elizabeth, I did not realise everyone could hear me," said Georgiana, stopping immediately. "I did not mean to be quite so loud. I was not really paying attention to what I was doing."

She shuffled her music around and struck the notes of a pianissimo piece. But she had scarcely played more than a few bars before the volume rose to in a crescendo.

"I cannot help it," she said. "My fingers are too heavy." She rose from the bench and walked across the room to the window.

"Do you ever feel as if nothing will ever satisfy you?"

Elizabeth, seeing an opportunity to question Georgiana about her moodiness, sat down and replied with interest.

"I often feel that nothing will satisfy me. I will pick up a book, expecting to find enjoyment in the pages, then find it does not live up to my expectations. Then I will go to the theatre, to view some piece everyone is raving about, and find it is of little interest at all."

Georgiana was not listening.

"I suspect you mean something entirely different," said Elizabeth, hoping to encourage Georgiana to speak.

Her hopes of receiving a disclosure were not to be satisfied, for the words fell upon thin air and disappeared.

When more circumspect measures fail, one can always turn to direct questioning.

"Georgiana, is there something troubling you?"

Her question sounded lame even to her own ears. But having brought the proverbial cat out of the bag, she persevered. "I could not help but notice that you are not as cheerful as usual."

If anything, this statement was surely even lamer than the other, which at least had the virtue of being direct. But Georgiana's continued silence unnerved her.

Georgiana was on the verge of saying something, when a footman brought in a letter for her on a silver salver.

Georgiana, surprised that anyone would know where to address the letter, opened it quickly. It was from Anne.

> *Dear Georgiana,*
> *Clarissa has written to me to reveal the unfortunate consequences of your visit. I am sorry to hear that I have been the cause of so much unhappiness. I would not in*

the world wish to come between you and someone who is important to you. You must reveal the reason for your visit to Richmond to Mr G—. I know of his reputation in Kent, and I believe him to be a trustworthy, honourable gentleman, so I do not hesitate to entrust him with my secret. Only do not let him speak about it to anyone else. You understand, of course, the continued need for secrecy. I hope that you will be vigilant always. My sincerest wishes for your future happiness,

Annabelle Williams

"Excuse me," said Georgiana, to Elizabeth. "I must speak to Clarissa."

Georgiana stalked down to the saloon. Controlling herself with an effort, she asked Mrs Gatley if she could steal Clarissa from her for a few minutes.

"Certainly," said Mrs Gatley. "The weather is very fine. Why do you not go for a long walk?"

Georgiana had only enough patience to wait until the door of the Manor had closed behind them. Then she whipped round and stopped Clarissa in her tracks.

"You wrote to Anne?" said Georgiana. "Without even consulting me? And you told her—what exactly did you tell her?"

"I told her that you had quarrelled with Mr Gatley—I did not reveal his name, I am not such a dunce as all that—because you had to conceal the reason for the trip from him and that the only way to repair the damage was for you to tell him the truth."

"Anne knew you were speaking of Mr Gatley. Oh, Clarissa, it

was not well done of you at all." She began to walk again, in long quick stride, forcing Clarissa almost to run to catch up with her.

"You know, you resemble your brother when you look like that, all stern and virtuous. Come, Georgiana. You do realise what this means. You may now explain the circumstances to Mr Gatley, and all will be well."

"Really?" said Georgiana, stopping abruptly. "And how do you propose that I do so? Shall I write him a letter and have him condemn me for that? Or shall we find some excuse to go to visit him in London?" She set out again.

Clarissa shook her head helplessly and followed. "There must be a way to reach him. You *must* explain the circumstances to him."

"Even if I could," said Georgiana, "which I cannot, I would not explain the circumstances. You do not understand the situation at all. It has nothing to do with telling him the truth."

"If *you* will not explain the circumstances to him," said Clarissa firmly, "then *I* shall find a way to do so."

"Stop! You have grasped the wrong end of the stick. My quarrel with Mr Gatley is about something else entirely, which is his willingness to think the worst of me at the slightest provocation and to believe that his moral superiority allows him to point out all my faults whenever he chooses. You misunderstand completely if you believe that such a situation can be salvaged simply by telling the truth about Anne. I have thought about the situation a great deal, and I realise that it cannot possibly be salvaged."

"But you love him."

"You know as well as I do that loving someone is not always the wisest of courses. Your Mr Parker is a case in point. No, I have begun to think that love and marriage are incompatible. I have determined that next Season, I will accept the hand of any young gentleman who is half-way agreeable and who wins the approval of both my brother and Elizabeth. *They* will be my guide."

"Phew! What nonsense is this? You cannot give up your dreams of happiness merely for a silly quarrel. If you do, then I will think you more ninny-headed than I imagined."

"Think of me whatever way you like," said Georgiana, rising and walking back to the house.

⁂

It was one of those days destined to produce surprises. Everyone was assembled in the saloon, partaking of afternoon tea, when the bell rang. It was the wrong time for regular calls, so all eyes turned to the doorway in expectation.

Mrs Moffet entered, carrying her embroidery set, from which threads dangled in disarray.

"Forgive me for calling so very early," she said. "I know it is not correct form, but I really could not wait. I knew you would want to know as soon as possible, so I have come over as quickly as I could to be sure that you were the first to know."

Mrs Gatley requested her to take a seat. Mrs Moffet sat down, and taking up her embroidery, tried to sort out the tangled thread. In her agitated state, however, she only succeeded in tangling the threads further.

"Pray tell us the news, Mrs Moffet," said Mrs Gatley gently.

Mrs Moffet abandoned all pretence at embroidery and set everything aside. "You will think me bird brained, to become all excited about nothing at all, but there you are. I have come to tell you that Mr Channing has spoken to Mr Moffet and has requested Athena's hand in marriage. Mr Moffet had no objection—and why should he?—and so Athena accepted, and now they are engaged. I can scarcely believe it! My daughter to marry Mr Channing! Who would have thought it could happen? I am quite over the moon with happiness."

Georgiana, alarmed, looked over to Clarissa. Clarissa, however, gave no indication that anything was amiss, and so Georgiana was able—once her turn came—to wish Mrs Moffet her sincerest congratulations.

"I told you the name would bring her good fortune, did I not, Miss Darcy? Is it not fortunate I called her Athena? Do you see how things worked out for her? Was I not right?"

"You were, Mrs Moffet," said Georgiana, smiling warmly, the happiness in the proud mother's eyes proving quite contagious.

"I hope you will find happiness too, for you deserve it." She lowered her voice. "You must not think I am upset with you at all for turning my Odysseus down. He is still too young to think of marriage, and you would not have suited at all. I know the gentleman you've set your sights on, and I hope with all my heart that you get him. I wish you very well, my dear."

Georgiana's happiness dimmed, and tears came to her eyes. She turned away quickly, not wishing Mrs Moffet to see them.

※

In the midst of the confusion and effusions of Mrs Moffet's announcement, Georgiana signalled to Clarissa to join her, and they slipped through the French doors into the garden.

"I hope you are not upset by Mrs Moffet's announcement," said Georgiana to Clarissa.

"No, not at all. In fact, I was very relieved to hear it. I stayed up most of last night trying to reach a decision, but every time I thought I had resolved on something, I would come up with a reason not to do it. I thought I would drive myself to madness. Thank goodness I no longer have to decide."

"But how could he do this," said Georgiana, "when you had not even given your answer?"

"It is as you said. It was not meant to be," she said. "He is not for me."

Georgiana laughed. "It was Mrs Moffet who said it, you know."

The two young women linked arms.

"I wonder what is to become of us," said Clarissa. "I would like so much to do something with my life. Not just to marry—though clearly that is something I wish for—but to accomplish something, to have a purpose."

"Well then you must find one, and then you must find someone who will help you fulfil it."

"That is easy enough to say but almost impossible to carry out."

"If there is anyone who could do it," said Georgiana, "then it must be you."

Clarissa grinned. "I suppose you are right. Though I must admit I did not quite achieve my purpose in helping *you*."

"Oh, *that*," said Georgiana. "I am glad you did not achieve your purpose, or it would have been my engagement that was being announced, not Miss Moffet's. Imagine me marrying Channing!"

It really was most incongruous. Georgiana could not imagine at all why she wanted to win Channing's attention so badly. She could only laugh at the thought.

❧

Gatley waited impatiently for the footman to let down the stairs so he could leave the carriage. He was just about to take the stairs into the Manor when the distinct sound of Miss Darcy's laughter reached him, coming from the garden. Drawn by an invisible string to that laughter, he began to move in that direction.

As she came into view, he came to an abrupt halt. She looked *happy*. Of all the things he had expected, it had not been that. She looked so happy that he could not bring himself to talk to her. Whatever pangs of anxiety *he* was suffering, it was more than clear that *she* was experiencing nothing like that. She was laughing.

He backed out of the garden to return to the main entrance and almost ran into Mrs Moffet, who was leaving. She looked ecstatic.

"I see by now you have heard of the engagement," she said, looking towards the young ladies. "I am the happiest mother alive."

He followed the direction of her eyes.

His world fell apart.

When a person is uncertain in love, there is nothing easier than for him to put one and one together and to make three out of them. Which is precisely what Mr Gatley did, looking into Mrs Moffet's smiling face.

It was not Mrs Moffet's fault that his life was ruined. He should not glare at her as he did. He struggled to say something, because it was expected, but he could not.

There was a stone in his throat. How it came to be lodged there he could not imagine, but he had lost the ability to swallow. And to speak. He tried again to utter the necessary words.

"Congratulations," he croaked.

"Oh, Mr Gatley," said Mrs Moffet. "You are coming down with a cold. You should go to your room and rest at once. Rest is the only cure for a cold, if you manage it in the early stages. I fear I must go. I have several visits to make, you know. I can't wait to spread the news."

The stone lodged in his throat seemed to have grown larger. He bowed to Mrs Moffet, hoping he would never have to exchange another word with her in his life.

No wonder Miss Darcy had looked so happy.

Not that he thought Mr Moffet was right for her. Not by any means. But he was honest and decent, and he would make a good—though probably agonisingly dull—husband.

It was all too late now. There was no point anymore in apologising to her. She had never even given him a chance.

The only thing he could do now was congratulate her. Though how he could do so without seeming like a bull ready to vent its rage at a red rag, he had no idea. He had seen a bull fight once, when he was in the Peninsula. The bull had been preparing for an attack. Right at this moment, he knew exactly how that bull had felt.

She looked so happy.

There was nothing else he could say to her. It was all over.

Chapter 30

Gatley stalked into the house. His first impulse was to call Oskins and ask him to prepare to travel back to London. In fact, it was the only thing he could do. He should escape before anyone else set eyes on him.

But he could not do it to Oskins. Not again.

He would go upstairs to his room, wash, change his clothing, and have something to eat. Then he would be able to deal with this whole issue in a far more logical manner.

He requested some warm water to be brought up, then he climbed the stairs to his chamber, where he found his valet beginning to unpack his trunk.

"I need some time alone, Reid."

Reid threw him a questioning look as he left. He had never noticed before, but his servants were an impertinent lot, all of them. Why did they think they were entitled to know everything about him? As if he was obliged to account for all his actions. Could not a man rest in his own chamber without having to give an explanation?

He pulled off his boots with great difficulty—he should have asked Reid to do it before he left—and went in stockinged feet to look out of the window.

The young ladies were still there, sitting in the garden on a stone bench.

He stared down at Miss Darcy, or at least, at her bonnet, which was a sensible one, for once. He looked down at that neat, quiet form which had become so familiar to him, and his heart began to tear. There was no denying it to himself anymore. He was in love with her. Oskins was quite right—besotted. Not that it would do him any good now, when she was engaged to someone else.

Moffet, of all people! Was she so desperate that she had to marry someone like Moffet? Anyone could tell he was not right for her. He needed a wife that would be obedient, and she—she was too independent spirited for him.

The thought struck him like lightning. When had he come to that conclusion about her? When had he decided that Miss Darcy was too independent? He did not know. But it made no sense at all. All those accusations at the inn—they had been about her following in the footsteps of her cousin.

They were all wrong. She was right. He had jumped to the wrong conclusion. He had judged her without knowing the truth.

It was very obvious, now that he knew it. Miss Darcy had always stood up to him, right from the beginning, and she had never backed down in one of their arguments. She was too obstinate to be a follower.

Other things fell into place, now that he was willing to see them. There had been no engagement. Clarissa had not been married to Channing. That could only mean one thing. Something else had happened that day, and Darcy knew that Clarissa had not been planning an assignation with Channing.

He was an utter and complete fool. He had stayed away all this time for no reason at all. And in the meanwhile, Moffet must have insinuated himself into Miss Darcy's good graces and convinced her to accept him.

The young ladies were rising and were beginning to move towards the house.

A sense of urgency gripped him. He had to say something to her now, before it was really too late. Perhaps something could be done. Perhaps he could convince her...

He opened the window.

"Wait!" he said. "Do not go inside. I will be down shortly."

The young ladies turned astonished faces towards him. He could not tell from here, but it seemed to him there was a stubborn lilt to Miss Darcy's chin.

It was not a good beginning. Shouting commands to her from the window was not the right way to gain her attention. Very likely, Miss Darcy would deliberately decide to ignore him and would return to the house.

"Please?" he added a little hoarsely, that pebble threatening to block his voice again.

He darted down the stairs as quickly as possible. He would intercept her if she tried to return. Everything suddenly seemed to depend on her not coming back inside. If she did, he knew he would never be able to convince her of anything at all.

❧

There was a grating sound, the sound of a man with a very sore throat trying to clear it.

Georgiana looked towards the door of the Manor. There was Gatley, looking exactly as she had seen him yesterday but without a cravat and in stockinged feet. She stared at him, unable to look anywhere else.

"May I—" There was that throat clearing sound again. "Miss Darcy—" The throat clearing again, then a grinding sound that came from between his teeth "—to you."

"Elizabeth is waving to me from the window," said Clarissa, walking with very quick steps towards the house. "I will be back very soon."

"Yes," said Georgiana not paying attention at all. She was too busy wondering what in heaven's name Mr Gatley was trying to say.

He sounded so strange, so unlike himself. But perhaps it was simply that the very sight of him—leaning out of the window and shouting out to her to stay—had brought back that relentless iron fist again, and she could hardly breathe.

And then there was that thudding sound in her ears—the sound of her heart clamouring to get out.

She stood immobile. She could not have moved if a stampede of horses had come her way.

Gatley watched Clarissa leave, wondering how she could possibly have heard him. He was sure that his request to see Georgiana alone had been too garbled for anyone to understand.

Perhaps he was making more sense than he thought. Perhaps, in that case, he did not have a stone in his throat after all.

"Miss Darcy," he said, trying it out. The words came out more clearly, though his voice still rasped. "I owe you...I have wanted to apologise since that terrible episode at The King's Arms...my behaviour on that occasion..." He drew himself up. This was going nowhere. "I can only account for my contemptible behaviour by recalling that I had suffered a blow on the head after falling from a carriage, and I had been unconscious for some considerable time. Perhaps that will go some way towards explaining why I was not thinking clearly."

It was really quite pathetic of him to use his accident as an excuse.

It was quite despicable. He was trying to ring every ounce of sympathy he could from her. He was disgusted with himself for doing it, but he could not help it. He needed every advantage he could think of.

His words had some of the desired effect, for Miss Darcy put a hand to her mouth and turned quite pale.

"Oh—why did I never think—I cannot believe that I forgot—but of course!" she cried, staring at him in dismay "No—it is I who should apologise. To think that, after what happened—I did not even consider that you were experiencing shock—after the blood loss—and that your head was—how are you feeling now?"

He was completely taken aback by this very mundane question.

"I am perfectly well, thank you."

She smiled. Oh, how he loved this particular smile of hers. It was so genuine, so *simple*, and yet it had the power to wrench his heart.

"I am very glad you are fully recovered," she said in a very polite tone.

He could bear it no longer. He had to hear it, from her own lips, so that his fate would be sealed, and he would walk away from there and put it all behind him. Even if it would wrench him apart.

"This engagement..." he said, leaving it open, unable to speak the words and make them true.

"Oh, you already saw Mrs Moffet," she said, grinning broadly, *grinning*, for heaven's sake, just because she was going to marry Moffet. He half turned away.

"I suppose I should express my good wishes."

"I suppose so," said Georgiana, looking faintly puzzled "It is not *urgent*, surely? You can stay for a while, can you not?"

He must be imagining things because he thought he had heard the tiniest hint of pleading in her voice. So tiny that he must have made it up, just because he wanted it to be there. He had thought his injury completely healed. But now his head was beginning to throb, just where the cut had been when he was injured.

"If you meant, am I going to ride straight over to offer Moffet my felicitations, then, no, of course not."

Not over his dead body.

"Moffet?" she asked. "Is Moffet engaged too? Goodness! Who is he going to marry?"

It took him a long moment to translate her words into some semblance of meaning. Then, as the meaning sank in, the oppression in his head and the throbbing, all slid away as if by magic.

In a few long strides, he was in front of her.

"You are not engaged to Moffet?" he said, standing very, very close to her.

"No, though he did propose—"

A fierce sense of triumph swept through him. She would not be able to wriggle out of it this time. He would make sure she did not slip through his hands.

"Then you will marry me," he said, making it very clear that it was not open to discussion.

She took a step backwards, then another.

"Mr Gatley," she said, in a tone that made it very clear that she *did* mean to argue. "I would like to know by what right you come barging in here and ordering me—commanding me—to marry you. Just because I accepted your apology—"

His heart sank. Why had he thought that just by apologising, everything that had happened between them would conveniently melt away?

He should have known that matters with Miss Georgiana Darcy could never be simple. He looked into hazel eyes speckled with anger and understood that nothing but the absolute truth would do.

"I said earlier that my injuries partly account for my behaviour that day. But it was not true. They were just a convenient excuse. The fact was, I was taken by surprise. I overheard Darcy's accusations, and I—I was bitterly disappointed. I believed at the time, you see, that I had finally found someone I would like to spend my life with. That you were—and then suddenly the carpet was pulled from under my feet. It never occurred to me to doubt Darcy, not for a moment."

He shut his eyes, partly because he did not want to see her expression, partly because he wanted to hide the pain that sprung up whenever he even thought of that afternoon. "And I believed you then to be under your cousin's power."

He opened his eyes and shook his head but carefully avoided glancing at her face.

"I can scarcely believe myself capable of such folly. Perhaps I wilfully allowed myself to be misled because I did not want to face the reality—which was that my feelings were threatening to overcome my reason. I believed you then to be too easily influenced, and I have always promised myself never to marry a woman who was not as strong as I, for that is the road to unhappiness. I have seen it only too well in the case of my aunt. Darcy's words only confirmed to me what I feared, and I did not stop long enough to question them.

"When I look back at it, it seems ludicrous. Why would you have me drive you all the way to Richmond for an assignation, when you could easily arrange one somewhere in London? It is not as if London lacks establishments where this could be accomplished. And then to think that Miss Clarissa—" He paused, a tinge of colour darkening his cheekbone. "It is really quite embarrassing to recollect what I believed at that moment."

He turned and looked at her now, straight into her eyes. "I can only hope that, once again, you can bring yourself to overcome your resentment—however well deserved—and to forgive me, even if this time, I hardly deserve forgiveness."

She shook her head vigorously. "Enough!" she said, sounding pained. "You were not so entirely to blame. We *did* lie to you. We did deceive you. And then I did not offer you any explanation at all. What were you to think?"

She hesitated. "I still do not feel comfortable telling you the truth. Suffice it to say that we were visiting a young woman we know, and that I had promised not to reveal anything about her to anyone. You can reach your own conclusions about this, but I can assure you that we had no ulterior motives except to see her. I am sorry, but I do not feel that I can reveal our reasons to you even now."

"Then in heaven's name let us put the whole thing behind us!" said Gatley. "I do not need to hear anything more. It does not matter. As you pointed out then, it is all a matter of trust. I can assure you now that I would trust you with my life."

"You say so now," said Georgiana, her brow creasing, her whole expression lacking conviction, "but how am I to know that the next time something like this occurs, you will not yet again point the finger of accusation at me? How do I know that it will not happen again?"

"If it ever should occur again, you must remind me of this moment. But beyond that, one can never be certain. I have given you my trust. I can do nothing else but ask you to trust me in turn."

She stood before him, considering.

He wanted to take her in his arms and kiss her until every doubt inside her dissolved, but he could not. He forced himself to stand apart, hands at his sides, until she reached her own conclusion. If she decided against him, he would surely have to accept her verdict.

If he could touch her, she would know how he felt about her.

If he touched her, however, he would not know how *she* felt without being swayed by him. He wanted the decision to come from her alone.

She considered for so long that his resolve began to crumble.

But then, with a strangled cry, she stumbled forward and put out her arms to him. He stepped into them and pressed her fiercely against him.

"How could I not trust you, when I love you so very much?" he said, his lips moving against her hair.

She burrowed her head into his chest. He relished the feeling for a single moment longer, then he pulled her away from him. He needed to know what she felt.

"I want to see your face," he said. It sounded too much like a command. "Please?" he said.

She looked up then. Her eyes flickered, different emotions rippling through the different shades in her hazel eyes.

"Can you bring yourself to trust me?" he asked again, since she had not answered. He had to know that at least, if nothing else. If she could not give him more, then so be it.

"I trust you," she replied shyly. Then, more confidently, with a smile trembling on her lips, she repeated, "Yes, I trust you, Mr Gatley."

It was the only answer he needed. To still the trembling of her lips, he bent forward and steadied them with his own. He meant only to kiss her gently, to give her just a hint of his feelings. But to his surprise she flung her arms around his neck and drew him closer, standing on tiptoe to intensify the kiss.

His senses reeled. Only the certain knowledge that Darcy was in the house and would be upon them any moment, prevented him from surrendering to the moment. He pulled away from her gently.

"I think we ought to stop now," he said, "before matters progress too far."

She stepped back. He expected her to be embarrassed, but instead she had the look of a woman who is very well pleased with herself.

It put him at a disadvantage because he was not satisfied at all, not by a long margin.

"I am glad we have resolved things," he said with just a touch of vexation.

"But we have not resolved things at all," said Georgiana. "We have only resolved the question of trust."

"What more do you want?" he cried. "I have told you I love you. Does that count for nothing?"

Her eyes darkened again. "It counts for a great deal," she said.

"And?" he said, waiting for her to say something more. But she did not.

Everything was suddenly uncertain. The next few instants would determine his life. What if she meant to say no? He could not bring himself to say the words.

"Yes, Mr Gatley, I will marry you," she answered, even though he had not asked the question, at least, he had not asked it now.

Georgiana knew she had rushed into it. She had been driven by a compulsion to say the words because for a moment there he had looked so hesitant and there had been too many misunderstandings between them. Besides, he had already asked her before. So yes, she had jumped in and answered. Before he changed his mind.

She expected him to look pleased, but instead a frown had settled on his brow.

"Mr Gatley?" He really was not behaving as she expected at all. He was quite inattentive. Or was it disapproving? Perhaps she ought not to have answered his question before he asked it.

Her temper flared. Well, if her outspokenness had put him off, it was really too bad. Because that was who she was. He had lectured her about being herself, and now that she was being herself, he was looking dissatisfied instead of being happy. It was a good thing she had discovered the truth, before it was too late.

"Actually, Mr Gatley, I take it back. I take it back. If you are to behave yet again like some boorish"—she could not think of the right word—"*bull* just because I anticipated your question..."

She started to walk off. He held onto her hand firmly and pulled her back, putting his arm around her waist and laughing.

"No, silly goose. You will not take it back. You have already given me your word, and I will not let you go back on it." He considered her affectionately. "I was upset at myself, not at you, since I realised that you deserved better than this."

Georgiana looked confused. He drew himself up to full length and gave her a lopsided smile. "You deserve a far better proposal than this. If I had known it, I would have prepared a speech."

A new, tender kind of laughter rose up in her at the sight of his rueful face.

"Oh, well—that," she said, sneaking her own arm around his waist and cherishing the feel of his strong muscles against her. "Perhaps if you are really kind to me and you undertake not to deliver any more lectures, at least not until we are married, then I may overlook such a lamentable lapse."

He stopped and turned towards her, his other hand now encircling her completely. He gave her such a long, searching glance that she almost pulled away.

"But are you sure of this? Do you really want to do this? Do you care for me, at least a little?"

Her breath caught in her throat. She was swamped by the emotions that had welled up in her at that question, by the uncertainty in his gaze.

Again, she stepped forward, pulling him against her.

"Of course I am sure," she said in a choked whisper. "I love you. I do not know how or when it happened, but you cannot imagine how miserable I have been, thinking I might never see you again."

His arms tightened. He kissed her on the brow, aware that they could be seen from the house. He let go of her and took her hand.

"Come then, we should tell the others," he said.

They walked hand in hand towards the Manor, laughing and retracing the past they had already built with each other.

"I have been a bit in love with you since that first moment I saw you in church," said Gatley. "You looked so chagrined at your cousins' behaviour and wished yourself someplace else entirely."

Her lips twisted at that. "And there I was, thinking you were passing judgement on me."

"I was," he said. "And my judgement was that you were the most adorable creature I had ever set eyes on."

They slowed down to a crawl, wanting to prolong the moment as much as possible, and reluctant to face all the questions that they knew were coming. But it was inevitable, and eventually they reached the steps and began to ascend.

"I would suggest that you put on your boots before you speak to anyone," said Georgiana. "And you should find yourself a cravat."

Gatley stared down at the stockings that had become dirty and half-torn without him even noticing.

"Stockings," he said grandiosely, "who needs them? They are far more interesting as handkerchiefs."

The two of them dissolved into laughter.

He let go of her hand as they entered the house. Georgiana felt bereft of that warm contact immediately. Until now, Georgiana had only half believed in what had happened. But now that they were to tell everybody, she knew that it must be true.

"Would you mind very much if we inform my mother first?" said Gatley. "It may come as a surprise to her, and I would rather tell her in private."

"Of course," said Georgiana. "But you need to change first."

When he came down a few minutes later, his cravat was hastily knotted and not at all up to his usual standard. Georgiana refrained from pointing it out however. She too was too nervous to delay their announcement any longer.

They inquired about Mrs Gatley's whereabouts and were informed that Mrs Gatley was upstairs in her bedchamber, taking her afternoon rest.

"Shall we go, then?" said Gatley.

Georgiana took a deep breath and nodded. "I will wait for you outside in the hallway. You can talk to her first, and then you can call me in when you are ready." Gatley scratched at the door and entered.

"Mother, you should be the first to know—I have told no-one else yet. Miss Darcy and I are engaged to be married. I hope you have no objection."

Mrs Gatley's eyes wrinkled in a smile. "Thank heavens! I have expected this news for some time now. I knew you would come round eventually. You have an obstinate streak, but fortunately you have too much sense to let it affect you when your future happiness is at stake. Where is Miss Darcy? Why did you not bring her with you? I would like to congratulate her."

"She is waiting outside," he said, "I just wanted to be sure of your approval first."

"Of course I approve. Why do you think I invited everyone to stay at Ansdell? I was hoping you would show up at some point and put an end to all this folly."

Gatley gave a rueful smile and went to the door.

"My mother would like to congratulate you. She is very happy for us," he said, smiling.

Georgiana stepped into the room, hoping that Mrs Gatley was indeed as happy as he believed.

"Come in, come in, Miss Darcy. Or should I call you Georgiana? Best wishes! You cannot believe how delighted I am to know the daughter of my dearest friend is to marry my son." Tears gathered in Mrs Gatley's eyes. "I know your mother would have wished it very much if she were still with us. And my dear husband too. I really miss them at times like this."

Georgiana felt her chest tighten. Mrs Gatley's words reminded her keenly of her absent father, and her mother too.

"I suppose you can call *me* mother now," said Mrs Gatley, wiping away her tears.

The words could not have fallen on more receptive ears.

"I would be more than happy to do so," replied Georgiana, taking the hand Mrs Gatley held out to her and pressing it firmly.

"You cannot call her mother yet," said Gatley. "It would be rather improper to do so before the wedding. In fact—"

"For goodness's sake, Gatley! I do not know how you came to be so strait-laced! You certainly did not get it from me!"

"Strait-laced? Surely you are not referring to me?" he said in mock astonishment. "Next, I suppose, you will be calling me a curmudgeon. What do you think, Miss Darcy? Do you still think me a curmudgeon?"

"As a matter of fact," said Georgiana, "if you will allow me to be completely candid, you are. Just a touch, mind."

Mrs Gatley's laughed. "I can see you will do very well together, especially since you seem to have taken his measure, Georgiana. There will be no surprises."

"Oh, I would not be as sure as all that," said Gatley. "She has sprung a few surprises on me already."

Georgiana protested laughingly and said it was because he had wilfully misunderstood her.

"Well, Georgiana," said Mrs Gatley. "Have you found what you were looking for?"

Georgiana's eyes sparkled. "Yes, indeed I have," she replied.

❧

Buoyed by Mrs Gatley's happiness at their news, the couple headed downstairs to announce it to Georgiana's family. As they reached the hallway, the footman informed them very officially that Mr Darcy was awaiting their presence in the drawing room.

The chilly reception they received quickly smothered the smiles on their lips. Darcy and Elizabeth stood by the window. Darcy's expression held rigid disapproval, while Elizabeth looked decidedly grim. Clarissa put down the book she was reading rather ominously, and squirmed uncomfortably.

Georgiana, bewildered, searched her mind for a reason behind the dismal mood in the room.

"Mr Gatley, I hope you have a perfectly good explanation for taking my sister upstairs unaccompanied," said Darcy harshly. "It seems to me we still have unfinished business. I believe, the last time we met, we agreed to fight a duel. We never resolved our disagreement in the The King's Arms. You owe me an apology or I am afraid my honour will need to be satisfied."

Georgiana's mouth fell open in dismay. She could feel Gatley stiffen next to her.

"As a matter of fact—" he began.

Everybody in the room burst out laughing.

"My dear Gatley," said Darcy. "I hope you do not intend to call me out again, for I do not think I can resist it this time."

Gatley, relieved to realise that Darcy was joking, let out a deep sigh.

"I can see I will have nothing but trouble if I join this family."

Georgiana threw him a sharp glance. "It is too late now to regret it. You have already told your mother."

"We have told no-one in your family of our engagement yet. I can withdraw at any time."

"Well then," she said defiantly, "we'd like to announce that we have decided to marry. Now let me see how you can get out of it."

Warm congratulations followed. Clarissa dashed across the room to embrace Georgiana, her eyes dancing, and told her how glad she was that matters had worked out. "I had the hardest time keeping a serious face when you came in. But your brother insisted on his little joke."

"You really ought not to have done that, Fitz," said Georgiana. "I actually believed you were serious—for a few seconds at least."

Darcy smiled. "Blame Elizabeth if you must blame someone. It was *her* idea. In any case, I am very happy for you. Gatley is as worthy a suitor as you could possibly have. I know him well, and I do not think you will come to regret it."

He turned to Gatley. "I am glad you have overcome your quarrel. I am quite tired of Georgiana's moping."

"And I am quite tired of her piano playing," said Elizabeth, kissing Georgiana on the cheek. "We have both been quite beside ourselves, trying to find a way to resolve the problem. Fortunately, Mrs Gatley was very helpful," she added in a half whisper.

As if the name itself had conjured her up, the door opened and Mrs Gatley entered. Everyone's attention turned to her. She was dressed in a splendid red net ball gown and was escorted by two liveried footmen. Their polished buttons glittered, as did the silver trays on which they carried the champagne bottles. The crystal flutes glinted and clinked as the footmen glided into the room.

Clarissa shot Georgiana a significant glance, and Georgiana hid a grin. Mrs Gatley had perfected the Grand Entrance.

Mrs Gatley's solemnity, however, soon reminded her that this was, indeed, a very serious occasion. Georgiana understood that her life was about to change irrevocably. She looked towards Darcy's and Elizabeth's familiar faces and for a moment felt terrified that she was about to lose them.

"To the happy couple," said Mrs Gatley, raising her glass in a toast.

The gloomy moment passed, and Georgiana put her fears behind her.

"Let us also toast the other happy couple," said Mrs Gatley. "It is not remarkable, that you should both be engaged on the same day?"

Gatley looked around him in confusion. "Engaged? But who is it that is engaged?" He looked around, his eyes alighting on Clarissa.

"Do not look at me," said Clarissa. "*I* am not engaged."

"Then who on earth do you mean? Do enlighten me, Mother!"

"Why, Channing, of course."

Gatley, who had just taken a sip of champagne, choked as the bubbles went up his nose.

"Channing? Why on earth would he do such a thing? And without even consulting me?" He set down his glass. "Who knows what kind of a scrape he has fallen into! I really must go to see him immediately."

Georgiana began to laugh. "It will have to wait," she said. "You are in the middle of celebrating your engagement." Then, in a half whisper, she added, "I think it is time you let Mr Channing make his own decisions. After all, it would not do for your cousin to be under your thumb, would it?"

"How dare you throw my words back at me?" he said in a mock-rebuke. But he looked shamefaced.

"I am afraid you shall have to grow accustomed to it."

"If our newly engaged couple will deign to give us a moment of their time," said Mrs Gatley, "it is time to discuss the wedding. Since we are all assembled together under this roof, shall we take advantage of this opportunity and start to make plans? Where do you think we should hold the wedding? How many people shall we invite?"

"In my opinion," said Miss Darcy, with a sideways glance at Gatley, "we should not make it too complicated. I would by far prefer something *simple*."

A great deal of argument followed. Both Darcy and Mrs Gatley wanted large weddings in London with a great deal of pomp and ceremony.

"I have only one sister," said Darcy. "The least I could do is celebrate her wedding in style."

But Georgiana was adamant. She wanted to be married in Hunsford, for this, after all, was where the two of them had met.

In the end, the argument that swayed everyone was Elizabeth's, who pointed out that surely, if they were to have the wedding here, Lady Catherine could be convinced to build at least a small bridge to overcome the quarrel between them.

⚜

The day of the wedding, which had seemed so far away when they had all spoken about it, came all too soon. For it is generally true that, the more preparations one has for an event, the more inconveniently fast the event will occur.

Georgiana stepped quietly into the church and looked down the long aisle, all the way to where Lady Catherine sat regally at her pew, her head crowned with a turban. So she had kept her promise at least not to make the schism between the families visible. Georgiana let out the breath she did not know she had been holding. Even Georgiana's uncle the Earl had honoured the ceremony with his presence.

Mr Collins stood in the front, fussing with his collar and throwing little sideways glances at Lady Catherine, who stared fixedly before her, quiet and pale.

Elizabeth sat next to Colonel Fitzwilliam. Robert and Caroline sat on the pew behind them, whispering to each other. On the other side, in the opposite pew, sat Mrs Gatley with Gatley's sister, Isabella, and her husband, and Gatley's brother Peter, who had returned to England now that the war with France was over.

She remembered that first time when she had seen Gatley sitting there. He was not sitting at that pew now, and for a moment a slight pang passed through her. But then she looked round and there he was, looking spectacularly handsome in his dark coat and his carefully knotted cravat. Next to him stood Channing, smiling in that playful way of his at Miss Moffet, who was in one of the front rows.

The door opened behind her, letting in the sunshine and a few yellow-brown oak leaves. Georgiana looked back. It was her cousin. Clarissa stepped in with a smile and a wink, dropped the flowers she was carrying, and, stooping to retrieve them, let go of the door. A gust of wind nudged it, just a little, and with a reluctant squeak, it slammed shut.

Everyone looked their way.

"It's your Grand Entrance," whispered Clarissa, and Georgiana swallowed down a sudden bout of nervous laughter.

Just then Darcy emerged from the shadows at the side of the aisle and put out his arm to her, and there was no more time to be an observer. Her brother was about to relinquish her. She would no longer be his little sister.

It was the last moment of her childhood. She held on tight to her brother's arm, dismayed to find tears filling the corners of her eyes.

Then from the front, Gatley smiled at her. Her heart reeled in response. She smiled back, brushing aside the tears. Her step quickened, and she started to pull Darcy along with her, impatient with his slow pace.

Her life as an adult stretched before her, and she walked forward to embrace it.

The End

About the Author

As a literature professor, **Monica Fairview** enjoyed teaching students to love reading. But after years of postponing the urge, she finally realised what she really wanted was to write books herself. She lived in Illinois, Los Angeles, Seattle, Texas, Colorado, Oregon, and Boston as a student and professor, and now lives in London.

For more from Monica Fairview, read on for an excerpt from

The Other MR. DARCY

Now available from Sourcebooks Landmark

Prologue

CAROLINE BINGLEY SANK TO THE FLOOR, HER SILK CREPE DRESS crumpling up beneath her. Tears spurted from her eyes and poured down her face and, to her absolute dismay, a snorting, choking kind of sound issued from her mouth.

"This is most improper," she tried to mutter, but the sobs—since that was what they were—the *sobs* refused to stay down her throat where they were supposed to be.

She had never sobbed in her life, so she could not possibly be sobbing now.

But the horrible sounds kept coming from her throat. And water— *tears*—persisted in squeezing past her eyes and down her face.

Then with a wrench, something tore in her bosom—her chest—and she finally understood the expression that everyone used but that she had always considered distinctly vulgar. *Her heart was breaking.* And it was true because what else could account for that feeling, inside her, just in the centre there, of sharp, stabbing pain?

And what could account for the fact that her arms and her lower limbs were so incredibly heavy that she could not stand up?

She was heartbroken. Her Mr Darcy had married that very morning. In church, in front of everyone, and she had been unable to prevent it.

He had preferred Elizabeth Bennet. He had actually married her, in spite of her inferior connections, and even though he had alienated his aunt, Lady Catherine de Bourgh, whose brother was an earl. Caroline simply could not comprehend it.

She had that tearing feeling again and she looked down, just to make sure that it was not her bodice that was being ripped apart. But the bodice, revealing exactly enough of her bosom as was appropriate for a lady, remained steadfastly solid. So the tearing must have come from somewhere inside her. It squeezed at her with pain hard enough to stop her breathing, and to force those appalling sobs out even when she tried her best to swallow them down.

She rested her face in her hands and surrendered to them. She had no choice in the matter. They were like child's sobs, loud and noisy. More like bawling, in fact. Her mouth was stretched and wide open. And the noise kept coming out, on and on.

On the floor, in the midst of merriment and laughter, on the day of William Fitzwilliam Darcy's wedding, with strains of music accompanying her, Miss Caroline Bingley sobbed for her lost love.

※

A long time later, someone tried to open the door. She came to awareness suddenly, realizing where she was. The person on the other side tried again, but she resisted, terrified that someone would come in and catch sight of her tear-stained face. No one, *no one*, she resolved, would ever know that she had cried because of Mr Darcy.

Whoever was on the other side gave the doorknob a last puzzled rattle, then walked slowly back down the corridor.

She rose, straightening out her dress, smoothing down her hair with hands that were steady only because she forced them to be.

She needed to repair the ravages her pathetic bawling had caused. At any moment, someone else could come in and discover her. She moved to look into a mirror that hung above the mantelpiece.

And recoiled in shock.

For the second time that day, she lost control completely. Her hand flew to her mouth and she squeaked—for that was the best word one could honour it with—squeaked in absolute horror.

For there he was, reflected in the mirror, sitting with his legs stretched before him, watching her gravely. He was a complete stranger. He had sat there, all that time, silent witness to the one moment in her adult life when she had broken down in such an utterly demeaning fashion.

Like the snap of a riding-crop, her surprise jolted her into motion. The heavy sensation scattered. She spun round to face him.

"How dare you sit there and watch me, sir, without the courtesy of letting me know of your presence!"

The stranger stirred and came to his feet. His face, which had been in the shadows, entered the light as he shifted, and she drew in her breath. In her befuddlement, she thought for a moment it was Darcy himself. Then she knew it was not, merely someone who resembled him, somewhat, someone with a clear family relationship.

"You are entirely correct," said the stranger. "I have been very remiss. I realized my error after the first minute. But by then it was too late. I could not interrupt such an outpour, and I felt it would be ill advised of me to try."

"If you were a gentleman," she remarked, with as much haughti-ness as her anger would allow her, "you would have left the room."

He waved his half-empty glass towards the door. "Unless I left through one of the windows, I really had no option but to stay." His hand indicated the rest of the room as if to prove to her the truth of his words. Because she was still befuddled, her eyes followed it, noting that the room had no French doors, and that the windows were quite narrow.

"Well," she persisted, but her anger had abandoned her, to be replaced by exhaustion, "you ought to have thought of something."

"I did try," said the stranger. "Believe me, I tried. It was not a spectacle I relished."

The spark of anger rekindled, along with the sharp sting of shame. "And you have the gall to refer to me as a spectacle?" Those deplorable sobs were threatening to burst out again. They made her voice uneven and appallingly unfamiliar to her ears.

His eyes remained grave, though the corner of his mouth moved, just marginally. "I was not referring to you. I was simply remarking that I would have rather been anywhere else than a witness to your grief."

His statement mollified her. Indeed, she could think of no response. She rearranged the wrinkled skirt of her dress around her, gathering together the shreds of her dignity. What did it matter, after all, what this stranger thought of her? She would most likely never see him again.

Then it crossed her mind that he had complete power over her, that he was in fact free to disgrace her completely if he revealed her outburst to the assembled guests.

"I would be grateful to you, sir, if you would be good enough to keep this episode to yourself," she said, her gaze lowered to the ground, abject in her fear.

He came forward and with a touch of a gloved finger, raised her chin so that she looked up into his eyes. There was sympathy in them.

"You may consider this episode forgotten," he said. "But if at any time you wished to speak about it, I would be honoured if you would confide in me."

She did not want pity. Nor would she let him take advantage of her weakness. She stepped back out of his reach, stood up straight, and answered, her voice quite distant.

"That would be highly unlikely, sir. We have not even been introduced."

With that she swirled round and, her footsteps deliberate, she walked to the door, opened it, and closed it firmly between them.

Mr. Darcy, Vampyre

Pride and Prejudice CONTINUES...

Amanda Grange

"A seductively gothic tale..." —Romance Buy the Book

A test of love that will take them to hell and back...

My dearest Jane,

My hand is trembling as I write this letter. My nerves are in tatters and I am so altered that I believe you would not recognise me. The past two months have been a nightmarish whirl of strange and disturbing circumstances, and the future...

Jane, I am afraid.

It was all so different a few short months ago. When I awoke on my wedding morning, I thought myself the happiest woman alive...

"Amanda Grange has crafted a clever homage to the Gothic novels that Jane Austen so enjoyed." —*AustenBlog*

"Compelling, heartbreaking, and triumphant all at once."
—*Bloody Bad Books*

978-1-4022-3697-6
$14.99 US/$18.99 CAN/£7.99 UK

"The romance and mystery in this story melded together perfectly... a real page-turner." —*Night Owl Romance*

"Mr. Darcy makes an inordinately attractive vampire.... *Mr. Darcy, Vampyre* delights lovers of Jane Austen that are looking for more." —*Armchair Interviews*

Mr. and Mrs. Fitzwilliam Darcy: Two Shall Become One
SHARON LATHAN

"Highly entertaining... I felt fully immersed in the time period. Well done!" —*Romance Reader at Heart*

A fascinating portrait of a timeless, consuming love

It's Darcy and Elizabeth's wedding day, and the journey is just beginning as Jane Austen's beloved *Pride and Prejudice* characters embark on the greatest adventure of all: marriage and a life together filled with surprising passion, tender self-discovery, and the simple joys of every day.

As their love story unfolds in this most romantic of Jane Austen sequels, Darcy and Elizabeth each reveal to the other how their relationship blossomed from misunderstanding to perfect understanding and harmony, and a marriage filled with romance, sensuality, and the beauty of a deep, abiding love.

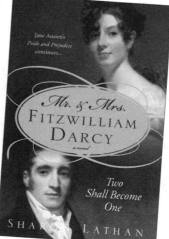

What readers are saying:

"This journey is truly amazing."

"What a wonderful beginning to this truly beautiful marriage."

"Could not stop reading."

"So beautifully written...making me feel as though I was in the room with Lizzy and Darcy...and sharing in all of the touching moments between."

978-1-4022-1523-0 • $14.99 US/ $15.99 CAN/ £7.99 UK

The Pemberley Chronicles

A Companion Volume to Jane Austen's **Pride and Prejudice**

The Pemberley Chronicles: Book 1

REBECCA ANN COLLINS

"A lovely complementary novel to Jane Austen's *Pride and Prejudice.* Austen would surely give her smile of approval."
—BEVERLY WONG, AUTHOR OF *Pride & Prejudice Prudence*

The weddings are over, the saga begins

The guests (including millions of readers and viewers) wish the two happy couples health and happiness. As the music swells and the credits roll, two things are certain: Jane and Bingley will want for nothing, while Elizabeth and Darcy are to be the happiest couple in the world!

Elizabeth and Darcy's personal stories of love, marriage, money, and children are woven together with the threads of social and political history of England in the nineteenth century. As changes in industry and agriculture affect the people of Pemberley and the surrounding countryside, the Darcys strive to be progressive and forward-looking while upholding beloved traditions.

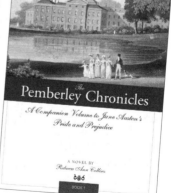

"Those with a taste for the balance and humour of Austen will find a worthy companion volume."
—*Book News*

978-1-4022-1153-9 • $14.95 US/ $17.95 CAN/ £7.99 UK

Mr. Darcy Takes a Wife

LINDA BERDOLL

The *#1 best-selling* Pride and Prejudice *sequel*

"Wild, bawdy, and utterly enjoyable." —*Booklist*

Hold on to your bonnets!

Every woman wants to be Elizabeth Bennet Darcy—beautiful, gracious, universally admired, strong, daring and outspoken—a thoroughly modern woman in crinolines. And every woman will fall madly in love with Mr. Darcy—tall, dark and handsome, a nobleman and a heartthrob whose virility is matched only by his utter devotion to his wife. Their passion is consuming and idyllic—essentially, they can't keep their hands off each other—through a sweeping tale of adventure and misadventure, human folly and numerous

mysteries of parentage. This sexy, epic, hilarious, poignant and romantic sequel to *Pride and Prejudice* goes far beyond Jane Austen.

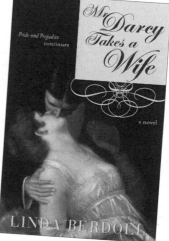

What readers are saying:

"I couldn't put it down."

"I didn't want it to end!"

"Berdoll does Jane Austen proud! ...A thoroughly delightful and engaging book."

"Delicious fun...I thoroughly enjoyed this book."

"My favorite *Pride and Prejudice* sequel so far."

978-1-4022-0273-5 • $16.95 US/ $19.99 CAN/ £9.99 UK

WILLOUGHBY'S RETURN

JANE AUSTEN'S *SENSE AND SENSIBILITY* CONTINUES

JANE ODIWE

"A tale of almost irresistible temptation."

A lost love returns, rekindling forgotten passions…

When Marianne Dashwood marries Colonel Brandon, she puts her heartbreak over dashing scoundrel John Willoughby behind her. Three years later, Willoughby's return throws Marianne into a tizzy of painful memories and exquisite feelings of uncertainty. Willoughby is as charming, as roguish, and as much in love with her as ever. And the timing couldn't be worse—with Colonel Brandon away and Willoughby determined to win her back…

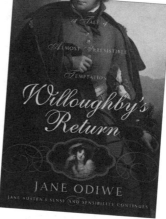

Praise for *Lydia Bennet's Story*:

"A breathtaking Regency romp!" —Diana Birchall, author of *Mrs. Darcy's Dilemma*

"An absolute delight." —*Historical Novels Review*

"Odiwe emulates Austen's famous wit, and manages to give Lydia a happily-ever-after ending worthy of any Regency romance heroine." —*Booklist*

"Odiwe pays nice homage to Austen's stylings and endears the reader to the formerly secondary character, spoiled and impulsive Lydia Bennet." —*Publishers Weekly*

978-1-4022-2267-2
$14.99 US/$18.99 CAN/£7.99 UK